FASHIONABLY DEAD DOWN UNDER

BOOK TWO OF THE HOT DAMNED SERIES

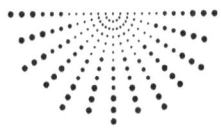

ROBYN PETERMAN

Uproariously witty, deliciously provocative, and just plain fun! No one delivers side-splitting humor and mouth-watering sensuality like Robyn Peterman.

This is entertainment at its absolute finest!

~ Darynda Jones, NY Times Bestselling Author of the *Charley Davidson Series*

DEDICATION

This dedication is twofold. First, for my Mom and Dad—everything that is good and right about me came from you—learned and inherited. Everything that is profane and nutty is completely my own fault! I love you both till the end of time.

And second, for Donna McDonald—you are my Siamese twin from a past life. You calm my panic and you feed my brain. As long as you laugh, I know I haven't taken the non-stop train to Crazytown and bought property. Thank you for being you.

ACKNOWLEDGMENTS

Writing may be a solitary sport, but putting a book out is not. I am grateful and blessed to have many amazing people in my life. *The Hot Damned Series* is the series of my heart and writing it is a joy.

My beta readers, Candace, Donna, Kris, Christi, Jowanna, Jim, Kim and Jennifer are the bomb. I adore all of you and thank you for the time you give me.

Rebecca Poole, my cover is everything I ever wanted and more. We are a warped team and I am so grateful for your creativity and your friendship. To many, many more!

My Pimpettes are amazing! You delight me and I write for you!

My critique partners, JM Madden and Donna McDonald, you ladies are brilliant and when I grow up, I want to write like you.

And my girl-crush, Darynda Jones… your cover quote humbled me and made me cry. You are an amazing writer and a beautiful friend.

Last but not least, I want to thank my family. Hot Hubby, you are my real life hero and you are hotter than Satan's underpants. My kids, I love you. You are my finest accomplishment. None of this would be any fun without you guys.

BOOK DESCRIPTION

Welcome to Hell. Literally.

The Hell where the Prince of Darkness is hotter than Hades, Hell Hounds smell like brownies and the Seven Deadly Sins are addicted to Facebook...Not to mention the soundtrack in the Underworld is Journey. For real.

I should have known no good could come from offing my parents in the space of twenty minutes no matter how psychotic and evil they were...

Now I find out my family tree includes almost every deity and mythological being alive while Ethan, the one and only love of my undead life has a limited time down under before he turns to dust.

In the land of Sin, you'd think I'd get some nookie time with my man, but no. Baby Demons, cousins and grandparents put the kibosh on that. Blue balls are the new normal. What the hell does a Half-Vampyre slash Half-Demon have to do to catch a break?

Apparently find a freakin' sword, calm Mother Nature's unmedicated mood swings and make sure Mister Rogers keeps his sticky fingers to himself during weekly poker with the Devil. And I have three days to do it.

By all that's unholy, I thought Ethan's Vampyre family was crazy... Trust me, they have nothing on the Demons.

CHAPTER ONE

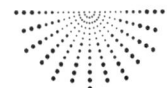

Pain—then ice—then intolerable heat.

A second took years, yet time stood still.

The claws of those that trapped me were razor sharp. They tore through my flesh as the ones who owned them grunted and screamed with delight. I struggled for balance, but realized I was standing on air.

Violet and silver dust engulfed me as I choked on smells of burning flesh and anger.

How was this happening? I was supposed to be planning my wedding to my hotter than Satan's underpants Vampyre Prince... not taking a ride to Hell with smelly and disgusting Demons.

Shitshitdamnitshit.

Journey? The soundtrack in Hell was Journey?

I would have thought Nine Inch Nails or AC/DC, but certainly not Journey... Don't get me wrong, I loved Journey, but *Don't Stop Believing* just didn't seem like an appropriate anthem for the Underworld.

Was I even in Hell? Maybe this was Purgatory or some other random plane of existence? Although I would expect Barry Manilow, John Tesh or Kenny G if I was stuck in Purgatory.

"Where in God's name am I?" I muttered as I gingerly pried my dry eyes open.

One thing I was absolutely sure of—I definitely wasn't on Earth. The ride to wherever the hell I was with the stinky Demons had sucked the big one. It was violent, smelly and it hurt like a son of a bitch.

Easing my body to a sitting position was difficult but doable. Now, to figure out where I was…

"You've got to be kidding me," I moaned, both from the pain shooting through my limbs and the simple fact that *Faithfully* was blasting from invisible speakers hidden somewhere in my cell.

Wait. Was this a cell? A trap? A bedroom?

A bedroom? I was in a bedroom?

This couldn't be Hell. It had to be some kind of holding area. The Underworld was supposed to smell like sulfur and look like post-Armageddon. This place looked more like some douchenoggle with big bucks and debatable taste had shopped at all the most expensive home stores on Fifth Avenue … while they were drunk.

My body ached like I'd been beaten and I checked myself for wounds. Surprisingly I was fine. Maybe all that flesh tearing had been an illusion. Being a Vampyre I healed quickly, but the trip to Hell, or wherever I was, had been rather turbulent. Turning my head took effort, but I needed to figure out my location and how to get out.

Interesting. I was on a large bed draped in cheesy and predictable slippery black silk. The walls of what I decided to assume was a massive bedroom were all done in burnished gold leafing. Thick and ornate crown molding framed the walls. The shades of the molding were more muted and depicted horrific scenes of mutilation and decapitations of some kind of animal-looking thing. Okay, this was more like the Hell I expected. The artwork added to the ambience—frescos of orgies and graphic depictions of group sex and death graced what had to be twenty foot high walls. The floor was so highly waxed it literally sparkled —the uninviting cold black marble stretched from one end of the huge room to the other.

Trying to block out Steven Perry singing *Lovin, Touchin, Squeezin'* was almost impossible. I had a bizarre urge to sing along...

Wait a fucking minute... were the walls breathing?

Stop. Pull yourself together—walls didn't breathe. I needed to deal with the situation at hand. I would not let Steven Perry or walls with a heartbeat derail me from getting the hell out of Hell.

First things first—I needed to get up. I wasn't chained to the bed. I was able to move as freely as my battered body would allow. I suppose the most unnerving part was that no one was around... or were they? I hadn't seen anyone or anything since my forced arrival. Could Demons cloak themselves like I could?

"Astrid," a disembodied voice hissed from out of nowhere.

"Holy Hell," I screamed and dove under the bed, slamming the side of my head on the metal frame and bending back all the fingers on my left hand. "Who's here?" I shouted, nursing my painfully throbbing fingers and head, not to mention the rest of my body.

"Al Pacino."

"Al Pacino lives in Hell? I didn't even know he died." Plus, he seemed more like a Purgatory guy to me. "Bullshit," I muttered, cautiously peeking out from under the bed. There was no one in the room but me. Maybe the walls were alive. "You are not Al Pacino. You don't even sound like Al Pacino. Who in the hell are you?"

"I'm part of you," the wall whispered.

"I'm a fucking wall?"

The wall laughed heartily. So heartily it pissed me off. "So, did you enjoy your trip, Astrid?"

"Are you kidding me? It sucked," I snapped and scanned the room for a hidden Demon. There had to be someone in here. Walls did not talk.

"What on earth did you expect, my dear? You'd just killed their leader who happened to be your father," the voice informed me. "Not to mention you offed your psychotic bitch of a somewhat human mother not even ten minutes before your father arrived."

"My father was no prize either. He was a gross, stinky, disgusting and evil Demon and wasn't even upset that I snuffed out my mother," I shot back. Fine. I'd lost it. I was talking to a wall...

"Darling girl, if you were able to kill both your parents, why didn't you stop the Demons from taking you to Hell?"

"Well, Wall, you seem to know quite a bit already. I'm sure you know exactly why I couldn't stop the Demons."

"Couldn't or didn't?" the wall inquired politely.

I'd had enough of the wall. "What does it matter? I was a bit tired from offing my parents and I had, um... other reasons." Damn it, this was impossible. Was I really talking to a wall? Yes. Yes, I was.

"Ah yes," the wall said lovingly. "Your unborn child. That child will also be part of me."

"Look, no offense, but you're a freakin' talking wall. I don't really see the connection between you, me and my baby."

"If you're not going to be pleasant, I'll leave," the wall huffed and the heartbeat disappeared. WTF?

Fucking. Awesome. The wall was gone because I pissed it off. Not only had I made myself an orphan earlier and earned a lovely unplanned trip to the Land of Damnation, but I'd made a talking wall in Hell angry with me. What did a girl have to do to catch a freakin' break? I'd done everything that was expected of me and still I got the shaft... I'd fulfilled the crazy Vampyre Prophecy. I'd saved the Vampyre King and proved I was indeed their Chosen One. Although I might have reconsidered the job had I known ending up in the Abyss of Darkness was part of the description.

"Are you screwing with me?" I shouted at the wall as *Open Arms* surrounded me on all sides. The incredible urge to sway and sing along was almost debilitating. There had to be something subliminal going on here... Was Journey part of some evil plan? Was it laced with hidden references to Hell and debauchery? Was Steven Perry an incubus? Either someone down under was obsessed with 80s pop music or I wasn't in Hell at all.

"Oh my God," I gasped as I crawled out from under the bed. I very slowly stretched out my cramped legs and arms. "I clearly fucked someone over in a former life to have to deal with this."

"Why would you think that?" the disembodied wall voice hissed.

"Motherfucker," I screeched, grabbing a pillow off the bed and hurling it at the wall. "Do not scare me like that. I've had enough surprises today."

The wall chuckled in reply.

The Demons had unceremoniously dragged my ass through the portal to Hell insisting I was their new queen—*like that was ever going to happen.* If they hadn't arrived in such large numbers, I might not be sitting in Hell right now talking to a wall and trying to make my body work, but I was... and I was furious.

However, as unhappy as I was about my new address, I would hazard a guess that my beautiful mate Ethan had gone ballistic. He would have arrived at the caves by now where my deadly family reunion had taken place and would know that I'd been abducted. My gut clenched at the thought of what he would do. His father, the King of the Vampyres, would have clued him in to the somewhat unbelievable story of my pregnancy and Ethan would... Shit, I didn't know what he'd do, but I needed to get out of here quickly before he attempted to come to Hell and rescue me.

I'd lost enough. I would not lose the man who was my world and I flat out refused to lose my baby. Unease skittered up my spine like little mice and I shivered involuntarily as Steven Perry began to belt out *Wheel in the Sky*. OMG.

Could the talking wall keep me from leaving? Time to find out.

On the far left side of the room was a bay window. I wondered how high up I was and if I could jump. What was I thinking? I could fly, for fuck's sake. I grimaced and stood. I just needed to find a way out of the garish bedroom and make my way to a portal that would take me back to Earth.

Of course since I had no idea what that portal might look like or where to find one, that might prove to be a clusterfuck in the making. Awesome. I needed to figure out where I was.

Walking hurt so I decided to fly to the window and check out the landscape. After two pathetic attempts that resulted in my ass hitting the floor—hard, I realized my powers weren't the same in Hell as they were on Earth. Not. Fucking. Good.

"Looks like you lost some power, my dear," the wall said.

"Ya think?" I snapped. Why was I even talking to the wall? It was a wall. I would ignore it and if it got mad—so be it.

My eyesight, hearing and sense of smell were still bionic, but my ability to cloak myself was gone along with my ability to fly. I needed to get the hell out of the room. Staying low and away from the walls just in case they had hands too, I slipped out of the bedroom and made my way down a massive hall. Ironically—or maybe not—Steven Perry belted out *Separate Ways*. Who in the hell knew Journey had so many hits?

Something was off besides the fact that the walls talked. Why was I able to breathe and why in the hell did Hell smell so good? Was I even a Vampyre anymore? If descending to I-have-a-shit-ton-of-money-and-no-taste-and-Journey-is-the-best-band-ever-land meant that I had turned into a full Demon, someone was going to pay.

Not wanting to show fear, but filled with dread that made my heart beat like the drum section of a percussion happy high school band, I stood in the center of the dimly lit hallway. If the Demons had wanted me dead they would have already killed me. I was creeped out that I'd been talking to a wall and had seen no one. It felt like I'd plopped down in the middle of a game with no rules...

This world was filled with dark magic and Steven Perry... and strangely, I found that combination appealing. Very appealing. It was unlike the foul magic of my mother or my father and his minions. This was smarter and a whole hell of a lot more dangerous. Thankfully my body was becoming my own again. The pain was receding although I was still without my undead powers...

Voices. I heard voices... and they didn't belong to Steven Perry or anyone from Journey as far as I could tell. A man and a girl.

Oh, I wanted to go home. Where were my ruby slippers or at the very least a fairy godmother? This was bad... very, very bad.

Moving quietly toward the sound with as much outward calm as I could muster my stomach roiled. Why, why, why did shit like this seem to happen to me on a daily basis? My karma couldn't be that bad... Suck it up and deal with it. I'd just defeated massive evil. I killed my vicious father and my bat-shit crazy mother in the space of twenty minutes. Not something I was proud of or wanted to brag about, but it was me or them and clearly I had more to live for... I was a kick butt half-Vampyre half-Demon who was pregnant. I was a virtual impossibility. I could do this. I'd talk my way out and go home. Or I'd whack a bunch more Demons and go home. Done. No fucking problem.

However, when I reached the source of the voices my courage disappeared. The sheer amount of magic in the room was like nothing I'd ever felt. The darkness wound around me like a perfectly cut cashmere wrap and the magnetic pull was intoxicating. There was no turning back. It felt right to be where I was in this very moment. I was positive this was where I would get some answers. Luckily I slipped into the room unnoticed. In the spirit of self-preservation and utter terror, I quickly hid behind a massive black brocade curtain as Steven Perry appropriately busted into *Who's Crying Now.*

"DIXIE, THIS BEHAVIOR IS UNACCEPTABLE!" THE MAN BELLOWED.

He was magnificent and frightening. His magic was stronger than any I'd ever witnessed. I slipped farther into the shadows so I wouldn't be seen. Fuckity fuck fuck. Every instinct in my body screamed at me to run away, but that was impossible... they would see me. This was a mistake—possibly a deadly one. But I'd been drawn here by an unmistakable pull. As much as I wanted to disappear, I wanted to stay even more.

The beautiful man stood at least six feet six inches tall and had long raven black hair—identical to the girl named Dixie he was displeased with. She was stunning, yet her demeanor was meek. Their eyes were golden like mine, although his turned a ruby red as his anger mounted. Was the girl related to the man? Who in the hell were they?

Their skin color differed. His was more of a pale mocha and hers was a peaches and cream. They were both long and lanky and reeked of magic. The girl, Dixie, appeared to be about nineteen or twenty and the man? Who knew...

"I'm sorry," she muttered, staring at her fingernails. She picked nervously at the chipped black polish.

"Would you like to explain these grades?" The air crackled with his anger and energy. He threw the paper to the ground at her feet.

Grades? WTF? This was Hell... people got report cards in Hell?

"Um... I studied?" she whispered, ducking her head to avoid a blow.

"No child of mine receives straight As." His voice was soft and menacing.

I was so fucking confused I almost stepped out from my hiding place, but sanity prevailed and I stayed put.

"I said I was sorry, Dad. I'll try harder to fail next time."

One question answered...

"Where did I go wrong?" he lamented. I watched him pace. His presence filled the room completely, leaving little space for anyone or anything else. His very expensive black leather pants and black silk shirt matched his hair perfectly. It was clear the girl loved him and was upset with his displeasure.

He threw his hands up in disgust, "I've given you everything, and this is how you repay me?"

"Didn't realize there was a price," she muttered quietly.

"Everything has a price," he hissed.

Damn, he had really good hearing.

Dixie shrunk down low and waited. I held my breath, wishing I hadn't chosen this particular room to explore.

"You will drop the goody-goody act. You will be rude, promiscuous and scandalous. You will not be compassionate unless I am concerned and I expect you to flunk out of the Demon College just like all of your sisters did. Do you understand me?" he demanded.

"I'm really sorry, Dad." She sounded like a broken record—this was clearly a familiar conversation for them.

"I am Satan," he bellowed and the room vibrated. "I have a reputation to uphold. You are a Demon Princess, you have a Porsche, your own bungalow in the most exclusive zip code in Hell and certainly more money than anyone your age should have access to and yet you throw all this in my face? Why Dixie, why?" He wearily dropped down on the couch next to the girl and she put her arms around him.

"I love you," she whispered.

A ghost of a smile touched his lips. "And I you." He wrapped his arms around her and looked into her eyes. "Is it true that you donated one million dollars of my money to feed hungry humans on Earth?"

"Yes," she said and buried her face against his chest. "I did."

He heaved an enormous sigh, "I have to punish you, you know."

"I know."

He put his finger under her chin, forcing her to meet his eyes. "If I don't punish you, all hell will break loose down here. No pun intended," he grinned.

"Daddy, that pun was totally intended," she giggled.

"That it was." He stood up and ran his big hands through his hair and turned his mesmerizing gaze on her. "You are so like your mother."

"And that's a bad thing?" she challenged.

"It's an... interesting thing," he conceded. His voice was melodic and hypnotizing.

"Dad?"

"Yes, Dixie?"

"What's my punishment?"

He gave her a terribly evil and intoxicating smile. "I'll have to think about it." He turned and walked toward my hiding spot. Shit. Why did I have to be so freakin' tall? Please walk by me. Please. He stopped a foot from where I hid. I held my new found breath and prayed to everything and anything I could think of... including him.

"Come out, Astrid. I've been expecting you."

Sweet baby Satan, this day couldn't get any worse. Actually, it probably could.

CHAPTER TWO

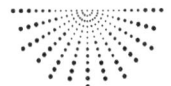

Shitfire, hell and damnation. This was bad. Satan was expecting me? How was that even possible? And how did he know I was hiding behind curtain number two? Although he was Satan or Lucifer or Beelzebub or the Prince of Darkness or...

"I prefer Satan. Lucifer is fine on Tuesdays and the Prince of Darkness will do in a pinch," he said smoothly in his dark, rich voice.

Son of a... I quickly slammed my brain doors shut and hoped I still had at least that ability. Test it, my filterless and quick to come up with horrific ideas brain told me. Fine... *Satan is a douchebag who wears ladies underpants and picks his nose...* Nothing. No reaction. Thank you Jesus and Buddha and Moses and Judas and whoever else was kind enough to be helping me out at the moment. Wait. I take back the Judas thing. Don't want to pray to a dude who gets people crucified. Dumb, dumb, dumb. I idly wondered for a moment if Judas lived down here. Focus. Satan was on the other side of the curtain I was hiding behind and he'd requested the pleasure of my company. Fuck.

I was Southern and I had manners. If I could teach art to genitalia obsessed seniors, I could converse with Satan. Right?

Right. If he was expecting me, he was probably aware of my recent patricide and matricide... Would he be impressed or pissed? After all, my father had been in charge of Hell. Wait. How was my stanky father in charge down here if Satan existed? This made no sense. Were the Vampyres wrong? Was my father a big fat hairy liar? Who in the hell did I kill an hour ago? Was he even my father?

"I'm waiting," Satan informed me in a tone that got my feet moving quickly.

"Hi," I said as I burst from the curtains and shoved my hand out to shake his, acting like it was the most natural thing in the world to be eavesdropping on the King of Debauchery's conversation from behind black brocade. "I'm Astrid and there was clearly some major fuc...mistake. I don't live down here and I'm not dead. Well, actually I am dead, but not dead-dead. I'm undead and my undead, um... husband is going to be pissed. I'm a newlywed of sorts in a Vampyre undead way and I need to go home, your Honor of Darkness. Now." I expelled a loud and long breath as I hadn't inhaled through my insane diatribe.

"Interesting," he purred and watched me. He hadn't taken my hand and I let it drop limply to my side. "So you're the Chosen One."

"Apparently," I snapped, annoyed that he didn't have the decency to shake my hand. "And you're the bad guy."

"Occasionally," Satan laughed and all the air left my lungs. God, he was beautiful... and scary.

"Cigarette?" he offered, holding a pack of my favorite brand out to me.

I was soooo tempted. I could breathe for God's sake. Would one measly cigarette hurt me? Um, yes. Yes, it would. In my struggle with temptation, I'd all but forgotten I was pregnant. Would I have taken it if I didn't have my little miracle inside of me? I'd like to think no, but I wasn't too sure. Hell was going to be hell.

"No, I quit," I said, looking away from my former vice.

"Such a shame," he replied, watching me intently.

It was if he could read me without diving into my mind. Shit. Time for a change of subject... "I thought my dad was in charge down here."

"You do realize *down* is a misnomer," he informed me. He was in my space and I itched to take a step back, but knew in my gut if I moved away I would lose a few points in whatever fucked up game we were playing.

"I'm not following," I said politely, very aware he avoided my statement.

"My dear beautiful creature," Satan said, moving even closer. "It's a misconception that Hell is below and Heaven is above. What does that even mean? Nothing is up or down, that's just mundane human mythology. Most likely the poor mortal fools made the mistake because Hell is occasionally called the Underworld. So very literal, those humans... Hell and Heaven are simply on different planes, accessible through portals. Earth was modeled after a combination of the seasons, climates and terrains of Heaven and Hell. We all share the same moon, sun and stars."

"Interesting. So about my father... " I said, ungracefully changing the subject. Again. Although what he said was fascinating and I did want to know more I was in a bit of a time crunch. The faster I could get out of here the better. I was certain Satan already knew if he was going to kill me, so I had very little to lose. I wanted answers, not a history lesson.

"Yes," he replied silkily. "Tragic ending."

"Who was he?" God, the Devil was more cryptic than the Vamps. "I thought he was in charge down here."

That stopped the Devil in his tracks. "Did he tell you that?" he demanded in a voice that made my stomach drop to my toes.

"Um, no... not exactly. I guess I just assumed, or maybe my mom told me." Under no circumstance would I tell him the

Vampyres believed my dead pappy, Abaddon, was the leader of the Underworld.

"How rich," he laughed, going from deadly back to blindingly beautiful in the matter of a moment. "Your father," he spat derisively, "was definitely not in charge here. He was my minion and managed a certain—how shall I put it—area of Hell... but he was weak and stupid—unfit to rule."

I stayed silent. The way he stared at me made my skin heat. He was breathtaking, but I wasn't pulled to him in a sexual way. It was a power thing... I think.

"Daddy, you should tell her more," Dixie said quietly from across the room. I'd forgotten she was still here. Her father's presence was so large and overwhelming everything around him disappeared.

"She's on a need to know basis," he informed his daughter. "Welcome to Hell, Astrid. Say hello to your cousin Dixie."

"My cousin?" WTF? If she was my cousin then he was my...

"Uncle," Satan supplied as I quickly re-shut the faulty doors in my mind. Damn it to hell, I was one walking defect... nothing worked.

"That's just awesome," I gushed, inching my way to the door, "but I have to go. It's been kind of lovely meeting you and I seriously hope we don't have too many get togethers and... "

"Halt," my uncle the fucking Devil hissed.

I did.

"Don't you think it only fair that you learn about the other part of your heritage?" he half asked-half insisted, turning his back on me.

"Um, no, that's okay. I've seen enough in the last couple of hours to last a lifetime... a long one—like mine."

"Unacceptable," he replied so quietly I wasn't sure I heard him, but if the look on Dixie's face was anything to go by, things were about to get hinky. Shit. "You will stay here until I deem it reasonable for you to leave. You will immerse yourself in the Demon culture and you will get to know your family."

"There's more than just the two of you?" I asked, hoping there wasn't.

"Oh yes, my lovely niece. Many more."

"There will be people looking for me," I said, wracking my brain for any excuse to leave.

"That should be fun," Satan grinned and I almost fainted. His charm was addictive.

"The longer I'm here the better the chance that there will be problems for you."

"Trust me, my dear, there are already problems... Plus, time runs differently here than it does on your chosen plane," he said and turned to leave.

"What the hell does that mean?" I demanded. I had no clue if he knew I was pregnant, but if time was screwed down here what did that mean for my baby?

"It means," my uncle replied slowly while staring me down, "that I determine how much time you miss on Earth. A week here could equate with a minute in your world... or it could equate to a year or ten. That, my dear, will be up to you."

"To me?"

"Yes, good behavior will be in your favor. Remember that."

With that he disappeared in a blast of black glitter and smoke. Son of a bitch, this day just kept getting worse...

"Come with me," my cousin Dixie said. "You'll stay at my place during your visit."

I rolled my eyes at the use of the term visit but didn't correct her. There was something fragile and trusting about Dixie. Honestly I kind of liked her, but more than that I was hoping I could use her to get the hell out of... well, Hell.

CHAPTER THREE

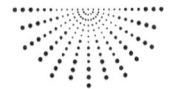

Dixie's bungalow was really freakin' nice. Gorgeous and graceful—very much like her. Actually, all of Hell was lovely. It reminded me of Kentucky in the spring... on crack. Blooming trees and roses and climbing blossoms everywhere. Literally. The scented air calmed me with its familiarity and I wondered how in the hell my father fit in here.

Dixie drove us from the Devil's estate back to her place in her Porsche. That's right, a Porsche.

"Um, Dixie, did you know my dad?"

She paused and considered her answer. Her body language was stiff and childlike. "Well, I'd met him, but he lived in another area."

"Another area? Like a different state?"

"Kind of," she hedged. It was clear she had no clue what she could tell me and what she couldn't. This could work to my advantage... use the naive cousin. Find out what I need to know and get the hell out of Dodge.

"Look, I won't tell anyone what you tell me. I thought I was supposed to learn about my, um... heritage. How exactly am I supposed to do that if no one answers my questions?"

"Good point," she agreed. "Listen, I have my therapy group coming over for a session. How about we talk afterwards?"

"Fine." I caved. Maybe if I was agreeable I could make her like me and she would slip up and tell me how to find a portal... "Can I sit in on your session?"

She giggled and shook her beautiful head. "Yep, but stay over on the side of the room. It gets somewhat violent at times."

"Noted." Hell was weird and I was about to discover how right I was.

THERE WERE THREE IN DIXIE'S GROUP BESIDES HER AND THE therapist, who was sporting a full body cast. WTF? They were as curious about me as I was about them. We all chatted a bit, then Dixie simply introduced me as her cousin. Nothing more. Nothing less. That was fine with me. I eyed the strange Demons and wondered if any of them would accept a bribe to get me to a portal.

Carl, Myrtle and Janet... I dubbed them the strong man, the bizarre little one and the bearded lady. Literally. Janet had a beard... Then there was the very angry therapist, who if she had a name I was not made aware of it. Again, fine by me. She was creepy and she smelled strange. I sat back in my corner and watched Hell's version of The Jerry Springer Show unfold.

The tension in the room was palpable. I scanned Dixie's living room for exits just in case this wonky little party of weird got out of hand. Carl, the Strong Man, rubbed his bald head the same way I rubbed my calf when it fell asleep. He rubbed so hard and fast, I was sure the skin was going to come off and his brain would fall out. I waited in anticipation and fear to hear what he had to say. I hadn't heard him speak yet. He did a few bizarre dance moves when I'd asked him a question earlier. I'd bit down hard on the inside of my cheek so I didn't laugh at him and I backed off. Janet, his bearded girlfriend, interpreted for him but no more. The therapist, sporting a bad attitude and a thin reedy voice, was very clear. Carl had to speak for himself.

I wondered if this wrinkle would cause a violent episode. I kind of hoped it would. A small zap of something warm shot through my body at my destructive little thought. I dismissed it and continued to watch the scene play out. Janet squeezed Carl's hand and smiled.

"I enjoy uthing my metal detector at family functionth. Preferably not my family. I made forty-nine dollarth and theventy-two thenth in jutht under nine hourth at a family reunion latht Auguth." Carl smiled. He actually had beautiful teeth and cute dimples, but the lisp… Hoo baby, now I knew why he preferred to communicate through interpretive dance. On Earth he could have had speech therapy, but in Hell I'm sure he got the crap beat out of him.

"All right then, Carl," the therapist snapped, "have you ever considered just stealing the money from the purses and wallets of the party guests? Or perhaps holding them at gunpoint and demanding their money and jewelry?"

"Um… no," Carl muttered, "I can't thay that hath ever occurred to me." He scratched his bald head in confusion.

As far I could sense, Carl didn't have magic or power. Hmmm.

I watched the therapist jot down notes and make disapproving tsking sounds. She avoided looking at me at all. Acted as if I didn't exist. Interesting. She clearly didn't want me here. Maybe she was the one to bribe…

"Janet," the therapist smiled nastily through her bandages, "you have a waxing and electrolysis appointment after this session."

"But I like my hair," Janet stammered. Her stubby little fingers instinctively went to her face to protect her beard and stache. Was she going to cry?

"Yes, but you've had over three hundred years to become evil and you have not succeeded. Your hair," the smelly, bitchy counselor sneered in disgust, "seems to be your most prized possession, so it will be taken from you." She smiled. She really was a bitch.

"Forever?" Janet whispered. Her little body trembled and Carl draped a big muscley arm around her, pulling her close.

"Forever," the therapist wasped.

"I am so glad I busted your ass with the coffee table," Myrtle muttered under her breath.

"What was that, Myrtle?" the therapist hissed.

"Nothing." Myrtle smiled and gave me a covert thumbs up. Again I had to chomp down on my cheek to keep from laughing.

I found myself happy that Myrtle had nailed the therapist with a coffee table of all things. Myrtle was my kind of girl. My guess was that it had been quite an entertaining show. A burst of magic rushed through my body as the violent thought manifested itself in my brain.

Glancing down at my fingers I noticed a black glitter coating them. WTF? Was this Demon voodoo magic? I quickly rubbed it off and tried to focus on the meeting. Satan had sent me with Dixie for a reason. There must be something in all this strangeness I was supposed to learn...

"Soooo, Janet," the nasty shrink challenged, "do you have any hobbies you'd like to share?"

Janet took a deep breath, regained control of her shaky little body and got back up in the saddle. "I too enjoy taking other peoples money, but I really enjoy working in television. I spend all of my free time, plus some of the time I'm supposed to be stoking the Hell Fires, following news trucks around and appearing in the background of live news reports!"

"She's been on TV at least forty-two times in the last three months alone," Myrtle gushed, giving Janet a high five.

Did Hell have its own TV stations?

Janet, gaining confidence from the high five, proudly shouted, "All of the local stations have taken restraining orders out on me!"

"Interesting," the mean ho-bag therapist droned. "Have you ever attacked a reporter or shouted obscenities on live television?" Janet was crushed. "No. I haven't."

"I thought not," Miss Meanie replied, writing in her notebook. "I'd like to point out that Muffy the Contortionist is no longer part of our group. She has graduated. She blew up a Dairy Queen on Earth last night. Apparently she felt she had been overcharged."

"Lucifer's Bouncing Balls, I hadn't even noticed her absence! Was anyone hurt?" Janet gasped and pulled on her beard in distress.

"Unfortunately, no," the icky therapist said, "but we hope she makes better choices next time." She took a pause, giving each of the group the evil eye through her bandages while still ignoring me as if I didn't exist. "Myrtle, you're next."

Myrtle fidgeted in her chair. I figured she had to be a couple of hundred years old like Janet, but she looked like she was about fifteen. Most Demons, like Vampyres, stopped aging somewhere between twenty and thirty, so it was difficult to determine true age. I wasn't sure why Myrtle looked so young.

"Um... well, I enjoy going to Earth and playing dead in public places. When I'm surrounded by humans I take perverse pleasure in jumping up and scaring the fucking shit out of them as they wail in anguish over my perceived death."

WTF? These Demons were nuts.

"Have you caused any heart attacks or strokes doing this?" Miss Bitchy Shrink grilled Myrtle.

"No, I can't say I have. A couple of them have wet themselves," she offered meekly.

"Anything else?"

"Ummm, sure." I watched Myrtle wrack her brain. "I do enjoy kidnapping people's dogs and cats. I groom them and dye their fur so they resemble wild animals. I then return them to their rightful owners in the dead of the night. I derive huge amounts of satisfaction watching our citizens walk their tigers, skunks and panda bears around town."

Everyone was speechless. That had to be one of the weirdest things I'd ever heard.

"Do you ever eat any of the animals you kidnap?" the therapist asked.

"No, I'm a vegetarian," Myrtle informed the group.

"A vegetarian Demon?" the bitch from hell shrieked, her eyes turning blood red.

Myrtle cowered behind the chair she'd formerly been sitting in. Janet started crying and braiding her beard, Carl looked mighty uncomfortable and Dixie looked like she wanted to do some damage. I suppose a veggie-Demon was an anomaly, but this shrink was a hag.

"I've heard of that," Dixie piped up, ignoring the look of hatred from the therapist. She tried not to fidget, but I could tell she was lying from a mile away. I was actually enjoying myself. These people were fucking crazy. "Those Demons get their protein from soybeans." Dixie had a captive audience so clearly she decided to elaborate. "I've heard of Veggie-Demons destroying thousands of acres of soybean fields on Earth just for an appetizer." She had to have yanked that whopper right out of her rear end.

Myrtle glanced over at Dixie gratefully. The lovely therapist looked as if she wanted to nail my cousin's ass to the wall, but she didn't dare. Dixie might have issues, but she was the head honcho's daughter. No one was stupid enough to fuck with that... or were they?

"Sooo, Your Highness," the bandaged skank began, "let's go over your list of problems...or should I say virtues. Shall we?" She laughed wickedly. "You're a straight A student, you remember birthdays, you clean your room, people describe you as kind, you pioneered the first Meals on Wheels in Hell, you donated a million dollars to feed *humans* on Earth, and you're a virgin," she sneered. "What do you have to say for yourself?"

How on Satan's Red Earth did she know Dixie was a virgin? Was Dixie a virgin? Wait. That was none of that bitch's business... and why did I even care? I barely knew my cousin, but I was pissed. I glanced around the little bungalow for something to throw at that woman's already injured head and I felt a dark power and magic run through me. Different from my Vampyre magic. Stop. This was not good. Did Satan send me here so I'd get pissed and turn fully into a Demon? If I pulled on the dark magic and destroyed the therapist would I be permanently stuck in Hell? I took a deep breath and said nothing. Thankfully I didn't have to. Myrtle stepped in.

"I don't know about you guys," Myrtle grunted, "but I'm feeling the need to bust on Dixie's coffee table and beat the living hell out of our therapist again."

Carl, Janet and Dixie grinned from ear to ear and I couldn't suppress the giggle that escaped my lips. Miss Bitchy Pants stood up and backed her way towards the front door.

"All of you, including the *Vampyre* have to report to the Dark Palace," she haughtily informed us.

"Now?" Janet asked hopefully. I assumed she hoped to avoid the enforced hair removal she was about to endure.

"No!" Meanie snapped. "This evening. After you get de-haired, you repulsive..."

"Enough," Carl shouted advancing on the horrid woman. She turned and ran from the house. Like a coward... foul, disgusting, bandage covered cowardice hag.

We stood quietly and looked at one another—the Princess, the Strong Man, the soon to be hairless Bearded Lady, Myrtle... and me.

Myrtle broke the silence. "So you're a Vampyre?"

"Apparently," I answered, hoping she didn't attack. I kind of liked her and really didn't want to kill her.

"Cool," she muttered and the rest of the freak show nodded their approval.

"She's part Demon too," Dixie added, giving me a shy smile.

"Very small part," I explained. "And I need to get home. Soon."

"I'm sure Daddy will send you home. I think he just wants to know you better."

"That's just awesome," I replied in a voice laced with sarcasm.

"He's really not that bad when you get to know him," Dixie said.

"He's worse," Myrtle mouthed to me out of Dixie's line of vision.

Fucking great. This was going to be a good time.

CHAPTER FOUR

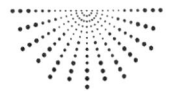

"YOUR POCKETS ARE TALKING," DIXIE SAID AS SHE TOSSED ME A PILE of dresses to try on. The therapy crew had left and we had several hours before we had to be back at the estate. From the looks of the clothes my cousin dropped on me, it was a formal affair.

"Yep, I know." I examined the goldmine Dixie had deposited in my lap and hoped that ignoring my Baby Demons in my pocket would make my cousin follow suit.

No such luck.

"Are they hungry?"

"Is who hungry?" I asked as I stuck my hands in my pockets and attempted to quiet my tiny monsters.

"The little Demons in your pocket. Are they hungry?"

"I have no idea what you're talking about," I replied as I pinched Abe, Ross, Rachel and Beyonce. They didn't help matters by giggling and poking their little heads out. "Fuck," I muttered and shook my head in disgust.

"They're adorable." Dixie giggled and reached out to them.

"No," I shouted and slapped her hand away. I quickly grabbed my little Demons before they ate my cousin. "Dixie, stay back.

They eat Demons and I kind of like you... so just back away. Slowly."

"We no eat her," Ross screamed and laughed like he was on crack. "She pretty and she good. Me like to touch her boo... "

"Enough," I snapped before Ross waxed poetic about my cousin's hooters. "You won't eat her?"

"Course not, Moooommmmmyyy," Beyonce chimed in. "She not evil. She be sweet and funny and me like her."

My Demons crawled out of my pockets and slowly made their way up my body. The tiny three-inch monsters perched on my shoulders and watched my cousin with intense curiosity. My little monsters were a recent and constant addition to my new Vampyre world. Much to my great surprise and delight, I could see Demons that others could not.

In my FUBAR undead life, my little Demons brought me joy and hours of laughter—not to mention the gifts of more power than I knew what to do with. I'd forgotten they were in my pockets when I was dragged to Hell and my gut clenched in fear. What on earth could happen to them in this place? Would they be safe? It was overwhelming enough to have to take care of myself and my baby living inside me... how was I going to manage to keep my little monsters from harm too?

Out. I needed to get out of Hell. Now.

"She is sooooooo pretty," Rachel whispered loudly.

"Thanks," Dixie said. "Can I touch you?"

"Yesssssssssssss," Rachel squealed and hopped off my shoulder into Dixie's open hand. "Don't touchy Ross or Abe. They like boobies."

"Um... okay." Dixie laughed. "Are they yours?' she asked me as she gently stroked Rachel's little head.

"Yes, they're mine and they're innocent, so if you have any ideas of turning them into evil little shits, you'll have to go through me," I snapped and took Rachel back.

Dixie was stunned by my anger and stood mutely in front of

me. My Demons began to laugh hysterically and pummel each other.

"Ohhhh, Mommmmmy so funny," Abe screamed and began to twerk on my shoulder. I plucked him off and put him on the floor. Breakdancing was one thing, but shoulder twerking was an entirely different matter.

"She no hurt us and nobody can make us bad," Ross explained to me and rubbed his little Velcro head on my cheek.

"You're sure about that?" I asked.

"Absofuckinglutely," Beyonce yelled as she flipped off my shoulder and onto Dixie's.

"Language," I hissed at them and they shrieked with delight.

"Mommmmmmmy has mouth like drunk sailor man," Rachel told my now amused cousin. "She know all the bad words ever made!"

"Great," I muttered. "That's just fucking great."

"Seeeeeeeee," Abe grunted as he twerked a figure eight around my feet. "Mommy has filthy poopy mouth. That's why we love her."

"Well, maybe she can teach me a few things," Dixie said as she lifted Beyonce off her shoulder and cradled her like a baby. Beyonce, *the traitor*, purred like a kitten and promptly fell asleep. "Do you think they're hungry?"

I paused. How to answer that… They were probably *not hungry* considering they'd eaten my very large and evil father not all that long ago. I was still coming to terms with the fact that my adorable little monsters ate bad Demons—more specifically, my father. Although I hadn't watched, the sound of the cannibalization of my pappy would stay with me for eternity…

"Well, I'm gonna go with a no on that one," I said and grimaced as I relived their last meal.

"We still full from eating your daddy," Ross crowed as he yanked up his shirt and slapped his little round belly. "He was sooooo tasty. Taste like chicken."

"Wow," Dixie said. "That's a bit unexpected, but, um… interesting and gross."

"Yeah, well, at least you weren't there," I snapped.

The silence was deafening. Several times I started to explain, but decided against it. I didn't owe Dixie or anyone in Hell an explanation for anything. The less everyone knew about me the better. I grabbed the pile of clothes and made a no-way pile and an oh-my-God-I-love-this pile. Ridiculously expensive clothing could take my mind off of almost anything. Almost.

"We no need to eat for weeks," Abe said as he humped my ankle. "And I no think your daddy taste like chicken. He taste like stinky cheese."

"Me say fish tacos," Rachel chimed in.

Okay, ewwww. "Me say enough," I said before they gave a play by play.

Dixie laid the sleeping Beyonce down on the couch and flipped through my "good" pile of eveningwear. Pulling out a drop dead Stella McCartney, she held it up to me. "Wear this. You'll be stunning."

"Look, I'm sorry if my manners are lacking, but I need to leave and going to a shindig at your daddy's is not high on my priority list."

"Astrid, Satan is fair and he is not demanding anything unusual of you. I think you should just play along until you can leave," Dixie said as she rifled through some jewelry.

She was probably right. Was she as sweet and innocent as she appeared to be? She was the daughter of the Devil. How could she be so freakin' nice?

"How old are you?"

She stopped and heaved a weary sigh. "I'm twenty."

"Twenty plus what?" I asked. Did she think I was an idiot? Every immortal looked somewhere in their twenties.

"Twenty plus nothing."

"Wow, you're a baby."

"Not much more so than you," she replied and handed me a diamond necklace and earrings. "These will be pretty with the dress. What size shoe do you wear?"

"Seven. So you haven't been alive very long."

"Nope."

"And there are more of you?" Stop being bitchy and learn something. Something helpful. Something that will help me get the hell out of Hell...

"No, there's only one me, but I do have sisters. Seven of them." She stared at me expectantly.

"What am I missing?" I asked. Was this a game show? Did I have to guess everything? I pinched the bridge of my nose to ward off the headache that was threatening.

"You don't know?"

"No." I rolled my eyes. "If I knew I wouldn't ask."

"Seven," Rachel screamed, waking Beyonce from her slumber which led to a baby Demon smackdown of epic proportions.

Ignoring the violent wrestling match at my feet, I stared at my cousin. "I'm sick of cryptic. Just fucking tell me."

"The Devil has seven daughters. I have seven sisters."

"Actually he has eight," I corrected her.

"True, but for thousands of years he had seven. I'm very new," she said. "I wear a six and a half shoe. Do you think you can squeeze your feet into these?"

I was momentarily speechless as she held up the hottest Prada pumps I'd ever seen.

"Oh my God," I gasped. "Are those this season?"

"They're next season." She grinned and handed them over.

"I'd consider cutting off some toes to fit into these babies."

"That would be gross," she giggled. "Did you figure out the seven yet?"

"I think so," I said as I attempted to wedge my size seven foot into her size six and a half shoe. "But it's so appallingly cliché it's pathetic."

29

"Then you got it right."

"Your sisters are the Seven Deadly Sins?" I laughed and then groaned. My toes were on fire. "Shitfuckshitshit, these are way too tight."

I felt like the ugly stepsister from Cinderella as I tried in vain to shove my foot into the slipper... no fucking go.

"Yes, they are. I can call Greed and see if she'll loan you a pair. I'm pretty sure she wears a seven."

"Someone named Greed is going to let a random cousin she doesn't know borrow her shoes?" I asked and reluctantly handed her back the gorgeous footwear.

"She doesn't like to part with her possessions, but getting to meet you before all the rest of them should be enough incentive for her to agree." Dixie grinned with glee and texted her sister.

"What about Sloth?" I asked. "Would she just sleep through us pilfering her shoes?"

"Trust me, you don't want Sloth's shoes."

"Why? No. Don't answer that. The less I know about all of you, the better. I'll just wear my own."

"You're wearing black Converse. I don't think that will work with Stella McCartney." Dixie laughed and sat down on the floor with my exhausted Demons. Beating the living daylights out of each other tended to wear their little monster asses out.

"I think Converse goes with everything," I said and joined her on the floor. "Why are you nice? Aren't you supposed to be evil and mean?"

"You think I'm nice?" Dixie's eyes lit up and she grinned happily.

"I do," I admitted, biting back my own grin. I really didn't want to like her, but she was making it difficult. "However, you've been kind of useless to me so far. Aren't you supposed to bring me up to speed about my heritage so I can get the hell out of Dodge?"

"What do you want to know?"

The floor and walls of Dixie's bungalow shuddered. I scooped up my babies and held them to my chest. Big mistake as Abe and Ross took that as a cue to feel me up.

"What was that?" I demanded as I peeled my little boys off my boobs.

"I have no idea." Dixie literally disappeared and rematerialized by her window. "It felt like a Hellquake, but it's the wrong season for those."

"Hellquake?" I laughed and rolled my eyes. "Is that Hell's version of an earthquake?"

"Yes, Miss Smarty Pants, it is. Well, nothing is on fire out there and my security team is still in place so no one has breached the barrier and tried to kill us. We're fine."

"Fine? We're fine?" I asked in a voice that sounded weird even to me. "We are not fine. I don't belong here. I have a mate and a family that will be looking for me and I have no time for this crap."

"You're going to have to make time," Dixie said. "If you don't, you'll find that time is all you have."

"Oh, for shit's sake," I groaned, "you sound like a freakin' fortune cookie."

"Whatever," she huffed. "Ask your questions and I'll answer what I can."

"Why aren't you evil?"

Dixie rolled her eyes. "Not all Demons are evil and not all Angels are good. Nothing is that simple. There's no such thing as pure evil and no such thing as pure good."

"Mommy is good. She kill her mommy and daddy today," Rachel chimed in. "They baaaad mamba jambas."

"Do you consider yourself evil?" Dixie inquired.

"Absolutely not," I shot back.

"But you committed murder."

Wow, harsh, but correct… "It was self defense. Me or them."

"I didn't realize the Ten Commandments had a self defense clause."

31

"Okay, fine. I suck. I'm evil. Next question, did you… "

"It's about balance, Astrid," Dixie cut me off. "You can't have good without evil or you wouldn't even know what good meant. One cannot exist with out the other. Satan and God. Heaven and Hell. It creates a balance."

"But your father creates death and hatred," I countered, trying to remember what I'd learned in Sunday School a million years ago. Fuck. I couldn't remember anything.

"Nope. My father punishes those that choose to do evil. God, your uncle and mine, gave man free will. Man has a choice and his choice determines his afterlife. This little ditty was a huge mistake on God's part and my father takes great pleasure in his brother's faux pas."

"How is free will a mistake?" She was crazy and had clearly drunk the Kool-Aid. "And did you say God was our uncle?" WTF?

"Yep, I did. And personally I don't think it was a mistake at all, but God is pissed that so many have chosen the *wrong* path. His words, not mine, but it's too late. What's done is done."

"So God's mad that humans suck and Satan is happy he gets to punish them."

"That's a little simplistic, but kind of accurate." She nodded her head and went on. "Technically, Demons are forbidden to create or cause true evil—we're only allowed to siphon off the energy from evil caused by humans. But Demons, like humans, also have free will. While mild violence, deceit, stealing, promiscuity and cheating are typically overlooked, acts of terror, mutilation or hobbies resulting in the death of others are strictly forbidden. Trust me, there are plenty of Demons residing in the Basement of Hell. It can be difficult and tricky to control something that thrives on evil, yet isn't supposed to commit it."

"Hell has a basement?" I asked, trying to absorb the massive amount of info she'd just spit out.

"That's your question after what I just told you?"

"Yep."

"Ooookay," Dixie laughed. "Yes. Hell has a basement."

"And nine other levels?"

"Um, no. Dante was completely wrong."

"You're kidding me," I gasped. Was everything I knew about Hell a fairy tale?

"Dante will be here on Thursday. It's poker night. You can grill him then. He's been pissed for ages. He went ballistic when he found out the actual layout."

"So much of what you just said was screwed on so many levels."

"Nine?"

"Touché," I laughed. "Dante lives in Hell? And he plays poker?"

"No and yes. Dante resides in Heaven, but comes over every Thursday to play poker with my dad."

"God lets people out to play poker?" This was too much for even me to believe and I was a Vampyre. A myth...

"Free will, Cousin. God has no say if his residents want to vacation in Hell."

"Does that work both ways?" I asked, still amazed that Satan played poker with Dante.

"Absolutely not. God doesn't let evil touch his doorstep." Dixie sniffed with disdain.

"Who else plays poker with your dad?"

"It depends. Most of the time Hemingway comes. Occasionally Marilyn Monroe, Elvis, Picasso and Mother Teresa."

"Back the fuck up. Mother Teresa plays poker with the Devil?"

"Why wouldn't she? My dad is charming and throws a great party. Besides, she's always trying to reform him." Dixie giggled and shook her head. "Oh, and one time Nixon came."

"How'd that work out?"

"Dad says he cheats."

"Of course he does," I muttered, wondering if she was just pulling all of this out of her ass and fucking with me...

"With all that being said, it would be a grave mistake to assume

Demons are goody goodies. They're not… alright, I kind of am, but I'm a freak here."

"I have no issue with freaks. I ride that train too," I told her.

"Here's the bottom line. I've been raised to be grateful to evildoers, because without them Demons wouldn't exist. We derive our power and magic from the chaos and evil of humans. So while we don't necessarily cause it, we thrive on it or feed on it, so to speak. Don't forget that our Uncle God dealt out the free will thing, not my dad. And now to combat his error in judgment, God and his army of Angels keep trying to end evil so my dad and his people, including me… and you, will cease to exist. No offense, but God really screwed himself by letting men and women choose their own paths. If he wanted everyone to be good, he should have come up with a better plan. Daddy thinks that particular subject is hilarious."

"I bet he does," I mumbled and wondered how to broach the what-does-a-portal-look-like subject without seeming too obvious.

"There's a ton more for me to tell you, but we only have a couple of hours before we have to go and not to be rude, but you need a shower. Your hair is kind of wild and there's soot all over your face and you've got some dried blood on you."

"Um, you waited till after your therapy session to tell me I looked like a homeless person?" I snapped.

"No, I did that on purpose. You look dangerous and crazy with all that hair and blood. I thought it might throw our bitchy therapist off her game… and it did." Dixie grinned and gave me a thumbs up.

I couldn't bite back my grin. Dixie wasn't quite as nice as I thought and I was glad. "Fine. Show me to your bathroom and I'll get spiffied up for your evil shindig."

"Wait till you see your hair," she giggled and led me deeper into her home.

"That won't happen," I told her as I examined her house. It was awesome—all done in earthy colors with bold slashes of chocolate brown and dusty rose woven in. "I'm a Vamp. No reflection."

"Oh, that's too bad," she said. "The red streaks in your hair rock."

"What red streaks? I don't have red streaks."

"Um… you totally have red streaks."

"Son of a bitch," I muttered, running my hands through the tangled mess. "Is that some kind of Demon gift?"

"Don't know, but I sure wish I had them."

Her bathroom was huge and better than any bathroom I'd ever been in. On one side were floor to ceiling mirrors and Dixie was right—I was a fucking mess. I mean I was still hot in that Vampyre undead way, but I was covered in dried blood and my clothes were torn. But my hair… holy Hell. My hair was its usual dark brown, but there were blood red streaks running through it. She was right—it was hot, but it shouldn't be there.

Wait. WTF? I could see myself?

I grabbed the counter for purchase and heaved in a huge unsteady breath—another thing I shouldn't be able to do. My body shook as I peered at myself. The self I hadn't seen since before I died. What did this mean? Was I still a Vamp? Had I become a Demon? Fuckityfuck, I needed to get back home soon before all of this was irreversible.

"Are you okay?" Dixie asked, running over to me and easing my quivering body to the floor.

"I can see myself," I whispered. "This is not good."

"Okay," she said and sat down next to me. "What can I do?"

"Help me get out of here."

"Oh, Astrid, I can't," she said with remorse.

"Then just get away from me," I hissed and put my hands over my eyes and my head between my knees. Anger boiled inside me and black glitter covered my fingers and traveled up my arms. Coating them like sparkling black sleeves. It was beautiful in a macabre way. I felt the dark power weave its way through my body and settle next to my dormant Vampyre power.

"Oh shit, Astrid," Dixie gasped and backed away quickly. "Be careful. You could blow us to Kingdom Come with that much magic."

"What are you talking about?"

"What do you mean what am I talking about?"

"Oh my God," I shouted. "If I ask a question, it means I don't know the answer. I don't talk just to listen to my own voice. So just spit it out, Cousin."

"You have dark magic," she said reverently. "And you have tons. I've never seen sleeves like that. Ever. Not even on my dad."

"How in the fucking hell do I make them go away?" I demanded, terrified that I would blow us up without even meaning to. I had no idea how I had this magic, what to do with it or how dangerous I was.

"Think good thoughts," she insisted frantically. "Think of people you love. Now."

I closed my tired eyes and willed Ethan to appear. I reached for him and he gently ran his hands over my stomach. Our child. Our baby that shouldn't be, but was—against all odds and reason. I let my mind wander to my nana who was in Heaven and then I floated to my dearest friends, Gemma, Venus, The Kev and Pam... and the tension left my body. The sleeves disappeared. I was calm... I was okay.

I opened my eyes to see a flabbergasted Dixie trembling in the corner of her bathroom.

"What?" I asked.

"What are you?" she asked so quietly I was sure I misunderstood.

"I'm sorry, what?"

"What are you?" she repeated.

I glanced over at myself in the mirror, shrugged my shoulders and laughed humorlessly. "I have no fucking clue, but I'd like you to keep this little episode to yourself if you wouldn't mind."

"Not a problem," she said with a shaky smile. "No one would believe me anyway."

"Awesome. Now leave so I can shower and then stare at myself. I haven't seen myself in a while."

"Will do," she said, backing out of the bathroom. "Will do."

CHAPTER FIVE

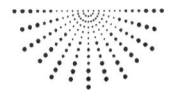

CLEAN AS A WHISTLE AND CONFUSED AS ALL GET OUT, I SAT DOWN
in front of the mirror to inspect myself. I traced my reflection and
wondered if all Vamps could see themselves in Hell or if I was so
freaky I was the only one. I was yanked right out of my pity party
by voices. Female voices. Voices I didn't recognize. Had Dixie told
my secret? Had they come to get me and destroy me? Fuck.

"I refuse to accept Einstein's Snot as my cocktail name," an
angry voice shouted.

"That's nothing," another chimed in. "My fucking cocktail
name is Hobbit Nipple."

"You are both imbeciles," yet another snapped. "Mine is the
worst. I'm Rancid Orgasm."

"But that's actually fitting," the first voice squealed with glee.

What in Satan's name was going on out there? I heard
something explode and Dixie scream. I yanked on the sweats that
my cousin had left for me and raced from the bathroom to the
living room where two very gorgeous women were slapping the
fire out of their hair while another supermodel-looking gal
laughed hysterically. Dixie stood in the middle, clearly furious
with all of them.

"This is exactly why I don't invite you over here," she yelled and helped put the fire out on the gals sporting the flames. She raised her hands and water shot from her fingertips, soaking the last of the burning embers from their heads.

"They started it," the one who had clearly caused the blaze whined.

"If the three of you weren't addicted to Facebook and playing those stupid name games there would be a lot less fire in Hell," Dixie snapped at the girls.

"I'm not addicted," the dry one said, pointing at the unhappy wet ones. "Those slutty cock knobs are."

"You have some nerve, you dicknose turd waffle," the wet one on the right screeched.

I watched in shock as the wet one on the left frantically scrolled for something on her phone.

"Got it," she said and read straight from her phone. "You are a pie-eating fuck clown and a smelly crotch goblin. Take that."

"Help me, Satan," Dixie muttered, removing the phone from whom I surmised was one of her sisters. Which Deadly Sins these were I had no clue...

"I'll take that and do you one better, you tone deaf rectum captain," the dry one shot back.

"Enough," Dixie ground out through clenched teeth. "These are disgusting and you all sound like uneducated idiots. I mean really—an insult creator on Facebook? For real? All of you are at least a thousand years old."

Wow, these chicks were ancient.

"And now that you've made asses of yourselves in front of our cousin, let me introduce you."

Three sets of eyes shot to me and examined me so intensely I grew uncomfortable. Their fascination wasn't unexpected, but it was loaded. With what? I wasn't sure.

"Astrid, these are some of my sisters. The two wet ones are Lust and Greed and the dry one is Envy."

I stood my ground and studied them with the same razor sharp focus that they had leveled at me. I refused to be the first to glance away. Everything here was a game and the price for losing was high.

It was obvious the girls were related, but by no means were they identical. Envy, the dry one, was a stunning brunette with golden cat eyes and a very voluptuous body. Her bosom practically spilled from her top and her curvy figure was one that drove men to kill.

Greed was equally as gorgeous but different. Her locks were auburn, but her eyes matched the others and her body was sleeker and lankier than Envy's. She had an air about her that dared someone to cross her. I didn't plan to put that theory to the test. I'd just go with my gut on that one.

Lust... Lust was breathtaking, even soaking wet. Her hair was dark and curly and her lashes defied nature. She was tall and thin, yet curvy in all the right places. Her appeal was immense and I would think she wasn't often denied anything... ever.

"She's not all that," Lust sniffed disdainfully, eyeing me critically.

"Um... yes, she actually is all that and then some," Envy dismissed Lust's underwhelming description with a wave of her hand. She circled me and I stood very still, prepared to defend myself and my baby to the death if I had to. These gals were scary and slightly unstable. "You're gorgeous and crazy powerful, I do believe."

I stayed quiet. There was no way I was going to be Chatty Cathy with these dangerous women.

"Cat got your tongue, pretty girl?" Greed asked.

"Nope." I smiled and decided the less I said the more power I would wield. And considering I wasn't in possession of my Vampyre gifts at the moment and I had no control over my emerging Demon magic, it seemed the smartest move.

Shitshitshit. I quickly scanned the room for my Baby Demons.

I did not want these gals to know about them. No trace. Clearly they'd hidden. They were far smarter than I gave them credit for. Part of me worried these Deadly Sins might be a little more appealing to my babies' palates than Dixie. I grinned as I imagined the clusterfuck that would cause. How would I explain to the Devil that my little buddies had eaten his daughters... My grin disappeared as the gravity of that being any sort of reality set in. Note to self—do not leave Baby Demons alone with Sins. Ever.

"If she doesn't talk, how will we ever get to know our new cousin?" Lust asked as she glared at me with undisguised hostility. What the hell had I done to her?

"Shut up, you nasty and ungracious bitch," Envy snapped at her sister. "Astrid, what's your last name?"

"Um... Porter."

"Umporter or just Porter?" Greed asked, snatching her phone back from Dixie and scrolling quickly. Envy and Lust crowded her and tried to see the screen.

"Porter." What were they doing?

"Alrighty then, your Sexy Pet name is Donkey Lips," Greed informed me.

"Well, that's just lovely," I deadpanned. "What's yours?"

"I'm Smelly Cha-chas," Greed moaned with disgust.

"Snuggle Cha-cha's here," Envy added.

"Bulky Cha-chas," Lust chimed in angrily. "And little precious Dixie is Honey Cha-cha's... of course. She even gets good names. It's just not fair. My cha-chas are far superior to any of yours in this room."

"Can it, sexy," Greed told her whiny sister.

"What's your last name?" I asked all of them. I had no idea the Devil had a last name. I wondered if God did too...

"Syn with a Y," Dixie said, taking all of her sisters' phones away from them. I suppose she'd had enough of the Facebook games. I declined to make a comment or a joke about their surname. I didn't want to get my hair fried.

"So, I hear you need some shoes," Greed said, reaching into a bag at her feet. "You're a seven?"

"Yep," I said, wondering if her shoes were as incredible as Dixie's. I shouldn't have worried. She yanked out some Jimmy Choos that made me salivate.

Greed grinned and handed them to me. "It's nice to see you're a whore for lovely things. I like a materialistic girl."

The compliment was somewhat of a slap, but the shoes were hotter than hell. "I've been called worse," I grinned and slipped my feet into the insanely awesome four-inch stilettos. They were amazing and made my legs go on for days. Ethan would love them... My stomach dropped to my toes. What in the hell was I doing getting excited over shoes? Ethan had to be going out of his mind. Time to learn a little more about my heritage so I could get back to my real undead life.

"So Daddy has a big announcement to make tonight," Envy said, rolling her eyes.

"It's probably about Astrid's visit." Dixie squeezed my hand and gave me a small smile.

"Nope," Envy cut her off. "He's been keeping a secret for at least a week. Astrid just got here today. Oh, and Astrid, Wrath can't wait to meet you! When she heard you killed your parents she was wildly impressed. And just so you know, we all thought your father was an asshole."

"Good to know," I muttered and meant it. I would have been screwed if I'd offed a favorite uncle. "Where exactly did he rule down here?"

The silence was long and their eyes were round. Why was that such a difficult question? Then the laughing started. And it went on until they were doubled over on the floor in tears. Dixie was the only one who wasn't amused.

"Oh, that's rich," Lust said, wiping her eyes. "He didn't rule anything. He was a guard of sorts in the Basement. He was an angry loose cannon."

Pot. Kettle. Black.

I had no fond feelings for my father—none—but he was my father and Lust's total disdain for him didn't sit well with me. Her insults went far deeper than my father. I knew it and she knew it… She couldn't stand me and the feeling was mutual.

I had to let my anger go before I developed my glittery black sleeves in front of my cousins. Furthermore, I needed to learn a lot more. "So what's in the Basement?"

"I believe our pretty little cousin needs a History of Hell lesson," Envy said as she made herself comfortable on Dixie's couch. "Dixie, you've been shirking your duties."

"No," I countered. "She's explained quite a bit. We just hadn't gotten to the geography section yet." I wasn't going to let them come down on Dixie. It seemed that they took far too much pleasure in doing that. "She's been lovely."

"Of course she has," Lust hissed and shoved Dixie to the side as she took her place next to Envy. Greed sat down on the arm of the couch leaving the armchairs for me and Dixie. I sat and waited.

"Wrath and Pride enjoy the Basement." Greed shuddered. "It's the lowest level."

"So there are levels?" I asked and wondered if Dante had gotten some of it right.

"Yes," Greed nodded, "but if you're thinking Dante, think again. The man is an idiot. You should have seen his face when he realized how wrong his little work of fiction was. Priceless."

"Anyhoo," Envy took over, "the Basement sucks. You know, the Hellfire and brimstone, screaming in agony, burning for eternity Hell. The Hell from the movies… That's where the most evil go when they die. Those bastards are punished in fire until the end of time. Nobody can give an exact definition on what the end of time actually means. You would assume that my dad or his brother Uncle God would have an idea on that one, but if they do, they're playing it close to the chest."

"And my father did what down there?" I asked, sickened by the thought of the Basement.

"He controlled the thermostat," Lust spat. "He burned people alive, and from everything I've heard he enjoyed it." She stared at me with such contempt my fingers itched to smack her. Thankfully I didn't. Good ideas in the moment often turned out to be shitty ideas in the long run. The others seemed nonplussed by Lust's viciousness. I suppose they were used to it or she was like this with everyone. Lovely.

"So he killed people?"

"No. They're already dead. They're souls," Greed explained. "He doled out punishment..." She paused and glanced at her sisters. Dixie nodded at her. She hesitated but continued. "Demons can't actually kill. We just siphon energy."

"My father killed people and his minions killed people."

Greed sucked in a weary breath. "Your father was an anomaly. A problem—which is why he was relegated to the Basement. He wasn't supposed to leave, but he was crafty and... well, he was stupid. He had free will just like the rest of us and chose to use it unwisely. You actually did Satan a rather huge favor by killing him. My father would have loved the honor, but as I said... we can't actually kill. We all have a purpose in the balance between good and evil."

"What in the hell was his purpose?" I clenched my fists at my sides. This was simply too much information, but I knew I needed to hear it as much as I didn't want to.

"Possibly to sire you—I'm not sure."

"Fucking awesome." I had more questions, but I didn't know if I wanted the answers. "Did I really kill him? Is he gone for good?"

"Oh, yes," Envy said. "You did excellent work."

"I'd say thank you, but I'm not exactly proud of what I did."

"Now your mother is a different story," Lust said, enjoying the look of horror on my face at the mention of my mother. "She's down here. I'd love to take you for a visit."

"Lust…" Greed warned. "You have no jurisdiction over those matters. I'd suggest you back off," she added in a voice that sent chills down my spine.

My mother was here. It wasn't unexpected. I certainly didn't expect her to go to Heaven. I searched my heart and realized I felt very little. Had I become hard or had she just beaten any feeling out of me? I assumed she was in the Basement, but I refused to ask. My parentage was so appalling, I just wanted to avoid the topic altogether.

"She's really quite pretty… well, she was," Lust purred, making me want to beat her senseless. I was now quite sure my mother was burning in the Basement. I knew she deserved it, but… As much as I couldn't ratchet up any feelings for my mother, I wanted to destroy anyone who spoke badly of her. I was the only one who was allowed to do that.

"Back to the lesson," Envy said, cutting off any more input from her nasty sister. "The next level up is the Sub-Basement. The Sub-Basement is for lesser evil souls when they die. There's fire there too, just not as hot. The lucky humans who reside there weren't quite bad enough for the Basement, but not quite good enough for Purgatory. I know, many doubt Purgatory, but it exists."

Dixie piped up. "I've been there and trust me, you don't want to go. It's boring and beige, it smells stale and they play bad cheesy elevator music 24/7." She giggled and shuddered. I gave her a smile and Greed nodded her head in agreement.

"Kind of like nails on a chalk board. Too close to Heaven for me," she said and winked.

I liked Greed. I mean, I wasn't into greedy people but the girl was funny and a lot nicer than the others.

"Ohhhh, don't forget about the Rehab Room," Dixie said.

"Daddy likes to pretend that one doesn't exist," Lust laughed. God, she was really beautiful. As much as I didn't like her it was almost impossible to dismiss her appeal.

"Right," Dixie agreed. "It's a room where souls do penance so they can leave Hell and ascend to Purgatory... then possibly Heaven. It's a major long shot, but there are some who I do think end up down here by mistake. Not that I would share that with my dad—my good report cards are about all he can take. The flip side of that is that some in Purgatory end up becoming violent and have to descend into Hell. Personally, I think the constantly piped in elevator music causes some souls to snap. It would make me want to tear my own head off."

"Agreed," Envy said. "And why in the hell are you still getting good report cards? Did you not listen to my lecture on skipping class?"

"I like learning," Dixie whispered, clearly afraid of ridicule.

"Listen, sweetie," Greed told her. "You can still learn everything you want. Absorb all of it. I did. You just need to blow your tests—on purpose. It will get Daddy off your back and it's what's expected of you. We have a reputation to uphold, dear."

Greed really was nice, but had a fucked up idea of what was right... Although what did I know? Hell was not my territory and I didn't want it to be.

"Don't forget the main floor." Envy stood up and walked over to me. "That's where we are now. It's as big as the United States, but most of the action takes place in the northeast corner in an area about the size of Washington D.C. This is where the Demons live. We're born in Hell and we are the loyal army of Satan, my dad. Many Demons take the portals back and forth to Earth all the time. Personally, I'd rather stay in Hell with my family no matter how dysfunctional we might be." She eyed her sisters and they all laughed.

"I like going to Earth," Lust cooed. "Humans are such a delight to fuck... and so are Vampyres."

"You've slept with a lot of Vampyres?" I asked. I could see Vampyres being attracted to her. I could see almost anything being attracted to her. Although once they got to know her...

"A few." She laughed and examined me like I was a science project. "I could go for some more Vamp sex. In fact... "

"Give it a rest," Envy snapped. "You're such a slut."

"Jealous much?" Lust snapped back.

"Enough." Greed stood up. "It was lovely to meet you, Astrid. We'll be seeing you at the gathering shortly. Enjoy my shoes and remember, everything comes at a price." She winked and all three of them disappeared in a flash of glitter and smoke.

"Holy shit," I muttered looking at Greed's shoes and wondering what kind of hellish price tag they came with.

"That was nothing," Dixie said and flopped down on her couch. "They were on good behavior. Just wait till you meet Wrath."

I glanced over at my cousin and gave her a smile that I was sure resembled a grimace. I had a lot to digest from this little get together and it exhausted me. "I can't wait. Truly. I can't fucking wait."

CHAPTER SIX

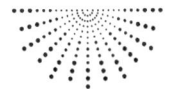

THE DEVIL'S ESTATE WAS CALLED THE DARK PALACE. FROM THE WAY Dixie picked at her nail polish on the car ride over made me think being called to the palace wasn't a good thing. At all.

"The Dark Palace is Daddy's main residence," Dixie explained as she ripped off a large intact piece of polish while driving. "I grew up there."

"Is the weather always so nice?" I asked the most benign question I could think of, wishing I had some of my own polish to rip.

"Yep. Warm, breezy and balmy all year round. We have more varieties of exotic plants and animals than Heaven. That really pisses Uncle God off royally." She giggled and seemed to relax a bit.

I glanced out the window of the car and took in the beauty. The palace property was loaded with streams, ponds, rolling hills and meadows filled with blindingly colorful wild flowers. Dixie's bungalow was tucked into the far northwest corner of her father's land. Her yard boasted huge weeping cherry trees, orchids and scads of bougainvillea. Absolutely beautiful and the total

ROBYN PETERMAN

antithesis of what I expected in Hell... although the Basement might cause me to reconsider.

I learned the palace itself sat on forty very manicured acres. It looked like a giant gothic cathedral. It was the grandest castle in the world, including Heaven and everything in between.

"We're a little early," Dixie said as she handed her keys to a valet in front of the massive doors of the palace.

I was a bit nervous, but my cousin was a wreck. She was chewing her nails like she hadn't eaten in a month. "Are you okay?" I whispered and pulled her fingers from her mouth.

She giggled and wrung her hands. "I'm just a little nervous that my dad is going to hand down my punishment for feeding the hungry humans tonight."

"Surely he wouldn't do that at such a public event."

"You don't know my dad."

Shit—and I really didn't want to.

Dixie had dressed with care. Her very fitted Prada cocktail dress was the bomb and her Lanvin stilettos were the stuff my dreams were made of. I knew I was no slouch either. The Stella McCartney rocked and Greed's shoes capped it off perfectly. I suppose if I had to be in Hell it was nice to dress up in clothes that equaled my entire salary as an art teacher for two years...

Of course the jewelry my cousin had lent me made me a bit uncomfortable. From the size of the rocks in my ears I'd assumed they were fake... Never assume. That makes an ass out of you and me. To my horror they were real. Six freakin' carats in each ear. I was wearing a house—a really nice one. I tried to take them off, but Dixie insisted I wear them and informed me I'd be keeping them... as a gift from her and her father. She was in for a rude awakening because she was getting them back. I couldn't even imagine the price that would go along with that gift.

As our Jimmy Choos and Lanvins clicked on the fieldstone tiles that led to the huge carved teak door, I jerked to an abrupt halt.

50

"What the fuck?" I gasped. Two of the most vicious looking animals flanked the door and watched us with beady little yellow eyes. I was so not walking past that.

"What?" Dixie asked with alarm.

"Those things," I said under my breath, just in case they understood English. "Those things look hungry... and pissed off."

"Oh, the Hell Hounds?" Dixie laughed and leaned in close. "You can't tell a soul, but the Hell Hounds are just big ugly puppies with razor sharp fangs and claws. I love them and they love me. Those two are my favorites, General George Patton and Bambi. They slept in my room until I moved out of the Palace a couple of years ago."

"For real?" I asked doubtfully. They did not look anything like puppies to me. "What in the hell do they eat?"

"Cheese pizza." She giggled. "I want to go love on them, but Daddy would be furious if word got out that the Hell Hounds were big cuddly, slobbery babies. I don't mean to imply they're wimps—if anyone even looked at me, my sisters or Hell forbid, my dad sideways, the Hell Hounds would kill them in two seconds flat. Other than that, they're sweet."

"Awesome," I said, still not moving.

"Come to think of it, they'll automatically protect you too."

"Right."

"No, they will. You and I have the same blood. We're related. They can tell."

General George and Bambi purred as we passed. I instantly relaxed. Dixie giggled and blew them covert kisses, bumping into Bambi on purpose. I gently ran my hand over General George's head. His fur was soft and silky and he smelled like brownies. Who was I to judge things by the way they looked? I was in love with my Baby Demons and they were definitely not winning any prizes in the looks department, but they were beautiful to me. I glanced back at the Hell Hounds and they both gave me a slobbery smile and a quick wink. Of course I made friends with the weirdos...

I took a deep breath and followed Dixie inside. My pace was slow, but I felt like I was walking to the guillotine.

A very well put together woman clad head to toe in designer Chanel made a beeline for us.

"Dang it," Dixie moaned. "That's Daddy's new consort. What is her name?" Dixie's fingers flew back into her mouth. "It's something like Sandra or Miranda or... crap, I'm sure it ends in an A."

"Hello Dixie," the consort ending in A said while ignoring me completely. She was dressed to the nines and she was short. Even with her four inches heels, she was still a good deal shorter than both me and my cousin, but then again, we were on the tall side. I had a tough time seeing what Lucifer saw in this gal. I would assume he could have his pick of anyone. She was definitely pretty in a blonde Barbie doll kind of way. She did have big boobs and a nice backside, but she was a mean Demon. My Baby Demons would definitely find her appetizing... Note to self: leave Babies at Dixie's while in Hell. This one, whatever her name was, seemed smart. Mean and smart. Well, not so much smart as sly and greedy. She eyed my ears with great interest.

"Those are lovely earrings," she purred, addressing me and the rocks in my ears that could feed a small country. She made a lovely face as if I either smelled bad or she was in serious pain.

"Yep." I grinned, then sniffed the air around her and gagged.

She pressed her overly enhanced lips together and decided to ignore me again. Fine with me. She rolled her eyes and stared daggers at Dixie.

"Oh, right," Dixie stammered. "This is my cousin Astrid. Astrid this is, um... this is... "

"Amanda," she hissed. "My name is Amanda."

"I knew that." Dixie smiled at her. "And I have to agree with you, Astrid's earrings are lovely. They're a present from my dad."

"My, my, my," Amanda choked out. "Such a lovely gift for one so distantly related... and a *Vampyre* to boot."

Dixie shifted uncomfortably back and forth on her stilettos, but I'd had enough of the icky Amanda. I flashed her some fang and smacked my lips together hungrily. She was gone in a heartbeat.

"That was awesome." Dixie giggled and hugged me tight. "I can't stand her. I hope Daddy doesn't keep that one around for long. I preferred Kitty, the last consort. She was as dumb as a box of hair, but she was a great cook and she smelled like honeysuckle."

I really had nothing to add to that.

"Hey Dixie. Hey Astrid." Myrtle, the bizarre little gal from the therapy session, ran up to us and slapped me on the back with such force I almost hit the deck. Holy Hell, she was strong.

"Sorry," she muttered and grinned sheepishly. She wore a black tracksuit with black Pumas on her skinny little body. Her hair was pulled away from her face. She had a pretty face. I hadn't noticed that earlier. "This place gives me the heebees," she said. "No offense, Dixie. I know it's your dad's crib and all, but damn."

"None taken." She laughed and hugged Myrtle. "Thank you."

"For what?" Myrtle was confused.

"For being you."

"Oh, okay," she said. "Hey, do I...um, look alright?" she asked. Her face turned blotchy red in embarrassment.

"You look great," I told her. Dixie nodded in agreement. "I didn't realize how pretty you were until tonight with your hair away from your face."

"Oh." Myrtle was speechless. She looked like a fragile little girl and I felt an overwhelming need to protect her. Great... now I wanted to protect Demons? Home. Soon.

"Hey, um..." she continued, abruptly changing the subject, "is there a john around here? I've gotta take a leak."

"Yes," my cousin said, trying not to laugh. I sucked my bottom lip into my mouth to keep from giggling. Myrtle really was quite disgusting. "Go down that hall and you'll find several johns."

"Thanks." The little Demon wandered off with a spring in her step and a new air of confidence about her.

Dixie took my hand and we made our way through the foyer. The foyer of the palace was tremendous. A huge curved marble staircase dominated the enormous space. The ceilings were three stories high with violent religious frescos painted on them.

"Oh my God." I was shocked at how many works of art I recognized. "The paintings. Are they copies?"

"Nope. Real," Dixie told me. "Quite a few famous artists have spent time in Hell. Some because they deserved it and others came for a visit out of curiosity. A couple of the visitors have chosen to stay on the main floor in Hell much to our Uncle God's dismay. Apparently unless you're burning in the Basement, Hell is a lot more fun than Heaven."

"Huh," I said, still shocked by the sheer amount of priceless art everywhere. "What the hell is hanging in the museums on Earth?"

"Forgeries."

I thought the Vampyres were opulent... they had nothing on Satan. Thick burgundy red brocade curtains rained down from the windows that were at least thirty feet high. The curtains boasted heavy golden fringe and masterpieces dotted the creamy ivory walls. A mix of my favorites—van Gogh, Goya, Basquiat, Botticelli. And to my utter amazement—Da Vinci's *Mona Lisa*. Clearly the one I'd seen in the Louvre was a fake. Much to my chagrin, I realized I was not so discretely grooving to *Lovin', Touchin', Squeezin'*... WTF?

"Dixie, what's the deal with Journey?" I asked, pressing my hands to my sides so I didn't raise them over my head and sway.

"Daddy *loves* Journey. You could say he's obsessed. He can't wait till they all die and he can have his own personal Journey concerts in Hell. He was heartbroken when Steve Perry quit the band. He didn't come out of his suite for a month."

Wait. What? That was just weird. So weird I didn't know what to say. Hell had rendered me speechless several times in one day. Ethan would be impressed. My gut clenched at the thought of what he must be going through. I wondered if there was a way to communicate with him. Were there phone lines to Earth? Would Satan let me use one? Would Dixie? Would Myrtle?

The foyer was full of Demons, from the most high ranking, who were sipping expensive champagne, to the lowliest, who were serving it. I didn't see my Uncle Satan anywhere, but I did catch Amanda the consort greeting guests as if she owned the place. Gross.

"Thank Beelzebub, Cole is on her," Dixie muttered as she snagged two champagnes for us.

"What do you mean?" I asked, staring stupidly at the glass in my hand. Did I try to take a sip? Could I eat down here? I could breathe and see myself…

"The man tailing Amanda, the wanking bitch, is my dad's second in command, Cole. I'm glad that someone who has my father's ear can see what an opportunistic skank she is."

"Right," I said, still eyeballing my glass.

"Drink it, it's wonderful champagne. Daddy has the finest vineyard on all the planes of existence."

"That's lovely, but I'm a Vampyre. I drink blood, not grape juice."

"Okay, ewww, but you're a Demon too and you're in Hell. Try it."

I lifted the glass to my lips feeling like I was somehow betraying my Vampyre heritage, but when in Hell… Forcing a bright smile I took a sip and it tasted like ass. Not that I knew what ass tasted like, but it was bad, stinky and gross and I couldn't have been happier. There was still some Vamp in me. I spit the offending liquid back into the glass and grinned.

"Bad?" Dixie laughed.

"Very," I choked out.

"And that makes you happy why?"

"Because I haven't totally lost myself."

"I don't get it, but I'm glad you're happy. Come on, let's get this evening over with."

"Lead on, dear cousin."

CHAPTER SEVEN

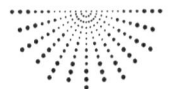

THE GRAND BALLROOM WAS EVEN MORE ORNATE THAN THE FOYER. The marble floors were encrusted with precious gemstones; rubies, sapphires, emeralds, and diamonds and ten of the most gorgeous crystal chandeliers I'd ever seen spilled down from the ceilings. It was waaay over the top in my book, but Demons clearly enjoy the sparkly.

I was guessing by the looks of things that everyone who was anyone in Hell was here and I had a bad feeling that I was going to be part of the festivities. The covert pointing and whispering didn't help. They made me feel like a freak. Speaking of, I spotted Carl and... *Sweet Baby Cousin Jesus*, was that Janet? Carl had his arm around the most delicately pretty woman I'd seen in Hell yet. She wasn't a knockout like Dixie and her sisters, but she was a timeless beauty.

She was small with a Cupid's bow mouth, glittering gold eyes, rounded pink cheeks and a gorgeous mane of chestnut hair. The only giveaway were her stubby little fingers. I recognized those from the therapy session earlier. She wore a simple black dress and flats and looked extremely uncomfortable and insecure. Carl

ROBYN PETERMAN

kept his arm tightly around her and growled at any male Demon
that even glanced Janet's way.

"Dixie, look. There's Carl and Janet," I said, pulling her to a
stop so she could see.

"Oh my Hell," she gasped. "She's beautiful without the beard
and stache."

They were too far away for us to call out and I quickly lost
sight of them as more Demons filed into the Grand Ballroom.

"Follow me, we'll find them later," Dixie instructed as we
moved to an area near a gothic three story stained glass window
that was reserved for Lucifer's family. I spotted Greed, Envy, Lust
and four others who had to be the rest of the Sins. They were
stupidly gorgeous and waving us over. My gait slowed.

"Don't worry, Astrid. They have to behave here," Dixie said,
pulling my reluctant body toward the Seven Deadly Sins.

"Did you know when a male octopus finds his mate he rips his
own penis off and throws it at her? She then inseminates herself
and he grows another one," Envy told her sisters, much to their
disgust. "Oh Astrid, you look to die for," she gushed.

"Already dead," I replied, hoping she was done with her sea
creature sex stories. My response elicited laughter from my gaggle
of dangerous cousins.

"Isn't she lovely, girls?" Envy asked, looking directly at Lust
who turned away in anger. What was that about?

A breathtaking blonde eyed me with interest. She had the
same eyes and build as her sisters, but her coloring was vastly
different. "I've been waiting for you," she said in a voice that was
even more hypnotic than her father's. "I'm Wrath."

I stood and stared mutely at her. She was one powerful
Demon. Wrath stood and approached. Every instinct I had was to
step back, but I held my ground. Being tested repeatedly in Hell
was wearing me out.

"Nice to meet you, Wrath." I held out my hand, but she took
me in her arms and laid a big wet one dangerously close to my

mouth. *Alrighty then.* Her arms around my body were drenched in magic—strong magic. "You are very powerful," she whispered in my ear, sending shivers of sheer terror down my spine. "It's good to have you here."

"Um, thanks," I said, extricating myself and moving away. I knew I may have lost a few points by moving out of lip range, but I had no intention of making out with my Cousin Wrath.

"Did you realize that huge penises were thought to be disgusting in Ancient Greece? That's why all the statues are sporting itty bitty marble man junk," Envy said, reading straight from her phone.

"Give me the phone before I zap it and shove it up your ass," one of the sisters I hadn't been introduced to said. It had to be Gluttony, Pride or Sloth... I was betting on Sloth. Although beautiful, she was a wrinkled mess and looked as if she'd just rolled out of bed.

"That's Sloth," Dixie said, confirming my guess. Sloth grinned and nodded. "And the other two are Pride and Gluttony." All three girls had varying shades of dark brown hair and golden eyes. They were identical for all intents and purposes, only little things made them differ. It was difficult to tell them apart except for Sloth's sloppiness. "They're triplets," Dixie added.

"Wow." It was all I could think of to say. This was a whole new world of strange. I was a bit overwhelmed by my new family and not in a warm and fuzzy way.

"So Dixie," Greed said with her hands clasped in excitement. "I think you're going to be assigned tonight."

"But I'm too young," she gasped. She grabbed my arm so tightly I was sure a bone would snap. Her dismay and fear were so evident that I stayed still and let her maim me. I was a Vamp. I'd heal.

"Oh, honey child, I was fourteen when I got assigned," Greed laughed and kissed her forehead.

What the hell did assigned mean? Clearly Dixie wasn't on board with it.

"That was eight hundred years ago," Dixie said.

"You're twenty," Envy chimed in, "and for whatever reason, Daddy thinks you're going to come into a bunch of power very soon."

"Wouldn't it be better if I was at home when my powers emerged?" my sweet and terrified cousin asked.

"Nope." Envy smiled and ran her beautifully manicured hand down Dixie's cheek. "There are things happening that need to be dealt with and Daddy thinks you're the gal to do it."

Dixie was on the verge of tears and I was sure my arm would never be the same. I was tempted to ask what they were talking about, but I was afraid if I opened my mouth I would scream in pain.

"I haven't had much training and I suck at being a Demon," Dixie said desperately.

"Oh baby," Sloth cooed, pulling her close and thankfully disengaging her from my arm. "You're a beautiful Demon. None of us were trained before we were assigned. Lucifer believes in on-the-job training. You can't conquer the world without failing miserably first, sweetie."

"What if all I do is fail?" she whispered.

"You won't, my darling." Wrath smiled and gave her baby sister a quick hug.

"Of course you can bring your imaginary friend," Lust said and elbowed Pride with glee. Dixie blushed a deep red and stared at the floor. She certainly seemed a little old for an imaginary friend, but who was I to judge? Growing up in Hell surrounded by nightmare inducing siblings had to be hard.

"Shut up, Lust. Stop being a bitch." Wrath turned on Lust so quickly the air around us cooled. Lust closed her mouth and stared daggers at her sister. "You do not want to fuck with me," Wrath hissed, advancing on Lust.

"Enough," Greed snapped and separated her sisters before they had a go at each other. If this was good behavior, I would hate to see the alternative.

"Ohhhh, here he comes," Sloth said, causing all to stand at attention.

A hush fell over the room as Satan entered. His beauty was absurd. Demons were an extraordinary looking race, but Satan put all to shame. His black Armani suit fit to perfection and he wore his black silk shirt open at the neck. It wasn't just his looks, it was his aura—something intangible. Sheer unadulterated power. It was obvious by the reaction in the room that he instilled rabid loyalty, adoration and fear. He was beloved by his people and despised by his enemies. And he clearly loved being in charge.

"Good evening, my Demons," Satan laughed, showing even white teeth and dimples that brought women to their knees. My cousin Greed snuck up behind me, poked me in the ribs and made a gagging sound as all the women in the room swooned over her father—my uncle. I stifled my grin and watched the drama unfold.

"Greed," Dixie whispered in a panic, "am I getting assigned because I sent money to feed humans?"

"Of course not," Greed whispered back. "Now hush."

She did.

"Welcome my people," the Devil's voice boomed through the Grand Ballroom. His second in command, Cole, stood on his right and the skanky consort Amanda stood on his left.

"That's certainly new," Envy said under her breath.

"What's new?" I asked, looking around. Dumb question because everything was new to me, but I was curious and Envy was approachable… kind of.

"I've never known a consort to stand so close to him at a public event. She has some big balls." Envy glanced around at her sisters who were watching their father and mistress with great concern.

"Tonight is a night for celebration." He grinned and my breath

61

caught. His beauty was ridiculous. "My consort carries my child and she tells me it's a son."

A gasp went through the crowd and my cousins froze. A giant wave of applause engulfed the ballroom.

"How is that possible?" Wrath hissed. "He's never sired a son. Only daughters."

"I don't know," Envy shrugged in confusion.

"Is it his?" Sloth asked.

"If it's not, she's dead." Lust laughed. "Personally I hope it's not. I can't stand that bitch."

Amanda smiled at the crowd and rubbed her yet to pop belly. Damn, as much as I didn't like her, I had to agree with Lust. Amanda was gross. The crowd eyed the consort with distrust. The applause continued, but there was much speculative whispering. She moved to Satan and put her arms around him, trying to establish ownership, but apparently that was a little premature for one who had not yet borne him a child. My uncle peeled her off and walked away, leaving her humiliated and alone.

"Is this how it was when I was conceived?" Dixie asked her sisters.

"No, we didn't know anything about you till Daddy brought you to Hell when you were three years old."

"Where was I for my first three years?"

"Probably with your imaginary friend." Lust laughed at her cruel joke.

"Why don't you leave her alone," I snapped. I'd had just about enough of her and her shitty attitude. Dixie had just learned something shocking she never knew before.

"Why don't you make me," she shot back. Her eyes turned red and dark magic seeped out of her. I knew my own eyes turned green and I itched to take her out.

"My pleasure." I stepped toward her.

"While I'd love to see Astrid kick your skinny ass," Wrath grinned, "now is not the time or place."

We both backed off, but this was far from over.

"We don't know where you were," Greed told Dixie, ignoring the fact that a girl fight had just been averted. "But we're happy you're ours."

"I wonder if Amanda got the memo that once you bear Satan's child that he kicks your ass to the curb." Pride muttered and straightened her immaculate hair.

"Clearly big fake lipped and fake boobed Amanda doesn't think that applies to her since she plans to blow out a boy," Wrath said thoughtfully.

"You do realize that her Sexy Pet name is Donkey Nipples," Envy grunted, trying not to laugh. I bit down on my lip and held my own laughter in. I suppose it was good they were funny considering they were as dangerous as all get out.

"Yes, that had occurred to me." Greed giggled and high fived her sister. "I dare you to call her that," she challenged.

"I'll do it," I said with pure immature bravado, imagining the horrified look on Amanda's face. "Wait... can I get killed for that?"

"No," Wrath said. "You are a guest. We don't have guests killed very often."

"Good to know," I mumbled and wondered why I offered to put my head on the chopping block. Did I want them to like me? Was I so desperate for a family that I would risk my life to make them laugh... Apparently yes. I needed to get out of here. I had a much nicer, if slightly unstable family on Earth.

"Holy shit," Gluttony gasped. It was the first time I heard her speak and it was like music. "Did you realize that the main characters in Sponge Bob Square Pants were based on us?" She was *of course* on Facebook. The sheer irony...

"Who am I? Patrick?" Sloth asked with a huge grin.

"Yep," Gluttony told her. "And I'm Gary."

"Am I Plankton?" Wrath asked.

"Nope, you're Squidward. Greed is Mr. Crabs, Envy is

Plankton, Pride is Sandy and Lust is Sponge Bob," Gluttony sputtered.

"How in the living Hell am I Sponge Bob?" Lust demanded. "There isn't one sexy thing about Sponge Bob."

"Don't know, sexy pants, but that's what Facebook says, so it's true."

"Bullshit," Lust griped. "Facebook sucks."

"Quiet, Daddy's not finished dropping bombs." Envy shushed her sisters.

"He's losing his fucking mind," Wrath hissed with disgust.

"I couldn't agree more," Lust added.

Were they serious? Was Lucifer insane? If he was, what did that mean for me? Would I ever get out of Hell if he'd lost his marbles? Shitshitdamnshit. I moved stealthily behind Wrath and Lust just in case they had anymore nuggets of wisdom to impart. I needed to be armed with everything and anything I could learn.

"Another reason I have called you here tonight is to celebrate my beautiful daughter Dixie."

The Demonic crowd went wild. She may not be evil, but she was certainly well liked. Satan held his hand out to her and she went to him like a moth to a flame. His magic filled the room and his power was undeniable. If he had gone crazy we were all in for a hell of a ride.

"It is your turn to be assigned," he told Dixie. "You shall transport to Earth in six months and serve me well."

Dixie's chin dropped to her chest and her shoulders slumped forward. I barely heard her whisper, "Yes, Father."

Two large fingers lifted her chin, forcing her to meet his gaze. "This is not a punishment," he said quietly, "it's your birth rite and your duty."

"I know, Daddy," she replied, "and I'm honored to serve you."

"You have no idea who you are yet," he told her.

"Would you like to give me a hint?" Dixie gave him a lopsided smile. A wash of light laughter went through the crowd of Demons watching the exchange between Satan and his daughter.

"It's not my way to pave a path of ease," he said. "I fear I may have done too much for you already."

"I would quite agree with that," Amanda hissed under her breath.

Oops, guess Amanda didn't get the memo about Satan's super duper mega hearing skills. His body stiffened in rage and his power and anger bounced off the walls of the Grand Ballroom. The crowd of Demons gasped in delight, dying for a bloody showdown. I couldn't help that I hoped he would destroy her as well. I felt a strong strand of magic and power jolt through my body as I owned my evil thoughts about Amanda. It felt good—entirely too good.

The Devil slowly turned to his consort and with a deadly calm ground out, "You will never interrupt me when I am talking to one of my children. Ever again."

Amanda blanched and dropped to her knees. Satan stared at her for a moment as a snicker went through the crowd of Demons. She trembled with fury. Her fisted hands pressed to her sides were a sure giveaway. She was an idiot of epic proportions.

"She had better have a boy and it better be his or Amanda is toast," Greed snickered.

Satan raised his eyes to the room, clearly dismissing his furious consort. "Who will accompany my prized daughter Dixie to Earth in six months? Who will earn my favor by risking their immortality for a Child of Lucifer?"

The crowd murmured and looked around to see who was brave enough or stupid enough to go with her.

All of what I assumed to be Satan's generals including his second, Cole, stepped forward immediately. That was to be expected and Satan nodded his approval. What came next I didn't expect.

"Who of my people will pose as a family for my daughter so she may continue her education and embarrass me with her appallingly high grades?" He grinned at Dixie. A giggle escaped her lips and she blushed. Methinks he might be just a little bit proud of her brains...

"I will protect her," I heard a familiar male voice shout, "and tho will my Mate."

"I too will lay down my life for the Demon Princess Dixie," another familiar voice added.

WTF? I turned to see Carl, Janet and Myrtle standing in front of Satan. He stepped menacingly toward Dixie's therapy group and much to my great surprise, they held their ground.

"Why," he bellowed, "should I let my prize go with three Demons who are not evil?"

"Because we will not betray you or Dixie," Myrtle told Satan without batting an eyelash. "And with all due respect, you know full well we are evil, we're just a little out of practice." Myrtle was on a roll as she straightened her tracksuit and pulled on a piece of her hair. "We are as evil as any Demon in the room, but we also feel compassion. Which quite honestly makes us far more dangerous to an enemy and more useful to you than a Demon who is only out for himself." She rocked back and forth on her black Pumas and waited.

SATAN LAUGHED. HE LAUGHED HARD. THE DEVIL WAS SO BEAUTIFUL when he laughed I had to struggle to breathe. His allure was alarming—not sexual, but addictive. He picked up a shocked Myrtle in his huge hands and kissed her. First her left cheek and then her right. She blushed a furious red and looked down at the floor.

"Yes," he said, his melodic voice still coated with mirth. "You are right, Myrtle, Keeper of Secrets. You, Carl the Destroyer and

Janet the Atrocity Maker will go with my child. Kneel to me," he commanded and they did. He laid his hands on each of them and they shuddered as a glittering black mist wafted over them.

"What just happened?" I asked Envy.

"He made them stronger," she replied.

Satan glanced over and crooked his finger at me. His charm was magnetic and I drifted to him in the same way Dixie had. The crowd began to murmur with fear and displeasure as I approached my uncle. I held my head high and ignored the dissent around me.

"This is my niece, Astrid," Satan bellowed, effectively ending the chatter. Every eye in the house was trained on me. "She is a Demon and a Vampyre. She is the Chosen One of the Vampyre lore. She is my guest and will be treated with utmost respect. She has the ability to kill and has done us a great service."

Oh shit, did they not know that I killed my daddy? How was that going to go over?

"She has eliminated my brother and for that I am most grateful."

The crowd gasped and dropped to their knees. If this was for me, Satan or my dead evil pappy, I was unsure.

"Is he gone for good?" A Demon yelled from the crowd.

"Oh, yes." Satan laughed and embraced me. "He was eaten."

"She ate her father?" someone else yelled.

I gagged and almost threw up in my mouth a bit at the thought.

"No, she did not, but that is her story to tell if she wishes."

I glanced at my uncle, grateful that he didn't out my Baby Demons. I was sure that if he knew my dad had been eaten, he was aware I had instructed my Baby Demons to do it. I did not want them to be a target. The applause started slowly, but crescendoed into a deafening roar. Well, my dad definitely didn't have any friends in Hell. Nice.

"I think it's an abomination to host a bloodsucker," Amanda said, stepping forward. She held her head high and her bulbous lips settled in an unattractive sneer.

"Is that so, my consort?" Satan asked, enjoying her hostility. His arm tightened around me, but for all intents and purposes he looked completely relaxed to the crowd.

"Yes," she said and coyly batted her eyelashes at him. "She is below us and doesn't belong here."

"Interesting. Would you like to challenge her?" he asked.

Challenge me to what?

Amanda blanched and glanced around the room looking for support. A fairly large number of Demons clapped, the rest watched warily. I tried to catalog some of her supporters. They were possibly the ones who would happily lead me to a portal if my presence was such a blight on the community.

"If I wasn't with child, I would destroy her," she hissed.

I'd had enough between Lust and the cheap silicone floozy insulting me. I didn't want to be here and it was quite obvious I wasn't wanted. There was no way in hell I would reveal that I was with child too, but her cakehole needed to be shut. "Well first of all, Pamela… whoops, I meant Donkey Nipples, although I could level your ass with my eyes shut I don't think I'd have too much fun, but I'd love to take you out after you give birth, so please by all means pencil me in."

"My name is Amanda," she ground out through clenched teeth.

"That's what I said." I grinned when I saw all my cousins from Hell giving me the thumbs up.

"Enough," Satan insisted, but his eyes glittered with amusement. "My consort shouldn't be upset." He released me and took her in his arms. She melted into him and he whispered something in her ear that made her purr like a kitten. She sauntered back and took her place near Cole smiling like a Cheshire cat.

"So," my scarily beautiful uncle told his people, "Astrid is to learn the ways of her people. We are indebted to her and shall treat her accordingly."

I glanced over the crowd. They weren't pleased, but it didn't seem that there was going to be a riot. No one was stupid enough to cross Satan. With a nod from my uncle, I went back to my cousins.

"Enough with formalities," Satan shouted to his adoring crowd. "Let the party begin."

The Demons surged the area where Satan stood, trying to get a word or a touch in. He was a god to them. A living, breathing, beautiful, evil god.

"That was outstanding," Wrath said, coming in for another lip lock. Thankfully Dixie pulled me into a non-sexual hug and I escaped Wrath's lovin'.

"She hates you," Greed said. "Look at her."

Sure enough Amanda was sneering at me, her teeth bared in what I guessed to be blatant Demon aggression. I smiled and winked. She turned an unattractive mottled red and mouthed, "You're dead."

"Did she just threaten my life?" I asked Wrath who was watching with great interest.

"I believe she did," Wrath answered. "What ever shall you do about it?"

Killing her was out of the question. Too many witnesses, plus I was working without my Vamp powers and she was pregnant. But wait—when in Hell… I let Amanda's anger and discontent wash over me and I absorbed it. A strong wave of dark magic ripped through me and it felt good. I glanced over at Lust and let my body take in her ire too. This was almost too easy. My fingers tingled and I saw the black glitter covering them. Could I do it? Should I do it? I may as well try something small to figure out if I could protect myself in real danger.

I raised my fingers and pointed at Amanda's overly blown up sneering lips and I flicked. I watched my magic, a gorgeous mist of black glitter, travel from my fingertips to her mouth...and it popped. I popped her enhanced lips and they deflated like a flat tire. She looked ridiculous and I laughed. She quickly slapped her hand over her mouth and shrieked.

Satan turned his attention to her. "What's wrong?" he snapped impatiently.

"Nothing," she said from behind her hand, staring daggers at me. "I bit my lip, excuse me." She left. Quickly.

"What was that about?" Satan turned to where we were huddled laughing. We all shrugged innocently, but his gaze narrowed in on me. Holy Hell he was magnetic. To hide my fear and guilt, I smiled and waved. Thankfully his attention was demanded by his people and I was safe—for the moment.

"Brilliant," Greed congratulated me. The rest looked on with approval.

"The sheer fact that you called her Donkey Nipples makes me love you," Pride offered dryly. "You're alright with me."

Dixie squeezed my hand and grinned. I was fitting in with the Seven Deadly Sins and it felt good. Was this what it was like to have sisters?

"Has Astrid met Grandpa yet?" Sloth inquired as we began to head out.

"We have a grandpa?" Help me Cousin Jesus. I couldn't imagine he was going to be delighted that I'd offed his son.

"Oh, yes," Sloth told me, clenching her teeth like she was talking to a puppy or a baby. "You'll love him. Why isn't he here?" she asked her sisters.

"Because there are too many of us present. Besides, he's still recovering from the broken ribs and concussion you gave him," Gluttony snapped.

"You broke his collarbone last month," Sloth countered nastily.

WTF? They beat up their grandpa?

"Whatever. He heals."

Groping with the thought of these gals performing a smackdown on their grandpa, I revised my thoughts about having sisters.

CHAPTER EIGHT

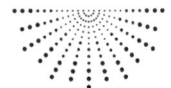

THE PARTY HAD BEEN INTERESTING BUT EXHAUSTING. MOST OF THE
Demons kept their distance, but a few adventurous Minions of
the Devil offered up their necks and begged to find out if being
bitten was as sexual as they'd been led to believe. I politely
declined and stuck close to my cousins. Not that I really wanted
to hang out with the Facebook addicted freaks, but everyone gave
them a wide berth due to the simple fact that they were scarier
than Hell itself and they were using the Facebook Insult Creator
to all in their path. My favorite of the evening was Dicknose
Boner Socket. I would store that one for future use.

Uncle Satan held court with scads of fawning women. His
magic and power filled the room to the point I almost felt
claustrophobic at times. Amanda never came back. I idly
wondered if they had plastic surgeons in Hell or if she'd have to
take a trip to Earth to fix her kisser. Next time I'd pop her boobs.

"So why did your sisters beat up your grandpa?" I asked.
Curled up on Dixie's couch with a borrowed pair of comfy sweats,
I was much happier than I'd been a short hour ago.

She giggled. "They didn't beat him up. He's just so adorable
that they get overexcited and squeeze him too hard."

"I'm sorry, what?"

"It's difficult to explain. You'll get it when you meet him."

"Look, here's the thing, I'm not staying around much longer so if you want me to meet Grandpa and Grandma you should call them and invite them over."

Dixie blanched and put her hand over my mouth. "Sweet Baby Satan, do not mention grandma. Don't even whisper about her. The last time she was here Daddy had to rebuild his entire mansion."

"Your, um… the person married to your Grandpa knocked down your dad's monster party house?"

"Yes."

"I was joking," I said, trying to wrap my head around the kind of power Grandma must have.

"I wasn't." Dixie shuddered and peered fearfully around her living room.

"Is she here?" I asked, worried that I'd conjured up something better left alone.

"No, but she can hear everything."

"Demons can hear everything?" I gasped and looked under the couch. Fuck, Dixie was making me nervous.

"She's not a Demon." She giggled, but didn't let her guard down. She searched the room carefully.

"What the hell is she then?" What else was in my bloodline besides Vampyre and Demon?

"Shhh," Dixie said, rushing to her window. "No more or she'll hear us and that would suck beyond anything you could imagine."

Her fear was real and my curiosity was piqued. Was my grandma on my daddy's side as heinous as my mother? My mother was here in Hell… A stupid, pathetic and needy part of me wanted to see her, but I assumed she was in the Basement and that could be an image thousands of years of therapy would be unable to erase. The simple fact that I still wanted her love to me was mind-boggling. However, since I'd been the one who killed her and inadvertently sent her to the Basement, I knew that wouldn't bode well for a mommy-daughter get together.

"Okay, relax your crack," I told her. "Let's talk about me getting out of here before my mate takes it upon himself to come and get me."

"He can't," Dixie said, still staring out of the window.

"What do you mean?" My heart sank and I placed my hands over my secret inside my tummy. Without my power, I suppose I somehow thought Ethan would be able to save me.

"Vampyres can't exist in Hell. Wait, I think they can survive for a couple of days, but I can't remember how many."

I jumped up and yanked her away from the window. "What would happen to a Vampyre in Hell and why isn't it happening to me?"

"Astrid, you're half Demon—you're fine," she said reassuringly. "But a pure Vampyre will suffer a brutal death down here."

"What happens? Is it at the hands of the Demons?"

"No, Demons can't kill."

"Bullshit," I hissed. "My father was a Demon and he killed so cut the crap about how sweet and harmless you people are." I paced the room. I had to move or I would burst. I wanted to crawl out of my skin. I wanted to go home. I needed Ethan.

"You're one of us," she whispered, backing away.

"No. I'm not," I shot back, getting angrier by the second.

"Look at your arms."

Lifting my hands in front of me, I gasped. The black sparkling gloves were back which meant the place could blow any second.

"Son of a... " I muttered and quickly shut my eyes and pulled images of people I loved to the forefront of my mind. It was harder this time. The glitter crawled up my arms and began to cover my chest. Ethan, Nana, Gemma. Not working... Pam, The Kev, Venus. It crept higher and I felt the warm dark magic on my neck. The problem was that it felt good. I liked it. I wanted it. No. No, the darkness didn't own me. I owned it. Motherfucker... My baby. My beautiful sweet little boy. I pictured a perfect tiny replica of Ethan and the heat that tried to control my body began to recede.

"You're amazing," Dixie said. "How did you do that?"

"Which part?" I asked, making sure my evil gloves were gone.

"Either."

"Not sure," I told her. "Although it seems to have something to do with getting pissed off."

"Can you absorb evil and anger around you?"

"I did at the party. That's how I popped Amanda's lips."

"Which by the way was awesome." Dixie grinned and I joined her.

"Thank you. Dixie, have you ever heard the walls talk?"

"Are you making fun of me because I have an imaginary friend —who, by the way, isn't imaginary?" she huffed.

"No." I decided to ignore the imaginary friend thing. "The walls were talking when I first got to Hell at your dad's."

"That's odd. I've never heard that."

"Must have imagined it," I said, knowing full well that I hadn't.

"Well, I'll listen harder next time I go to the Dark Palace. That's really kind of neat. Anyway, I'm going to bed. The second door on the left is your bedroom. Do you need anything? You haven't really eaten anything," she said, worrying her lip. "Do you need to bite me or something?"

"Or something," I muttered, wondering how long I could go without blood. I was unsure what Demon blood would do to me and wasn't willing to chance it and find out. "No, I'm fine... for now."

"Okay." She hesitated and picked at her nails. "I know you don't want to be here and I know you'll be leaving soon, but I'm really glad to know you."

Realizing she was expecting an answer, I surprised myself. "I'm glad to know you too. Maybe this was worth it somehow."

She gave me a small smile and left. I was happy to know her, not necessarily the rest of the bunch, but it was kind of interesting to learn about my fucked up family tree. God, wait till Ethan found out I was the niece of the Devil himself. That would be fun.

CHAPTER NINE

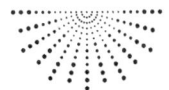

MY BEDROOM WAS LOVELY. COOL BLUES AND WHITES MIXED WITH dusty rose. The furniture looked Amish—beautiful and well built, but that was it as far as sparse went. The bed was soft, squishy and inviting. The walls were covered in a faded striped fabric instead of paper and the ceiling was tin. A dresser, desk, chair and vanity with a mirror finished off the suite. It smelled wonderful—like clean sheets and summer breezes. Before I got used to Hell being so lovely, I probably needed to visit the other levels.

I glanced up at the tin ceiling and looked for my Baby Demons. They weren't there.

"Abe, Beyonce, Rachel, Ross?" I whispered. Nothing. Where had they gone? Did they know their way around Hell? Why hadn't I thought to ask them that? I'd bet they knew what a portal looked like. Shit. Where were they?

"Guys, I need you." Nothing. They'd always come before. Crap, did something happen to them? If I'd remembered that they were in my pocket when I was unceremoniously dragged to Hell, I'd have tossed them out. I'd never forgive myself if something happened to them...

Catching a glimpse of myself in the mirror, I turned away.

Looking at myself seemed to make me more Demon than Vampyre and I didn't want that. Ever. Although I hadn't tried eating food yet, I was curious. I knew liquid was out, but I wondered if I'd be able to taste solid food. I'd been jonesing for peanut butter and jelly since I'd been turned.

Only one way to find out.

Dixie's kitchen was awesome. After a short search I found bread, peanut butter and jelly. I rounded up a knife and a plate and I was ready for my experiment. Holding the most perfectly made peanut butter and jelly sandwich in my hand, I froze.

"Astrid," an eerie voice that sounded exactly like the one from the palace whispered.

I whipped around, quickly grabbing the first weapon I laid my hands on. A butter knife... A butter knife? Crap, couldn't I do better than a freakin' butter knife? Where in the hell were my Vamp powers?

"Who's there?" I demanded. My stomach clenched. I clutched my pathetically dull blade, dropped low and waited to do battle with my killer.

It laughed.

You have got to be kidding me. I was so not in the mood for this. Far too many people, and I use that word lightly, had laughed and given me crap lately and I was done.

"Who are you?" I spat. Fear began to seep away, slowly replaced by anger. "Show yourself, asshole."

My temper flared and my hands began to tingle. Good. The freaky gloves had shown up. I wasn't exactly sure how to use them, but they were better than nothing. I didn't feel like dying tonight.

"Feisty," the disembodied voice hissed.

"I'll show you feisty, you butthole."

Damn it, butthole sounded kind of junior high. Asshole was way better—or fucker. I didn't want whatever invisible freak show that was in the kitchen to know I was basically power free at the moment. Butthole kind of put me in the league of 'I won't really kill you because I'm too nice.' Not good, not good. Maybe if I call him an asshole again, or maybe shithat... Sweet Baby Beelzebub...shut up. I needed to turn off the inner monologue and focus or I was going to end up so dead.

I scanned the kitchen, but my intruder was invisible or just hidden very well. I felt an energy but it was all over the place. I was unable to locate the source. This was new. Did the glitter gloves make me aware of energies?

"I said," I ground out through clenched teeth, "show yourself and I mean it."

"And what will you do if I don't?" the voice whispered ominously.

My fingers were tingling and sparks began to fly. Shit, shit, shit.

"I'll blow up the entire house and burn your sorry ass alive." No clue if I could actually do it, but bluffing worked occasionally...

"There are a few problems with that plan," it said quite matter-of-factly.

Was the voice critiquing my methods or offering advice? Could this get any weirder?

"Oh yeah, what?" I countered with way more confidence than I was feeling.

"Well, for starters," the voice said, "you have no idea if fire would even kill me, but there's a fine chance you'd kill yourself and your cousin Dixie in an explosion like that."

Damnity damn it, the voice was right. Wait a minute. "Why in the Hell would you care if I killed myself or my cousin?"

"Because I love you."

"Okay, eeewww. Are you some kind of disgusting pervert weirdo stalker who loves the people he kills?"

I quickly rescanned the room. Why couldn't I find him? I inched toward the archway next to the foyer which led to the living room which in turn led to Dixie's room. Maybe she would know what to do.

"Don't. Move," the voice bellowed.

I'd had just about enough of being the victim. It was time to go Clint Eastwood on the monster in my cousin's kitchen. I didn't care what it was, it had to go. Now. I dropped the useless butter knife, closed my eyes, raised my flame throwing fingers and began to chant. I was chanting in a language I'd never heard, although it was distantly familiar. The words flowed freely from my body and it felt wonderful, powerful, dark and fucked up.

With my eyes closed I was able to locate the source. The melodic chant gave me a different kind of sight. Not being able to see with my eyes heightened every other sense I had. I was able to see everything around me with a clarity that was as alarming as it was accurate. My creepy killer was cloaked in invisibility and stood about three feet away. I couldn't tell what he looked like, but I knew where he was. That was all I needed.

I pointed my fingers at the energy and a fireworks show exploded from my hands. I hit my intruder. I didn't want to kill him. I wanted to question him before I destroyed him. And if I was perfectly honest with myself, I wasn't sure I could kill him. I had no clue what he was.

"Very good!" the voice yelled.

Why in the Hell was the voice happy? I blasted it with some kind of Demon magic. I mean that shit had to hurt. Right? Come to think of it, why in the Hell did the voice all of a sudden sound familiar to me? It sounded like the Sprite I met at my mother's funeral. What was a Sprite doing in Hell?

I gritted my teeth and waited for him to show himself. "Materialize. Now."

He did. My annoyance increased with the smug satisfaction on his face. It was that little Sprite shit. I was going to kill him. "Did you think that was a good joke? Because I didn't."

"Darling Astrid, you were wonderful!" He clapped his adorable little Oompa Loompa hands and grinned from ear to ear.

As cute as he was I was not about to let him off easily. "Clearly you know my name, but I'm at a loss about yours."

"I'm your grandpa."

"What? You're a Sprite." He was so full of shit.

"I'm a Demon Sprite and I'm most definitely your grandpa." He grinned with delight and held his arms out for a hug.

"Nope. No bonding until you answer some questions, little man."

"I prefer Grandpa, but I've answered to much worse."

My Grandpa was the cutest man alive. I pressed my fists into my sides so I wouldn't start squeezing him. It didn't surprise me that he spent a lot of time in traction because the Deadly Sins had squeezed and loved on him too hard. I had a horrific compulsion to grab him and cuddle him. I knew my jaw had clenched and my lips had pursed. The same way they would if I saw an adorable puppy or a super cute baby. I had to bite my tongue so I wouldn't start spouting baby gibberish to him.

"You want to hug me to your bosom and shower me with kisses," Grandpa informed me smugly.

"Ewwww," I groaned, "do not say bosom. That's disgusting."

"You have a mouth like a sailor and you're offended by bosom?" he asked with a twinkle in his eye.

"No. Just when you imply that I'm going to connect you to mine. It sounds wrong—like illegal wrong."

"I do see your point," he agreed. "But I meant nothing of the sort."

"Good to know." I rolled my eyes and stared at the little man who called himself my grandpa. "Was that you in the bedroom of the Dark Palace?"

"Yes!" He was positively gleeful. "I wanted to show myself, but it wasn't the right time."

"So wait, you're Satan's dad *and* God's dad?"

"Oh no dear, Satan and God share the same mother. They're half brothers."

"And their mother is?"

Grandpa glanced around the room in terror. "Mother Nature," he whispered.

"Right." I laughed and rolled my eyes.

"For the love of everything evil," he moaned and shuddered, "don't do that. If she's hears or sees you, we're all screwed."

"For real?" His fear was rubbing off a bit. Although I was having a hard time believing Mother Nature was real.

"Yes, my dear. Let's leave that subject for now, shall we?"

"Ooookay, um… I killed your other son." I figured just getting it out on the table was for the best.

"Yes," he agreed. "Thank you for that. He always was a problem child."

"You're not mad?"

"Absolutely not. Now, his mother may be a bit put out… "

"And his mother is?" I asked, hoping he was also Satan's half brother.

Grandpa glanced around and then mouthed "Mother Nature."

Fuck.

"I suppose that meeting will turn out just peachy," I muttered, praying that day never came.

"We'll try and avoid that at all costs," he said. "How are you controlling yourself around me? Dixie is the only one who doesn't cause me bodily harm."

"No clue," I answered. "I would like to squish you, but maybe if you stay over there I'll be able to abstain. And why in the hell didn't my fireworks show hurt you? You should be dead."

"Yes, yes." Grandpa's eyes sparkled with joy.

"So?"

"So," he continued gleefully, "on any other Demon that would have worked, but not on me. In fact," he pondered seriously, "I believe there are only several beings in the entire universe that your power will not work on."

"And they would be?" I asked.

"Oh yes, of course," he giggled. "What's the difference in a True Immortal and an immortal?" he asked, eyeing my sandwich.

"Is this a test?" I moaned.

"Of sorts," he replied, picking up my PB&J and examining it.

"I have no idea." Was he going to steal my sandwich before I had a chance to see if I could eat it? I think he was... I watched him stare lovingly at my late night snack and I rolled my eyes.

"A True Immortal can't die. Did you know that?" he asked.

"Why do you answer my questions with questions?"

"Because it's fun," he grinned and sniffed my sandwich. "True Immortals can die—they just can't be killed."

I pushed my hair out of my face and groaned. "Like that makes any sense."

"It makes perfect sense, my love. A True Immortal can only die if they choose to."

I pondered that as I grabbed a spoon and scooped some peanut butter out of the jar. I'd given up on getting my sandwich back. "Why would a True Immortal want to die?"

"It's quite simple," Grandpa replied, "a broken heart."

"You're joking," I laughed... He didn't.

"No, Little One, I wouldn't joke about that."

"Wait." I swallowed a big glob of peanut butter and almost threw up. A big no on the eating, not to mention it tasted like dust. "You just get a broken heart and drop dead?"

"Sweet Baby Satan," he threw back his head and let out a great peal of laughter, "it's a bit more complicated than that. It's a three part finale. One, your heart must be truly broken. Two, you must choose to die and three, The Sword of Death must be plunged into your heart."

"Holy crap." I was still choking on my peanut butter.

Grandpa slapped me on the back and I went flying. For being

such a little guy, he had one hell of an arm. "I've never heard that before. Hell, I thought my father was in charge down here."

"Did he tell you that?" Grandpa asked, totally offended.

"No, I just kind of assumed."

"Never assume, dear, that makes an ass out of you and me."

He was definitely my grandpa.

"Anyhoo, the Sword thing is a secret. That's not information we want getting out," he replied. "In the wrong hands that could be a real problem."

"Right." Why couldn't I have a normal family? "All of that sounds awful."

"Oh yes," he agreed, "but if you think that's bad, there's something even worse." He took a dramatic pause and pressed what used to be my sandwich to his chest. "The Sword of Death is missing."

Without asking, I somehow knew that was part of the reason I was here. "Do we have any idea who might have it?"

"We have an educated guess." He flattened the PB&J into a pancake. What in the Hell was he doing? His sandwich etiquette was gross.

"Shall I guess?" I asked. He tilted his head and watched me. "My guess," I inhaled deeply, "is that it's a Demon and that I'm here to find the fucking Sword because I can off people and apparently you can't."

"Correct," he smiled ruefully. "You are correct, but enough about depressing things—let's get back to your history lesson."

I didn't stop him. I knew this was all connected. I just didn't know how, and if Grandpa was as vague as the rest of the immortals in my life, he was only going to tell me part of it. I would have to figure the rest out for myself. Cryptic Demons sucked.

"So, where was I?" he inquired, carefully tearing his PB&J pancake into four equal squares.

"Broken hearts, Sword of Death missing, have to want to die, sandwich stealing..."

His mouth quirked with humor. "Yes, yes, of course." He pet his flattened sandwich pieces with affection, "there are only seven acknowledged True Immortals right now, but more exist."

"Is that important?" I tried to figure out the significance, but I couldn't.

"Oh, yes," he chuckled. I waited for more, but none was forthcoming.

"Grandpa." It felt odd, but nice to say the word grandpa. "I'm assuming there is a reason you're telling me all this..."

"Of course, darling."

We sat in silence while I waited for him to continue. It was clear I was going to be waiting a long time. I wiped the frown off my face. A change of tactic was in order...

"Alrighty then," I clapped my hands like a kindergarten teacher and slapped on a big smile. You get more bees with honey, right? "I'm guessing you're a True Immortal and that Satan and his brother God are too."

"Yes Astrid, that's accurate."

"I think Cousin Jesus must be one," I added, trying to hold back my smirk. Saying cousin and Jesus in the same sentence just seemed wrong.

"No," Grandpa cut me off. "Jesus is an immortal, but not a True Immortal. He is the only being in the universe that embodies flawless purity and goodness. He is beyond reproach and would never be touched, but he is not a True Immortal."

"Do you know him?"

"Of course, I spend a good amount of time in Heaven. That's how I know your Nana."

"I thought Demons weren't allowed in Heaven."

"Ah yes, but I'm also a Sprite which is genetically close to an Angel."

I didn't want to touch that.

"Wow, neat." I was stuck. Who in the Hell were the other True Immortals?

"God begat two Angels, The Angel of Death and the Angel of Light. They are True Immortals. Your Grandmother is also one."

"Does she like to be called Grandma?"

"Oh hellfires, no. She's a colossal bitch." Grandpa gave me a sly grin.

"You like her!" I accused, laughing.

"No," he insisted. "I don't like her at all. She's very difficult," he smirked. "But I do love her."

"Is she your true love?" I asked quietly, thinking about Ethan.

Grandpa stared at his snack. "Yes, Astrid, she is...but that doesn't mean I can live with her. I'd kill her... Dixie's mother is a True Immortal."

"Her mother is alive? Does Dixie know her? I haven't heard her talk about her."

"Oh no, Dixie knows nothing about her."

"But she's alive?"

"As far as I know, my sweet. I'm sure I would have heard if she bit the big one. Although if you ask me, she may as well be dead considering how she's neglected her duties and the mess she's made." He finally took a large bite out of the PB&J and closed his eyes in ecstasy. "Why does food taste so much better when someone else makes it?"

"I have no idea, Grandpa, but we need to back up a little bit." He was excellent at avoidance, but he was not avoiding this.

"Fine, darling, what can I help you with?" He finished off the sandwich and made another.

"Do you have a good reason for showing up and scaring the Hell out of me?"

"Oh yes." He took my hands and stroked them lovingly. "I was testing your abilities. You need to be ready. I'm so worried for you and so is your nana." He let go of my hands and took another huge bite of his sandwich.

"Am I?" I asked, holding my breath.

"Are you what?" he replied with a mouth full of PB&J.

"Am I ready?" I huffed in exasperation.

"Oh, For the Love of Everything Repulsive, No," he laughed.

I deflated like a balloon and dropped onto a kitchen chair. My head fell to my hands and I gave into the impulse that had been clawing at me since I arrived in Hell. I cried.

"Oh, my baby." Grandpa smoothed his little hand over my hair.

"I'm okay," I said, wiping my tears.

He giggled with relief and squeezed himself. Holy Hell, he'd better not do that. I wasn't sure I could curb my hugging impulses if he was going to rub my face in it by loving on himself.

"I'm not going to be of much help," I told him. "I can't use my Vampyre powers down here."

"Of course you can," he corrected me.

"Um, nope. They're gone."

"You must accept your Demon powers and you will find your Vampyre powers have been with you the whole time."

"What do you mean? Accept my Demon powers... "

"It's more mind over matter," he explained. "You don't need to have control of your Demonic power, you simply need to accept and embrace your Demon heritage."

"You want me to accept evil?"

"No. I want you to accept that there is a balance—a Balance of Chaos, if you will. We are all good and all evil."

His answer was simple, but I knew by now nothing was simple and nothing came without consequences.

"I saw no good in my father or my mother."

"At one time your father was very good. Time and choices made him dark and quite honestly unredeemable."

"Why did he look like he did? Do you look like that too?"

Grandpa was silent for a long moment and if I'm not mistaken a flicker of sadness crossed his face. "That was choice, not necessity. Your father chose his physical appearance and after a while he was stuck with it. The outside often ends up being a manifestation of what lies within."

"How do you control what you become?" I asked, wondering what had really happened to my father.

"That, my beautiful child, is a question we all wrestle with for our entire lives. And some of us have very long lives with which to wrestle."

"So if I accept this, I become one crazily powerful mistake of nature?" I asked, unable to imagine what I might be able to do.

"That's one way of looking at it," he said thoughtfully. "Or you become the arbiter between Heaven and Hell. The voice of reason between those who can't—or refuse to acknowledge or even see the other side."

"You do realize I'm basically a Prada whore with a mouth like a sailor who teaches art to genitalia loving senior citizens… "

Grandpa's laugh made me want to tackle him and love on him for hours. "You are the Chosen One of Vampyre lore. You have proven yourself to be loyal with a moral strength that is beyond compare. You are very special indeed."

"I have more than myself to think about," I murmured, unconsciously touching my stomach.

"Then all the more reason to make the Universe a better place," he said gently. "May I?" His hand tentatively reached for my stomach and I nodded. The need for him to touch me and to touch him back was overwhelming.

Gently running his small hands over my stomach, he sighed in contentment. "This child will be the future. He will be the one who will maintain the balance that you create. Leave him his legacy, for if you don't, you will take his purpose from him and he will have no choice but to follow the darker part of his heritage."

"That sounds a bit like blackmail," I said, pulling away.

"Emotional blackmail," Grandpa corrected. "But true nonetheless. Accept your fate and the world will be yours.

However, at every turn will be a choice and only you can make the right one."

"Jesus Christ," I groaned. "You sound like fucking Mr. Miyagi from *The Karate Kid.*"

"I loved that movie!" Grandpa clapped his little hands joyfully. "And you really shouldn't take your cousin's name in vain."

I rolled my eyes and tried not to laugh. I failed.

"Think about what I have said, Astrid. I am so happy to be able to reveal myself to you. I have waited many years for you."

"Little overwhelming, Gramps. You're making me nauseous. Now a bit more about the Sword... "

He handed me a small book. "Everything you need to know is in there. The rest you will have to discover."

"Awesome," I said sarcastically.

"Oh, but it is, my dear. It really is."

With that he disappeared in a mist of black and golden glitter. This had turned out to be the biggest clusterfuck of a day I'd ever had and I'm counting the day I was turned into a Vampyre. I suppose my vacation in Hell was going to be a bit longer than originally planned. Ethan will not be pleased.

CHAPTER TEN

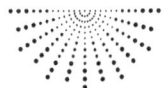

I SPENT THE BETTER PART OF THE NIGHT TRYING TO MAKE SENSE OF the little book my grandpa had given me. I was not a big non-fiction reader. Give me a romance and I'm a happy girl, but this crap... I was having a hard time understanding even the smallest details. It was as if it had been written in code—overwritten, flowery purple prose everywhere.

"Okay, the Sword of Death," I said, talking to no one since my babies still hadn't shown up. Luckily I had found several passages I could comprehend. "The Sword lives in a secret place full of temptation very close to the mouth of Hell. That's dumb. Why in the world don't they put it in a neutral safe place..." Immortals had rules coming out of their asses and many were completely antiquated.

I found out the Sword could kill any immortal with a mere prick of the blade. Its power and magic were unsurpassed. It had been created by the first True Immortals, giving them an out if they so chose. It didn't clue me in to who the first True Immortals were, but I guessed that would be Mother Nature and possibly Grandpa. Everyone else seemed to have been created in one way or another by those two or their offspring. Mother Nature,

Grandpa, God, Satan, the Angel of Death, the Angel of Light and Woman. Woman? I supposed that was Dixie's mom, but what a shitty name. It was interesting that even in the book her identity was hidden. Whatever. Not my problem. Oddly, there were three more spaces for True Immortals, but they were blank.

However, there was a caveat. I had to read the passage six times to decode what the hell it meant. If my deduction was correct, on the lunar eclipse, which occurred at least twice a year, the Sword could be used to kill a True Immortal if he or she was stabbed through the heart three times. Lovely. I'd lay money that we were due for a lunar eclipse…

Who was the target? Satan? God? Grandpa? Mother Nature? The Sword was stored near Hell, so my assumption was Satan or Grandpa. Not good. I kind of liked Grandpa and if I was being truthful, my uncle fascinated me too. Would destroying a True Immortal throw this Balance of Chaos that Gramps spoke of off? Would it bring on Armageddon? Could good and evil switch places or cease to have meaning? Could I possibly confuse myself any more…

Enough. Enough of the book for now.

I couldn't absorb any more information if I tried and there was no sex in it so I was getting bored. Realizing I needed to communicate with home, I decided that would be first on my agenda in the morning. Only one day had passed in Hell, but I was unsure if that equated with one day on Earth. Second on my schedule would be finding my Baby Demons. They were the key to something. What? I didn't know, but I was learning to trust that very little was an accident.

"No, there are no phones to Earth." Greed laughed as she bit into some kind of Danish from the platter off of Dixie's kitchen table. She was dressed to the nines in some kind of sexy power suit with thigh high stiletto boots. Thankfully I was able to hold my own in the fashion department due to the pile of rockin' clothes Dixie had left in my bedroom. I was still wearing my black Converse, but they were paired with some insane Prada black pants and a Stella McCartney fitted t-shirt. "Silly girl. Even if there were, which there aren't, do you really think Daddy would let you do that?"

"Am I a prisoner here? Or a guest?"

Greed exchanged a look with her sisters, Wrath and Envy, who'd shown up uninvited and unwanted to breakfast. All of the gals were dressed to kill... hopefully not literally. Dixie stood to the side completely ignored by her sisters.

"Would anyone like coffee?" she inquired, changing the subject.

"Yes, be a dear and fetch me some," Wrath instructed her youngest sibling. "Don't forget the sugar," she called after her.

I liked them and I didn't. I didn't trust them a bit, but I was definitely going to find out what I could from them. "So you're the Seven Deadly Sins, what does that make Dixie?"

"A spare heir," Envy snorted and seated herself next to me.

"Meaning?"

"Meaning if one of us bites it, she becomes a Sin," Envy explained and poked at the plate of pastries.

"Has that ever happened?" I asked, a little shocked at the implications. I had assumed each cousin embodied her Sin and was born that way.

"Nope," Greed cut in. "Never and it would be a total ugly turd waffle if it did."

"Facebook?" I asked.

"How'd you guess?" Greed grinned and took another Danish. "I understand that you met Grandpa last night."

"How'd you hear that?" How did she hear that? I hadn't even shared with Dixie yet.

"I feel his energy," she said. "Don't you?" she asked her sisters.

"Definitely," Wrath said and Envy nodded.

"Yes, I met him and he was just as cute as Dixie said he would be."

"Did you break anything?"

"Nope, I'm fine."

"Not on you. On him." Greed blew out an exasperated breath at my stupidity.

My stupidity was on purpose and that's the way I wanted it. Everyone seemed to buy my flightiness except Wrath. She watched me closely with an odd expression on her lovely face.

"No, he left in one piece," I told them and turned away to avoid Wrath's intense scrutiny.

"What did you speak of?" Wrath asked.

"Not much. You know, 'Welcome to Hell, learn your heritage, blahblahblah.'"

"Did he give you any gifts?" Envy asked in a tone I didn't like.

"No books? No baubles?" Greed wanted to know.

What were they angling for? I had no intention of telling them I had a book. Unsure why, but trusting my instincts, I played dumb.

"Nope, nothing," I said. "Why? Does he usually come bearing gifts?"

"No, but he always tries to pawn this stupid little book off on us," Greed said and rolled her eyes.

"It's written in some ancient script that none of us can read. I suppose it's some kind of test," Envy added.

"I can read a bit of it," Wrath said, still watching me closely.

"Probably because you're thousands of years older than the rest of us," Greed snapped.

Swallowing back my surprise at Wrath's age I wondered if I had been given the very same book... If I was, why in the hell was I able to read it? Bad feeling number one—and I was certain I'd have many more before the day was done.

"Coffee," Dixie sang and passed cups to her sisters. "Would you like some, Astrid?"

"Nope. Vampyre."

"Right." She giggled and served her sisters dutifully.

"Do you need blood?" Wrath inquired as she put an alarming amount of sugar in her coffee.

"No, not at the moment. Are you offering?" Her head snapped up and there was serious interest in her eyes.

"I might be," she answered silkily. "Let me know if I can be of service."

"Will do." *Will not.* There was no way Heaven or Hell I would drink the blood of a several thousand year old Demon... not to mention I was fairly sure she had some kind of icky girl cousin crush on me.

"What are your plans for the day, dear?" Envy asked.

"I'll spend the day with Dixie and rest. This has been overwhelming so far."

"Very well then," Greed said and gave me a light squeeze. "We shall see you soon."

With that, they stood and vanished in a blast of black glitter. I let out the breath I'd been holding and sagged in relief in my chair.

"Do they come to breakfast often?" I asked a similarly relieved Dixie.

"Never," she admitted and scrunched her nose. "Sorry about that."

"I can handle them."

"Better you than me." She giggled and picked at a Danish. "Did you enjoy your visit with Grandpa?"

"Actually I did and I didn't break one single bone in his body." I grinned and sniffed the coffee. "God, I miss caffeine."

"Do you want to try it?"

"No," I interjected quickly. "I tried peanut butter last night and almost hurled."

"Well, I have my therapy group coming later this afternoon and I want to go to the grocery and buy some snacks. Would you like to join me?"

"Hell has grocery stores?"

"Yep, we even have malls," she said with great pride.

"But you're a princess—can't you have your stuff delivered?"

"I can." She nodded her head. "But I want to live like a normal person and I enjoy getting out. I do take a bodyguard, but I drive myself."

I gave her the thumbs up and she giggled. I had no desire to go to the grocery and I wanted to find my little ones. "Have you seen my Baby Demons?"

"No, but I'm sure they're fine," she said, grabbing her purse and keys. "If you want to walk the property make sure you take a bodyguard. They say there was a mild Hellquake during the night and I don't want you to get lost or hurt."

"Are those common this time of year?"

"Hellquakes are never common. The first time I felt one was yesterday with you. Word is that it wasn't a Hellquake at all. It was some kind of unnatural phenomenon. Something bad."

"Well, that's great and especially since it coincides with my arrival."

"Yeah, unfortunately that's the word around town too," she shrugged and gave me an apologetic smile. "You take a guard if you want to wander the grounds. Okay?"

"You got it." *Not.*

CHAPTER ELEVEN

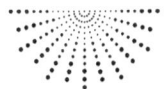

MAKING PEACE WITH MY DEMON SIDE WAS DIFFICULT—MAINLY because I had no freakin' clue how to do it. The book was of no help whatsoever. It was just history and gobbledygook. Although it did have a detailed picture of The Sword of Death—one of the most impressive pieces of deadly art I'd ever seen. If I was to find it, I definitely didn't want to touch that sucker… way too evil for me. In my gut I knew this was the book the Sins were talking about. It was probably significant that I could read it, but that was the least of my problems at the moment. After Dixie left I paced her house trying to pick up on the energy Grandpa left behind. I felt things, but I wasn't sure which energy belonged to which Demon. Shitshitshit. I was worried about my little Demons. I needed to find Ross, Rachel, Beyonce and Abe and I was hoping to be able to use that nifty little energy trick to find my babies.

"Hell's bells," I muttered. I hopped around, hoping to release some tension and become one with my inner fucking Demon. "How hard can this be?"

Hard.

I tried walking and talking and yelling and meditating. Nothing. I couldn't make the black glitter gloves show up at will and my Vampyre powers were still MIA. Ten more minutes. I'd give myself ten more minutes to try and get this shit and then I was going out anyway. There was no telling what kind of trouble my tiny monsters could get into in Hell.

Peeking out of the window, I sized up the bodyguards. They looked more like gun-toting, bodybuilding male models than they did bodyguards. I was certain they knew their job. Satan wouldn't leave just any old guards with his daughter. The one on the far left looked the weakest. He was who I wanted to be my escort. Ten minutes...

What were some of the things Grandpa said? Come on... think. Mother Nature was a colossal bitch... my dad had made his own evil bed... seven True Immortals... mind over matter. Wait. That was it. Mind over matter. Could it really be that simple? I laughed at the possibility.

"I choose to accept both my Vampyre and Demon heritage," I mumbled. "I choose to accept my Vampyre and Demon heritage," I said a bit louder.

A tingling started low in my spine and travelled up to the base of my neck. It wasn't uncomfortable, but it was unfamiliar. I moved faster around the room wondering if this would be as debilitating as when I became a Vampyre.

"I choose to accept my Vampyre and Demon heritage," I shouted, uncaring if all the guards outside could hear my lunacy. It was working. And I felt fine and my... shit. I jack knifed over in pain as wave after wave of nausea ripped through my body. Everything appeared blurry and red and I grasped for purchase on the carpet. Fuck, why did everything immortal have to hurt?

"I promise to be good or evil or vapid or anything," I screamed, praying to every deity I think of... Just stop. Please stop. The burning was branding my soul and I planned to rip my cute little son of a bitch grandpa to shreds with my bare hands if this turned me into a full Demon. Wait. Why in the fuck did I even listen to him? Was it because he was cuddly? I was an idiot of epic proportions.

Crawling across the floor, I gasped for air. The burning slowly subsided, but the tingling in my spine remained. Please God, Satan, Jesus, Moses, Steven Perry and all the rest of Journey, don't let there be a Round Two of fire consuming my body. Sitting still I waited. And waited. Nothing. Why the guards hadn't stormed the house was odd. I knew I'd been screaming, but the duration was fairly short. Was screaming in pain a common occurrence at Dixie's house? I certainly hoped not.

Time to test the new me.

I closed Dixie's shades to be on the safe side, shut my eyes and took a flying leap. Thankfully I could fly, but I learned a valuable lesson. Flying with your eyes closed is a no-no. Bashing into a wall hurts and causes damage. I moved one of Dixie's paintings to cover the busted plaster and moved on.

I was still breathing and my reflection was still there, but when I cloaked myself my image disappeared. Positive that Steven Perry had been the lucky charm in my prayer, I silently thanked him and forgave him for quitting the band.

Flying. Check.

Cloaking. Check.

Crawling into the minds of other Demons? Only one way to find out...

Peeking out the window I focused on the strongest looking one I could find and I slid in. Bingo. He was bored and was attracted to the male guard named Tony to his right. He knew Tony was seeing a woman, but felt that with his skills he could turn Tony...

I slipped right back out. TMI. Next experiment... I willed my sparkling black gloves to appear. I did need to find my inner-angry-bitch to do it, but she was readily available. However my inner-slut had all but disappeared. Thank God, because Ethan was nowhere in sight. Closing my eyes I silently commanded the

gloves to disappear. They did. Score. Grabbing the little book and
shoving it in my back pocket in case I needed it I cloaked myself
in invisibility and stepped outside.

No movement from the guards I could see. I was sure there
were many that I couldn't see so I planned to stay invisible until I
found my babies and had to reveal myself. Then I'd cloak their in-
trouble little asses and bring them home. Wait. This was not my
home. I'd bring them back to Dixie's.

I easily walked right past the guards and through the
manicured yard. The uncanny resemblance to Kentucky was
bizarre. The flowers and trees and rolling hills were lovely and
strangely familiar. Did it look this way to everyone or was it an
illusion catering to the likes and needs of those it hosted? What
the hell did it matter to me? I planned to do whatever I had to do
to help out and then leave. Permanently.

Slowing my pace, I tried to detect the energy of my babies. I
concentrated and let my mind wander... I sensed them, but they
weren't nearby. The thread of energy was distant and weak,
although it was stronger to the north. Moving quickly through
the overgrown grass on the outskirts of my cousin's property, I
felt the connection to my little Demons increase. I'd probably
travelled several miles away from Dixie's house before the terrain
went from manicured-lovely to wild-beautiful.

The scent of the grass tickled my nose and I giggled. No one
would ever believe me if I told them how stunning Hell was.
Running toward the energy, I froze when I saw a free-standing
door approximately twenty feet ahead. What was a door doing in
the middle of a field? It stood about eight feet tall and was made
of intricately carved wood. The shiny black lacquer finish
glistened in the sun and the handle looked as if it was encrusted
with jewels. Was that a portal? There was no fucking way it could
be this easy.

Approaching slowly in case it was a trap I moved closer. I kept
myself cloaked and levitated off the grass so I didn't accidentally

rustle anything on the ground. The air on either side of the door shimmered and moved in the gentle breeze. Was something there? I couldn't tell. I floated around the door. It truly was freestanding. There was nothing but grass behind and all around it... and it was making me horny. My nipples hardened and a tingling started low in my abdomen. What was happening here? Was the door a succubus? Could an inanimate object be a succubus? When had I lost my mind and thought humping a door might be a good idea? I realized it wasn't the door I want to do the horizontal mambo with and I heaved a huge sigh of relief, but what was it?

The aroma of freshly baked brownies accosted my nose and... Brownies? No way.

I needed to become corporeal if I wanted to open the door, but was unsure if the owners of the brownie scent would be happy to see me.

"General George Patton? Bambi? Is that you?" I whispered, hoping to God I wasn't attracted to them. "It's me, Astrid. I'm Dixie's cousin and she said you wouldn't, you know, um... eat me because we have the same... "

They materialized and I screamed. They were heinous. I hadn't remembered the Hell Hounds being quite so big. Moving away slowly while keeping my eyes on them, I debated on whether or not to run or hump them. Please tell me I didn't just consider humping Hell Hounds... Their eyes narrowed and they lifted their bulbous snouts in the air.

"Astrid, it's lovely to see you again," a deep goofy male voice said. Neither one of the Hell Hounds mouths moved. I whipped around to find the owner, but no one was there.

"It's me, General George," the voice huffed. "I speak through my eyebrows."

WTF?

"You have eyebrows?" I asked, stepped closer and noticed the bushy wiry tufts of hair above his beady eyes.

"Yep. All Hounds speak through the brows."

He was right. They bounced in rhythm with his words. Bizarre.

"If you talk with your eyebrows, what do you do with your mouth?"

"Eat pizza and destroy those that threaten the life of my master."

"Right." As much as I was repulsed by the duo, my inner slut was telling me a different story. Shit. This was not happening.

"Um, I was wondering where this door led. Do you know?" I asked, dying to run my hands over my breasts. I slapped them to my sides and held on to my pants. I wasn't attracted to them last night. Why was I attracted to them now?

"Are you okay?" Bambi's eyebrows asked me in a high squeaky voice.

"Not really," I whispered. "Do you guys feel anything weird?"

"Always," General George told me. "Why? What are you feeling?"

Truth or dare? If I came clean and they felt the same way this could be a clusterfuck of massive proportions. Pun intended. But if I lied would they know?

"I'm, um... " I wrung my hands and cursed Satan for making me stay in Hell. There was no way I could tell animals that I thought I wanted to do the nasty with them, no matter how much they smelled like brownies. Omission is not lying. "I lost something important to me and I was looking for it."

"It or them?" Bambi's brows jiggled.

Did they know something? My gut told me not to fear them, but I was in Hell where nothing was as it seemed. "Them," I told her. I was at a dead end. I could feel my little monsters slightly, but it had faded. "My Demon Babies."

"Are you speaking of Abe, Beyonce, Rachel and Ross?" General George's waggly eyebrows inquired with great fondness. Hopefully it wasn't because he'd just eaten them as an afternoon snack.

"Maybe," I answered. "Have you seen them?"

"Oh yes, my dear," he said. "Abe was quite sure you'd be coming. We've been waiting for you."

"You have?"

"Yes." Bambi giggled, if you could call a snort that spewed slobber a giggle. "We are here to guide you."

"Why would you help me?" For the second time in less than ten minutes I wondered if this was a trap.

"Something is afoot and it's wrong," General George grunted, shaking his ginormous furry head.

"I thought you guys were okay with evil stuff."

"Oh, we are, but this goes far beyond evil," Bambi added.

"Are my babies okay?" I asked, heading for the door to go find them. I was going to kill those little shits if they weren't already dead.

"For now," Bambi assured me, stepping into my path. "Tell me what you're feeling."

I halted and again I considered lying, but something stopped me. They were trying to help me. They said they were my guides. Maybe they would be flattered if they knew I thought they were hot... but I didn't think they were hot at all. I just had a disgusting compulsion to scratch my itch, so to speak.

"Well," I hedged. "I'm not sure and I'm actually mortified to say this, but I might be just the tiniest weeniest bit, um... "

"Attracted to us?" George asked, his eyebrows dancing a jig.

"Possibly," I muttered almost inaudibly. How was I going to live this one down?

"Excellent," Bambi screeched. "The little Demons were correct. Let's go."

"Wait," I yelled. "You're just going to let that slide?"

"Yes, we are," General George said, avoiding eye contact.

As grossed out as I was with myself, I was also completely insulted. Clearly they weren't attracted to me and I wanted to know why. But how in the world did I broach that one?

"It's your chest bumps and your stench," he said, intently examining his hooves.

"Can you read my mind?" I snapped. Wait. Did he actually just refer to my boobs as chest bumps and call me stinky?

"You need to shut your brain doors," Bambi told me sweetly. "And you do smell odd, but so do all Vampyres."

"Chest bumps?" I pointed to my offensive mammaries.

"Yes, dear." She giggled as her brows shimmied on her forehead. "Do you find us attractive?"

"Well, um… no, not exactly."

"We find each other very appealing," she cooed, nudging a now embarrassed General. "You are not attracted to us and we are not attracted to you. You are attracted to something behind the door."

"Thank Satan," the General snorted. The ego part of me wanted to smack him and the sane part of me wanted to laugh. The laugh won out.

What was behind the door? As relieved as I was that I didn't really want to get down on it with General George and Bambi, I wondered if the alternative was worse. Enough about my libido. I didn't plan to satisfy it no matter how horny I was. My mate was on Earth and I was a one Vamp girl. Period.

"Are my Babies behind the door?"

"Not directly," Bambi explained, moving her huge hairy body to the left of the door.

"But they did go in there?"

"Yes." George shook his head sadly. "I begged them to wait till you came and we could all search together, but they insisted."

"Why?"

They were silent. Not gonna work for me. Had they lied to me? Did they eat them?

"Why?" I demanded.

The Hell Hounds exchanged furtive glances and Bambi sighed dramatically. "They said he needed to eat. They were going in there to sacrifice themselves."

"What?" I shouted, grabbed the handle and tried to push the door open. "To who? Who in the Hell are they going to sacrifice themselves to?"

"I think the name they used was Ethan."

My world spun and I landed hard on the ground. The Hounds got me back on my feet, but the ringing in my ears was deafening and I wouldn't have known if they had taken a big chunk out of me. My body shook and real fear grabbed hold of me and held on tight. Why was he here and why was he behind this door?

"Where does this door lead?" I asked, wanting to know yet dreading the answer.

"To all the other levels of Hell."

"Can you take me to Ethan?"

"That is why we are here. Is he important to you?" General George asked.

"He's my world—my entire world."

CHAPTER TWELVE

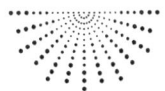

THE DOOR WAS LOCKED.

"What the hell?" I groaned and rattled the diamond and ruby covered knob. "It's locked."

"Do you trust us?" General George asked, watching me with a thoughtful expression.

Did I? Kind of… I didn't really have much of a choice. They knew where Ethan and my Baby Demons were. I needed them. Staring at his bulbous head and hairy body, I made a decision to throw my normal caution to the wind and go with it.

"Yes."

"With your life?" Bambi inquired, licking her lips.

That lip-smacking thing didn't really inspire undying allegiance, but when in Hell…

"Sure." Dear Sweet Baby Cousin Jesus, please let me survive this…

"Put one of your hands in each of our mouths," the General instructed.

What? "Um, will your slobber lube them up so I can open the door?"

They laughed so hard I actually joined them. WTF? I was

about to potentially lose both of my hands and I was cackling like a hyena. I mean, I knew they'd grow back, but that took time and hands were kind of important at the moment.

"Can I ask why I need to do this?"

"No," Bambi said.

"Fine," I grumbled and shoved my hands into their mouths. Time was of the essence and if they wanted to eat my appendages, I was quite sure they could do it without my blessing.

The insides of their mouths were spongy and warm. The scent of hot brownies grew stronger and I closed my eyes. If this turned out to be a bad move I planned to conjure up my black gloves and fry their asses. The light pressure of razor sharp teeth scraped my palms and rough tongues bathed my hands in what truly felt like brownie batter... ewwwww. Every instinct I had was to yank my hands out, but their lips had closed around my wrists in a seal-tight lock.

"Fuck," I shouted and futilely tried to disengage as their teeth pierced my skin. A rush of something cold shot through my body and landed right between my eyes, giving me one of the worst brain freezes I'd ever felt—black raspberry chip ice cream had nothing on the Hell Hounds.

Gasping in pain and dropping to my knees, I lamented my utter stupidity. I attempted to use my varied and sundry magic on them, but I was blocked. No matter how hard I tried to call upon my power, nothing happened. My eyes were screwed shut in agony from the headache pounding in my skull. Prying them open took everything I had, but I needed to look at them while they killed me. I wanted them to see how much I hated them.

The love and compassion on their hairy faces threw me and made me second guess for a brief moment, but the icy cold shooting through my veins brought me back to my bleak reality. I had trusted the bad guy... or rather bad dog. And then it stopped... The shock of being released was jarring. I quickly scooted away and cloaked myself in invisibility.

"Are you alright?" Bambi asked kindly. WTF? I heard her voice, but her eyebrows were still. I didn't answer.

"We can see you," General George said. And just as with Bambi, his bushy eyebrows were immobile. *"We can also hear you, so if you're going to be rude you might want to rethink it."*

"Why?" I yelled. "Will you sink your teeth into my ass or my head next time?" That hairy bastard had one hell of a nerve. And how could they see me? I was cloaked… and furthermore how in the hell could I hear them when they weren't actually talking through their eyebrows? Shit. Were we connected? Did the freezing cold bite connect us somehow?

"It did," Bambi snorted gleefully. *"When we descend to the lower levels, we need to communicate. It will be the simple difference of you making it out alive or dead."*

"So that excruciating chomp was a love bite?" I snapped, still not willing to let bygones be bygones.

"Exactly," she agreed and rubbed her big soft head on my leg.

"You'll have to stay cloaked and just think your thoughts at us. We can speak as much as necessary and no one will be the wiser." General George's voice bounced around inside my head.

"Okay," I said internally. *"Can I ride on your back?"*

"If it pleases you." He chuckled. *"We used to ride Dixie around for hours on end."*

"Can she talk to you?"

"Oh no, dear," Bambi said. *"Not yet, but soon."*

It was clear that was as much of an explanation as I would get from them about who could hear them and who could not. Whatever. There were far more important things pressing at the moment.

"Are we ready?" I asked, wishing I had weapons on me. I would just have to defend myself and my furry friends with magic.

"The question is, are you?" George countered.

"I was born ready." I grinned and hopped on his back. Bambi

pushed the door open with her hoof and we descended into the abyss.

$$\sim$$

WHATEVER I HAD EXPECTED, IT CERTAINLY WASN'T THIS. LINES OF desks and filing cabinets littered an area roughly the size of a football field. Harsh fluorescent lighting bathed everyone's skin giving it a greenish hue. Demons hustled around in a business-like manner. Wearing suits and ties and conservative dresses, they manned computers and phones. Most of the Demons looked like humans, but there were a few who resembled my father. I watched in shock as they all worked like a very well oiled machine. Several of the heinous Demons had human looking hands or hair. Maybe they were wearing wigs… but the hands were real. But the strangest thing of all was the purple and red and black darts of light flying around the room bashing into everything. The demons seemed to take no notice of the spastic lights, but occasionally swatted them away if they got right in their faces. WTF?

"What's the deal with the ugly Demons?" I asked, wishing we could get a closer look.

"They're trying to redeem themselves. The ones that have grown back some skin are successfully on their way to being able to visit the Main Floor of Hell," Bambi explained. *"It takes hundreds of years and raw determination to come back from the skinless evil they had chosen, but a few actually make it."*

"My father looked like that."

"Yes," the General said tersely.

Bambi said nothing, but I was sure they exchanged some kind of mental telepathy that they chose to leave me out of. There was a fuzzy noise and I knew they were communicating. I could care less if they were insulting my father. Hell, I'd had my Baby Demons eat him…

112

"It's okay, you guys. I know my dad was bad. Don't hide your thoughts."

"You heard us?" Bambi stuttered and stopped moving.

"Not what you said," I answered, alarmed. Was that bad? *"It was more like a blurry signal. I knew you were talking, but you blocked me."*

General George's head bobbed and his body shuddered. Bambi gaped at me as I sat astride her boyfriend's back.

"What? Is that a big deal?" They were making me a little nervous. Why do I always talk before I think?

"It is," George said reverently. *"It is."*

"You gonna expand on that, big guy?" I asked, already knowing the answer.

"Nope."

"Fine," I snapped. *"Where are we and where are Ethan and my babies?'*

"They're still a ways away. This is the processing center. When a soul enters Hell they come here and get assigned a level."

"Are the souls those obnoxious little lights flying everywhere?"

The General gasped and Bambi's snout paled. That was freakin' weird. I was so obsessed that her nose went from pink to white I forgot I had yet again apparently said something wrong.

"You see the souls?" Bambi asked blankly.

"Um... maybe," I said, not wanting to commit to the wrong answer. They could still eat me if they wanted to.

"What colors do you see?" General George demanded.

"Why? Is this some kind of problem?" I shot back. I had places to go and shit to do. What in the hell was the big deal?

"No," he answered carefully. *"It would just confirm our suspicions. What colors do you see?"* His voice was gruff and quite honestly scary. Was there an incorrect answer? Fuck. The truth will set you free... or get you eaten by Hell Hounds.

"Fine. And by the way, if you look over your shoulder you'll see me rolling my eyes... I see purple, red and black."

They were silent. Did they hear me? General George started to chuckle and Bambi's beady little eyes swam with tears. WTF?

"*Amazing,*" he murmured.

"*Let me guess,*" I said dryly, "*you have no intention of explaining why I'm so fucking amazing.*"

"*Correct, but know that you are not exactly what we expected,*" he said.

"*Story of my life. Can we get moving?*" Time was wasting and I needed my mate and my monsters.

"*Do you trust us?*" Bambi asked.

What's with that question? Last time I answered that little ditty I got a massive brain freeze from Hell Hound teeth...

"*Will it hurt if I say yes?*" I asked, bracing myself for something horrific.

"*Possibly,*" she said, smiling.

At least she was honest...

"*Sure. I, um—trust you to...* "

The searing crack of pain at the back of my skull came from her paw that felt like a ton of bricks as it connected with my head. The room went blurry and the Demons appeared to have grown extra heads and lips. The soul lights looked like a Christmas tree in a cyclone. This was the last fucking time I trusted dogs... Slumping forward on the General's furry back, everything went dark.

CHAPTER THIRTEEN

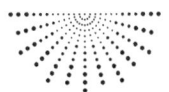

"She's dead, you know. It was so deliciously violent and bloody. She screamed and begged… such a coward. They had to decapitate her just to shut her mouth," the woman said in a tone laced with sex. "She's not coming back."

"Interesting," a familiar male voice answered. "You do realize I would know if that was true."

"Fine," she hissed. "But she will be dead soon if you don't comply with my wishes."

The man said nothing. Was he considering going along with the woman's plan?

"I can make it so good for you," she purred. "I can make you forget her. I promise."

"No," he replied. "You can't. No one can. And if you kill her, I will know. I will come after you every day of my life and destroy you until there's nothing left to reanimate."

"Are you flirting with me? That makes me wet," she giggled maliciously. "You do realize with you chained up like an animal I could simply straddle you and fuck you."

"You're forgetting my species, darling. I direct the blood flow and you do nothing for me."

Was that Ethan... and Lust? I tried to open my eyes, but they wouldn't cooperate. I was on some kind of fur rug with a heartbeat. Where was I and why were Ethan and Lust talking? And why in the hell was she trying to have sex with my mate? Again, I tried to sit up and speak. Again, nothing happened.

"Have it your way," she shrieked and a wave of dark magic engulfed wherever the hell I was, "but you will be mine. No one denies me, you bastard. No one."

"Good luck with that," he replied in a bored monotone.

A crackle of lightning burst and my eyes shot open. My body was still useless, but I could see. Ethan was chained to a wall with iridescent chains binding his body. I assumed they were enchanted. He was gaunt and pale. There were open gashes on his beautiful arms and torso. Why hadn't he healed? The lightning hit him in the chest and his body jerked. He grunted, but refused to make any other sound. My need to go to him was overwhelming, but my body refused to agree.

"You stupid, stupid man," Lust ground out between clenched teeth as she pressed her breasts against his chest. Her eyes were dilated with desire and she cupped him in her hand. He was mine and I was going to kill her.

Except nothing worked—not my body, not my mouth and my brain was mushy. How did I get here? The damn Hell Hounds... I wasn't laying on a rug with a heartbeat. I was sprawled across General George's back. I knew I was still cloaked—I was cognizant enough to recognize that magic.

"*George, you fucker, help me wake up. I need to kill Lust. Now.*"

"*Do you think that's wise?*" he asked, seemingly unconcerned that the slut was dry humping my mate.

"*Um, yes, I think it's wise you jackass and I'm going to make it hurt,*" I snapped. "*Help me or I'll...*"

"*What will you do, Little Astrid?*" he inquired.

He had me there. Shit. What would I do? What could I do?

These freakin' dogs had more unexplainable woowoo magic than I'd ever witnessed. I was clueless how to even fight them.

"Please, just help me."

"Why don't we think this through for a moment," George suggested reasonably.

Not feeling reasonable in the least, I imagined myself killing Lust and then kicking George's ass until he begged for mercy.

"General," I replied as calmly as an insanely angry woman could, *"If some skanky dog was mounting Bambi against her will, what exactly would you do?"*

"I would kill him."

"So, why is it that it's cool for you to off a skanky ho and not me?"

"What feels satisfying in the moment is often the wrong move in the long run."

"Is there some kind of prerequisite that if you live in Hell you have to talk like a fortune cookie?" I groused.

General George chuckled, but didn't lift his hairy paw to help me in any way.

"You enjoyed me last time we were together," Lust cooed, running her hands all over the chest that belonged to me.

Wait. What?

"That was a long time ago and quite honestly I can't recall much of it. Wasn't that memorable," Ethan said.

"You bastard," she shrieked, slapping his face hard. Her fingernails tore across his chest drawing more blood and leaving angry red welts. "You turned me away when you found out I was a Demon. Well, your precious Astrid is a Demon. Why can you fuck her and not me?"

"I don't love you."

My heart tripped at his admission, but he was in the doghouse for popping my slutty cousin…

"Love has nothing to do with it," she whispered as she licked the blood from his chest. "Your time down here is running out, and if you ever want to see your little whore Astrid again, you'll have to satisfy my needs. It'd be a shame to watch such a fine specimen of man turn to dust."

"Do not call my mate a whore." Ethan's eyes blazed and the room began to tremble. "Did you hear me?" he shouted in a tone that scared me, and if I'm not mistaken made the General and Bambi flinch as rocks fell from the ceiling and the floor rumbled ominously.

"Stop it," Lust screamed as she dodged a chunk of rock that would have done some damage to her lovely face. "Stop it," she screamed. "Someone will come."

"Answer the question," he roared as the floor began to separate.

"Yes," she hissed. "I called her a whore."

One wall of the room caved in completely and Lust looked terrified. Was she not supposed to be here? Did my lovely Uncle Fucking Satan know about this?

"Never call her that again. Do you understand me?" Ethan's voice could have cut ice.

"Yes," she spat angrily, but her body still shook with shock and fear.

Ethan was the Hellquakes…

"Did Ethan cause all the Hellquakes?" I demanded. Did that mean every time Lust hit on him parts of Hell disappeared?

"Yes."

"You win this round, pretty boy, but as your time runs out you'll change your tune," she told him and backed right into Bambi, who growled. Lust jumped away and paled considerably. "What are you filthy dogs doing here?"

Bambi continued to growl low in her throat and General George joined in on the chorus. Lust was furious, but kept her distance from my furry friends. Did they talk to her? It certainly didn't seem like it.

"Are you spying on me?" Her demeanor was pure evil, but she still stayed as far as she could from the Hell Hounds. Interesting.

Maybe the General had been right about listening and learning, not that I'd ever tell him.

"You don't have to. I'd say I told you so, but... " George's voice danced in my head. Shit—we were still connected.

"Can't she speak with you?" I asked, assuming all Demons or at least Satan's family could talk to the animals.

"Absolutely not," Bambi said indignantly. *"She is not special. None of those girls are except for our Dixie."*

And apparently me. I'd mull that one over another time. *"Can you get rid of her so I can help the man I love?"*

"I'm on it," Bambi said as she advanced menacingly on Lust. Bambi was one scary dog when she wanted to be. Her teeth were bared and her growl was vicious.

"Get away from me, you putrid beast," Lust demanded.

Bambi didn't listen. Not one little bit.

"Fine," she hissed, realizing she was backed into a corner. "I'll leave." In a blast of glitter and smoke Lust disappeared.

The General laid my body at Ethan's feet. His scent calmed me.

"Astrid, this will be uncomfortable," George explained.

I tensed and waited. I was sure his idea of uncomfortable would be excruciating, but this time he was right. It burned as my coordination and control came back, but it wasn't intolerable. Now standing in front of my mate, my blood lust and libido went haywire...

"Why can't he see me?" I asked

"You're cloaked."

"But he can see through that."

"Astrid, shockingly he maintains some of his Vampyric powers, but not all of them. He cannot see you."

"And he grows weaker by the hour."

I closed my eyes and willed my corporeal body back. His gasp and anguished cry made my heart leap to my throat.

"Astrid," he whispered. "My Angel."

"Oh my God, Ethan," I said, running my hands gently over his body. He felt like home. "Why aren't you healing?"

"The chains keep most of my magic in check. I can't regenerate while I'm bound."

"Then I suppose those sons of bitches have to go," I muttered, reaching for the glowing nightmare that kept him immobile.

As my fingertips connected with the shimmering metal, a vicious shock rocked my body and I was thrown across the room.

"Astrid," Ethan shouted and struggled to free himself.

"I'm good," I gasped. "I'm okay."

"Goddamnit," he roared and dropped his head to his chest.

I stumbled to my feet and moved quickly back to him. "Look at me," I said, gently raising his chin. "I'm really okay. Are these chains painful to you?" I examined them without touching.

"There's a low level constant burn, but nothing like what it did to you. I don't want you touching them again," he said in a tone that expected no back talk. Clearly he'd forgotten who he was mated to...

"Your Highness." I grinned cheekily, even though my body still hurt. "There is no way I am leaving you here like this so you can spank me once you're free."

"*TMI*," George groaned inside my head.

"That's what you get for listening to my thoughts." I turned and glared at the General.

"*My dear child those were not thoughts. You spoke aloud.*"

"Whoops." I shrugged in apology and turned back to my man.

"Are you talking to the Hounds or me?" Ethan asked, confused.

"The hounds. I stuck my hands in their mouths and the hairy bastards bit me and then we had the communication mojo going. Kind of weird, but apparently there was a fine chance of me dying on this level if I was visible. Of course then they knocked me out and I didn't get to see any of the horrors. By the way," I said turning to George. "What level is this?"

"It's a subfloor below the main level," he said through his

eyebrows in a voice that could clearly be heard by both Ethan and myself.

"But I thought there was the Basement, the Sub-Basement, the Rehab Room, Purgatory and the main floor," I said, wondering if Dixie had kept information from me.

"So Dante had it all wrong," Ethan muttered.

"He'll be here on Thursday night. He plays poker with Satan."

"What?" Ethan asked.

"I'll explain later," I told him with a wave of my hand. "So General and Bambi, this isn't an actual level?"

"It's Hell's waiting room. Of course there are cells to hold prisoners here too," Bambi explained.

I glanced around at the destroyed room and panicked. "We need to get Ethan out of here before someone comes in to check on him... Wait! Where in the hell are my monsters?" My stomach roiled and I ran around the room looking beneath the rubble. "Damndamndamn."

"Astrid, stop. They're here." Ethan's voice snapped me out of my frenzied search.

"Where?"

"They're hanging onto the back of my pants I believe... are they about three inches tall with a breast obsession?"

"Just Abe and Ross," I sighed, relieved that they were okay. "You can see them?"

"Apparently." He laughed and shrugged. "They're quite amusing."

"Tell me about it. Come out, you little shits."

They crawled to Ethan's broad shoulders, careful to avoid his wounds.

"Mommmmmeeeeeeyyyyy," Abe gushed. "We so happy to see you."

"Me like Mommy's mate. He pretty," Beyonce cooed, giving Ethan little wet kisses.

"We'll discuss your disappearing act later. Get in my pockets. We're getting out of here."

"Doggies," Ross shrieked and waved wildly at General George and Bambi. The Hell Hounds woofed and wagged their enormous puffy tails. They had tails? How had I not seen those? They were huge. As soon as they were done greeting my babies the tails disappeared. Question answered.

"How you get the chains off the pretty man?" Rachel asked, pointing to the luminous metal while blowing gleeful raspberries at the Hounds.

"I'm not sure, but I'll figure it out," I mumbled, staring at the intricate knotting on the chains.

"You will do no such thing," Ethan snapped, going all alpha Vampyre on me.

"Listen, sweetie," I shot back. "I would die for you, so a couple of shocks won't hurt me."

"And our child?" he asked, staring at me with an expression of wonder mixed with anger.

"I was going to tell you," I said quickly, "but then a bunch of stuff happened, you know—I killed my mom, then my dad and then the icky Demons showed up and..."

"And?"

And... I had no excuse. I should have told him the minute I found out. "I'm so sorry." Tears flooded my eyes and I leaned into his body, avoiding the chains. "I'm sorry."

"I'm not sorry," he said gruffly and kissed the top of my head. "I am beyond words. I am more in love with you than I thought possible. I will not let you harm yourself or our child."

"There's got to be a way," I insisted. "General, Bambi, can you undo the magic on the chains?"

"No, child, but you can," George informed me.

"You gonna tell me how?"

"Now where would the fun in that be?"

"You're a dick, George. I suppose I have to use some Demon voodoo?" I moaned.

"Yep." He gave me a Hell Hound grin that would have scared the Cousin Bejesus out of me if I didn't know him.

"Will my black gloves help?" I asked, already knowing the answer.

"Go for it," Bambi cheered me on.

Mad. I needed to get mad. Well now, that wouldn't be too hard...

"So you did my cousin?" I asked Ethan.

"I'm sorry, what?"

"You played hide the salami with Lust?"

"She's your cousin?" He was surprised.

"Do. Not. Answer. My. Question. With. A. Question." I yelled. "Did you hit that?"

"Dear God." Ethan rolled his eyes. "It was over three hundred years ago and I truly don't remember it."

"Beside the point," I said, picturing it. Ewwwww.

"Astrid, you didn't exist three hundred years ago. Surely you realize I have a past," he said in that obnoxious Vampyre way that normally turned me on, but not this time.

"But my cousin?"

"Would you mind explaining that?"

"Sure," I snapped, furious that I couldn't control my jealousy. "Satan is my uncle and the scarier than hell Seven Deadly Sins are my cousins, along with Beelzebub's other daughter Dixie who I actually like. Of course, I'd hate to leave out Uncle God and Cousin Jesus, but I haven't exactly met them yet. And apparently my grandma, Mother Nature, is a ginormous bitch... Did I forget anything? Oh yeah, my grandpa, Satan's dad—not God's, likes to pretend he's a wall and screw with my head. Happy?" I shouted.

For the first time since laying eyes on my beloved Vampyre, he was speechless—utterly speechless.

"Enough about my delightful family tree," I added, boiling with anger. "Let's get to work."

I closed my eyes and felt the dark magic mold itself to my body. It was warm and whispered seductive promises to me I knew it wouldn't keep. As long as I used it but kept my soul hidden, I would be okay. I hoped.

My Baby Demons gasped in awe as the black sparkles appeared on my arms and chest. Opening my eyes, I saw Ethan's look of dismay. I had no time to deal with that now. I was what I was and if we were going to have that problem again, I would kill him myself... Tearing my eyes from his, I focused on the chains.

The magic was complicated and woven in a deadly way. Do I just blast the fucker? Will that harm Ethan? Will it harm me? I glanced over at George.

"Go with your gut," he said simply.

My gut told me to blast the fucker, but my gut had also told me to get hypnotized at a seedy strip mall to stop smoking. That decision turned me into a Vampyre... But wait, I was glad I was a Vampyre. I had Ethan, a family and a baby on the way. Maybe my gut wasn't so bad after all.

Taking a huge breath, which also surprised Ethan, I closed my eyes and found a very dark place inside my mind. It glowed red and felt wonderful. Opening my eyes so I didn't inadvertently blow someone's head off, I aimed at the chains and let her rip. A blaze of sparks flew from my fingertips, unlike the magic I'd used on Grandpa. This was focused, evil and deadly. Ethan's body jerked violently as the now flaming chains dropped from his body. He lurched forward and fell to the hard ground as the Baby Demons went down with him. They screamed with joyous abandon like they were riding a roller coaster. God help me.

"Again," Abe shouted, jumping up and down and clapping his little claws.

"Hush," I told Abe as I ran to Ethan's crumpled body. Please God, let him be okay. "No, no, no," I cried as he refused to wake up. My fangs dropped. I ripped into my wrist and placed it over his lips. "Drink," I yelled. "Drink."

Slowly his throat moved as my blood poured into his mouth and ran over the sides. The relief was massive. My body sagged, but I kept my wrist firmly clamped to his lips.

"He'll be okay," I whispered. "He'll be fine."

"We need to leave," Bambi murmured.

"He needs to get his strength back," I told her.

"No time," she said. "It's far better for him if he doesn't see anything else down here. Can you cloak yourself, Ethan and your babies?"

"Yes."

With Bambi's help, I loaded Ethan's massive frame over George's back. I popped my monsters in my pocket and I made our sextet invisible. I felt shaky, having expended so much magic, but there was no time to rejuvenate. I briefly considered drinking from Ethan, but he was so weak I decided against it.

"Are we ready?" George asked.

"As we're ever gonna be," I answered, hoping we'd make it out of here but having no clue what to do after that.

"Then let's go," he grunted.

And we did.

CHAPTER FOURTEEN

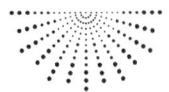

NOW I KNEW WHY THEY KNOCKED ME OUT THE FIRST TIME
through. It was not pretty. If this was the waiting area, I knew I
never wanted to see the rest. The thought of my mother in the
basement sat heavy on my heart. I was sure if I was cast down
there she wouldn't have given me a second thought, but I was not
my mother. She got what she deserved, but I couldn't shake the
constricted feeling in my chest when I thought about her.

Dark and smoky hallways filled with Demons and soul lights
were all I could see for what seemed like miles. No one was
actually doing anything wrong, but the smell of sex and blood was
everywhere. It was depressing and quietly terrifying. Unable to
put my finger on exactly why, I attributed it to the muted
moaning and crying. I missed the overplayed Journey soundtracks
from the main level. The Hounds walked the corridors as if they
owned them and were given a wide berth by everything and
everyone we passed. The fear they instilled was palpable. Clearly
no one knew them the way I did.

"*Is your reputation earned?*" I asked.

"*Yes,*" George said.

"*Nice.*"

"*Thank you.*"

After a long while we entered the area with the desks, Demons and soul lights. I breathed a sigh of relief only to be followed by a sharp intake of breath.

"*What's wrong, Little Astrid?*" Bambi asked, concerned.

"*Where will I take Ethan? Can you take us to a portal?*"

"*Your mate is not strong enough to make it home through a portal and I do believe you have offered your services to help find the Sword of Death. I would have thought you were a woman of your word,*" the General huffed indignantly.

"*I am,*" I hissed. "*My intention was to send him home and stay till I finished whatever was expected of me here.*"

"*Do you really think the most powerful Vampyre in the world would go for that plan?*" George chuckled at my lack of foresight.

"*I hadn't thought that far,*" I muttered, hating that yet again the General was correct. "*Okay, Smartypants, where will he be safe?*"

"*There is a guest house on Dixie's property. We will go there.*"

"*Fine. Go fast. I don't want to run into anyone I'd have to kill. I'm not in the mood right now,*" I said, hoping Ethan would stay knocked out till we arrived.

"*As you wish.*"

THE GUESTHOUSE WAS CHARMING—ONE BEDROOM, A LIVING AREA, kitchen, dining area and a huge bathroom with a sunken tub. God, I wanted to get in the tub and wash the stench of Hell's waiting area off of my body, but there was no time for that at the moment.

The Hounds helped me get Ethan to the bed and I wrapped him in blankets after I cleaned his now healing wounds. I tried to feed him more blood, but in his exhausted and unconscious state he refused to cooperate.

"You will need to cloak the house," Bambi told me through her eyebrows as she peed on the front porch wrought iron furniture.

"Um, is that necessary?" I asked as she continued to mark the flowerbeds, the bird feeder and the small garden shed.

"The cloaking? Yes. The peeing? No, but it's fun." She giggled and finished up by urinating on the welcome mat. It smelled like brownies, but it was still gross.

"Once you've cloaked the house we shall leave. All you have to do is call us in your mind if you need us. We will come," George said, admiring Bambi's work.

"Why?"

"What do you mean?" he asked, lifting his leg and hitting a few spots Bambi had apparently missed.

"Why are you helping me?" Everyone had an ulterior motive here. What was theirs?

"Because you're special," his eyebrows bounced, answering logically.

"What does that mean?" I blew out an exasperated sigh and wondered why everyone was so fucking cryptic.

"It's for me to know and you to find out," he grunted and then laughed uproariously at his own joke.

"What are you? Five?" I snapped.

"I am far beyond five, but your lack of maturity seems to be rubbing off on me." He grinned and bowed. "Thank you for an eventful day, Little Astrid. Good luck to you, you will need it."

"Me want to play with doggies," Abe screeched from my pocket. Hell's Bells, I'd forgotten they were in there.

"Me tooooo. Me ride the doggie and jump on him and tickle him," Rachel added enthusiastically.

"My doggy. Me have the doggy," Beyonce yelled, flying out of my pocket and landing on the General's snout.

"Me kick your assssssssssssss," Ross grunted, dive bombing Beyonce and starting a slap fight of epic proportions on George's head.

"Enough," George roared. The Demons froze and looked

curiously at him. "If you promise to behave and Astrid okays it you may come for a play date at the Dark Palace."

A chorus of, "Pleeeeeze Mommmmy," made my head ache.

"Will they be safe?"

Bambi and the General rolled their beady eyes at me and shook their bulbous heads.

"Fine." I gave in. The Hounds would probably be able to keep a better eye on them than I could. "You little turds behave," I said, kissing them. "Will you bring them home tonight?"

"Absolutely." The Hell Hounds were excited to have little guests and the little guests were screaming with joy so loudly I had to slap my hands over my ears.

In the most beautiful blast of magic and glitter I'd seen yet, the Hell Hounds disappeared with my monsters. *Good luck... you'll need it?* That did not sound good. At all. For now I felt relatively safe with the guesthouse cloaked. Dixie would think I'd gone for a walk and I had at least an hour or so to wake Ethan up and get him up to speed.

Locking the doors and windows seemed silly considering I was in a place where people popped up magically, but it made the former human side of me feel more secure. Ethan was still out. He'd kicked off the covers and his muscle bound body was in full view. I ran my fingers over the light sprinkling of blond hair on his chest. I breathed in his scent and snuggled up next to him—warm and safe. He made me whole.

"I love you," I whispered.

"I love you too, you crazy Vampyre." His voice was hoarse, but laced with amusement.

I bolted up and took his face in my hands. "Are you okay?"

"I've been better, but I would feel very happy if you were naked."

"You're a sex addict." I grinned and whipped my shirt over my head.

"I'm your sex addict," he shot, back removing his pants and

boxer briefs since he was already shirtless. I was stunned motionless. How had I forgotten how beautiful he was? Perfect.

"Pants need to go," he said, sliding them and my panties down my legs. "Stand up," he commanded gruffly. I stepped back and let him look. He reverently placed his lips on my still flat stomach and bathed it in sweet kisses. "So gorgeous. So beautiful. Mine."

With Vampyre speed he put me underneath him. His lips and hands were everywhere and I shuddered in anticipation. His fangs scraped my breasts and my hips bucked involuntarily. His erection pressed into my belly and I moaned.

"No foreplay, Ethan. Please, I need you now."

The sexy sound he made set my lower regions on fire. I was wet and so ready. My head spun as he trailed his mouth from mine to the place on my neck that made me senseless.

"Now," I hissed, spreading my legs and wrapping them around him.

"I aim to please," he growled, lifting my ass with his strong hands.

"Excuse me, kids, I know this might be a bad time and all… "

WTF? Grandpa?

"Oh my God," I shrieked and rolled out from under Ethan. Wrapping a sheet over my naked body and putting a pillow over Ethan's privates I glared at my grandfather. "Grandpa, get out!"

"Right. Of course. I'll meet you in the living room," he said, giving Ethan the thumbs up and winking at me.

"Who was that?" Ethan demanded, frustrated and pissed. "And how in the hell did he get in here?"

"My grandpa, and I have no clue. I cloaked the house and locked the doors. Shit," I groaned, looking at my still fully erect mate. "We're going to have to get back to this later." I ran my hand lightly over his ragingly hard erection and damned my grandfather to Hell. I laughed as I realized how redundant that was.

"You think this is funny? I'm not sure I can walk. And if you touch me again," he threatened, "I don't care if all of Hell is out there. I'm going to fuck my wife."

"I like when you say that." I giggled and grabbed my clothes.

"Which part?" he asked as he retrieved his torn pants and pulled them on.

"Um... all of it, but especially the wife part."

"You are my wife and my mate and everything that matters to me. Always," he said, pulling me into his strong arms and kissing me thoroughly.

"Oh, Ethan," I gasped and pulled back. "We had all the history of Hell wrong."

"What are you talking about?"

"Too long to tell you everything now, but my dad, Abbadon, was not in charge. He was Satan's mentally imbalanced brother. He lied to your father."

"Are you quite sure?"

"Very. Apparently he was a loose cannon and everyone, including Satan, is delighted that he's gone."

"That explains the Uncle Satan thing," Ethan mused, still mulling over the fact that his race had believed what turned out to be fiction for hundreds of years. "Does God exist?"

"Yep. He's Satan's brother and he's good and lives in Heaven. Oh, and Heaven is not up above, it's just a different plane. Just like Hell isn't below... different plane. We share the same sun, moon and stars."

"You're making me dizzy," he said, sitting on the edge of the bed.

"Trust me, I know. Totally screwed up, but I didn't want you sounding like an idiot out there."

"Why thank you," he said sarcastically. I realized it was going to take him hundreds of years to get used to me not kissing his ass.

"No problem, sexy. Now come meet my certifiable grandpa."

CHAPTER FIFTEEN

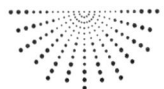

"You're a fucking Sprite," Ethan bellowed in disbelief. That certainly wasn't the best first line when you meet your mate's extended family...

"Um... Ethan," I stepped in front of him just in case he decided to punctuate his anger with a little magic or a fist. I knew my grandpa was a True Immortal and I had no clue if that came with extra super powers. I just got my mate back and I was taking no chances. "He's a Sprite and a Demon. He's the one who helped me at my mother's memorial service."

"How did he help you?"

"He gave me the clue about how to kill her," I told him. This seemed to calm him down a little bit...

"Have you grabbed her ass?" Ethan demanded of my grandpa, who was highly amused by all of this.

"Most certainly not," he huffed. "I am far too busy avoiding my shrew of a wife to be grabbing anyone's ass. And I would never grab my granddaughter's ass. Ever."

"Okay then, now that we've all met and sniffed each other's butts, why are you here and how in the hell did you get through my cloaking?" I asked my cute little bastard of a grandpa.

"Darling, nothing keeps me out of where I want to be," he explained, making himself comfortable on the couch.

"You answered half. Why are you here?" I demanded. Keeping my grandpa on track was similar to herding greased cats.

"Fucking Sprites," Ethan muttered under his breath.

"I can hear you," Grandpa snapped.

"I certainly hope so," Ethan replied politely.

Help me, Cousin Jesus.

"Enough." I glared at Ethan and then turned my ire on my gramps. "Spit it out or leave."

"Fine, dear," he sighed dramatically. "When it came to my attention that you busted your boyfriend out I was worried about both of you."

"You knew he was being held? Like an animal? Being molested by a slut named Lust?" I shouted.

"Yes. No and no," he answered, looking a bit put out.

"What exactly are you upset about?" I asked. "The fact that he was being held or the torture he was being put through?"

"I'm quite perturbed that I didn't know this. I am sorry that the father of your child was treated disrespectfully, despite the fact that he is rude. That was not ordered by anyone to my knowledge."

"Would my Uncle Fucker have ordered this?"

"Astrid, I'd avoid that endearment," Gramps admonished. "Lucifer's sense of humor isn't that broad."

"I wasn't joking."

"Yes, well... let's get back to the matter at hand," Grandpa was flustered. It was incongruous with what I'd seen of him thus far, but what did I know? I thought he was a wall. "How long do you feel that you've been here?" he asked Ethan.

"A day—maybe two. Do you run consecutively with Earth time?"

"Not exactly," Grandpa told him. "But you confound me. You

have your power. Vampyres are always rendered magic-free in Hell. Why are you different?"

"Because of me," I said. Both men looked at me and waited. Ethan wasn't going to like what I was about to say, but... "He's had my blood. Would that make the difference?"

Ethan's jaw worked silently, but he said nothing. Grandpa sat quietly and considered.

"Yes, it would make a difference if... " He stopped himself.

"If what?" I asked. The time for half stories and 'Let's Let Astrid Figure It Out On Her Own' was over. "If what?" I repeated.

"I'm not at liberty to say," he muttered and rubbed his cute little head, making his hair stand on end.

"Oh, for God's sake," I yelled. "I've got a little problem here and if you can help me I would really appreciate it."

"That's Uncle God to you," he corrected. I rolled my eyes and plastered my arms to my sides so I wouldn't slap him.

"The issue is that I can survive a week in Hell. I need to know how time is running," Ethan said, avoiding eye contact with me.

"You can only be here a week?" I shrieked and Ethan nodded. "Can you find out or adjust the time thingie?" I asked Grandpa frantically.

"That is very complicated." Gramps looked pained and frightened.

"If he dies I join him."

"What? You can't die." Gramps was shocked. Clearly he didn't know everything.

"We're mated—if one of us dies the other follows. So as I see it, you have a couple of choices. Take us to a portal so I can send Ethan home and complete whatever I have to do here... "

"Not an option," Ethan snapped.

"Alrighty then, Pops, you have one choice. Stop time on Earth until I find your stinking Sword of Death."

"Shit." Grandpa turned green and then ghostly white. "There's only one way."

"Will it hurt?" I asked, expecting something hideous.

"Not you, my dear. Me."

That stopped me. As much as I wanted to throttle the tiny man, I had fallen a little in love with my grandpa. "Will it kill you?"

"Oh no," he laughed. "I actually enjoy a bit of pain."

"TMI, Gramps. What do we have to do?"

"I have to call in a favor with your grandma," he whispered. His head snapped around and he fearfully searched the room.

"Is she here?" I asked quietly, backing into a corner in case the ceiling caved in.

"What's happening?" Ethan asked, picking up on the terror.

"Not sure," I muttered, "but come stand by me just in case."

He hopped up and joined me. Grandpa swallowed several times, ran his hands through his already messy hair and then chanted in a language that was vaguely familiar to me. The melody was transfixing and I found myself swaying.

Slowly the carpet turned to grass and the furniture to boulders and bushes. The curtains transformed from brocade to blindingly colorful flowering vines. The scents were divine. Trees sprouted and burst through the ceiling. Heavy unfamiliar orange and blood red fruit hung from the branches. Pastel colored birds flew gracefully around the room and tiny monkeys hopped from the limbs to the bushes. I idly wondered if the house would ever go back to normal, but this was so gorgeous, I didn't really care.

"It's beautiful," I said as a purple bird landed on my shoulder.

"Son of a bitch, shit, hellfire and damnation," a female voice screamed. "I was in the middle of *Jeopardy*. This had better be good, or I'll turn your ass into a tree."

The voice, hypnotically beautiful, did not match the words flying from the mouth of the disheveled beauty standing in the middle of the forest that used to be a guesthouse. She wore a gown made of a sheer sparkling fabric like none I'd ever seen. Yards and yards of the tulle-like material floated around her. Her hair was a wild mass of fiery red curls and her skin was a pale porcelain. But her eyes... her eyes were the clearest, brightest blue and they glittered. She was the most beautiful woman I'd ever seen and she was pissed.

Her magic filled the room. It had an earthy scent to it with a distinct undertone of malice. Every move she made was sensual and dangerous. Shit, I hoped this was the right decision.

"Bill, this is not good timing," she hissed. "That smug bastard Alex Trebek mispronounced a word and I was watching the gas filled douchewanker squirm. It was glorious."

Grandpa's name was Bill? Satan's father was named Bill? How was that possible? I bit back the hysterical laughter that was trapped in my throat and prayed that she wouldn't notice us.

"Gaia, lovely to see you," Grandpa Bill stuttered.

She eyed him critically and then gifted him with a smile. A smile so brilliant, it would have killed a mere mortal. Grandma had some major mojo going on...

"I prefer Gigi," she snapped, turning to me. "Grandma sounds old."

Fuck, another mind reader.

She laughed with delight and then sucked in a quick startled breath. Her eyes narrowed and she walked toward me. Ethan being an alpha dude and my mate stepped in front of me, staking his claim and warning Mother Nature.

"Silly, silly Vampyre," she murmured, pushing him away with a mere flick of her finger. "You. You are so pretty."

"Thank you, so are you," I said and then went for the big one. "I, um... killed your son—my father."

"Yes, yes. Thank you, dear," she muttered searching my face.

Wow, not what I expected. No one liked my dad... not even his nutty mother. "Why in the hell is everyone so scared of you?"

I heard Grandpa's gasp and Ethan's moan of displeasure. I rolled my eyes. By now they had to know I was a loose cannon.

Having no clue how long Gigi was going to stick around, I decided to get right down to business.

"Because I'm a woman with power and a monthly cycle," she said, adjusting her ample bosom. Bill cleared his throat. Twice. "Alright, fine, I'm a little unstable and prone to fits that result in earthquakes, typhoons and volcanic eruptions. Happy?" she snapped and glared at her husband. He winked and she giggled. Bizarre.

I shut my brain doors, knowing at some point I would think something that would piss her off. Could I just ask her to stop time? Did Grandpa need to ask? What would I owe her?

"So is anybody going to tell me why I'm here? There is a *Full House* marathon coming on and I think that show is so heinous I must watch it."

Mother Nature watches *Jeopardy* and *Full House*... How did I end up here? Only short months ago I was a single art teacher with nothing exciting on the horizon. Now I was a Vampyre-Demon who turns out to be related to every mythical and religious figure imaginable. WTF?

"Well, um... we were wondering, you know, since my mate, Ethan, can only, um... " She was making me nervous. What if I caused a tsunami? I'd be sick about that.

"Forgive me, son," she muttered and made the sign of the cross, "I'm about to sin... again. Goddamnit, I don't have time for this. Get to the fucking point or I'll blow up the left side of Hell and let you explain that to my other shit of a son who NEVER comes to visit me."

She stomped around the room. Her little monkeys followed her faithfully and the birds flew in a halo formation around her head.

"I am sick and tired of nobody visiting. It's fucking boring in Nirvana and I need chocolate," she yelled.

I glanced at a terrified Ethan and Grandpa. Gigi had progressed to a kicking and screaming fit on the grassy floor and her monkeys had gone ballistic. She was C-R-A-Z-Y and we needed her help. Awesome.

Dashing to what used to be the kitchen I scrounged around, and praise Cousin Jesus, I found chocolate. Gigi was nuts and dangerous, but she didn't seem evil like my mom. Honestly, she needed a good kick in the pants and most definitely some chocolate.

Her fit had escalated to a degree that was nothing short of terrifying and the monkeys were shrieking and fighting. The birds were no longer graceful—they were dive bombing Grandpa and Ethan, both of whom were hiding under bushes. Enough was enough. This shit was ending now. I was certain her tantrum was going to bring every Demon in Hell to my doorstep and I needed to have time stopped before that happened.

Panic settled in my throat. A True Immortal and a Master Vampyre were hiding from her. Was I an idiot to think I could stop her? Yes. Yes, I was. The ramifications of her fit were a big unknown and that scared me. Could she cause some horrific destruction on earth because she was rolling around on the floor stringing more swear words together than even I knew? She didn't seem to be the kind of gal who destroyed the world on purpose—she simply appeared to be completely out of control. I wondered for a second if she'd ever tried hormone therapy… would that even work on an immortal?

"Gigi," I shouted in a harsh voice I pulled out of my butt. "Stop it. NOW. Is it any wonder nobody visits you? You're a fucking disaster." I heard my grandpa whimper and Ethan groaned. That took some nerve. They were hiding… the cowards.

Mother Nature sat up with a look of shock on her face that was priceless and damned scary. Was she going to zap me dead or listen to reason? It was anyone's guess…

"Did you just call me a fucking disaster?" she asked in a very low tone. My gut clenched and I felt a little lightheaded.

"Yes. Yes, I did. You are acting like a two year old and I'm worried that you're going to blow up half of the continental USA if you don't get a handle on your tantrum."

"No one has ever called me a fucking disaster," she shouted.

"Well, then no one that you hang with has balls," I shouted back.

There was a long silence where I calculated the odds of how much longer I had to live. I slowly handed her the chocolate, hoping she didn't bite my hand off.

"Do you really think this is why no one visits?" She sounded like a lost little girl for a moment, but she was no child. She was a dangerous, slightly deranged woman with a ton of magic. She broke off a small piece of the chocolate and popped it in her mouth.

"Yes, I do. Would you want to visit you?" I squatted down next to her and helped her to a sitting position. I was sure I heard Bill squeak in fear.

"I suppose not," she pouted. "It is a tiny bit unnerving."

"Exactly," I told her as I adjusted her dress and tucked her hair behind her ears. "You need to ease up on the fits and maybe try some yoga or meds or something."

"Do you think that would help?"

Damn, she was pretty.

"I would think so. Do you have any friends? Or hobbies?"

She thought hard and then shook her head sadly. Her red curls bounced and her perfect mouth pursed. "No. No friends or hobbies although I've always wanted to take up knitting and pole dancing."

"Well," I stuttered, biting down hard on my lip so I wouldn't laugh. "You should try that. You might even make some friends if you take a pole dancing class."

"I think I will." She laughed and her monkeys clapped wildly. She tossed them the rest of the chocolate and they munched happily. The birds again created a halo around her head. "I like you, Astrid. You will be my new friend. Of course you are my granddaughter, but more importantly, you will visit me in Nirvana or I'll come to Kentucky. We will shop and go to movies and I will babysit your child once it's born and we will go to spas and wrestling matches. What do you think?"

She waited anxiously for my reply. Most of it sounded good except for her babysitting and the wrestling matches.

"Yep, I'm in." I heard Ethan gasp and I grinned. "But I have a problem."

"Oh dear, are you hormonal and want to kill people or drown a city?" she asked with great sincerity.

"Um, no. I was wondering if you would stop time on Earth while I… "

"Done," she said.

"Don't you want to know why?" I asked.

"I already know," she trilled and took my face in her hands. "But I only bestow gifts on those who are worthy. You, my child, are worthy. Time will resume when the mission impossible has been accomplished. Ohhhhhhhhhh, I love that movie. Don't you? Tom Cruise is such a cutie."

Grandpa harrumphed from under his bush and Gigi giggled.

"Anyhoo, I'm horny and I want the Sword of Death tucked away in the Den of Iniquity where it belongs. I'm so not in the mood to be killed when you've given me a new lease on life, Astrid."

Deciding to ignore the horny part I touched on the storage of the Sword instead. "Why on earth would the Sword be kept in The Den of Iniquity? Seems a little dicey to me," I said, surprised the True Immortals would be fine with that.

"Oh no, dear, it's perfect. Trust me."

Clearly it wasn't perfect if someone had taken it, but I didn't want to kill her happy buzz.

"Bill, you'll be coming home with me," she cooed to Grandpa. "I have an itch that needs to be scratched for about a week or so."

"My pleasure." Grandpa grinned like a teenage boy about to score big and moved quickly to her side.

"Astrid darling, we'll be in touch. I'm going to get us signed up for pole dancing classes!"

"Great," I said, pulling Ethan out from under the bush. "This is my mate, Ethan."

"Ohhhhhh, he's dreamy. Take care of her or I'll smite you." She smiled sweetly, blew me a kiss and in a burst of rose and turquoise colored glitter she and Grandpa disappeared.

"If I hadn't witnessed that, I would never have believed it," Ethan muttered.

"Um, me neither." I giggled and dropped to the couch. WTH? The house had been totally returned to a house. Aside from a few gorgeous plants that had appeared in shimmering pots, you'd never know we'd been in a forest only moments ago.

"What's next?"

"I'm not sure. I suppose I should have a chat with Uncle Fucking Satan."

"I have been called many things, but that one is new to me," Satan said, standing in the doorway. "I'm not quite sure I like that."

"Oh my God," I shouted. "Have you ever heard of knocking?"

"Now where would the fun in that be? Introduce me to your Vampyre."

"Ethan, Satan. Satan, Ethan," I said warily.

"Lovely to meet you, Ethan. Why don't we all have a seat and have a little get to know you time?"

I had a feeling this would either be a clusterfuck... or a clusterfuck.

CHAPTER SIXTEEN

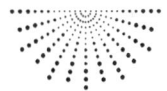

I SAT ON THE COUCH WITNESSING THE SURREAL EXCHANGE OF pleasantries between the King of the Underworld and the strongest Vampyre alive who also happened to be a Prince. The simple truth that one was my uncle and one was my mate was bizarre. Of course the other fact was that even though they were older than dirt, they both looked around thirty. Ahhhh, the life of an immortal.

"I'd like to offer my most sincere apologies for your treatment thus far," Satan said, clearly disturbed that he was unaware of the situation.

Mind you, the torture didn't seem to bother him as much as the fact he didn't know about it… Getting used to this side of the family was going to be a challenge.

Ethan simply nodded and watched my uncle carefully.

"Strong silent type," Satan mused, examining Ethan just as closely.

The beauty in the room was stupid. I exhaled the breath I was holding slowly because I hadn't realized I was holding it. I knew for certain my attraction to my uncle was in no way sexual, but his sheer charisma was shattering. Ethan was the only person so far to be unaffected. Uncle Fucker didn't like that.

"Ethan, my boy, do you play poker?"

Ethan's body tensed at the word boy, but he didn't lash out physically. No, he was far too clever for that.

"Actually I do, Uncle Fucker. May I call you Uncle Fucker?" he inquired politely. "I assume I'll be meeting so many members of Astrid's family, I'd like to get the monikers correct."

"Satan will be fine," my uncle answered tersely.

"Will Dante be there?" I asked, changing the subject. A fight was out of the question.

"Yes," Satan sighed dramatically. "He's an insufferable bore, but he always shows up and it would just be rude to turn him away."

"I've heard he's an ass," Ethan added. "I assume he went a bit girly when he realized his fiction was truly fiction."

"Yes, yes," the Devil laughed heartily. "The son of a bitch got his panties in quite the wad."

"Who else will be playing?" I inquired, happy the little powwow was going so well.

"I do believe Hemingway will be there and we may get lucky enough to be graced by Mother Teresa."

"Mother Teresa lives in Hell?" Ethan couldn't hide his shock.

"Sweet Nephew Jesus, no. None of my poker buddies reside in Hell. They just take the bus over once a week to have a little fun. It's a bit stuffy at my brother's house."

"Interesting," Ethan said.

"So are you in, my man?" Satan asked.

"What do you play for?" my mate asked warily. I didn't Vampyre-marry no dummy.

"Why, favors of course. If I win you make a little deal with the Devil."

"And if I win?" Ethan crossed his arms over his chest and waited.

"You make a deal with me."

"So technically either way it's a deal with the Devil…" Ethan grinned, sat back and ran his hands through his hair. "I'm in. It will be good to rub it in with Dante and to kick your ass."

"We shall see." Satan grinned back. "It's formal attire."

"Problem," I said.

My Uncle snapped his fingers and boxes and hanging bags full of clothing from the world's finest designers appeared before our eyes. "Problem solved. I will see you this evening."

With that he vanished. We sat in silence. I pondered the thought of meeting Hemingway and Mother Teresa and I wondered if anyone had ever beaten the Devil at poker.

"Today's Thursday?" I asked.

"Looks that way," Ethan muttered, letting his head fall back on his shoulders. "Do you think he cheats?"

"Most definitely," I said, eyeing the bags labeled Prada.

"Angel," he said in a voice that stopped me and made my tummy flip. "I believe we have some unfinished business."

"I believe we do." I slowly eased my shirt over my head as his eyes went from golden to green. "Should we adjourn to the boudoir?" I giggled as I slipped out of my pants and panties.

"Nope. I'd like to christen the couch, armchair and kitchen table for starters."

His arm muscles stretched as he removed his pants—corded and strong. He was Heaven and sin personified and he was mine.

"Sounds like a plan," I choked out. My body ached with need and speech was difficult. "Do you want me to come over there?"

"I want you to come everywhere—over and over again."

Oh my God, that was hot. My knees buckled and he was on me faster than I could blink. I moaned as he manhandled my ass and ground me into his very happy camper.

"I want you," he hissed in my ear. "I'm going to fuck you until you can't remember your name."

"That works for me," I gasped, grinding against him. "Why are you knocking on the wall?"

"What?"

"You're knocking on the wall," I said as I tried to pull him to the floor. "Stop. It's weird."

"I thought it was you."

"Why would I be knocking on the wall?"

"We're not by a wall." He groaned and stared at the ceiling. "We're in the middle of the fucking room.

He was correct. "Then what the hell... ?"

"Astrid?" Dixie called from outside the front porch door. "Are you in there? I just got out of therapy and Daddy told me you were back here."

"Shitshitshit, who did I screw over to deserve this? I'm gonna have blue balls," I snapped, grabbing my clothes and yanking them on. Pre-orgasm. Again.

"Who is that?" Ethan ground out, clearly suffering from a very real bout of blue balls.

"My cousin, Dixie. She's the one I like. Can you wait a little longer?" I asked, half hoping he'd say no...

"Can you?"

I nodded my head even though I wanted to cry in frustration. *Was this like that tantric sex shit I read about? If it was, it sucked.*

"It's against every instinct that I have, but I'll wait. However, when I have you later, it won't be pretty, gentle or nice.

I shuddered and almost tripped over my pants. "Promise?"

"Swear."

"Be right there, Dixie," I yelled. Making sure Ethan was as covered as he could be with his ripped pants, I pushed him down on the chair and slapped a throw pillow over his enormous erection. Giving him a wink and flashing him my boobs, I opened the door.

"Astrid, are you okay?" Dixie burst in the room and checked me over from head to toe.

"I'm good."

"Daddy told me you'd been to the waiting area and some

trouble went down. Did someone hurt you or try to force you to a lower level? Tell me what they looked like and I'll have them banished to the Basement. I'd like to destroy them if they hurt you, but you do look fine. Maybe a little flushed, but fine."

"Dixie, I…"

"I know I'm not supposed to actually kill anyone, but I swear to Uncle God, I'd do it if you'd been harmed. I promise I won't leave you again—not even for a moment while you're here. I'll keep my back turned in the bathroom, or we can just pee with the door open."

"I'm a Vamp. I don't actually do that."

"Right. Vamps don't pee. I forgot. Wow, that's got to be convenient on long car rides. Anyhoo, I'll still be here and just turn away when you need some privacy. Damn, if I had my power I could shapeshift into a dog or something cool like that, but my magic hasn't come in all the way yet."

"Dixie, are you through?" I asked, worn out by her diatribe and touched by her concern.

She bit her pretty lip and thought for a moment. "Yes. Yes, I am."

"I went to the waiting area with General George and Bambi. I sensed that my Baby Demons had gone there. The Hell Hounds were amazing and I found not only my little monsters, but also my mate."

"You found a mate in the waiting room of Hell?" she asked doubtfully.

"Um, no. I found *my mate* from my life on Earth. He was chained and being tortured by your… some Demons."

"No," she gasped. "I certainly hoped you killed them."

For someone who didn't kill, she was awfully bloodthirsty.

"No, not that I didn't want to," I said, remembering Lust slinking all over Ethan's bound body. "No, I'll take care of his torturer in a more creative and painful way."

"Good," she nodded with approval. *If she only knew.*

147

"Your offer to be my protector is lovely, but I do have my mate and he's a badass mofo."

"But he's only a Vampyre and their magic doesn't work here," she said.

"I beg to differ," Ethan said from the couch.

"Oh Hell," Dixie shrieked and jumped behind me. Peeking out, she grinned sheepishly and waved. "Guess I would have made a crappy bodyguard... "

"You make a better cousin," I teased, then took her hand and drew her over to the couch. "Dixie, this is my mate Ethan."

"Nice to meet you," she whispered, clearly awestruck by his beauty.

"Nice to meet you too." He grinned and she blushed. I even felt myself swoon under the spell of his wicked smile. "I want to thank you for being good to Astrid and my child. It will not be forgotten."

"You're the father of the Baby Demons?" Dixie sputtered. "Astrid, I had no idea that you'd given birth to those little cuties. I thought you found them. I guess it's kind of odd that you have three-inch kids, but maybe that's because you mated with a Vampyre. I'm kind of shocked you can have kids since you're dead and all... but I think it's great that you don't make them feel bad or inferior, not that you would... Oh my Hell, they actually ate their own grandfather." She turned a pale shade of green when she put that theory together. In truth, she had put nothing together, but she was talking so damned fast I couldn't get a word in edgewise.

"Done?" I asked.

"Um, sure."

"I most certainly did not give birth to the hooter obsessed Baby Demons," I laughed. "They have about fifty to sixty years on me and Vampyres have normal sized kids." I glanced over at Ethan for confirmation on this and he shrugged his shoulders. WTF? I was aware that Vampyres didn't normally have babies, but he didn't have to be an unsupportive dick about it. Now I was going to worry that I'd be blowing out an alien until the big day arrived. "Whatever," I huffed, and gave him the evil eye. He was going to be working those blue balls for a while. "Dixie, I'm pregnant now. It's a boy."

"When are you due?" Her body tensed with excitement. "I'll be coming to Earth in six months. Maybe I'll be there for the birth! I can babysit for you."

Did all immortals consider themselves good babysitters? Dixie was a vast improvement over Gigi, but...

"I met Grandma."

"No way." She backed herself up to the wall and scanned the room nervously.

"Yep. She wants to be called Gigi. Grandma makes her feel old. She's planning on taking up knitting and pole dancing and I suggested that she might want to try some meds."

"And you're still alive?"

"As a dead person can be. She offered to babysit too."

"Oh... um, I'm not sure you want to do that," she hedged. "Grand, um, Gigi is fucking insane," she said in a rush and then slapped her hand over her mouth in terror.

I laughed, but checked the room as well. Another visit would be one too many at the moment. "She took Grandpa home with her. For a week."

"That will be loud." Dixie giggled and rolled her eyes.

"Yep," I agreed. "So will you play poker tonight?

"No, normally I watch, but I'm meeting some friends." She picked very seriously at her nails as a slow blush travelled up her neck and landed squarely on her lovely cheeks.

"Friends?"

"Well, um... a friend, but my dad doesn't know and I... "

"Secret's safe with me," I told her, grinning.

She glanced over at Ethan. "My lips are sealed."

"Thanks."

"When do we have to be there?" I asked as I waded through the piles of clothes. Satan had thought of everything. There were undergarments as well as casual clothes mixed in with the formal wear. So much for going commando…

"In an hour. Go ahead and change and I'll be over to pick you up in forty-five."

I peeked over at Ethan as Dixie raced out. His grimace of pain made me smile. "No time for nookie," I purred. I need to shower and daydream about our three-headed, four-armed baby."

"Our son will be perfect," he growled as he tried to stand, only to hunch forward due to his unsatisfied hard-on. "I'm letting you play this little game, Angel, but the consequences will be devastating."

"Promises, promises." I laughed as he chased me to the bathroom. I couldn't wait to get back here tonight. I was going to ride him till he was blind.

CHAPTER SEVENTEEN

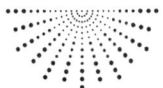

THE POKER ROOM WAS BRIGHTLY LIT, BUT THE AMBIANCE WAS anything but friendly. It was as overly opulent as the other parts of the palace that I'd visited. Highly glossed marble covered the floors and rich brocades and velvets covered the furniture and walls. The focal point was the table in the middle of the room—a heavy mahogany top with carved and bloodied headless cherubs holding it up. *Nice.* The dark atmosphere was in direct conflict with Steven Perry's voice belting out *Open Arms*. Ethan gave me the silent raised eyebrow and I shrugged and giggled. I'd forgotten to tell him about my uncle's Journey obsession.

I recognized Hemingway immediately. He sat silently at the table nursing a martini. His demeanor didn't invite chit-chat, so I kept my distance. A pompous, sullen looking man lounged on a furry black chaise lounge in the corner—had to be Dante. He was clearly pouting about something, but in ironic contrast, he sang along with the music.

Assuming Satan would make an entrance, I wasn't surprised he hadn't shown up yet. Neither had Mother Teresa... but Mister Rogers had. WTF? *Mister Rogers shouldn't be playing poker in Hell*

151

with Satan. *He should be feeding fish and making new neighbors in Heaven.* Did he even realize where he was?

"Ethan," I whispered. "That's Mister Rogers."

"Mister who?"

"Mister Fucking Rogers," I hissed, covertly nodding my head in his direction. He was wearing the cardigan and everything.

"His first name is Fucking?" my mate asked with a smirk.

"No. His first name is Fred and I can't believe he's here. I love him."

Ethan glanced over at Fred and waved. Fred smiled and waved back, then proceeded to change from his dress shoes into some tennis shoes.

"No one will believe this," I muttered.

As I gaped at my childhood idol, eight Demons entered the room and placed themselves in strategic areas. Interesting. Ethan's body tensed and for the umpteenth time since I arrived in Hell I wished I was armed.

"How much of a handle do you have on your power?" Ethan telepathically asked as he sized up the Demons.

"Why? Do you think I'm going to need it?"

"Unclear at the moment, but I'm assessing our arsenal."

"Apparently I have an assload of power. I need to get angry to use it and I'm not real sure how to control it."

"Outstanding."

"Sarcasm will not get you laid."

Ethan's mega watt smile made my knees turn to jelly. He'd get laid no matter what... and he knew it.

"I'd be surprised if Satan wants violence in his own home, but stranger things have happened," he said.

The poker quintet appeared to be Ethan, Mr. Rogers, Hemingway, Dante and the Devil. The Demons were the bodyguards and Dixie's therapy group was the staff. Wait. What? Carl, Janet and Myrtle were circling the room with trays of hors d'oeuvres.

"You look lovely, Miss Astrid," Janet tittered, complimenting the tight red Prada halter dress I wore. "Would you care for a Soy-Pig-in-the-Blanket?"

"I'm sorry, what?" I asked, taking a closer look at the tray. Sure enough it was loaded with little pastry covered cocktail weenies. "Satan likes tiny hot dogs?"

"Oh yes, but the fake meat kind. He also likes Velveeta cheese dip and s'mores. I think Carl is serving the dip and Myrtle is passing around the s'mores," she chirped happily and popped a soy weenie in her mouth.

"Wow." I stopped there, swallowing all the other things that came to mind.

"Want one? They're the bomb," she explained with her mouth full.

"Um, no. I don't eat food."

"Right," she said, mortified. "My goodness, I'm so sorry." In her nervousness, she shoved about six more mini dogs into her mouth.

"No worries." I gave her a quick squeeze and a hearty slap on the back as she choked on her mound of weenies. "So this is your job?"

"It is now." She swallowed and stood up straighter. "We're living in the Dark Palace preparing to go to Earth with Dixie in six months. Satan, my savior, wants us close so he can monitor our progress."

Satan, my savior? Sweet Cousin Jesus in a miniskirt, I needed to get the hell out of here soon. "Well, that sounds awesome. You guys doing therapy anymore?"

"Definitely." She nodded and popped a few more weenies in her mouth. "We have a new therapist though. Oh my, will you look at that?" She stared in shock at her serving tray. "The weenies are gone. I need to get more from the kitchen before the Devil gets here or there will be hell to pay." She guffawed at her pun and scurried away. I was tempted to tell her she'd eaten a dozen in my presence alone, but that would be rude and I liked her.

Dante refused food or drink, but Hemingway was chowing down on the s'mores. Mister Rogers had brought his own snack. He laid apples, peanut butter and carrots neatly on a plate that he pulled from his pleather briefcase. Tucking a napkin into the collar of his shirt, he dug in while Hemingway watched in fascination.

"Are you for real, man?" Ernest bellowed at Mister Rogers.

"Oh yes," Fred replied kindly. "Would you care for an apple? I may even have a protein bar in my bag."

"No, no. The s'mores are just fine," he grumbled and shoved one whole s'more into his mouth to punctuate his point. Fred just smiled and gave Hemingway a neighborly thumbs up.

Surreal didn't even begin to cover this evening. There were six chairs at the table and I wondered if Mother Teresa might still show up… Nope. That hope was dashed when one of the uptight Demon guards removed the sixth chair and took it from the room. The music pounding through the speakers stopped abruptly and a hush went through the room. I stuck close to Ethan for many reasons. He smelled amazing and I wasn't sure which one of us was stronger at the moment. There was no way in Hell or anywhere else I would let anything happen to him. Ever.

"Please rise for the King of the Underworld," one of the guards grunted in a menacing voice.

Everyone did.

Satan's entourage entered first; his second in command Cole, looking very foreboding, followed by an overly made up and scantily clad Amanda. I stared in wonder at her repaired lips. I was certain they were bigger.

"*That's Satan's consort,*" I told Ethan. "*She's pregnant with his child and claims it's a boy.*"

"*Would a male child knock one of the Sins out as the heir apparent?*"

154

"No clue, but that could be a clusterfuck." That really could be a clusterfuck...

"That's an understatement."

Speak of the Devil, pun intended, next came the Sins—all seven of them. They were dressed in evening attire and they were gorgeous. Lust in particular was striking. She glanced over at us and her eyes rounded for a brief second in shock, then narrowed to slits. I wanted to tear her ass apart. I knew that wouldn't go over too well at a party, so I decided to bide my time.

"Good evening," Satan shouted joyously from the doorway. He'd chosen his entrance well. The backlighting from the hallway bathed him in a golden glow, creating the illusion of an entire body halo. I grinned at his audacity. He was a first class beautiful bastard and I liked him. "Theodore, please share the rules with our guests."

One of the Demons stepped to the middle of the room. Satan waltzed in and trapped Amanda in a passionate embrace. Watching the Devil seduce a woman was like watching live porn. Holy Hell, I bit down on my lip to keep from shouting, "Get a room." The Sins did some massive eye rolling and Cole turned away in embarrassment or disgust—I couldn't tell which.

Theodore cleared his throat and Satan ended his little performance. "There shall be one winner. There will be ten rounds. The player with the most wins shall be the champion. If the winner is not Satan," Theodore paused dramatically, "the winner will decide the parameters in the deal with the Devil. If Satan wins, he shall make a deal with each and every one of you." Theodore stepped back to his spot.

"What the hell kind of rules are those?" Dante demanded petulantly. "I call bullshit."

"Then leave," Satan said and everyone froze. "But, Dante *my friend*, if you leave you shall never be allowed back."

Dante cleared his throat several times and shifted back and forth. His gaze narrowed and his face turned an unbecoming shade of red. "I can abide by the rules," he muttered and took a seat at the table.

"You're a fucking opportunist asshole, but I'm in," Hemingway bellowed with a shit eating grin on his face.

"Carl," Satan instructed. "Please bring Ernest a fresh martini. Use the chilled glasses and the cold onions. And make it dry."

"Good man," Hemingway grunted as he took his seat. "Good man."

"Now, neighbor, while I do find your rules a bit slanted in your favor, I've been looking forward to this for months. I'm in," Mister Rogers said sweetly. "And Carl, if it's not too much trouble, I'd love a glass of milk and some cookies."

"Thath no trouble at all, thir," Carl said, bowing to Mister Rogers.

"Thank you."

Ethan said nothing. He walked to the table and took his seat. Damn, he was hot. Unfortunately all my cousins and the skank-ass Amanda thought so too. Lust couldn't keep her eyes off of him and it made me feel a little crazy.

"Green doesn't become you," Ethan said.

"Everything becomes me," I snapped. His chuckle bounced around inside my head and I almost slapped him until he sent a visual of what he planned to do to me later this evening. *"Okay, fine. I won't kill her, but I want to."*

His wink made me smile. He was mine. I had nothing to worry about.

"Let the games begin," my uncle said.

The atmosphere shifted quickly to intense in complete juxtaposition to Journey's greatest hits that spilled out of the hidden speakers. I watched the players, but I also watched the peanut gallery. Cole kept his eyes firmly on Amanda as she stared moon eyed at my uncle. He clearly didn't trust her and I was curious what he knew. Dante kept glancing up at the Sins. From where I stood, it was unclear who he was making eye contact with. It was either Sloth or Greed. Greed. It was definitely Greed. Interesting. Was she helping him cheat? Would those girls work against their father?

Carl, Janet and Myrtle quietly made sure drinks were full and no one went without as many weenies as they wanted. Janet placed a large plate of pigs in a blanket next to Satan and he savored them the same way some enjoy fine caviar. Bizarre. Hemingway threw back his martinis and Carl kept them coming at the Devil's discreet nods. I was certain the drinks got stronger and stronger.

Dante sipped wine and Mister Rogers drank his milk and ate his cookies. Ethan was the only one who ingested nothing. He was of a Vampyre age that he could enjoy a blood-laced beverage, but that was not on the menu. The first two hands went to Ethan and the second two to Satan.

"Why have we lowered ourselves to play with Vampyres?" Dante groused, slamming his hand down. "Are we slumming it now?"

"Touché, Dante," Satan said in an overly polite manner. "Perhaps next time we can play on level eight or seven or six… Ahhh, but wait, they don't exist."

Dante's fists clenched and his jaw worked overtime. "Pardon my rudeness," he ground out. "It was thoughtless of me."

Ethan simply nodded and then ignored him. Mister Rogers shook his head sadly and Hemingway burst into laughter.

"My God, man, relax. It's a game. We're playing with the Devil—why not throw a Vampyre in for good measure?" Hemingway said and signaled to Carl for another round. "Who cares if you lose? I've been making deals with the goddamn Devil my whole life… what's one more?"

"Well said." Satan grinned at the famous writer and glanced over and winked at me.

It was the first time he had acknowledged my presence this evening and I'd be a liar if I said it didn't thrill me. My uncle was a magical evil man. He was temptation and all the sins of his daughters rolled into one. The safety I felt in his company was a lie. I needed to remember that everything down here was a game and the stakes were high.

Ironically Mister Rogers won the next two hands, and that's when that slut Lust made her move.

"Daddy," she purred. "I have a bit of a headache. Would you excuse me for a bit? I promise to be back."

"Of course," Satan said absently as he examined his cards.

Lust stood slowly and stretched. Every eye in the room except her father's was on her. She ran her hands down her body, spending a little extra time on her boobies. The guards were almost salivating and poor Mister Rogers looked like he might pass out. Ethan watched her in the same detached way I did and it was clear she didn't like that one bit. As she sauntered past the table she ran her hands over Ethan's shoulders and tangled them into his hair. Leaning forward, she kissed his neck. He roughly shoved her away as her sisters laughed. She hissed her displeasure and left the room in a huff.

Satan glanced up from his cards, having missed the exchange. He looked curiously at Cole, who gave him the 'everything's okay' look and he went back to his cards. Cole might think everything was okay, but I did not. It was time for the bitch to pay.

"I'll be right back," I muttered and quickly made my way to the door. Wrath smiled viciously. Shit, she wanted me to go kick her sister's ass. Well, I hate to disappoint so I gave her a curt nod and left.

"*Astrid*," Ethan said tersely. "*Do not do anything stupid.*"

"*Don't worry, honey. I got it covered.*"

CHAPTER EIGHTEEN

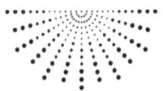

Son of a bitch, where did she go? I scanned the long hallway in frustration. Feeling helpless and human was not working for me—time to tap into my power free-for-all and let the chips land wherever they wanted. Lust was not getting away this time.

Finding my anger wasn't difficult. It was right on the surface, but I needed to dig deeper. I was asking my power to help me find something, not to destroy it. Although when I found her, all bets were off. The chant that I'd heard Grandpa say was caught in the far recesses of my mind. The angrier I got the further away it floated.

"Shit, why aren't there ever any fucking directions?" I groaned. The book Grandpa had given me had no guide on how to use my power. I was in Hell… fury should work. Shouldn't it? Wait. Balance… the balance between good and evil. Is that what I needed to find? Probably, but how was I supposed to do that? Forget it. I had to go with what I knew. My Vampyre skills were no longer dormant. However, I was worried that I'd need my Demon magic to truly deal with Lust. Shitshitshit. I closed my eyes, took a deep breath, let my mind wander outside of myself and slip into hers.

Got it. WTF? Lust was a riot of fury and emotion, but I knew exactly where she was. Unable to decipher any kind of linear thought from the commotion going on inside her, I turned to the right and moved with Vampyre speed in the direction she'd gone. What exactly I had planned when I found her... I had no clue, but she was going to lay off my mate. Period.

I almost laughed as I realized I avoided the talking walls. What I wouldn't give for the walls to speak right now. That would mean Grandpa was near, but that was impossible. He was in Nirvana doing the nasty with Gigi. The visuals were too disturbing so I shoved that sucker to the back of my mind and hummed along with Journey's *Any Way You Want It*.

As I drew closer my body trembled with excitement. The black glittering gloves appeared and I was drunk with power and fury. Wait. What the fuck was I doing? Was I really going to go and have a bitch fight over a man with my cousin? I froze. Ethan was mine. Lust was no threat to me. None—but the rage inside me demanded blood. Shaking my head, I tried to clear it. I had never been this person before. Vengeance and hate were alarmingly appealing to me. Is this what Hell did to people? Part of me cared, but a larger part of me didn't. Was I even in control of myself?

I stopped and leaned against the wall, letting my body slide to the floor. All I wanted to do was go home. Mortified by my desires, I sucked in several deep breaths and calmed down. I'd go back to the poker room and avoid Lust at all costs. She was not my nemesis. She was not a threat. She was an annoyance that didn't deserve my ire or the luxury of thought. If I could find it in myself to feel sorry for her, I'd really win, but I wasn't quite that magnanimous at the moment. I'd get there in a year or two...or ten.

"I knew you'd follow me," Lust hissed, standing over me with crazy written all over her.

"Oh my God," I shouted. "I changed my mind and you're about

to fuck that up." I stood and took a step away. Bad move. She was on me like a bad toupee.

"He was mine first. He'll be mine again. You don't hold a candle to me," she ground out through clenched teeth. "You're in my way and I want you gone."

So much for taking the high road... "You are delusional." I laughed at her as she tensed like a bomb about to explode. "You've been used so many times you probably give out frequent rider miles."

"Did you just use a 'yo mama' joke on me?" she yelled. Her face burned red and her fingertips sparked.

"Yep. Yep, I did." I grinned. "And I have more where that came from. Ethan is not yours. Never has been and never will be. Look, I get that you're horny, but you need to find someone who will appreciate your widely spread talents."

"My *talents* made him come till he begged for mercy and I'll have him begging again as soon as I get rid of you. You're just a stupid weak half-breed and I always get what I want."

Pushing the image of Lust and Ethan naked together aside was difficult, but since she was coming at me like a freight train, I had no choice. I tapped the angel wing tattoo on my chest, a gift from my Baby Demons, and prepared myself to either kick some ass or get mine handed to me.

Her anger made her sloppy. I stood completely still and let her advance. Right before she landed a mean right hook, I dropped low and took her out with my leg. The thud of her body hitting the wall and then the ground was music to my ears. Rolling over, I brought my elbow down on her face and took complete pleasure in the sound of bone crunching.

"Bitch," she screeched and raised her arms to the sky. A strong stream of sparks flew from her hands, but as she stood she was unsteady on her feet. Blood poured from her nose and lip. "You're going to pay for that."

"You really don't want another piece of me," I panted and

rolled my eyes. I stayed low in case she tried again. What I wouldn't give for a sword or a throwing star.

"No, I don't want any part of you, but I know some people who might." She flung her arms in a circular motion and a shimmering door appeared. It was translucent and golden flames licked up the sides. There was no heat and I wasn't sure if it was real or a mirage... Lust vanished and I had a bad feeling I was fucked. I backed myself against the wall and began to inch away. Why did I follow her out? Ethan was so damned right about green not being my color. It was an outstanding lesson, but would I live to tell? I didn't for one second believe she was gone. With my back plastered against the wall I had slightly better odds of seeing where she might attack from next. Of course from behind was the last thing I expected, but I was in Hell—a place where all your night-fucking-mares can come true.

She flew out of the wall and shoved me through the door with such force my head snapped back and I saw stars.

"Say hello to your mommy for me," she hissed as flames engulfed me. "It was good knowing you. I promise to take very, very good care of Ethan."

Fucking. Awesome. The crazy slut was sending me to the Basement and I had a feeling no one would be happy to see me there. I killed their leader, my disgusting daddy, and I was certain that as happy as Satan was about that, the nut jobs in the Basement would not agree.

I THOUGHT THE WAITING AREA OF HELL WAS CREEPY, BUT IT HAD nothing on the Basement. The ride through the portal had been violent, smelly and hot. While the flames didn't disfigure me, they practically destroyed my Prada halter. My boobs were being held up by threads. *Great.* Gonna flash my goodies at some evil

Demons. Never thought I'd put those words together in a sentence. Ever.

Crude stone walls and uneven rock floors were illuminated by torches. The odor was putrid and exactly how I had thought Hell should smell. Where were the Demons? With great caution, because of my heels, the floor and the simple fact that any slight movement could expose my knockers, I made my way down a dank hallway. Go toward the sound... the horrific sound of wailing souls being burned till the end of time.

How was I going to get out of here? The portal had disappeared once it spit me out and I had no clue where another one might be. As I passed the torches the flames extinguished. Did the Demons know I was here? Were they going to pop out and yell surprise? Fuck.

Silence. An eerie silence stopped me in my tracks. What happened? Why weren't the souls screaming? Did they get turned to ash? I was under the impression they had to burn for eternity. God, I wanted out of here, but that was clearly not in the plan thanks to Lust. Time to deal with the icky Demons and hopefully not have to kill a ton of them. I wasn't sure how that would go over upstairs.

"Hello," I called out. "Anybody home?"

As soon as I spoke the shrieks and wails resumed at a level even higher than before. Words were intermingled with the howling and I heard garbled begging and pleading. WTF? I was close to the mouth of what looked like a large room. It was lit up like Christmas, a holiday I was certain they skipped down here. *Go into the light, Carol Ann* kept running through my brain and I laughed without humor. This was not a movie. It was real life— my life. *Poltergeist* was G rated kiddie crap compared to this shit.

Taking a deep breath and tamping down my gag reflex at the stench, I sauntered into the bowels of Hell.

A huge wall of fire blasted out of a crevasse in the floor that had to be at least ten feet wide and spanned the entirety of the room, which from my estimation was the length of several football fields. The soul lights darted around in the flames wildly, although some were sluggish. Were those the older souls —the ones that had become accustomed to being on fire? My stomach roiled at the thought. Did Satan come up with this punishment?

The Demons roaming around were identical to the ones that had dragged me to Hell. Their bloody skinless bodies were muscular and oozing with pus and disease. They undulated in and out of each other, stabbing and prodding the less powerful ones with their sharp and filthy claws. Had they really looked like the Demons on the main level at one time? It was difficult to wrap my mind around that. Huge blood covered teeth clicked as they ate what looked like flesh and organs. *Fucking awesome, I had arrived in time for dinner.*

Had no one noticed me, or was I being ignored?

The Demons amped up their attacks on each other and the sounds of moans and grunts joined the wailing. As wonderful as all this was I had no time to watch a real life horror movie. I needed to get the hell out.

"Excuse me," I shouted over the cacophony. Everything halted, including the soul shrieking. Hmmm, not sure that was good. At least fifty pairs of beady bloodshot golden eyes turned to me.

A huge reeking Demon stepped forward. It took everything I had not to step back. Shitfuckshit. His eyes went red and his teeth clicked ominously. He had bits of skin on his arms and chest. They were rotten and peeling away. The edges were black and runny. Had he tried to redeem himself and failed or was he working on getting out of here?

"You've finally come," he said in a voice that hurt my ears and made my throat clench. It was like my father's. It sounded as if his mouth was full of glass shards.

"Well, I wasn't really planning on it, but, um… yep. Here I am. I was wondering if you knew where a portal was?" I was sure my smile resembled a grimace, but if he was being polite, I could certainly do the same.

He turned his back on me and addressed the crowd. "Our Queen has come home," he shouted. My stomach sunk and I felt sick. This was not going to end well.

The Demons cheered and dropped to their bone and muscle exposed knees. The souls began screaming again at a volume that vibrated through my body. I slapped my hands over my ears and bent forward.

"It will stop in a moment," the Demon told me.

"Why?"

"It is the way. They are given a moment of peace so each time they burn it will be more devastating than the last. They can never be allowed to forget what it feels like to be free of pain. It would defeat the purpose of the punishment."

"That is fucked up," I said before I could stop myself. I mean, who in the hell came up with this sadistic kind of torture?

"Yes," the Demon smiled and licked what I supposed were lips. "Your father was a brilliant man."

"This is my father's doing?" I gasped and wondered why I wasn't more screwed up.

"He took the more violent Bible passages quite seriously."

"Maybe he should have taken some meds more seriously," I muttered and scanned the room for alternate exits. "Look, um... "

"Lance."

"Right. Lance. I'm flattered that you want me to be your, ah... queen, but I am not queen material at all. I am so fucking grossed out by this," I said, gesturing wildly around the cave. "You really don't want me to be your queen."

"It is not our choice," he grunted dismissively. "You made that choice when you killed your father. We would have never chosen a woman to lead. Women are weak and inferior, but we will deal with what we have been given."

WTF? Was he kidding me? *Inferior, my ass.* I did not want to be the leader of Stinkyland, but I'd be damned if they didn't want me because I was a girl. "Look, Buster…"

"Lance," he corrected.

"*Lance*, I don't want the job. However if I did, I could lead the shit out of you filthy asswipes."

He growled and advanced. OMG, he picked the wrong girl to fuck with. I was done. Done. I'd been dragged to Hell, made to talk to walls, watched my mate get manhandled by a Sin, got bitten by Hell Hounds and then shoved through a flaming door into a place that ten thousand years of therapy couldn't erase. I was done. I mean WTF—how much was a hormonal pregnant half-Vamp half-Demon with semi-exposed breasts supposed to take?

"Back off," I hissed.

"Make me," he snapped and moved faster. He came at me with his claws raised and his mouth open.

He asked for it. I swung my arms and slashed through the air. I had no real idea what I was doing, but winging it had worked so far. The room turned a hazy red and I would bet my undead life that my eyes had turned the same color. Glittering black and crystal white sparks flew from my fingertips and attacked Lance with a vengeance. I closed my eyes when I heard him scream. I let my mind float and I entered his, fully prepared to destroy him. The pop of his body blowing into thousands of tiny pieces was so close and a sense of excitement filled me.

"*Do it*," his mind screamed to me. "*Do it*," he begged. "*End me.*"

What? He wanted to die? For real and forever?

I pulled my mind back from his and stared at him. My magic held him in a stasis and he writhed in pain. I touched my angel wings again and created a shield around myself. I didn't want one of these fuckers sneaking up from behind while I figured out what Lance meant and why I was becoming such a blood-hungry psycho.

The Demons made a menacing circle around us and I

wondered if I could take all fifty or so out at once. I seriously hoped I didn't have to find out.

"What did you mean?" I demanded. "Why do you want me to end you?"

"I know nothing of what you speak of," he snapped. The circle of love surrounding us growled and began to keen like mourners at a funeral.

"Yes. You do," I ground out. "Tell me." With a wave of my hand I increased the magic. He panted and convulsed on the ground at my feet. "Tell me."

"Fine," he gasped. "Look at us," he cried. "Look at us. See how many have tried to turn decent. Look at the tiny pieces of decomposing flesh on our bodies. We can't do it. There is no way out."

"We were lied to and used by your father," a Demon yelled from the circle.

I rolled my eyes. "It takes two to tango, idiot," I shot back. "Don't try to tell me you're simply innocent bystanders and got fucked over by my big bad daddy."

"We are not innocent." Lance wheezed some nasty goop. Whatever insides he had were beginning to come up. "But we were no more evil than the Demons on the main floor until your father came along."

"Free will, Mister. My dad may have been certifiable, but you had a choice."

"No," he groaned. "No choice."

"He ate my child," one shouted from the circle.

I almost threw up in my mouth. "He did what?" I whispered. I eased off on the magic trapping Lance. He now lay still at my feet. He watched me closely and his eyes still begged me to destroy him.

"He killed family members and threatened us with destroying each of our lines if we didn't comply," Lance explained.

"So, I'm supposed to believe that you were all blackmailed into becoming the lowest form of Demon imaginable by my dead pappy."

Not one of them said a word, but stared at me with eyes that had seen true horror. It was hard to buy. I was in a place where lying was the norm and most sins were overlooked. Why was I starting to believe this?

"How did he have so much power?" I asked, looking for a chink I could find in their story.

"He was Satan's brother. He had magic beyond the normal realm of a Demon and he had his brother's ear in the beginning... before Satan shunned him."

"Okay," I said, pacing back and forth, being careful not to get too close to the edge of the circle. "I get that he had you by the balls, but are you telling me you've done nothing wrong? You are innocents sent here by mistake?" I asked sarcastically.

"No, we no longer deserve another chance. Ever. But we don't deserve this. We were deceived and did not choose this of our own free will."

Holy Hell, talk about some gray areas...

"What do you do down here?" I asked.

"We watch," Lance said and shook his head in disgust.

"That's it? You just watch souls burn?"

"Yes. We watch and we go just a little more insane with each passing hour."

I glanced around at them. They were so disgusting it was nearly impossible to see the people they might have been at one time without the influence of my father. Could they be redeemed? Many of them did have decaying skin, so clearly they had tried. What did they want? Could I speak with Satan about them? Would he care? If I stayed with them I wondered if I could help them change. Was my purpose here to undo the damage my father had done? Hell, was that even possible?

"I can speak to Satan for you," I said.

"No," a smaller Demon yelled. "He cares nothing for us. He associates us with your father and will show no mercy."

"And you think I will?" I laughed and shook my head. What did they want from me?

"You have to," Lance said. "You are our only hope. We have nothing left."

"Look, Lance, I am sorry for the sins of my father, but I am not my father. I am not staying down here and if I have to kill each and every one of you to leave... I will."

An excited murmur went through the circle. I could swear the sons of bitches were smiling at me... or they all had gas. Every single Demon dropped to their knees and leaned forward. Placing their hands on the ground they began to weep. Some shuddered and some laughed with joy. What the hell was happening?

"Thank you," Lance said. "We cannot thank you enough."

"For what?" I asked, completely confused.

"For killing us."

Wait. WTF? When did I agree to kill them? "Um, Lance?"

"Yes, my Queen?"

"Not gonna happen. You guys can't just ask me to kill you and then I kill you. I wouldn't say that I want to hang with you, but I kind of like you and as alarmingly scary as you are... I feel sorry for you."

"Show us mercy, my Queen," someone cried out.

"Please," another sobbed.

What was I supposed to do? This could be a trick. I could kill the fifty or so Demons and five hundred more pissed off Demons could show up and kill me or, God forbid, want me to kill them too.

"Is this all of you?" I asked in a voice I didn't recognize. It was thin, tinny and far away. I was shocked I was even considering this. Did I truly need to atone for the sins of my father?

"The others are not here. They've been taken away," Lance explained.

"What does that mean?"

"I don't know," he admitted in his gravely voice. "One day they were here and one day they were gone."

"Like gone, gone. For real gone?" I asked, wondering if an army would seek me out for retribution.

"Probably not." Lance shrugged and forlornly laid his huge misshapen head back down on the floor.

Okay, think Astrid. You could right one of your father's many wrongs and kill a bunch of Demons... which in turn could piss off the Prince of Darkness and set in motion a large bounty on my head. That would suck asswads. You could try to escape, but you have no fucking clue how to get back to the main level and there could be other areas of the Basement worse than this one. Hard to imagine, but this was Hell.

Glancing around, I saw the Demons peeking up at me. They reminded me of little children... disgustingly ugly little children. Fuck.

"Stand up," I barked. "This feels like an execution and I am not at all happy about this."

The Demons stood with their hands clasped in front of them and a sense of peace about them.

"My Queen, we have waited thousands of years for this day. What you are doing is merciful. I can never go back to those I love. I am ruined... tainted by so much horror and death, I am no longer worthy of love. Mind you, I do still love. Deeply. That is why I have never tried to escape. The threat of harm to my wife and children is something that even someone as lost as I've become cannot fathom."

"But my father is gone. Why can't you go back to your loved ones?" I asked, hoping I'd discovered the magic ticket. Maybe they could all work hard and grow skin and then go to the waiting room and get jobs and then be reunited with their families. And maybe Leprechauns could fly out of my ass...

"Oh, young Queen, it was too late for that hundreds of years ago. I stand here begging your mercy, but I am by no means free of sin. Heinous sin."

"Open your mind, oh Queen," a Demon begged. "Come inside and see."

"Proof?" I asked.

"Indisputable," Lance answered.

I closed my eyes and let my mind roam free. Dipping in and out of the Demons thoughts, it was all I could do not to fall to the floor and break. Memories of children and wives and parents intermingled with the horror they'd been forced to perform leading to horrors they'd chosen and willingly performed. Horrific beatings from my father that shamed me and then the names... names flew at me. Names of loved ones, names of those they'd killed, names of the victims' families that they wished to beg forgiveness from, and then came their names... David, Michael, Josiah, Peter, Noah, Paul, and on and on. I didn't want them to become more than what they were. That would make what I knew I had to do harder, but they had become inhuman faceless nothingness. They needed to be seen for who they were— for who they wished to be. James, Adam, Leonardo...

"Stop," I commanded harshly. "Stop."

I wanted to forgive them their sins. I felt how truly remorseful they were, but I also knew if they lived on they would continue to commit sin after sin and I had no jurisdiction over mass forgiveness for that. I only had compassion and the unhealthy need to right my father's wrong.

"Tell me where a portal is," I said. "I'll need to leave when I'm... done here."

Lance shook his head. "I don't know."

"You have got to be kidding me." I sighed heavily and pinched the bridge of my nose. They wanted me to commit mass murder and then hang out with the dead bodies? They were going to have to think again. It would be hard enough without having to look at what I'd done for God knows how long.

"We will give you our power before the deed is done. It should be enough to help you find your way," Lance said.

"Whoa, Nelly." I stopped him before they all started magically sending their fucked up evil Demon mojo my way. I might empathize with them, but I didn't want to become them.

"Our power is pure," Lance assured me. "Our memories and our physical bodies are not."

"Are you all very sure this is what you want?" I asked. My hands trembled at my sides and my knees were unsteady. This was so much different than what I had been trained for. I still wasn't positive I could do it.

"You would put a suffering dog down, wouldn't you?" Lance asked quietly.

"Yes, I would."

"We are nothing more than animals at this point. We haven't been humanely treated in over a thousand years. Please... just please."

"Make the circle tighter," I shouted. I looked up at the jagged rock ceiling and prayed for a moment, but who or what was I praying to anymore? All my ideas of the afterlife had been altered. I didn't know what I believed. What the hell did good and evil really mean and how closely were they related? Were they actually the same thing?

A muttered chorus of 'thank you' wafted around me, but I could barely compute. My heart beat so loudly in my chest it was all I could hear. I closed my eyes and realized I had no anger, just sadness and fear. I realized I no longer needed anger. I only needed to know what I owned, how to use it didn't matter—I only needed to think of the outcome desired and the means to get there would become obvious.

Closing my eyes, I asked a God I wasn't sure existed in the way I wanted him to anymore for forgiveness—forgiveness for what I was about to do. My grandfather's chant that had eluded me was now at the forefront of my mind and I marveled at the complexity and the simplicity of it. I felt the release of power from the Demons and I let it in. Unsure if it was safe, I did it anyway. It felt right. A whisper of movement in my stomach startled and frightened me. My child, my son... I felt his love and strength and approval. Holy Hell, the moment was surreal. It was a very old soul inside me and his knowledge was far superior to mine, but he loved me and knew I was there to take care of him. He was sure I would do what was right. Would I always pay for the sins of my father? I hoped the score would be even and I could move forward without his taint touching my child's world, but only time would tell.

Was this the balance between good and evil... Was I doing evil for good? Or good for evil?

It only took an instant. I saw the outcome and the deed was done. Sparks flew wildly around me and the popping noises made me grind my teeth and scream in despair. I fell to my knees and beat the ground. I'd just killed fifty people. Did it matter that no one loved or wanted them anymore? That should have made it easier, but it didn't. Had I become the Grim Reaper, meting out justice as I saw fit? Who in the hell did I think I was? I slowly opened my eyes and they were gone. No trace of the ones who had begged for death. The floor was covered in icy white crystals and black glitter. The soul lights were momentarily quiet.

It was either shock or regret that consumed me and I gave in to my basest need. I lay down on the dank filthy floor and I cried... for the Demons, for my father and for myself.

CHAPTER NINETEEN

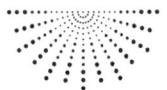

LITTLE WET LIPS KISSED MY FACE AND HEAD. THE SOFT FEATHER
touches tickled. I had no clue how much time had passed since I'd
committed one of the worst sins possible, but it felt like years.

"Me see your boobers, Mommy," Abe said with great
satisfaction. "Me want to touch."

"No," Ross shouted and kneed Abe in his little Demon nuts.
"Me massage Mommy's love melons."

"Ohhhhh, squishy," Rachel said as she poked at my chest.

"Mommy has nice balloons," Beyonce told everyone.

"No touching the boobs," I said as I pushed myself from prone
and pathetic to seated and slightly pathetic. I smiled and picked
my Baby Demons off of my chest. "How did you find me?"

"Easy peasy," Ross said. "My doggies felt your sad."

"The General and Bambi are here?" I asked, scanning the room
in alarm. How would they feel about what I had done? I struggled
to my feet and prepared to defend myself and my child.

"Sit, little one." George's soothing voice calmed me. "We are
not here to judge. We have come to take you back."

"You know what I've done?" I whispered. My stomach was
knotted with sadness and shame.

"I'm glad to see they didn't harm you. It was unwise of you to come here," he scolded.

While his sentiments were nice, his facts were fucked.

I took a slow breath in and gathered my thoughts. General George had protected me and helped me save Ethan, but he worked for Satan. His opinion of the Demons was as warped as his master's.

"I didn't come here on purpose and I was never in danger." I stood and put some distance between us. "Pockets," I instructed my little monsters.

"Mommy don't have no pockets," Abe informed me logically.

I glanced down at my shredded eveningwear and grimaced. He was correct. I had no pockets. I barely had a dress. Closing my eyes, I reimagined my beautiful dress. A faint heat surged through my body and a small burst of glitter burst from my fingertips.

"Very good," Bambi gasped with delight. "I like the one shoulder look far better than the halter."

"Mommy so pretty in pink," Rachel gushed.

They were spot on. Somehow my red halter had morphed into a hot pink one shouldered masterpiece. I had the magic—I was just missing the finer points of detail.

"Whoops." I shrugged and attempted a smile. Letting my head fall back on my shoulders I contemplated what I had done. Was it truly mercy? I had to believe it was... but why did I feel so awful?

"Self-defense is a necessary reason to kill. Your life was far more valuable than theirs," George said quietly.

Again his misinterpretation bothered me. I could nod my head and be done. Who would be the wiser? The screaming souls? Doubtful.

"It wasn't self-defense. They asked me to end them and I did." The silence was loud.

"What?" Bambi asked. "You just killed them for no reason?"

I felt ill. She was only voicing what I already thought, but she was wrong. I was wrong.

"I corrected the sins of my father. These people…"

"They were hardly people," the General sniffed dismissively.

"I beg to differ," I shot back defensively. Time to come clean. If they didn't understand, they could do whatever they chose. As each minute passed I grew stronger. What I had done, while horridly distasteful, was the merciful thing to do. I could only hope that someday if I needed the same favor, I could find someone that cared enough to end me. "While they were by no means innocent, they had been at one time until my father took that away. With blackmail, murder and threats he destroyed their lives. They had no free will where this was concerned. None."

"They didn't attack you?" George asked.

"No, not in any real way."

"And you believe this fantasy they wove?" he demanded.

I paced the cave. My anger rose and I was very aware the glittering gloves had appeared and my chest tingled. Calm down. Calm down.

"I went into their memories. Something maybe Satan should have done if he wasn't so fucking selfish," I snapped. "And to be fair, there was very little to redeem them at this point, but they tried. Over and over they tried. I am of my father's blood and he destroyed their spirit and their lives. All I did was give them the peace they were owed."

"And who owed them this peace?" George asked. His eyes narrowed. I was sure he took offense at my opinion of Satan or he was considering what was to be done with me. Whatever.

"I did," I shouted. "I owed them peace that no one else could give to them. I owed them the dignity in death that my father stole from them in life… and everyone can just fuck off."

Again with the silence.

I squatted down and picked up my Baby Demons. They were quiet and still. Amazingly, I'd wished pockets into my beautiful dress. I gently tucked them in and turned to face the Hell Hounds.

George was chuckling and Bambi was doing a bizarre doggie

jig. WTF? Their reaction was alarming and incongruous and I wondered if this was the pre-Eat Astrid dance... I also realized the souls had been silent since I'd destroyed the Demons.

"She is so far ahead of where she should be," Bambi sang as she shimmied, *if you could call it that,* around George.

"You are not what we expected," he told me.

"Yep, I get that all the time. You gonna eat me?"

"I'm sorry, what?" George choked out.

"If you're going to eat me, I'm going to fight back, but I'd like to know so I can put my little monsters somewhere safe."

The third silence was a charm...

"Um, no. We have no intention of eating you. We're vegetarians."

"That's not a well known fact," Bambi chimed in. "So don't let that get around."

"You are such a funny one," the General said, loping toward me. "We would die for you. It would be lovely if you didn't put us in that position, but we would gladly go there if necessary."

"You're not going to eat me?"

"No. You're too chewy." His eyebrows slapped open and closed as his huge body rumbled with laughter. "So very young to find the balance so quickly, but I should have expected no less."

"No less from what?" I asked, hoping to catch one of these freakin' immortals off guard so they'd cough up their cryptic secrets.

"Ah, I wouldn't want to ruin the surprise. It's like reading the end of a book after the first Chapter," he explained.

"How long is the book?" I asked.

He considered me for a moment then gently rubbed his head against my leg. The comfort it brought me was immense. "The book shall be as long or short as you make it."

I knew better than to be snarky, but God, how I wanted to...

"We should be getting back," Bambi said. "She's been missed."

George cleared his throat. At least I think that's what that sound was—either that or a weird burp. "Astrid, I would suggest you cloak yourself."

"Why?"

He rolled his eyes and I knew that's as much of an answer as I would get.

"Fine." I matched his eye roll and upped it by half. "I'll cloak. Anything else?"

"As a matter of fact and self-preservation, yes... Do not act before you listen."

"You do realize that I'm not wired that way," I said with a double down eye roll.

"Yes, my child. I realize that, but I'd suggest you start rewiring now."

"Yes, sir." I sarcastically saluted him and made myself invisible with a flick of my fingers. A shimmering door appeared behind them and cast a rosy golden glow on the depressing gray stone of the Basement. This time it wasn't engulfed in flame. The Hounds waited for me as I circled the area where the Demons had stood and died. I whispered silent goodbyes to the beings that ceased to exist anymore. And I...

"Wait," I gasped. A chill shook my body and nausea overcame me.

"Mommy?" My little Demons poked their heads out of my pockets in distress.

"General, I need to see my mother." Need was correct. I didn't want to see her. I wasn't even sure I could handle seeing her, but the pitiable small child that still lived somewhere inside me wanted to try to make amends. Again.

"Now is not the time, child. There are things above that must be reckoned with before it's too late. I promise I will bring you back."

My eyes filled with tears, not because I couldn't see my mother... No. I was so relieved that I'd been forbidden for the moment I was embarrassed. After what I'd already done I had no clue if I was strong enough to face her. Covering my face with my hands, I tried to hold back the waterworks.

"It's good to cry," Bambi cooed sweetly. "It's never smart to face all your Demons in one day, dear. Too hard on the digestive system."

"I thought you were a vegetarian," I blubbered through my tears.

"Oh, dear Satan." She giggled and rocked her head from left to right. "Too much stress can give you gas. It's not lady-like to fart up a storm."

The laugh burst from my lips and my tears were now from joyous disbelief and disgust. I had no clue if she was serious or trying to cheer me up. I didn't care, but made a mental note to stay clear of her bottom in taxing situations.

THE POKER ROOM WAS FILLED WITH DEMONS. THE TENSION WAS thick and ominous and the eight guards had been joined by at least twenty more, but that wasn't the interesting part. No, the interesting part was the show in the center of the room. The large ornate table had been tossed to the side of the room leaving a gaping hole in the plaster. Ethan held Lust by her throat with a dagger pointed at her heart. Satan stood back with his arms crossed over his massive chest looking highly displeased. Lust was babbling and crying. It was clear I'd missed all the fun.

Hemingway and Mister Rogers were no longer present, but Dante stood in the corner behind Greed, enjoying the potential bloodbath immensely.

"I leave for ten minutes and come back to find *this?*" Satan bellowed.

"My liege, let me destroy him," Satan's second, Cole said, clearly ready to make good on his threat.

"Not quite yet," Satan replied. "I hate to sully the house. Would you care to explain, Vampyre?"

Ethan's eyes slid casually to the Devil. "Not particularly," he answered smoothly. The smile on his lips didn't reach his eyes. "Why don't you ask your daughter?"

"I find that she has a tendency to lie. I'd much prefer to hear why you think it's an appropriate idea to gut a Sin in Hell."

Satan stood as still as a statue and waited. Ethan matched his calm. The dagger was a mere thought away from Lust's black heart. My instinct was to reveal myself, but I'd promised the General I'd listen. Fuck, that was a stupid pact, but I was well aware the Hounds, who had disappeared as soon as we were coughed up from the portal, didn't give unwise advice. I simply wasn't sure how long I could follow it.

"She tried to kill me," Lust choked out. Her lovely face turned mottled red as she struggled for air. "She beat me. She's jealous and unstable. Told me she'd turn me into a Vampyre."

WTF? Did she really think anyone would believe that pile of shit? She was a thousand year old Demon and I was a newbie half-breed. Only my curiosity kept me from unveiling myself and plunging the knife through her heart. I wondered if the blade could actually kill her.

"Vampyre, you do realize that if you slay my child, you have signed your permanent death sentence."

"Beelzebub, you do realize if she has killed my mate that my life means nothing. Your threat holds no weight," Ethan ground out and tightened his hand on her throat.

"I have to agree that my daughter's story has a few holes," Satan said agreeably, as if he was discussing something as mundane as the weather. "Let her go and we shall get to the bottom of this."

Ethan laughed. "I am nowhere near as old as you, but if you take me for an ass, you are gravely mistaken."

"I do enjoy a man with a death wish." Satan grinned and took a seat. "So how shall we solve this little dilemma?"

"Have your spawn tell me what she has done with my mate."

"Do you plan to kill her when she submits to your demands?" Satan inquired, completely intrigued and bizarrely excited with the unfolding events.

"Depends," Ethan winked and Satan roared with laughter.

"I hate you, Daddy," Lust spat.

"Well now, that's just rude," he said and tsked. "Address the Vampyre's concerns and I might let you get away with whatever you've done this time."

"I told you she… "

"I am well aware of what you told me," Satan said in an icy cold voice that made everyone in the room cower. "Now tell me what really happened."

"She hasss wha was mun." Her voice was ragged and she was difficult to understand. Ethan had obviously increased the pressure on her throat.

"Vampyre, could you let up just slightly on the trachea so we could understand her?"

"The Vampyre is mine," she gasped as she took in air. "She had what was mine and I pushed her to the Basement. She's dead by now." Lust smiled with smug satisfaction and tried to snuggle close to Ethan. OMG, she was insane and I was done hiding.

"I call bullshit," the Devil said, rolling his eyes. "This is utterly embarrassing. Lust, you are infantile. I suppose it's partially my fault for spoiling you and your sisters, but… "

"Amen," Amanda the consort muttered.

The Devil whipped around so quickly the room temperature dipped. "I have had enough of your unacceptable sacrilegious pro-Christian narration, darling. Remove her. Now."

Three of the guards dragged a mortified Amanda from the room. No one made a move to comfort her or even acknowledged her rough departure with a glance. "Now, where was I?"

"Call your mother in," Ethan demanded, changing tactics. My man was smart. Gigi loved me and she would not be pleased. My uncle blanched and grabbed the back of the chair for purchase. Everyone in the room paled and glanced around in terror.

"You have no idea what you ask," Satan hissed.

"Oh, but I do. Astrid found her quite delightful and I'm sure she'd have something to say about her disappearance. I'd be happy to call her myself." Ethan's smile now reached his eyes. Damn, he was hot when he got going. Hell, he was hot no matter what.

Damn it, I'd learned nothing I didn't already know yet... Ethan was hot, Lust was a lying sack of shit, Amanda was stupid and everyone was afraid of Mother Nature. It was difficult, but I stayed cloaked.

"Where is Astrid, Lust?" Satan demanded. "This grows tiresome and I have no intention of losing another home because my mother gets called in."

"The Basement," she said with glee.

"Son of a bitch," Satan roared and the walls trembled violently. Lust used the split second of chaos to get away from Ethan and began to chant a spell in the room that was going to be a doozy.

My turn.

Deciding that a grand entrance was in order, I created a tornado—a small but vicious little bastard. My Baby Demons bounced with glee in my pockets. The goal of the mini cyclone was to knock the smug out of Lust. Icy white and black crystals formed in the air and the wind started at a violent speed. Satan clapped his hands with delight and stood up. He put his hands up the way a child would on a roller coaster. He was fucking nuts. The rest of the Demons flew all over the room. The only immortals that stayed planted on the ground besides Satan were Ethan, Wrath and Dixie. I hadn't realized my sweet cousin had returned. I had no time to contemplate the makeup of the group left standing. I had more important things to do.

The screams and grunts were music to my ears, especially those of Lust. I flipped her and slammed her body against each of the walls. Her body flew like a rag doll around the room and I made sure her head connected with the massive silver chandelier as many times as possible. I knew she'd live... my purpose was not to kill, just to teach a little lesson. Most of the Demons had fallen to the floor and taken cover. This made me happy. I had no grudge with them. Lust shrieked and tried to use her magic to steady herself, but she was no match for a pissed off pregnant chick.

"Alright, Astrid," Satan yelled over the howling wind. "That's enough."

Wait. What? How did he know that was me? I was still invisible...

"Show yourself," he demanded.

I let the wind die down and revealed myself. The gasps of the windblown crowd made me think I'd lost my dress in the melee. Nope, still clothed. I held my ground and waited for my uncle to unleash his displeasure on me... or worse.

"I didn't try to kill her," I said calmly and felt Ethan at my side. His relief was palpable. "She attacked me and pushed me to the Basement."

"I did not, you bitch," she hissed as she tried to crawl to her feet. "You took what was mine and I punished you, which was my right."

"Can it, Lust," Lucifer snapped, examining me with wonder. "You are simply delectable."

"Back off," Ethan growled.

Satan stopped, clearly alarmed and impressed with Ethan's total lack of respect for him. "Not in that way," he assured my mate. "I may have no morals, but family is off limits."

"Good to know," I quipped. "Now about Psycho over there..."

"Yes, she'll be taken care of," he promised and tiredly ran his hand through his hair. "I shall see to her punishment myself."

That shut the entire room up, including Lust. Her bravado had disappeared and was replaced by naked fear. Wanting no information on what he might have planned, I nodded and accepted his offer.

"I want to go home," I said.

Satan considered me thoughtfully for a moment. He glanced around the room at the damage I'd done and winced. "At this very moment I'm tempted to send the both of you home, but I have a proposition. It shall wait till the morning. I'm quite worn out from all the excitement and I'm not used to losing at poker. I shall retire and see you in the morning." On that note he disappeared taking everyone in the room with him except for Ethan, myself, Dixie and Wrath.

"Holy shit, that was one hell of a trick," I muttered looking around for everyone.

"He does like to dazzle," Wrath said. "That was an impressive display. Congratulations and nice hair." With a slight movement of her delicate hands, she disappeared in glitter and smoke leaving the man I loved and the only Demon I trusted in Hell.

"What's wrong with my hair?" I asked.

Dixie looked uncomfortable and Ethan bit down on his lip. Was I bald? I grabbed my head and felt hair. Thank you sweet Cousin Jesus in a tube top, it was still there.

"It's blood red," Dixie whispered reverently. "It's beautiful."

"What?" I shouted, grabbing a fistful and bringing the long wild locks eye level. Motherfucker, it was red—fiery blood red. I was not in the mood for this. I would have never conjured up anything in the pink or red family to wear if I'd known my freakin' hair was crayon red. I must look ridiculous. Forget the fact that I'd just created an indoor storm and bounced Demons around the room like they were balls, I had horrific hair. The streaks were one thing, but my whole head… "Oh my God, this is awful. Are there salons in Hell?"

"Um… yes," Dixie stuttered, "but I'm pretty sure that's not going to help."

"This is unacceptable," I yelled. "I am wearing pink. I look like a walking fashion disaster."

"You are exquisite," Ethan murmured in my ear and I shivered. He took my hand and his eyes blazed green. "Dixie, take us to our accommodations."

"Will do." She grinned and led us to her car.

CHAPTER TWENTY

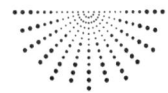

"Shut the fuck up," I laughed. "Mister Rogers won?"

"Indeed he did," Ethan said, lying back on the bed. "Satan's face was priceless when Fred made his deal."

It was all I could do to pay attention to the conversation. Ethan was shirtless and edible and I was in a towel. After washing my hair six times I gave up on the notion that the heinous red might not be permanent. I chose to ignore Dixie's unacceptable prediction and had her schedule an appointment at a salon. I crossed my legs and sat on my hands so I wouldn't jump the Adonis reclined on the bed. I really did want to know what had happened.

"So he has to go to lunch with his brother God and make nice?" I giggled as I pictured the scenario. Having not met my Uncle God yet, I still imagined him as I had when I was a child— long white beard, kind eyes and flowing robes.

"Mister Rogers will join them and Hemingway finagled an invitation as well. He said he wouldn't miss it for all the bull fights in Spain."

"Where will they meet?" I asked, wondering if God would let his morally corrupt brother set foot in Heaven.

"Satan suggested a neutral territory, like Earth, but Fred and Ernest are dead and that could cause a few complications." His grin of amusement sent the butterflies in my stomach into a tizzy. No one had the right to be so pretty.

"Or a tabloid writer's wet dream," I muttered.

"True... now you."

"Now me what?" I asked, knowing full well what he meant.

"Tell me."

Did I want him to know what I had done? I did, but I feared the consequences. Could I tell him without having to speak? That might be stupid, but if he wanted me, then he had to want me warts and all. If I was being honest, I was testing him...

"If I open the doors in my mind can you come in and see? I don't want to talk about it anymore."

He hesitated. "You won't be able to hide anything, not one single thought or feeling," he warned.

"I don't want to hide from you. Ever."

His smile melted my insides, but unease consumed me. What if he was disgusted that I had shown mercy?

"I won't judge. I will just watch," he said.

"Famous last words," I muttered and unlocked the door in my head. Seated in a chair across the room from him, I closed my eyes and pulled up the horrifically sad scene.

What felt like eons later, I sat still and kept my eyes tightly shut. Leaning forward in my chair, my stomach churned and I waited for the bomb to explode. He had seen it all and I felt ill at having to relive it. As sure as I was that I had done the right thing, it was still heartbreaking and frightening.

"Our son is amazing," he said softly.

I opened my eyes to find him kneeling in front of me. He was awed and his eyes blazed a brilliant green.

"You don't think I was wrong?" My voice sounded childlike and far away.

"I think I have much to learn from you. Your compassion and

bravery astound and humble me." He put his fingers under my chin and forced me to meet his eyes. "You are my world and I love you."

The waterworks flowed freely and I threw myself into his strong embrace. His strength and beauty overwhelmed me, but his love almost incapacitated me. How did this man feel this way about me?

His full lips gently feathered mine and I breathed him in. His scent made me dizzy with desire and his mouth was shorting out my brain.

"You're overdressed," he murmured as his fangs grazed my collarbone.

"I'm in a towel." I giggled and let my head fall back to give him better access.

"Exactly." He ripped the towel from my heated body and stared. The need in his eyes matched the enormous bulge in his pants. My breath caught in my throat and my limbs went watery. "You are mine."

"And you are mine," I said, slowly getting to my feet and pushing him toward the bed. "Stop. Don't move." I dropped to my knees and unbuttoned his jeans. The simple sound of the zipper coming down in the otherwise silent room was as erotic as anything I'd ever heard. "Hands behind your back," I ordered as he went to slide his pants down his legs. "I'm in charge."

"For the moment," he replied huskily and watched me through hooded eyes.

I released him from his jeans and boxer briefs and came face to face with one of the most gorgeous parts of his body. I eyed the monster with delight and anticipation. A slow heat coiled in my lower abdomen as I put my lips on the head of his cock. His hissed reaction and muttered curses made me want to make him lose his mind—the same way he made me lose mine.

I used my tongue to make him slippery and took my sweet time easing him to the back of my throat. The pool of moisture

ROBYN PETERMAN

between my legs made me squirm, and his groan as I took him deep in my mouth made me tingle all over.

"Astrid, stop," he said gruffly. "If you don't it will be all over before we begin."

"But you're a Vampyre," I teased. "You can go for days."

"This is true, but the first time I come tonight will be inside you."

In less than a second, he had me beneath him on the bed. I shrieked in protest and he pinned my arms over my head. His half smirk sent my girlie parts into fits and I wriggled beneath him for all I was worth.

"Tonight I will make you scream," he threatened. His fangs gleamed and his eyes were wild. "I will own you in every way a man can own a woman. Do you understand?"

"You already do," I gasped, more excited than I thought possible.

"No." He chuckled. "But I will."

I had no clue what he meant, but I didn't care. I would willingly give him whatever he desired—over and over again. His lips latched onto my breast and he sucked my tender nipple into his mouth with a harsh pull. My back arched and my hips bucked. When he sank his fangs into the soft flesh I cried out in pain mixed with intense pleasure. He brought me to the point where the two meshed and were indistinguishable. With my hands suddenly free, I raked my nails down his back. His muffled chuckle at my breast made me see stars.

I was on the verge of an orgasm and he hadn't even moved from my breast.

"Ethan, I'm going to come," I gasped.

"Be my guest," he said as he divided his attention between both breasts.

And I did.

Colors blew through my brain behind my closed lids and a scream tore from my lips. My body grew hot and everything clenched, drawing out the pleasure. It didn't matter where we were, he was my home and he always would be.

"I need to be inside you." His hands grasped my wrists again and forced them over my head. I opened my legs to welcome him, but he spread them wider with his knees. Keeping my arms pinned with one hand he stroked himself and watched all the expressions flitting across my flushed face. "Do you want to be fucked?" he asked in a strained voice. The veins on his neck stood out and my fangs descended. My voice was raw from my screams and I searched for sound as he waited. "Answer me."

"Yes," I croaked through my raw throat.

"You'll have to do better than that." He grinned and stroked himself with more force.

"Please," I begged. "Please."

"Please what?"

God, he was a bitch, but he knew how to push all my buttons. Undulating beneath him, I tried to press the issue, but his restraint was massive.

"Please fuck me," I whimpered. Everything felt swollen and needy and I wanted him to take me, to relieve me, to fuck me until I couldn't make a sound.

"Not quite yet," he said as he lowered his head between my legs. I gasped and tensed as I felt his fangs nip at my clit.

"Ethan, I... " I started, but his tongue took over and words left me.

"Shhhh, don't think. Just feel," he purred and the rumble of his voice on my sex made me shudder. My hips rocked and I tangled my hands in his thick blond hair to pull him closer. His fingers dug into my thighs as his mouth did magic things.

His hands left my thighs, grasped my ass and raised me off the bed, giving him more open and vulnerable access to the parts of my body he was plundering. His fingers slid between the cheeks of my ass, pausing at the area I fondly called no man's land. The pressure of his insistent fingers on the area he knew was off limits made me struggle helplessly as he held me tighter. Trying to get away from his fingers but closer to his mouth was impossible.

"Ethan, don't," I said.

"Am I hurting you?" he asked, glancing up at me with those damn eyes.

"Um no, but I... well."

"How about this," he suggested in a tone laced with sex. "I can promise you that I will make you feel so good you will pass out screaming. You can't stop me unless it hurts. Hurts in a way that you don't like," he added with a smile on his face I was tempted to smack off.

"I... "

"Say yes," he whispered, tracing my clit with his thumb. "Say yes."

This was the man that took me to heights that were unimaginable. He was magic, power and sex and he scared the hell out of me in the best way possible. "Yes."

"Good girl. Such a good sexy girl." His fangs scraped the inside of my thigh as his fingers found their way back to my bottom. I shuddered and closed my eyes as his teeth moved closer to my center. The sensations of his fangs teasing my clit while his fingers pressed into my ass made me whimper and moan. The thought of doing something I had always believed was forbidden added to the raging fire in my belly.

Trying to stay still was impossible and my body found a rhythm that pleased itself. I was spiraling to a place I didn't recognize. Ethan worked with Vampyre speed and I forgot what we had even talked about. I was one huge pulsing nerve open for him to use as he wanted.

I screamed. I screamed so loud I was sure I could be heard in the Basement of Hell. I screamed as his fangs pierced into parts of me that I was sure were illegal and his fingers probed inside of me with expert knowledge of how to make a woman lose her mind. My body flailed and twisted, needing less and more as an orgasm of epic proportions ripped through me leaving me with no coherent thought whatsoever.

"Oh my God," I gasped in a hoarse voice as aftershocks rocked me.

"That's just the beginning," he said, moving up my body and settling himself between my legs.

He pushed only the head of his cock into me and held still as my orgasm pulsed on. He moaned as my body contracted around his and the muscles in his neck strained as he fought to hold out.

"Fuck me," I begged. "Fuck me hard."

His concentration snapped and he slammed into my body. As wet and softened as I was, I was still never prepared for his size. I cried out in pleasure and pain as he sheathed himself in me to the hilt. His mouth found my neck and his tongue drew small tight circles around my veins as my body found his rhythm and I met him thrust for thrust. The heat in my abdomen unfurled and shot through my limbs.

The speed and intensity would have killed a mere mortal, but we weren't mortal. We were Vampyres and I wanted more than just sex. I wanted blood.

"Bite me," I moaned as I grew closer to another orgasm. "Now," I hissed as I tightened and clamped around him. He bit down and I cried out with what little voice I had left. The sheer electric force of all the things happening at once were too much. The pulse in his neck called to me and my fangs ached with need. I pressed my lips to his neck and bit.

His shout of pleasure as he came rocked me into darkness. Little explosions of bright golden light burst behind my tightly closed eyes and his lips found mine. I kissed him as if my life depended on it and our tongues tangled and fought.

With our bodies still merged as one, I held on tight. He showered my face and neck with kisses and I breathed him in. He was as essential to me as blood. I needed him to exist. I loved him with everything I had... and I knew he loved me too.

"Was I right?" he asked smugly.

"Um, yes... yes, you were," I admitted. If I was still capable of blushing I'd be as red as my hair. "You just about killed me." I giggled and buried my face in his strong neck.

"Come with me," he said, hopping out of the bed.

"Where are we going?" I followed him out to the living room.

"We're going to christen every square inch of this house," he informed me with an evil glint in his sparkling eyes.

"Oh we are, are we?"

"Yes, my love. We are."

And we did.

CHAPTER TWENTY-ONE

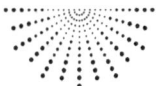

"I'm sure the bastard cheated, but I can't prove it," Satan said as he picked at his breakfast.

"You do realize that you just called Mister Rogers a bastard?" I laughed at the incongruity. My uncle was quite put out with losing and was even more displeased with the deal that had been struck.

"It makes no sense," he pouted. "I was cheating and he still won."

"Do ya think there might be a lesson there?" I asked and he rolled his mesmerizing eyes.

"Absolutely not."

The dining room was massive and as overblown as the rest of the palace. With only three of us at the table the room felt positively cavernous. The table had to seat at least thirty. A buffet was laid out for a king—exotic fruits, homemade breads and jams, pancakes and waffles, muffins and an array of freshly squeezed juices. The maple syrup sat in a bowl of steaming water. The smells were divine and I wished for the umpteenth time I could still eat food.

"I'd offer you some blood, but we don't keep it on hand," he said. "I assume from your rosy cheek color and the smell of sex you are both quite satisfied."

"Um, not that it's any of your business," I said, completely embarrassed. "But yes, we're fine."

"So, first things first," he said jovially. "You'll be delighted to know Lust has been appropriately punished and humiliated. Would you like to know what I did?"

"No," I said at the same time Ethan said, "Yes."

"Two against one." Satan laughed and clapped his hands. "I shall tell you. I do have to congratulate myself. It was quite a creative punishment and one she won't forget anytime soon."

I really didn't want to know, but Satan wanted to brag on his brilliance. I had no choice, but when the reality of what he'd done actually hit I was mortified. However, Ethan seemed quite pleased.

"What did you just say?" I yelled. "You did what?"

"Do you not understand English?" my uncle asked with a wolfish grin on his face. Ethan glanced down to hide his smile. I kicked him under the table and turned my furious gaze back on my uncle.

"Tell me you're joking," I snapped.

"Not even a little bit," he replied. "Think about it, beautiful niece, it makes perfect sense. In order to hit someone where it will hurt, you must tap into their basest desires."

"But it was an invasion of my privacy." I crossed my arms over my chest and narrowed my eyes at the Devil.

"Your disrespect is so invigorating," he shouted with glee.

"So you put her in a cage outside of our guest house and made her listen to us have sex all night?" I was flabbergasted, grossed out and a tiny bit impressed with his evilness.

"Yes, you are correct. And from everything I've heard it was quite vocal and completely out of control." He winked at Ethan.

"Oh my God," I muttered and pressed my fingers to the bridge of my nose. Last night had been a loud one, even for me. "That is just sick."

"Yes, well, I am rather proud. She won't be annoying you for a while." He poured an obscene amount of syrup on his pancakes and dug in as if all was peachy keen in the world.

Playing with the linen napkin, I did have to agree it was rather brilliant and the petty part of me enjoyed that she heard how good I actually was—Ethan had been very vocal during... Wait. This was fucked. Yesterday I put fifty Demons with questionable pasts out of their misery and then caused a tornado in a poker room right after Mister Rogers may or may not have cheated during a round. Like that wasn't enough... my evening of screaming sexual gymnastics with my mate ended up being a punishment for the slut who pushed me to the Basement of Hell. I. Needed. To. Go. Home. Now.

"So, Vampyre," Satan cooed condescendingly.

"Yes, Uncle Fucker?" Ethan replied with a smirk on his face.

Satan winced and pressed his palms to his temples as I slapped my hand over my mouth to hold back the burst of laughter that threatened to escape.

"Point taken," Satan muttered, shaking his head. "*Ethan*, you do realize your time is limited down here."

"*Satan*, with all due respect, you're wrong." Ethan picked up a cup of coffee and took a sip. Damn it, he was old enough to drink stuff other than blood. I was insanely jealous. I dipped my finger in the syrup and touched it to my tongue. Oh hell no, it tasted like butt. My gag caused both sets of golden eyes to land on me.

"Sorry," I mumbled and shoved my hands under my thighs.

"Anyhoo," Satan continued, ignoring Ethan's statement, "I'm quite sure I'm right, so you two will be under a bit of a time constraint to accomplish this little mission I have for you."

"You're wrong," I said.

He blew out an exasperated sigh and shook his head sadly at

us. "I don't know where you're getting your information from but I can... "

"Your mother."

Satan paled considerably and his eyes darted around the room in fear. "What are you talking about?" he whispered wildly. "Is she here?"

"Nope, she's doing Grandpa in Nirvana for a week or so."

"I'm sorry, what?" While my uncle's color had come back his voice was still barely audible.

"Grandma, who prefers Gigi, is doing the nasty with Grandpa this week. She stopped by the other day and we had a little chat." I grinned at his discomfort.

"You're alive?"

"Yep, even after I suggested she look into some meds." I ignored his look of shock and folded my napkin into a swan with droopy wings. I had never been good at napkin animals.

Satan was speechless. I was fairly sure this was a first for him and I had to admit I enjoyed it. He focused on his fruit and chewed as he thought. It was his turn so I waited.

"Did you talk to her?" he asked Ethan.

"Only at the end. She threatened to smite me." He shuddered at the memory.

Satan sighed in relief. "She threatens me with that all the time."

I blew out a frustrated sigh and slapped my hands down on the table. "Look, I'm tired of the bullshit and I want to go home. Gigi stopped time on Earth for me and there is no chance of Ethan dying. You, on the other hand, are in deep doodoo. Your mother is lonely and pissed. It would behoove you to visit her once in a while. You might curb her deadly tantrums if you showed a little respect or at the very least kissed her ass on a monthly basis. I'd recommend you get your pansy ass over to Nirvana. However, I wouldn't go this week because like I said, I believe she and Gramps are going to be busy."

"Did you just call me a pansy ass and use the term doodoo?"

Satan inquired looking flabbergasted.

I thought for a moment about lying, but decided that wouldn't really work. "Yes, I did."

"Would you promise to call God a pansy ass when he comes for lunch at the end of the week?"

"Will that help my case?" I asked.

"Yes, it would," he answered with a huge smile pulling at his lips. "It would make me very happy indeed."

Grinning, I shook my head. I was dealing with two year olds who could destroy the world. Who fucking knew? "Fine. I'll call God a pansy ass. Now I want to go home. Today."

"No can do, pretty one," Satan said, digging back into his pancakes with gusto. Clearly my agreeing to call his brother a pansy ass brought his appetite back.

"Should I call Gigi?" I asked politely.

"No," both Satan and Ethan yelled at the same time.

I shot the evil eye at my mate. I'd been bluffing and he was screwing me up.

"Sorry," he muttered and went back to his coffee.

"Listen, Uncle," I said with saccharine sweetness. "I'm pregnant and you're eating pancakes. This does not work for me. I would like to tear your head off right now, so start talking or I'm calling my grandma."

To say the Devil looked taken aback would be an understatement. "Fine. You win… this round. I have a little problem. The Sword of Death has gone missing and I need it back."

"Yes, and?" I said, knowing where we were going.

"I can't actually kill anyone to get it back and I need someone who can to find it and destroy the traitor who took it," he stated logically as if I'd understand and agree.

"So basically you want an assassin to go do your dirty work when you all were dumb enough to leave the damn thing in the Den of Iniquity."

"Yes, that sounds about right," he agreed, speared a piece of pineapple and ate it. It was good he was eating pineapple. I was allergic to pineapple. If he'd eaten bacon I would have used a little magic voodoo and sewn his lips shut. Glancing around the table I realized there was no bacon or sausage or eggs in sight. He was a lucky man.

"That is a tempting offer, but I'll have to pass. I'm not a hired killer and neither is my mate."

"I beg to differ. You killed fifty Demons yesterday and seem quite fine today," he said, watching me with curiosity.

Looking down at my hands, I wanted to cry. Ethan tensed beside me and the room filled with his heavy-duty magic. I squeezed his hand to let him know I could handle it. There was no getting around the fact that I had created the magic that destroyed those men... I looked my uncle in the eye and let my tears fall without shame. "That was not for money. That was for honor."

"Yes, I believe it was." Satan nodded and stood. Pacing back and forth he ran his hands through his hair.

"Ethan, I want to go."

"Listen to what he has to say. I have a feeling it's far more complicated than just finding a sword," Ethan answered.

"Nothing down here is what it seems."

"As is with most of life." He gave me a brief smile and took my hand in his.

"Are you two done?" Satan demanded impatiently.

"For the moment," Ethan said smoothly.

"There's a balance. Good and evil. The lines are constantly crossed and blurred. The Sword was created to destroy what can no longer distinguish the difference," Satan said.

"Its purpose is to kill a True Immortal?" I asked.

"True Immortal?" Ethan asked.

"There are seven True Immortals; myself, the pansy ass God, Mother Nature, The Angels of Light and Death, my father and the Woman. We cannot be killed by conventional means. We can either choose death and then use the Sword, or the Sword of Death can be plunged through our hearts three times and we would cease to be."

"I would assume that would be a difficult feat," Ethan surmised.

"Yes," Satan agreed, "but not impossible."

"Grandpa said there are three empty spaces," I lied, not wanting to reveal that I'd read that fact in the book. "Do those True Immortals exist yet?"

Satan gave me an odd stare for a moment and then shrugged. "Possibly, but I'm not quite sure. No one is. It is something we are all trying to discover. The worry is that the new Immortals could tip the balance."

"And that would be bad."

"Very." Satan's pacing stopped and his hand went back to his hair. "Losing any one of the True Immortals would upset the balance. Those ramifications would not just be felt in Heaven and Hell… they would decimate your world as you know it. This is far bigger than a missing Sword."

"Why in the hell are we the only ones looking for it?" I was shocked. I would think everyone would be freaking out… not eating pancakes and making lunch dates.

"No one else knows yet," he said and sat back down.

"Your mother and father know," I told him.

"Yes." He nodded wearily. "But God and the Angels don't."

"What about the Woman?"

He stared at the ceiling lost in thought for a moment and then rejoined us. "No one knows where she is."

Now there was a story I was sure I wouldn't be privy to. "How do you know one of them didn't take it?"

"Because every time it's gone missing, it's some idiot in Hell trying to overthrow me." He heaved a put upon sigh. "As much as I love deception and liars, it does get exhausting."

I rolled my head and tried to piece together what he had said and I realized it was a whole bunch of nothing. "Do you have any leads? I don't even know the territory here. How do you expect us to find the damn thing?"

"I know it's in Hell. I can feel it and I am sure that someone very close to me is the culprit."

A chill tickled my spine and I hated Hell just a little more than I did seconds ago. He was asking me to destroy a Demon close to him or, God *the pansy ass* forbid, a family member.

"No," I said. "I won't kill anyone that's not trying to kill me or Ethan or... " Shit. My reasoning didn't hold up. I *would kill* someone trying to kill Dixie, Grandpa, Gigi, and even the Devil himself. Was it the pregnancy hormones or was I losing it?

"It has very little to do with an individual life, Astrid. It has to do with the delicate balance of good and evil. Without it, none of us exist."

"So if we don't get it back, the world will end," I rolled my eyes and in frustration picked up my napkin again. I'd try for a simple fan this time.

"I'm disappointed at your simplistic thinking," he tsked. "Of course the world wouldn't blow up and be over. It's far more insidious than that. It would slowly morph into a place so filled with confusion and the inability to distinguish right and wrong, it would implode upon itself eventually. Most likely during the lifetime of your son."

That gave both Ethan and me huge pause, but how was I to be sure my uncle wasn't lying? "I would think all that debauchery would make you happy," I snapped.

"Then you don't know me at all. While I might lack in morals, I am not an evil man."

I snorted.

"Yes." He grinned at me. "Some may disagree with my self-assessment, but I speak the truth... this time. I am simply the keeper of those who choose the dark side. I do not force or coerce man to do evil. He doesn't need my help for that. I do thrive on it and punish it, but someone has to or the balance would be broken."

"*He makes perfect sense,*" Ethan said.

I shot him a surprised glance. "*You think we should do this?*"

"*Honestly, I don't think he's giving us a choice.*" He said exactly what I had started to think. "*But I do think we cut a bargain with him. I don't trust that he will let us leave even if we find the Sword.*"

"If we do this, what do we get in return?" I asked Satan, who was very aware Ethan and I could communicate telepathically.

"What do you want?" he asked, back in his element of wheeling and dealing.

I thought about it carefully. Wording was important. My Uncle was a master manipulator and I was not... What could I get that would be beneficial to my world and my child in the long run that wouldn't fuck up the balance?

"Well, I want my natural hair color back." I heard Ethan drop his head back and moan.

"I'm not done yet," I hissed and elbowed him. "We want to go home with no strings attached. You have to give us back our weapons. You will visit your mother on a regular basis—meaning weekly. You will delve into the minds of those Demons that my father ruined and if they seek forgiveness, you will end them."

"You're asking me to bend the rules of Hell." His voice was low and angry.

"No," I countered. "I have no issue with how you handle your sinning souls. That's your prerogative, but the Demons my father lied to and blackmailed... different matter."

"Their souls are not clear."

"True," I agreed, "but they never had a chance. Never."

"You drive a hard bargain, niece." He laughed and clapped Ethan on the back. "You are a very lucky Vampyre to have garnered her favor."

"I agree," Ethan said.

"So?" I asked. "Do we have a deal?"

He took a seat next to me and I was overwhelmed by his beauty and power. Who did I think I was to bargain with the Devil? I was a blip in time compared to him... hell, I was a blip in time compared to my mate. I should have let Ethan negotiate. Shit.

"I shall agree with all but one point," he said. His proximity was intoxicating and I found myself leaning toward him. "No weapons."

WTF?

"You will only need your magic here. Have you seen any weapons in Hell?" he asked.

Thinking hard, I realized I hadn't. I would think Hell would be armed to the teeth.

"We have no weapons here. We have no use for them. They are made to kill. Magic can do both, but there is a choice. Weapons leave little choice."

"Jesus, that's profound," I muttered.

"Actually, he is." Satan nodded in agreement.

"Wait. What?" I was completely confused.

"Your cousin, Jesus. He's quite profound. I like him. Now his father is another story... sanctimonious shit."

"You have a deal," Ethan said quietly. "We will return your Sword and then we will leave. Forever."

"Astrid?" Satan stared at me.

"Yes. Yes, you have a deal."

He stood and moved to leave the room. "Oh, there is one more little thing."

Of course there was.

"We need to return the Sword to its home before my brother God graces Hell with his pansy ass for lunch."

"And that would be when?" I asked, hoping he wouldn't say today.

"In three days on the lunar eclipse," he replied. "The son of a bitch will be here in three days."

CHAPTER TWENTY-TWO

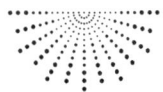

"We have three days to save the world. It sounds like the plot of a cheesy action flick," I groaned and flopped down on the couch in our little guesthouse.

"I think it's a test," Ethan mused.

"A test?" I sat up and watched him move around the room. The fluidity of his movement and his ass in his jeans made me want to jump him, but there was no time for nookie right now.

"For you," he said. "Satan is testing you for some reason."

"Do you think the Sword of Death hasn't really gone missing?"

He sat down next to me and absently played with my red locks. "I think things are happening to you here and he is testing your ability. I do believe someone has taken the Sword, but it's gone missing before and he got it back. I find it interesting that he wants you to do it."

"Us," I corrected him.

"No, I'm incidental to him. His real interest is in you and I don't like it."

"Well, I'm not particularly happy about it either."

"Come here," he said.

I crawled onto his lap and looked at the man who was so much more to me than a mate. Gently, I ran my fingers over his perfect lips. Our connection went beyond sexual; it was elemental— necessary. Staring at him, I forgot where I ended and he began. Unsure what higher power even meant anymore, I instead thanked the stars, the sun and the moon for giving him to me.

"I love you, my Vampyre," I whispered as I lay my head in the crook of his neck.

"And I you," he said.

"Where do we even start to look?" I murmured as I snuggled closer.

"There are several family functions over the next few days," General George bellowed from the doorway.

"Oh my God," I shrieked, flying off Ethan and the couch, causing me to trip over the coffee table. "Does anybody in Hell knock?"

"Door was open," he informed me.

"No," I told him. "It wasn't."

His eyebrows flapped in laughter. "Fine. I picked it," he conceded. "But we have work to do."

"We?"

"Why of course, dear child. You didn't think our great ruler would send you into the trenches blind. Did you?" He moseyed into the living room and headed for the kitchen. "You have anything to eat here?"

"No clue," I muttered and watched him negotiate the room with amazing grace for such a huge monster. "I don't eat food. Is Bambi here?"

"No, she went to Nirvana to make sure Mother Nature hasn't killed your grandfather."

"Is that a possibility?" I asked, horrified.

"No." He chuckled. "But she has been known to incapacitate him for a few months due to her… uh, creativity."

"TMI." I shook my head and followed him to the kitchen. "What do you want?"

"Veggies, fruit or ice cream," he said, making himself comfortable.

"You really don't eat meat?" I asked as I searched the fridge.

"No, clogs the arteries."

I found some celery and oranges. "But you're immortal, aren't you?"

"Yes, but no reason to muck up the system," he said as he shoved three oranges into his large mouth, peel and all.

"Come to think of it, Satan had no meat on his table this morning either," Ethan said, watching in fascination as the General threw back six more oranges and three bunches of celery at the same time.

"We think alike on many matters," the General explained.

I was amazed that he ate with his mouth and spoke through his eyebrows, but thought it might be rude to point it out. "Can he speak to you like we can?" I asked as I handed him some apples I found on the counter.

"Thank you, dear. And yes, of course he can speak with me. He created me, in a way."

"You gonna expand on that?" I asked and contemplated licking an apple just to see if it tasted like butt.

"Nope." He grinned with both his brows and his full mouth.

"Figures. So, family functions?"

He finished chewing, swallowed and graced us with a burp to end all burps. Thankfully it smelled like brownies. "Yes, there will be a formal dinner this evening. Tomorrow there will be a fight exhibition followed by a concert by a Journey cover band. And of course on the day of lunar eclipse there will be the lunch with God."

He had almost rendered me speechless with the Journey cover band thing, but the fight exhibition and the impending lunar eclipse were more alarming. "What kind of fighting?"

"Hand to hand. No magic," he said.

"That sounds interesting," Ethan chimed in.

"Nope," I told him, moving on to the next item on my agenda. "The lunar eclipse…"

"Yes, dear?" George replied.

"That's significant, isn't it?" I said. "It's when the Sword of Death can be used to kill a True Immortal. Right?"

"Yes."

"Does your master have nefarious plans for his brother? Is that why he's given me three days to find the damn thing?" I was mad. Satan was a douche and I was done. I refused to be an accessory to offing God.

"My goodness, what an imagination you have!" The General laughed heartily. "Satan and God are not the closest of siblings, but neither one would kill the other. Ever. It would upset the balance more than the Sword being missing. Plus, they'd have to answer to Mother Nature." George shuddered and grunted in terror.

I considered what he said, but I wasn't sure who to trust anymore. I adored George, but he did work for Satan.

"Sometimes you have to go with your gut," Ethan said.

"What if my gut is wrong?" I asked. *"There's kind of a lot riding here."*

"True. How about go with your heart instead of your gut," he suggested.

"Shit," I muttered and he grinned.

My heart said to trust George. This entire thing would be a little easier to swallow if the fate of the world wasn't resting on it. A tiny flutter in my stomach made me catch my breath. Our baby was letting me know I was correct. Holy Heaven and Hell, what was I giving birth to? Would he even need me? He was so much wiser than me already. I cupped my slightly rounded belly with my hands and gently rubbed. The warm feeling of my son's contentment washed away my fear of inadequacy. He needed me as much as I needed him.

"Okay," I told George. "I believe you. Let's go get this shit done."

"Patience, my child. I made a promise to you and I intend to keep it." George shook his bulbous head sadly.

"What promise?" Ethan asked.

George said nothing, but he didn't have to. I remembered. "He said he would take me to my mother."

"No," Ethan said adamantly. "Absolutely not."

I put my hand on his arm. "Ethan, this is not for you to decide. I need to see her once more. Please understand."

Ethan paced the small kitchen in frustration and ran his hands through his hair. "Can her mother hurt her?" he demanded of George.

"Not physically," he answered.

"I don't like this, Astrid," he said. He leaned back on the counter and shoved his hands in his pockets. "If you go I will go with you."

He had seen most of me, but he hadn't seen the pathetic child who still longed for her mother's love. I wasn't sure I could take him knowing.

"I have seen her. I've seen her in your mind and that's why I don't want you to put yourself through that again," he said quietly, staring at the ceiling. "I love you—all of you. The little girl inside you breaks my heart. If you go... I will go with you. Period."

"Okay," I whispered. "Okay."

"Put your hands on my back," the General instructed. "This will not hurt... much."

GENERAL GEORGE WAS RIGHT. IT WAS FAR LESS VIOLENT THAN MY last trip to the Basement. Ethan looked a bit shaken up, but he wanted to come. Oh crap. I glanced down at my outfit and cringed.

I should have changed into a dress before seeing my mother. While I loved the vintage jeans, combat boots and fitted black t-shirt I wore, I knew she would not find me up to snuff. Although I didn't even think a designer ball gown would help much in this instance.

I recognized where we were. It was the same place I'd ended the Demons. Surprisingly, I didn't feel sick... I actually felt peace with what I had done.

"Are you ready?" George asked.

"No, but that doesn't matter." I stepped toward the crevasse. The lights wailed and bounced. "How do I find her?"

"Call to her," he said.

Could it be that easy? Would she just be a light or would she look like my mother? I hoped if she looked human, she wouldn't be on fire. Fuck, this wasn't a good idea.

"If you've changed your mind we could... "

"No." I cut George off and took two steps closer to the flames. I was amazed that the heat of the blazing fire didn't affect me. I searched for a happy memory of my mother from the past and couldn't find one. Was I a classic abuse victim coming back for more? Maybe, but I wanted one last try to make her hear me. I didn't need her love anymore, but I wanted her to know I loved her—as damaged as she was.

"Astrid," Ethan called from behind me.

My hand flew up to stop him. This was my battle and mine alone. "Mother?"

Nothing.

"Mother?" I called again. Wait. What in the hell was I thinking? She didn't like being my mother. In life she rarely let me call her mother. She didn't want people to think she was old... "Petra, it's me—your daughter. Astrid."

The fire grew wilder and I was tempted to step back, but I held my ground. I was certain it couldn't hurt me. The soul lights screeched and moaned and then went silent. It was so abrupt, I gasped... and then she appeared. Her beauty was undiminished, but bright orange burning embers clung to her. She was completely naked, but the only part of her that wasn't blurred with red haze was her face. She twisted and writhed as if in pain, but she smiled. Was she happy to see me? My heart lodged in my throat.

"Hi," I whispered.

She stared and said nothing. I wasn't sure she knew who I was. The other souls darted around her, but stayed silent.

"What do you want?" she demanded in a voice tinged with insanity.

That was an excellent question. Now that I faced her, I was no longer sure.

"I wanted to see you… to see if you were all right." My voice sounded child-like and timid. I gouged my nails into my thighs to punish myself for still needing her to want me.

"How do you think I am?" she hissed. "I was meant to lead—to rule. He promised me," she screamed. Her body became clearer and I realized she was covered in profusely bleeding cuts. I put my hand over my mouth so I wouldn't cry out. Her formerly perfect outside was now as damaged as her inside.

"Have you seen him?" she asked with excitement. "I've been waiting for him to take me out of here, but he's late."

"No," I said, trying to swallow back tears. "I haven't seen him."

"He'll come back and this time I'll behave. I'll kill everyone he wants me to and I will behave," she promised. She panted like a dog and swatted at the soul lights. "Leave me," she shouted at the flickering souls. "I'm talking to a woman who knows my lover. She will help me escape."

"Do you know who I am?"

She narrowed her eyes and tilted her head. "Of course—you're the one I should have killed when you were born. My lover wanted me to, but there was an old woman who kept saving you. I killed that bitch." My mother's laughter rang in my ears and my stomach churned. My nana had saved me in so many ways that I never even knew. The woman who floated before me was an abomination. She was pathetic and evil.

"I have to go," I muttered and turned to leave.

"Wait," she begged. "I could be your friend if you help me get out of here. We could find my lover and we could rule the world. It would be so much fun. He will beat you and rape you, but after a while you won't mind. If you close your eyes you can float to another place with ponies and fireflies. I promise to take my share. I always did my share. Will you help me?"

Oh my God. I dropped to my knees and my body curled in on itself as I tried to hold back the bile in my throat. Anger and a feeling of helplessness consumed me. I wanted to tear at my own skin. Was she a victim too? Had my father destroyed her long before she was my mother? I knew she'd been reincarnated many times. She went back to my father each life and they built an army to destroy the world, but had it been his idea or hers?

Tears stung my eyes and I realized she wasn't capable of love. It had been beaten out of her many lifetimes before she gave birth to me. Forgiveness was no longer difficult. She was so broken it was almost unfathomable. I knew without a doubt what I was going to do.

I glanced back at George and Ethan who stood quietly and watched. Every muscle in my mate's body was tense and the pain I saw in his eyes made me love him even more. He was going to be a beautiful father and I was going to be a beautiful mother. I just had one more thing to do here.

Letting my mind leave my body, I closed my eyes and searched for my mother. She was blocked. There was no way in. I pressed my hands to my forehead and tried again. Closed. Why couldn't I go in? She had no chance. My father had destroyed her the same way he had destroyed Lance and the other Demons. I wanted to give my mother one last gift. She was by no means innocent of guilt, but she was as much a victim as the ones I'd shown mercy on yesterday.

"You can't enter the mind of a soul," George said.

I whipped around and stared at him. How did he know what I was doing? Hell, I didn't even care. I just wanted his help. "Is there any way to end her suffering?" I asked desperately.

"None that I know of," he said.

"I was meant to rule the world," she screamed, coming completely unhinged. "Find my lover, girl. Bring him to me and he will reward you with immortality and riches. He promised." She was now foaming at the mouth and her beauty was marred by the blood and pus that poured from her wounds. She had smeared it all over her face and in her hair. It was all I could do to look at her.

"I will try to find him for you," I promised, telling her what I thought she wanted to hear. "I promise to find the answer to help you."

"You're a good girl," she grunted as she slapped at the flames. "I wish I'd known you better."

"So do I," I whispered. "Goodbye." I turned back to George and Ethan. "Take me out of here. Now."

"As you wish."

CHAPTER TWENTY-THREE

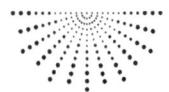

IT TOOK SEVERAL HOURS OF STARING INTO SPACE BEFORE I WAS ready to speak. Ethan sat next to me and General George lay quietly at my feet. I wanted to give mercy to the woman who had shown me no compassion in life. Putting the sad pieces of her story together made my heart break. I was no longer surprised at how happy everyone was that I had killed my father. He was horrific. Truly horrific.

"I want to end her—to give her peace," I said.

"I know." Ethan reached over and held me.

"She was already gone before she was mine and that wasn't her fault."

"She made choices," the General said flatly. "She went to him willingly."

"Yes, but under false pretenses. I know she was greedy and committed horrors over her lifetimes, but... after lifetimes of concentrated abuse and rape, do you really think she had free will to make a choice to leave? Do you?" I demanded.

"I do not know. It is not my place to condemn or forgive, nor is it yours," he said.

"I think nothing is black and white. You talk of balance and good and evil, who in the hell is keeping tabs here? It certainly doesn't seem like Satan is," I yelled.

George simply stared at me.

"I'm sorry. It's not your fault. Maybe it's not even Satan's. With as many people that are here who could really dig deep enough to figure all the nuances out?" I reached out and ran my hand through George's soft fur. "I'm just sad and angry."

"I know, child. I will leave you now to rest. I will see you this evening."

With that he disappeared in a burst of glitter. I glanced at where George had lain and saw something shiny.

"Did the General lay an egg or does he poop shimmering rocks?" I asked, leaning off the couch to peer at what looked like a small shiny egg or worse.

"I certainly hope not," Ethan said, examining the object. "Oh my God," he muttered. "The amulet."

"What amulet?"

"My father gave me this before I followed you to Hell. It will kill one. Only one. The one meant to lead," he said, remembering his father's words.

"Holy shit, that can kill Satan?" I picked up the stone and rolled it in my hand. It was smooth and gave off heavy vibes of magic.

"Now that I know of True Immortals, I'm not sure," Ethan admitted. "Quite honestly, I don't even know how it works."

"I'm going to assume that very little is a mistake as far as the General goes. He left that here on purpose. Do you really think he would give us the means to kill his lord and master?" I was fascinated with the amulet. It was as beautiful as it was deadly.

"He must have taken it from Lust. She had stolen it when I was beaten and chained."

"Did she know what she had?" I asked, still furious about what she had done.

"No, she couldn't have."

"What do we do with this thing?" I asked.

"We keep it until we need it," he answered logically.

"And if we don't?"

"All the better for everyone," he said.

"Put the damn thing away. Wait, I'll put it with the book Grandpa gave me. I shoved it under the mattress." I took the stone and ran to the bedroom. The bed looked inviting and I was freakin' exhausted.

"Would you like to cuddle?" Ethan stood in the doorway, looking every inch the sex-on-a-stick Vampyre Prince he was.

"Um, kind of." I smiled and crooked my finger. All of a sudden I wasn't so tired. "Come here."

His smile undid me. We slid into each other's arms and fell onto the bed. Jeans and t-shirts disappeared and it was impossible to get close enough. I wanted to crawl inside him and live there. Forever. He reverently ran his hands over my newly rounded belly.

"So beautiful," he murmured. "So amazing."

"Do you think he'll like us?" I placed my hand on top of his as he made lazy circles on my stomach.

"God, I hope so." He laughed and moved his hand to my breast.

"I thought you wanted to cuddle." I sighed happily and arched my back so he cupped me more fully.

"Ahhh, you're right," he teased. He removed his hand from my aching breast and wrapped me in a non-sexual embrace. "I'm not in the mood anyway."

"You suck," I giggled and rubbed my bottom on some very hard evidence that belied his words.

"You do realize that we have to be at your uncle's in a half hour."

"Can we be fashionably late?" I murmured, placing his hands back on my breasts.

"I'm good with that," he said and shimmied my panties to my ankles.

"I wannna be on top," I said as I straddled his body and felt the fire begin to unfurl low in my belly. "Do you mind?"

"I'd be delighted." His lopsided grin made my lady parts dance.

God, I loved this man. I loved him inside and out, but his outside was making me crazy at the moment.

"One rule," I whispered as I rubbed myself like a cat on his chest. "No breaking eye contact the entire time. I want to watch you come and I want you to watch me."

"That could be arranged," he said huskily. His eyes blazed green and hips moved in a slow fashion that promised really, really good things.

"Poke her boobie, it's squishy," a little voice squealed with excitement.

"Nooooooo, why he get to poke Mommy's melons? Mommy no let me grab her jugs," another whined.

"Pretty boy touches Mommy's butt. Me saw him smack it and Mommy laugh!"

"Was Mommy bad girl and get spank spank?" yet another asked with great concern.

"What the hell?" Ethan groaned and covered himself with the sheet. "You've got to be fucking kidding me." He slapped his hand over his eyes and tried not to laugh.

"Off," I yelled at my inappropriately nosy Demons. "Off the bed and out of the room. Now."

"But Mommy, it just getting good," Beyonce complained. Abe was humping the air and Ross was trying to pry Ethan's fingers from his eyes.

"Mommmmmy, how bout we be quiet and no touch. Can we stay?" Rachel asked sweetly as she pulled on Ethan's chest hair.

"No," I snapped. They were better than a vat of ice water as far as libido destroyers went. "You most certainly cannot watch. Ever... wait, have you been watching us?"

"Um, what you mean, Mommy?" Ross inquired innocently, slinking away from Ethan's head.

"I mean," I said as I pinched my thighs to keep from laughing or screaming, "have you been watching Ethan and me... umm..."

"Get jiggy?" Beyonce asked.

"Bump uglies?" Abe grunted and acted out his suggestion.

"Get some stankie on the hang down?" Rachel offered and Ethan choked.

"I know," Ross yelled. "She mean to say pound the duck!"

"Oh my God," I moaned as I scooped up my little monsters and tossed them out to the living room. Ethan's laughter followed me as I herded them out of the room much to their great disappointment at not being invited to the party.

"Are you guys almost ready?" Dixie was standing in the living room, fully dressed and ready to go. "It's a sit down dinner and Daddy has a shit fit if we're late."

My head dropped to my chest and I wanted to cry. I liked Dixie a lot. I was growing to love her, but right now I wanted to kill her. "Be there in a sec," I said and raced back to the bedroom. "Get up and get dressed. Our ride to my uncle's is here," I whispered and tried not to laugh at the incredulous expression on his face.

"We're finding the damned Sword tonight. I am done with being interrupted. My very impressive package is going to fall off soon if I keep having to ice it down." He swore and stomped into the bathroom to take a shower. A cold one. I wanted to join him, but that would add insult to injury.

"We'll be out in a sec," I repeated and pulled out a sexy black number. With my blood red locks, I had very little choice in the color department. I yanked on some hotter than hell thigh high boots and twisted my hair into a messy knot. I was pissy but good to go.

After a two minute icy shower Ethan came back a bit calmer. He took a long look at my ensemble, rolled his neck and closed his eyes. "The boots are not helping," he muttered as he retrieved the amulet from the mattress. "The stone can be worn as a charm. I want it on your neck."

"Is that smart? What if someone knows what it is?" I said.

"Fuck 'em," he said. He removed the thin gold chain from my neck and slid the amulet on. It was beautiful. "I'll feel better if you have this since we've been forbidden weapons."

It fell perfectly between my breasts and sparkled with magic. "It's a little scary." I laughed and glanced down at the tiny rock of utter destruction, but Ethan was right. If I needed it... I would use it.

"You ready?" he asked. He was dressed head to toe in Hugo Boss and I wanted to strip him with my teeth. Instead I sighed and grabbed a clutch.

"Yes, as ready as I'll ever be."

He grinned and gave me a quick but promising peck on the lips. "Let's go."

CHAPTER TWENTY-FOUR

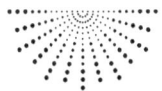

THE DINING ROOM WAS STILL MASSIVE, BUT LESS SO THAN THIS morning. Filled with Demons dressed to the nines, it looked like the set of a movie. Carl, Janet and Myrtle were on duty again making rounds with heavy silver trays laden with champagne and hors d'oeuvres. I was curious what Satan deemed appropriate eats for a formal dinner party, so I hightailed it to Janet.

"Would you like some smoked salmon, Astrid?" she asked.

"No weenies tonight?"

"No." She giggled and popped a perfect toast point smeared with cream cheese, salmon and capers into her mouth. "I like the soy weenies better, but Satan said we had to have classier fare tonight. Ohhhh, you look beautiful. Your hair is amazing."

"Thanks," I muttered ungratefully. Trying to ignore my hair color was impossible. There was no avoiding tresses the color of blood. "Do you know everyone here tonight?" I needed to start somewhere and I highly doubted that Janet had taken the Sword.

"Well," she whispered, "I know who everyone is. They wouldn't know me, because… I'm me, but it's the cream of the crop in attendance."

"Who are those people?" I pointed to a group of hard looking men sipping champagne and exchanging terse pleasantries.

"Those are Guards, like Cole." Her cheeks darkened with displeasure. "They think they run the show when the Master isn't around."

"Don't they?"

"Yes, but... "

"But what?" I asked. Were they cruel? Were they screwing with Satan?

"Nothing," she said, quickly recovering. With a big fake smile plastered on her sweet face, she gave me a small curtsy and hustled away.

"Anything interesting?" Ethan asked. He held a glass of champagne and eyed the crowd.

"Janet is afraid of the Guards over there. Possibility one or more might have delusions of grandeur about taking over Hell." I dipped my pinkie into his glass and touched it to my tongue. "Motherfucker," I hissed and choked. "How old do I have to be for food to stop tasting like butt?"

"Three hundred," he answered and arched an eyebrow in amusement.

"It's really not funny. I'm pregnant and I want pickles and ice cream. Only problem is I'm not fond of things that taste like dusty ass," I snapped.

"I can see how that might be a problem," he agreed. I rolled my eyes and elbowed him. His grunt of pain made me happy. "How many people know of the Sword?" he asked as he pinched my ass in retaliation.

"Good question." I gasped and smacked his hand. I considered tickling him or licking my finger and sticking it in his ear, but figured that was very immature and might be conspicuous.

"Hi guys, is this boring or what?" Dixie said as she tucked herself between us. "I hate these things."

"Dixie, how many people know about the Sword?" I asked.

Her head whipped to me so fast I felt a breeze. Her pretty eyes narrowed and she grabbed my arm in a vise-like grip. "What do you know about the Sword?"

"Ease up," I hissed and discreetly pushed her to a corner by a ridiculously large plant in a gold and jewel encrusted pot. The show of wealth in Hell was staggering. Ethan stepped in front and hid us from view. "Let go of my arm. I like you and want you to keep your hands."

She reluctantly released me, but her body stayed tense. "What do you know about the Sword?" she repeated.

"I know it's missing and I know I now suspect you of taking it." I watched a myriad of expressions cross her face, but the largest was disbelief. I relaxed a bit. My gut and heart knew she didn't steal it.

"I would never do that. It would put the Balance of Chaos in jeopardy, not to mention the lives of my father and grandfather," she ground out. "What else do you know?"

"I'm asking questions at the moment," I told her. "You'll get your turn. How many know of the Sword?"

"Most believe it's a story—that it doesn't really exist."

"Yes, and?"

"The True Immortals know." She glanced around in a slight panic. I wasn't sure if she was scared to tell me or terrified someone would hear her.

"Well, duh." I rolled my eyes. "I assumed they knew. Who else?"

"I'm not exactly sure." She shook her head and picked at her freshly painted nails. "I think my sisters know and most likely my dad's top advisors… "

"How do you know about it?" I asked. This was going to be a little easier than I'd originally thought—possibly.

She paused and gave me a hard stare before she went on. "Grandpa told me about it," she said. "I don't know if he was supposed to so I've never told anyone."

"Which sisters do you think have any knowledge of the Sword?"

"I can't be sure... why do you want it?" she demanded. "If you hurt my father, I'll... " Her fists clenched in anger and tears filled her eyes.

"Stop." I grabbed her by the shoulders and I got in her face. "Your father asked me to find it. It's been stolen. I would never hurt him. You have my word." I kept my voice low. The room was starting to fill.

She eyed me with distrust, but I saw the hope in her eyes. "You won't use it against him?" she whispered.

"I may be a loose cannon but I'm not an idiot. I want it back where it's supposed to be so I can go home. As lovely and over the top as Hell is, I really prefer Kentucky."

She took a deep breath and laid her head on my chest. "I knew something bad was happening. I felt it. I just didn't think it was this. I thought it was that Amanda was having a boy."

"Why is that bad?"

"It means she carries the true heir to Hell." Her body tensed. "Do you think Amanda has the Sword?" Dixie gasped and tried to pull away. "I'll kill her."

"Dixie, no." I held her firmly and got right back up in her face. "You will do nothing. I will watch Amanda and if she tries anything I'll take care of her. You are out of this. Do you understand me?"

"I know I'm not as magical as my sisters, but I love my father despite his shortcomings, and I will fight for him. Always." Her slim body shook and her eyes blazed red. She was gorgeous.

"Why would Amanda kill him? The child hasn't been born yet."

"Many doubt the child is his," she said. "If my father is gone they will have to accept the child as their ruler regardless."

"Okay, but a simple DNA test will solve that little issue. Whether Satan is here or not." Heaven help us all, maybe they did really need me here...

"Astrid, what you don't understand about Demons is a lot," she sighed and put her hand on my face. "Every Demon in Hell carries some of my father's DNA—even those he didn't sire. It's a magical ritual that happens when a child is born that determines who the true father is. Without my father... no magic or ritual. The child will have to be taken at face value and since it appears at this time my father believes the baby is his, the population will follow that lead."

"That is so fucked up, I don't know what to say," I mumbled.

"Just be happy you're half Vampyre," Ethan whispered over his shoulder. "You ladies need to finish your chat—we're getting some stares."

"Dixie," I urged. "Let me handle this. If I need your help I will ask for it, but I don't want you getting hurt. Promise me."

"I promise to let you do what you have to do," she said.

"Okay, that is a total bullshit answer because you just promised nothing and... "

"All rise for Satan," Cole shouted above the din of the crowd.

"We'll finish this conversation later," I hissed and pulled her and her grinning face out from behind the plant.

The crowd hushed as Satan entered with a radiant Amanda on his arm. I could tell nothing from the way she mooned at him. She was either a great actress or totally innocent. The Devil was dressed in Prada and so was his consort. Stunning didn't even begin to cover it and the crowd purred its approval. Satan's smile almost made me forget my name and I giggled as I recalled I'd told him he was a pansy ass.

He was followed by the Sins. They came in a close second to their father and his consort. They shone like jewels and I studied them carefully. This was not going to be as easy as I thought. I searched the room for Cole. I wanted to keep my eye on him too. He stood to the side and watched Satan and Amanda with intense interest. It may have been a mistake on my part not having gotten to know him a bit better. Well, no time like the present.

"You're more beautiful than all thoth bitcheth put together," Carl whispered in my ear and I jumped. Where in the hell did he come from?

"Carl, you just scared the shit out of me, but thank you."

"Your motht welcome, Athrid. I'd offer you a drink, but alath I have no blood," he said apologetically.

"It's okay," I assured him. "Hey Carl, why is Janet afraid of the Guards?"

His demeanor changed on a dime from sweet and harmless to furious. "Did they talk to her?"

"No," I said quickly as I realized I could be inadvertently opening a fucked up can of whoop ass.

He relaxed marginally. "Ever thince she had her beard and muthache removed they have perthued her. Janet ith my mate and I won't tolerate harathment. I will kill them."

"Oookay," I reassured him. "I'll keep my eye on them."

"Thank you. I mutht get back to work. Have a lovely evening, Athrid."

"Did he just say his girlfriend had a beard and mustache?" Ethan asked as we watched Carl slip back into the crowd.

"Yep."

"We need to go home."

"I couldn't agree more. How do my boobs look?"

"Edible, why?" he asked.

"Because if I can't have a sword I need some kind of weapon."

His mouth gaped open and his eyes blazed green in anger. "I am holding my shit together for the moment, but I need to understand what you just said. Tell me that you did not just ask a Master Vampyre, not to mention your mate, if your boobs would be a good weapon to use on other men in this room."

"Actually I did."

"Astrid, the temptation to put you across my knee and spank you and then fuck you so you won't be able to notice another man for the rest of your unnaturally long life is so very tempting at the moment. It will take everything I own not to do just that," he snapped.

"That sounds awesome," I said honestly. He closed his eyes and let his head fall back on his shoulders. "But we have a Sword to find and I need to figure some shit out. So, if my boobs will distract... I will use them."

"Shall I pull my dick out?" he asked sarcastically.

"Not yet." I winked and left him standing there in shock.

Cole was surrounded by Guards, but he stood to the outside of the circle and watched the room. He was as stupidly beautiful as the rest of the Demons in Hell, but there was something harder about this particular man. As a Guard, I wondered if he was permitted to use his magic to kill. I assumed so or he would be fairly worthless to Satan.

"Hi, Cole," I said and extended my hand in greeting.

He nodded his head curtly and ignored my outstretched hand. What in the hell did Demons have against polite greetings? Was it because I had Vampyre cooties? I let it fall back to my side, but kept my smile firmly on my face.

"Miss Porter, it is good to see you this evening," he said, barely giving me a glance as he continued to scan the room.

"Call me Astrid," I said. "Are you armed?"

"I'm sorry, what?" Now I had his attention.

"I asked if you were armed. As a Guard I wondered if the rules were different."

He considered me for a long moment. "No. I don't need weapons to protect my Savior. Are you?"

Oookay, he gave me the creeps, but that didn't mean he was guilty. "Nope, just my fangs." I grinned and gave him a quick peek. He wasn't impressed.

We stood in awkward silence and his eyes drifted back to Satan and Amanda.

"She's lovely," I said, hoping he'd let loose and dish on Amanda.

"I have no clue who you mean," he said in a flat voice that made it clear I was annoying him—so much for my boobies.

"Amanda. She's something else."

He glanced over at them and his eyes narrowed slightly. "Yes. She is." Turning back to me, he gave me another curt nod. "Please accept my condolences about your father. He was a misunderstood man. I must get back to work. Good evening... Astrid."

My mouth gaped open and words got lodged in my throat. What in Satan's name did he mean that my father was misunderstood? I was fairly sure he was not misunderstood at all. He was a psychotic loose cannon in Hell and everyone I'd come across thus far, including his mother, was pleased to hear of his demise. Cole was a weird one. It was also odd that Satan hadn't asked him to find the damn Sword. Did that mean my uncle didn't trust his second? This was a fucking mess.

"Did the boobs work?" Ethan asked, knowing full well they hadn't helped a bit. His supersonic hearing would have clued him into the failed conversation.

"My boobs were fabu." I smiled sweetly. "I think he's gay."

Ethan's laughter followed me as I made my way toward my cousins... and Dante?

What was Dante still doing in Hell and why was he with the Sins?

"All three of you have the same Offensive Leprechaun name because you're triplets," Envy informed Gluttony, Pride and Sloth as she scrolled Facebook on her phone. "You're Sharty O'Legspreader."

"That's absolutely foul," Pride sniffed. "I don't like that one."

"I do," Sloth laughed and ruffled her sister's perfect hair. "It's also accurate where you're concerned."

"Can it, bitch," Pride said as she scooted away from her sloppy triplet.

The Sins stood in a group isolated from the rest of the dinner guests. They looked like high fashion models with a bad attitude. I didn't blame people for avoiding them. If I had a choice I would do the same, but I didn't have one. I had a freakin' job and I was beginning to think the pay dirt might be one of the nut-jobs in front of me.

"Astrid," Wrath cooed. "Divine as usual." She leaned in for an inappropriate lip lock, but I was saved by Dante of all people.

"What is this Facebook you speak so highly of?" he demanded of Wrath before she was able to make the cousin love connection. She rolled her eyes in disgust and pointed at Envy.

"Ask her."

"What is your last name, Dante?" Envy asked. Her eyes sparkled with mischief. "And your birthdate. The day, not the year."

"Alighieri," he spat, completely insulted that she didn't know. "And my birth date is September fourteenth."

"Envy, don't," Greed warned as she sidled up to Dante and wrapped her arms around him. Well, now I knew why he was here. I'd called it correctly at the poker game. I wasn't quite sure what she saw in him. He was substantially shorter and his attitude sucked, but who was I to judge true love or a meaningless hook up?

"Dante," Envy purred, ignoring her sister's warning. "Your Leprechaun name is Slutty McKnobhobber Douchebag McShitsucker."

The entire group went silent as a highly unattractive purple suffused Dante's face. "I take extreme offense at that dreck. That is ungainly for a woman to use that kind of vulgar language and I shall not partake in this conversation." He put his rather large nose in the air and walked off in a huff.

"Holy hell," I gasped and sucked back my laughter. "Did it actually say that?"

"I embellished just a tiny bit." Envy giggled and tossed her long shiny locks over her shoulder.

"What exactly do you see in him?" Wrath asked Greed.

"Did you see the size of his nose?" She grinned suggestively.

"You've tapped that?" Envy asked, wrinkling her pert nose in disgust.

"No," Greed said. "But after tonight I will. Excuse me." She rushed off after the very disgruntled Dante.

In front of me stood Wrath, Gluttony, Pride, Sloth, Greed, Envy, but no Lust. I scanned the room for Ethan to make sure Lust wasn't stupid enough to try anything else. Ethan had joined a conversation with Cole and the Guards. Smart man. Boobs didn't work, but testosterone might.

"Who you looking for?" Wrath asked with a knowing grin.

"Santa Claus."

"Interesting. I think he's in Purgatory—with Lust."

I froze and stared at her for a moment to see if she was telling the truth. She was. My body relaxed. I hadn't realized how tense I was about bumping into Lust after what she'd heard. At least now I didn't have to. My guess would be that Satan didn't think she had the Sword or she would be here. I did need to have a little chat with my uncle, but that was going to be difficult. Shit.

"Dinner is therved," Carl called from the middle of the room. He was flanked by Janet on his right and Myrtle on his left. Myrtle gave me a covert thumbs up and I shot her one back.

"Take your seats, my friends and family. The show is about to begin," Satan bellowed joyously.

Lights. Camera. Action.

CHAPTER TWENTY-FIVE

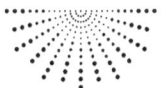

THANKFULLY I WAS SEATED NEXT TO ETHAN. THE GORGEOUSLY LAID out main table was for family and close friends. Several other tables, equally as lovely, were specifically for the Guards and their wives or significant others. The main table held Satan at one end and Wrath at the other. I assumed if he took Amanda as a mate that might be her spot. Amanda sat to the Devil's left and Cole to his right. Seated next to Amanda was Envy, then Greed, Dante, and Gluttony. On our side after Cole was Sloth then Ethan, myself, Dixie and Pride. That put me directly across from the delightful Dante. *Nice.* One chair sat empty down at Wrath's end. I assumed that one would have belonged to Lust.

The room seated probably forty or so and was now lit completely by candlelight. Janet turned out the electric lights as we were seated and Satan clapped his hands twice. A rush of magic that tickled my tummy blew through the room and hundreds of candles illuminated. The crowd applauded enthusiastically. It was beautiful. The crystal and heavy silver literally sparkled. The sheer amount of firepower in the room was a tad nervewracking, but the effect was stunning.

I tried to make eye contact with Amanda several times, but she avoided me like the plague. I suppose the whole lip popping incident had scarred her. Who knew?

"Ethan, did you learn anything from Cole?" I asked silently as I passed the basket of rolls that was making its way around the table. I wanted one badly, but knew that gagging at a formal dinner party would be considered bad form.

"Not much, but he seems to have a healthy obsession with Amanda," he replied.

"Really? I thought he didn't trust her." I glanced down at Cole and Amanda, but they weren't even looking at each other.

"I'm sure he doesn't, but it might go a bit deeper than that." He smiled and raised his glass. *"Astrid, pay attention. There's a toast."*

"Whoops," I raised my glass, then put it to my lips. There was no way in hell I was going to drink anything, but I wanted to fit in. Much to my great surprise it was blood. WTF? I glanced up in surprise and caught Satan's eye. He winked and I laughed, almost spilling my treat.

The dinner, which I didn't touch, smelled heavenly. Wine and conversation flowed freely and the atmosphere was light. However, as the meal wound down something changed. I felt a chill. A dark magic unfurled and wafted through the room. My hands felt clammy and my chest constricted painfully. What was it? Who was it? The desire to get up and move was strong. The magic was dissipated and not coming from any one direction. I glanced over at Satan, who seemed oblivious. Running around the room might appear odd, even for the *Vampyre* guest, so I stayed seated.

"Do you feel that?" I asked Ethan.

"Feel what?"

"Dark icky Demon voodoo."

"Did you say Demon doodoo?"

"Oh my God, no. Why would I say dark icky Demon doodoo?"

"You tell me."

"I said voodoo. Not doodoo," I snapped so loudly, his hand went to his forehead and he winced.

"Sorry, I'll keep my thought volume lower," I muttered. *"But do you feel it?"*

"No, I don't." He closed his eyes and focused. *"I feel nothing."*

The pressure on my chest eased, but the eerie presence remained. No one noticed, or if they did they showed no sign. Unable to hone in, I figured I'd continue to play Sherlock Holmes and delve back into the non-magic intel.

"Why does Wrath sit there?" I asked Dixie.

"She will become the leader of Hell when Daddy decides to retire or whatever," she said quietly.

"What if Big Lips has a boy? Does that fuck up the line?"

"As far as I know it would, but I don't think the baby is his. Amanda gets around—at least she did before she dug her claws into Daddy."

"Does Wrath think the baby is your dad's?"

"Nope, she's positive that Amanda will be in deep shit—her words, not mine—after she gives birth."

I was so happy I wouldn't be here for that shit show.

"Who's behind Wrath in line for the throne?"

"Envy. then Greed, then Lust, then the triplets, then me," she said.

I stored the information away and eyed the desserts that were coming out to the table. Shitshitshit. Black raspberry chip ice cream? Was someone screwing with me? That was my favorite and I almost threw a tantrum.

"You can do this," Ethan said, holding me back from the ice cream.

"I just want to sob," I whispered. "What the hell is wrong with me?"

"You're having our baby and he apparently wants ice cream." He smiled and squeezed my hand.

"I guess so," I pouted.

"I told you I'd give you what you want if you give me what I want," Dante hissed under his breath to Greed. He clearly didn't know about super duper immortal hearing skills. Although no one else seemed to be listening.

"Dante," she purred. "You get yours after I get mine."

Um, gross. I did not want to hear them discuss the arrangements or, God forbid, details of their rendezvous. Trying to tune them out, I refocused on the desserts I couldn't eat. Note to self... no more dinner parties while pregnant.

"I just want it. Now," he insisted. "If you don't give it to me my way then you'll get nothing."

Now, unfortunately, he had my full attention. I was about to throw up in my mouth and I didn't need the ice cream to help me. I had no clue what she saw in him. He was a douche.

"You are more trouble than you're worth," she snapped and turned to chat with her sister Envy, leaving the asshole with no one. Gluttony had turned her back to him at the beginning of the meal.

"So, Dante my man," Satan bellowed. "Are you here taking poker lessons or trying to find out if I've hidden some levels from you?" The crowd tittered and Dante fumed.

"I'm still here trying to figure out how to be a cheating, conniving, soulless bastard like you," he shot back and the room went silent.

After an uncomfortably long pause, the Devil threw his head back and laughed. The other Demons followed suit much to the great relief of Greed, who shot eye daggers at Dante.

"Those are some rather harsh words for someone trying to get into my daughter's pants," Satan added as the laughter died down.

"Daddy," Greed gasped.

"Yes, well... my apologies," Dante muttered insincerely. "Greed, a word?" he stood and pulled her chair out for her. The crowd stood and began to mill about as after dinner aperitifs were passed around.

"Something is off," I muttered and realized I was talking to myself.

Ethan had been drawn into an animated conversation with the Devil and the Seven Deadly Sins were chatting it up with Amanda the pregnant consort. No one back at home was going to believe any of this. I had a difficult time absorbing it. I watched as Dante roughly led Greed from the room and the voodoo stopped. The dark magic left the room with them. Bingo. It could not be this easy.

I quickly made my way out of the dining room. I caught Dixie's eye right as I reached the door. She arched an eyebrow in question, but I simply smiled and waved.

The hallway was dark. Thank God for Vamp vision.

I heard them from a distance and I made my way toward the sound. The hallway was thickly carpeted and I was able to move silently. Their voices were raised, but where was the magic? It had disappeared. Crap. It sounded like they were fussing at each other or someone was injured—it sounded horrific. Would they lead me to the Sword? Could I go home tonight? I was curious to meet God, but I wanted to get out of Hell even worse. Could it really be so simple?

No. Of course fucking not.

I picked up my pace and rounded the corner. If Dante had hurt Greed he was toast. I liked her and I... Oh. My. Hell. My first thought was that I would have to bleach my eyes... Dante's pants were at his ankles and Greed was on her knees in front of him. The slurping and moaning set my gag reflex in motion.

"Oh shit," I gasped. Dante's ass was nice, but extremely white. The entire situation was mortifying and would stay with me for centuries.

They turned and stared. Greed's expression was one of shock and Dante's was pissed.

"I am so sorry," I mumbled backing away. Dante had slapped his hands over his eyes and swore in what sounded like Italian.

Greed pointed to Dante's rather oversized manhood and gave me the thumbs up. I weakly returned the gesture and turned to go.

"Would you like to join us?" Greed called out as I hauled ass back to the dining room.

"Um… no, I'm good," I choked out. "But thanks."

"Maybe another time," she yelled as I picked up my pace to a sprint. I needed to go home. Immediately.

No Sword. No magic. Only eternal memories of my cousin giving a douchewanker a blow job in Hell. And now I was lost. How did I get lost? Granted, the Dark Palace was huge, but this was fucking ridiculous. I hadn't followed Greed and her boy toy very far and I was sure I went back the same way. Maybe in my haste to get away, I'd overshot the door.

A violent jolt of hazy black magic made me freeze. It carried the same signature as the magic I'd felt at dinner. It hadn't left the room with Greed. It had stopped and made me think it had been Greed. The owner of the magic had wanted me gone. Shit. Something was going down in the dining room and I couldn't find it.

When conventional means fail use magic. A shit ton of it. I lifted my hand and flicked my fingers and a glittery breeze engulfed me. It was warm and familiar. A giggle escaped my lips and I flicked my fingers three more times. Glitter spun wildly around me. The temptation to bask in the beautiful peach and rose colored magic was tempting, but I had places to be and Demon ass to kick. I just didn't know which Demon. No time like the present to find out. With one more flick, I transported back to the dining room.

CHAPTER TWENTY-SIX

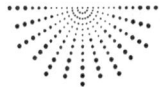

WELCOME TO HELL.

The dining room looked like the aftermath of a hurricane. Everything was still in motion so it was problematic getting my bearings. Violent winds swept the room. Debris and Demons were flying. Muffled screams and grunts assaulted my ears. The dust and glitter made seeing almost impossible, but there was a wall—a clear crystal wall. It stretched from one end of the room to the other and literally oozed magic. Iridescent goop dripped down the smooth facade, slightly blurring what lay beyond. The Guards and guests were on the opposite side from where I stood. Small fires from the candles burned and licked up the curtains and smoldered in the carpets. The Demons clutched at the walls to keep from being blown around and burned to death. The storm was far more violent on their side. The only immortals left standing were Satan, Ethan and Dixie. I tried to communicate with Ethan, but the wall blocked my magic. Whoever erected this sucker had some major mojo going on... The fury on the Devil's face at being helpless was like nothing I'd ever seen—beautiful, raw and horrifying.

What was happening? And why was I on the side where nothing was exploding?

"I should have given you more credit," a disembodied female voice hissed. I shuddered involuntarily at the malice in the voice. "I didn't think you'd make it back for the show."

Wrath? I whirled around and backed away. She was magnificent. Swirling gold and amber tattoos covered her pale skin and morphed from shape to shape. Her blonde hair flew wildly on her head and her gown billowed around her. She embodied her name.

In one hand she held Amanda. The consort was bloody and beaten and trembled with fear. In the other she held the Sword. Fucking awesome.

"You do that, you're gonna die," I said calmly, even though my insides roiled. She was strong and by the looks of it, insane.

"My father will never kill me. And you can't." She laughed manically and eased the Sword closer to Amanda's neck. "Only one prick—one touch of the blade and any immortal dies," she whispered as Amanda whimpered. "Just one and the whore dies."

Get her monologuing... bad guys love to tell you how bad they are. A few minutes—even seconds would give me time to think. Wrath had humongous balls to think she could get away with this. Everybody who was anybody in Hell had front fucking row seats. I refused to turn and look. One, I didn't want to see the worry on Ethan's face and two, I wasn't about to take my eyes off Psycho Cousin. Unsure if she'd actually kill Amanda, I was fully aware I could kill her even if she wasn't. I fingered the stone at my neck, *she was meant to rule...* I didn't want to use it and hoped she wouldn't make me.

"But the baby's not his," I pointed out hoping she'd forgotten that possibility.

"Probably not," she agreed and tightened her grip on Amanda's hair. "This is precautionary. A just in case."

The tattoos shimmered as her crazy increased. The glare off her skin intensified. I squinted and kept my eyes on her face.

"So, how's this gonna work?" I asked.

Wrath rolled her eyes and blew out an exasperated breath. "As attractive as I find you, Astrid, your stupidity is beginning to bore me. I am over a thousand years old, and some little hussy will not blow out a boy and take my birthright. It's quite simple. She dies and her child dies with her. Daddy won't retire for hundreds of years and I'll be forgiven by then. Done. Get it?"

"Why the Sword? Why don't you just kill her with magic or your hands?" Amanda moaned with despair.

"Nice of you to notice. I wanted to show all the Demons in Hell how magnificent I was and thought it would be a fun touch."

Deranged didn't even begin to describe her...

"Demons aren't allowed to kill," I reminded her.

"You bought that bullshit?" She cackled and my anger rose. "Of course we can kill. True Immortals are allowed to kill. Did Daddy leave that out of your lessons? Satan has blood on his hands," she snapped. "Why do you think he's in Hell?"

That was a surprise, but her logic was faulty. "You're not a True Immortal."

"Not yet, but there are three more unknowns and I plan to be one of them."

"I'm pretty sure that's not how it works, cousin, but good luck with that. Now, I'm going to ask nicely, mostly because I like my dress and getting into it with you might fuck it up... drop the Sword and let Amanda go."

"Who do you think you are?" she screamed. "You are nothing. A Vampyre hybrid—a wannabe Demon. I am Wrath and I can destroy you."

"Blah blah blah," I muttered. Her eyes widened in shock and I bit back my inappropriate laughter.

"What did you say?" she ground out between clenched teeth.

"I said blah. Blah. Blah." I smiled and watched her unravel.

"You," she hissed and dropped Amanda to the floor. Turning quickly she shot a spell at her. Amanda froze in a grimace of pain so awful, I felt myself viscerally react. I didn't like her, but she was pregnant and for the most part innocent. Being a bitch was not a crime to die for. This was not gonna happen on my clock. She and her unborn child didn't deserve death at Wrath's hand.

"You are scum," she spat at me. "You come from scum." Her hair whipped with wild abandon around her face and the tattoos raced even faster on her skin. The effect was dizzying. "Your mother was a whore. A greedy whore who traded her soul for power. That certainly ended up working out well for her, didn't it? She's looking a little worse for wear down there in the Basement. I do find it sweet that you still want her love." Her laugh made my teeth grind. My fangs descended and I knew my eyes glowed green with rage.

An acid-like burning started low in my gut and raced through my veins like fire. I sucked in a painful breath and finally accepted the darkness I'd avoided. It was liberating and frightening. I had no time to wonder if I was making a fundamental change in my chemistry. Honestly, it no longer mattered. I was what I was.

I eyed the lunatic Sword brandishing woman in front of me with rage. Wrath had been correct about my mother, but she was also deadly wrong. Yes, my mother's choices had been motivated by greed, but she'd been a mere child when my father got to her. Her free will had been destroyed by methodical abuse over lifetimes.

My body jerked forward as my Vampyre tried to reject what was happening to me, but I pushed her down. My hatred was consuming me and I let it.

"And your father," she hissed. "He was an imbecile. A stupid, stupid nothing. What could we possibly expect from you? You come from shit."

The blood roaring in my ears blocked all sound. Her lips moved, but I no longer had any desire to hear what she said.

It wasn't slow and it wasn't gentle. I called for the darkness and it came. I had control. I briefly closed my eyes and let the magic consume me. It was no longer just gloves. It was me—all of me. My skin was covered in a fine black glitter. I sparkled and vibrated with power from head to toe. Wrath's eyes rounded in fear and she took a step back. She was no longer the big, strong, evil bad guy... I was.

"What are you?" She pointed the Sword at me and took yet another step back.

"I'm the nothing that's going to take your Demon ass out."

Her scream was reminiscent of a battle cry and she came at me with a vengeance. It was too quick to call a spell and my body went into action like it had been trained to do. With Vampyre speed and Demon aggression, I back flipped out of her line of fire. As she turned, I cartwheeled and caught her by the neck in a scissor hold and knocked her to the ground. Her shock at my skill was all the time I needed. Her body hit the floor with a sickening thud and I rolled away as she shot a blast of lava hot voodoo at me.

She was back up and she was pissed, but I was done. Totally done. No more roughhousing. I had a baby to think about. I chanted as her eyes grew wide again. I pointed at her and she roared before my power even touched her. As if in slow motion, I watched a shower of black and crystal white magic flow into her. She dropped the Sword and fell to the ground. Her body convulsed and fluid began to gush from her nose and mouth. She was dying and I watched her dispassionately. I was happy.

Glancing up, I locked eyes with a horrified Amanda and I was jerked back into me. The real me. What the hell was I doing? I pulled back on the magic and Wrath's breathing resumed—erratically, but it resumed. The relief that I hadn't killed her was staggering. Would I have done it if I hadn't made contact with Amanda? Did it matter? I had made contact with Amanda and I stopped. Everything happens for a reason. Amanda was here to stop me and I was here to save her.

"Kill me," Wrath choked out. "Finish it."

"No," I said as I picked up the Sword.

"I will have nothing—no respect. They will laugh at me. I will have nothing." She sobbed at my feet and I gave her a smile that came nowhere near reaching my eyes.

"We can start a club. The Nothing Club. I'll be the president and you can be the treasurer. It will be fun." I raised my hands in the air and knocked down the wall dividing the room. Demons raced forward and threw what I assumed were magic blocking chains and ropes on Wrath. Satan went to Amanda and held her lovingly in his arms. I couldn't make out what he whispered to her, but she gave him a weak smile.

"Cole, take Amanda to my suites and have the women attend to her," he barked.

"Yes, my liege." Cole picked up a damaged but alive Amanda and took her away.

"Wait," she said as they passed me. "I don't know what you are… but thank you."

I nodded and felt strong arms embrace me from behind. "I could kill you," he whispered.

"Yep," I said as I leaned back into him. "I figured. Am I still all black and sparkly?"

"You are."

"Does that bother you?" I asked. My stomach knotted as I waited for his response.

"I actually think it's kind of hot," he whispered in my ear. Little chills ran down my spine and tears of relief pooled in my eyes.

Satan paced the floor in front of the disgraced Wrath and the crowd held its breath. The other Sins stood off to the side and watched with morbid excitement. All of them had enjoyed the show except Dixie. She stood away from them and trembled with fury.

"Things like this make me wish I'd had a vasectomy," Satan bellowed. "This is embarrassing and unacceptable." He turned to me and his gaze narrowed. "Why did you stop? Why didn't you kill her?" he demanded. An anguished cry ripped from Wrath's throat, but I had no sympathy left for her. She already received my mercy and I wasn't about to kowtow to the Devil. I was pissed at all of them.

"She didn't deserve it. She didn't kill anyone. And I'm not the judge of those who should die." I picked up the Sword and handed it to him. "Here's your damn Sword. I want to go home."

He turned so quickly I wasn't sure I was seeing things correctly. He touched the blade to Wrath's skin and slit a small wound. The gasps and cries from the Sins made my blood chill. Why would he do that?

"It's a fake," he said and dropped it to the ground.

It took a minute for me to find my voice. "Did you know that?" I yelled. "Or was that a test?"

He smiled his beautiful smile and shrugged. *Was he for freakin' real?*

"We have a deal. That sword was a fake. You will leave when your job has been completed."

CHAPTER TWENTY-SEVEN

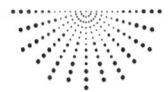

WE WERE STUCK. NO ONE FROM THE DINNER PARTY WAS LEAVING the Dark Palace until after God's visit. Most of the Demons had no clue why we were quarantined, but I knew. The Sword—the stupid Sword of Death. Satan was sure it was in the palace and he was taking no chances. The majority of Demons still believed the Sword to be a myth. As they grumbled and made their way unwillingly to their guestrooms they made that fact abundantly clear.

"I can sense it's here," Satan said as he paced the destroyed dining room and assessed the damage.

"Can you sense that I'm totally over this?" I muttered and pressed my fingers to the bridge of my nose only to realize my sparkly skin had reverted back to normal pale Vampyre chic.

My uncle threw back his head and laughed. "Thank you. I needed that."

"I wasn't exactly joking," I huffed.

He bent down and picked up a shard of glass that was at one point an exquisite crystal vase. He expelled a sigh and shook his head. "I've spoiled them rotten," he mumbled. "It's time for me to retire for the evening. I'm sure you'll find your accommodations satisfactory."

"Why me?"

"Pardon?"

"Why me? Why not have Cole or the Guards find the Sword?"

He played with the fragment of crystal in his hand. It caught the light from a chandelier that had miraculously weathered the storm and cast brilliant dots of color on the wall. "Because you're blood. I don't trust anyone but blood at this point. Besides, most of them don't believe the Sword exists."

"Does it?" I asked.

"Does it what?"

"Does the Sword really exist?"

He took my face in his hands and I leaned in, mesmerized by him. Ethan stiffened beside me but stayed quiet. "Indeed it does and if it's not found… "

"I know," I said.

His hand dropped down to my stomach and he gently placed it on my slightly rounded belly. "If the Sword is not found it will put the life of this child in peril."

"That sounds like a threat," Ethan said softly with an edge that made me uneasy. Neither one of us stood a chance against the Devil—at least I didn't think we did.

"Not a threat. It simply is. The child you carry is special."

"And by that you would mean?" I asked.

"Exactly what I said."

Son of a bitch, my child was special enough with his Vampyre-Demon heritage. He did not need any more special.

His hands left my body and I felt strangely bereft—sad. He was a link to my father no matter how I felt about my parentage. I wanted him to want me like a daughter. Wait. WTF? I wanted the Devil to be my daddy? Heaven and Hell help me… I needed some therapy.

My uncle considered me for a moment and I wondered if he

knew what I'd been thinking. "I find it interesting you didn't kill her when you have the power to do so."

"A killing machine with compassion is always such a big hit at parties," I quipped. I didn't want him to know that I might have destroyed her if it hadn't been for Puffy Lips. I didn't want to deal with that fact about myself yet.

"Ah yes, compassion... that pesky little habit." He smiled and then turned to go.

"Will what she did affect her claim to the throne?" I asked.

He paused and turned back. "No. Her behavior tonight will have no bearing on whether or not she succeeds me."

"Will having a son affect it?"

"Possibly." He nodded. "But probably not. In the end—and mind you, the end is many thousands of years away—it will not be up to me who shall succeed me."

"Who will choose?" He was a ball of cryptic and I expected no answer.

"You, Astrid. You will choose."

With that, he disappeared in a cloud of black glitter and smoke. I fell back into Ethan's arms and sucked in a huge breath.

"I didn't want to know that," I whispered and bent over at the waist so I didn't hyperventilate. "I'm going to stop asking questions."

"Quite honestly," Ethan replied, as shocked as I was. "I think that's a fine idea."

I WAS RIGHT BACK WHERE I STARTED WHEN I ARRIVED IN HELL. THE same room with the same predictably cheesy black silk sheets— only this time I knew exactly where I was, the walls were silent and I was with the man I loved.

"Ethan I... "

"Astrid, stop. The answer is I don't know. The only good thing

247

to come out of that conversation is the very likely fact that you will be around thousands of years from now. Everything else was alarming to put it mildly."

"I don't want that job," I whispered as I tried to pull the thigh high boots off my tired legs.

"Let me help," he said and unzipped my dress.

"What about my boots?" I whined as he slipped my dress over my head and tossed it on the floor.

"You're going to leave those on."

"I am?"

"You are."

Tilting my head to the side and batting my lashes, I feigned a huge yawn. "It will be awfully uncomfortable sleeping in stiletto boots."

"You won't be sleeping," he said and removed his coat and dress shirt. Ignoring me, he stripped off the rest of his clothing. My mouth went dry and my lady parts began to sing. The hard planes and edges of his body made me dizzy. A crooked half grin pulled at his lips. My breath caught in my throat and I grabbed the bedpost for balance. I smiled and began to back away from him. "You're playing a dangerous game, Angel. A game you won't win."

"Who says I want to win?" I continued to move farther away and he continued to stalk me. I was in danger of my knees buckling from sheer excitement and the look in his eyes. His erection lay flat on his stomach and his body was a perfect male sculpture come to life. He was the predator and I was his prey. A shimmer of panic and lust settled in my loins and I wet my lips with my tongue. His eyes darted to the movement and I realized the predator could be distracted...

Putting more distance between us, I ran my hands over my breasts and pinched my achingly hard nipples. My breasts had become tender with pregnancy and even more sensitive to touch. I hissed out a sound of pleasure and watched his eyes dilate and burn a beautiful green. He was no longer playing a game... it had turned serious. I stared at the lines of his sleek naked body and my heart bounced around in my chest. His muscled torso and biceps were the things dreams were made of. Someone as beautiful as he was should not exist.

He'd backed me into a corner, but that was as much my plan as his. I pressed my back to the cool wall and waited. I wanted him to take me and make me forget where I was, what I had to do and who I was supposed to be. I closed my eyes and inhaled his scent.

The feathering of light kisses across my belly startled me. I opened my eyes to find him on his knees worshiping the tiny bulge of my belly. His lips were warm and gentle and my throat constricted with emotion. Neither one of us had truly had time to bask in the miracle we had created. My eyes pooled with tears and I realized I was no less aroused, but I was far more deeply affected than I ever had been.

"Come with me." He took my hand and led me to the bed. I suddenly felt shy. Without a word he slid the boots down my legs and they dropped to the floor by my dress. His lips and teeth tickled my ankles and his hands massaged each part of my body till we were face to face. With his tongue, he teased the seam of my lips and I opened to him willingly. His taste was addictive and his large body covering mine made me feel safe.

He ran his open mouth along my jaw to my ear and I gasped in delight as his fang pierced the lobe. "You are my miracle," he whispered. "I have waited my entire lifetime for you."

His voice rumbled in my mind, sending little shockwaves of the purest pleasure I'd known. Wrapping my arms around him, I held tight to his body. The pressure in my chest verged on pain and I buried my face in his neck.

"What's wrong, my love?" he asked as he took my face in his hands and searched my eyes.

The simplicity of the moment was harder to deal with than if we'd been wildly out of control and all over each other. I had never been loved like this—so completely. Never been loved by someone who knew my weaknesses and didn't care. Someone whose strength matched my own and someone whose wisdom should have found me lacking, but didn't.

I traced his lips, nose and high sculpted cheekbones with my finger and I was free. I didn't need the love of a mother or a father. The love of a child would only be an added bonus to the overwhelming feelings I had for the man who lay atop me.

He shifted his weight to his elbows, but still covered me like a blanket. With his lips, he followed my tears from my eyes to my jawbone to my neck. My insides weren't big enough to contain everything I was feeling and I thought I might explode.

"Ethan, I... " Words were inadequate. I wrapped my legs around his waist and arched to meet him. I needed to show him with my body things that words simply couldn't convey.

As his body joined with mine, I gasped and cried out. The slow pace was more erotic and frightening than the wild coupling we were more accustomed to. Our eyes locked and our bodies moved in a rhythm that was age old but perfectly new. My body contracted and tightened around his. We merged and became one sexual and spiritual entity. Two bodies—one heart.

"I can't get close enough," I murmured as the pace of our lovemaking increased. The intensity burned and my legs clamped tighter around him as my fingers tangled in his hair.

"Don't close your eyes," he whispered. "Watch what you do to me. Watch what I feel for you."

My tears made him blurry, but the magnitude of what he felt could be seen without vision. It was in his magic, in the strength of his possession—in his essence.

We surged closer to crawling inside of each other than we ever had. He put his weight on one hand and skimmed my face, my breasts and hip with his other. He slid in and out and I raised my hips to meet his thrusts as the pressure built. His mouth came down on mine, hard and possessive. I bit at his lips as his body grew larger within me. The slow gentle lovemaking was over, but the ferociousness of our love and desire remained.

His inhuman beauty and strength sent my core into liquid meltdown and I writhed beneath him, unable to think or hold any part of myself back. His eyes never left mine and I struggled to keep mine open. The vulnerability was terrifying and raw. My insides danced and contracted around his girth and the sounds he made went straight to my most engorged and sensitive spots, unleashing a wild woman inside me that I gave to him freely— willingly and with every inch of my being.

I screamed as the orgasm hit. My eyes stayed open and I watched the explosion of pleasure rip across his beautiful features. With his fangs bared and his eyes hooded he came as hard as I did. I was more frightened and more satisfied than I'd even known I could be. The aftershocks of my climax continued to wrack my body as his mouth descended to my neck. My exhausted body reawoke as his fangs grazed the soft skin. The aftershocks turned into the feeling of a massive orgasm about to burst.

"I'm not sure I can… "

"You can," he muttered into my neck gruffly. "You will. I will take you there."

He grew rigid inside me and all of my nerve endings jumped to attention with need. My fangs dropped and we bit each other at the same time. I was sure this would end me. The sheer passion that tore through me was more extreme and acute than I'd experienced. Colors ripped across my vision and I cried out against his neck. The frenzied exchange of blood, lust and pure love sent me to heights that would have destroyed a mortal.

As I floated down I heard his chuckle of pure masculine satisfaction and it made me smile.

I was so fucking glad I was already dead… because that would have killed me for sure.

CHAPTER TWENTY-EIGHT

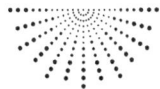

HOLY SHIT, CARL HAD THE HAIRIEST BACK I'D EVER SEEN.

"It looks like a fur rug," I whispered to Ethan.

"I'd have to agree," he muttered as he led us to seats beside the mats.

The fight exhibition was in full swing before we'd arrived. Our tardiness was due to a quickie meeting with the General who promised to get my Baby Demons and bring them back to the palace. I was concerned about them... actually that was inaccurate. I was more concerned for the Demons they might come across. I had no desire to be prosecuted because they munched on the wrong person.

The fight training room was impressive, although seriously over the top. I should have expected no less, but the gross show of wealth constantly surprised me. Padded bleachers with backrests lined both sides of the huge room. Padding was an understatement—the seats were covered in buttery-soft caramel leather. And from the thirty foot ceiling hung four exquisite crystal drop chandeliers.

Satan had yet to arrive, but the demonstrations had already begun. Carl's preparation for the next fight was doing his left and right leg splits… Janet and Myrtle stood by him and growled at anyone who dared to poke fun at Carl's unusual warm up. He wore a tight, fitted yellow wrestling suit that should have been burned in the eighties and, of course, the hair blanket on his back.

I poked Ethan. "I've never seen anything like that."

"He seems to be fine with himself," Ethan observed. "If he's smart he'll use it to his advantage."

"How in the world can a hairy back be an advantage?" I asked as I wracked my brain.

"Well, he could wear a cape and then reveal it at the last second, alarming his opponent and getting the upper hand. Or he could slick it back with a conditioner or gel so it would be impossible to take him from behind due to the slippage factor."

"That's either brilliant or just really weird," I muttered, trying to figure out if he was screwing with me. I looked around the room and got a wonky feeling. "Ethan… um, I think we were set up."

"I quite agree."

Everyone in the room was dressed casually, but not us. We were dressed in the workout clothing that had been delivered to our suite by a very timid Demon named Norm. Did my uncle expect us to fight? He was in for a surprise. I had no desire to fight unless it was life or death. Fighting for fun was not on my agenda today.

"Do you feel something odd?" I couldn't put my finger on it, but something was off.

"A dampening spell," he replied as he scanned the crowd. "Satan meant business when he said this would be hand to hand. The dampening spell prohibits magic."

"Oookay, that could be a clusterfuck if something hellish goes down."

"True. The Guards are the only others dressed as we are." He nodded in the direction of a group conversing quietly. Cole, standing in the middle, sported the same type of garb that we did —loose fitting black pants and tight black t-shirt.

"The Devil is always up to no good," I said. Ethan just grinned and shrugged.

"All rise for Satan," someone in the crowd yelled as Lucifer made his usual movie star worthy entrance.

"Good afternoon, my people!" He was dressed similarly to us and my stomach fell to my toes. Did he plan to fight today? Shitballs. "I see we've started, but I do believe I'm just in time for Carl and Moby."

The crowd went wild and Satan took his seat next to Amanda. The Sins, along with Dixie and Dante, were right behind him but Lust and Wrath were missing.

"What do you suppose he did with Wrath?" I asked Ethan.

"She's in Purgatory," a large male Demon behind me whispered with delight. "She'll be there for years." His grin made my skin crawl a little, but I was glad to hear she wouldn't be showing up any time soon. I nodded and gave him a polite smile. Everyone took way too much interest in others' pain and suffering here, but what did I expect? It was how they thrived.

The crowd was larger than the dinner party last night and I wondered if Satan had added more suspects or if these Demons might be staff. I shook my head and worried about how this would all play out.

"Begin," the Devil bellowed.

Carl, of the hairiest back I'd ever seen, and Moby, a sullen looking Demon, took the mat as Journey's *Wheel in the Sky* blasted from speakers around the room. I suppose it was in preparation for tonight's concert... The fighters bowed to Satan and proceeded to beat the living shit out of each other. What they lacked in finesse, they made up for in grunts and sweat.

"What the hell?" I mumbled, watching a bloody comedy of errors unfold before my eyes.

The mild mannered Carl I knew had disappeared and an out

of control violent wooly monster had taken his place. Moby didn't stand a chance. Janet and Myrtle jumped and cheered on the sidelines as Carl literally wiped the floor with Moby. Literally. The crowd roared their approval. I felt a little sick, but I was happy Moby wasn't wiping the floor with Carl.

A bell chimed and the fight stopped. Carl stood victorious in the center of the mat. He slowly slid into the splits with his arms raised above his head. Rolling out of the splits he hopped up, ran to the barely conscious Moby and picked him up. Cradling him in his arms, he hugged and kissed him, then encouraged the crowd to clap for the loser too. The Demons managed a light smattering of applause for the bloody Moby.

The next several exhibition fights were far more polished and beautiful. No less blood, but far more finesse. The partners were more fairly matched too. They fought with many of the same techniques we used and I got lost in the beauty of the movement. The lack of magic in the room let me relax and take in the show without worrying if a mystical tsunami was going to blow up out of nowhere. Amanda looked fine... *alright, she looked slutty*, but she didn't look like she been beaten and almost killed less than ten hours ago. Demons clearly healed as quickly as Vampyres. The music stopped abruptly, right in the middle of *Faithfully*.

"And now for the challenges," Satan shouted to the delight of the crowd. "Do we have a challenge?"

The denizens of Hell murmured with excitement and Cole stepped forward. A hush went through the crowd and I watched many Demons slink low in their seats so as not to be noticed by the Devil's second in command.

"My finest warrior has stepped up to the mat." Satan was positively orgasmic. This was not good. Was Cole going to kill someone? "Who do you challenge?"

Cole glanced casually around the room until his narrowed gaze landed on Ethan. Ethan grinned at him and winked. Oh my hell, I wasn't sure whether to laugh or groan.

"I challenge the *Vampyre*," he said smugly. The crowd gasped and the large Demon behind us patted my mate on the back.

"It was good knowing you," he sniffed sadly. *Was he crying?*

"Actually," Ethan said, still grinning from ear to ear. "You don't know me at all."

I shuddered. To anyone watching it would have appeared I was nervous for my man. They couldn't have been more mistaken.

Ethan stood and removed his shirt. I rolled my eyes at the gasps of appreciation for his ripped body. He was mine and I gave the stink eye to two buxom female Demons who were drooling. His ego was enormous and I suppressed a giggle. He sauntered slowly to the mat. The tension in the room was palpable.

Cole removed his shirt and I had to admit the sexy in the room had elevated greatly. Satan slashed his hand in the air and Steven Perry started belting out *Who's Crying Now*.

"Oh my, Astrid." Dixie slid into Ethan's seat and gripped my arm in distress. "Are you okay?"

"Why wouldn't I be okay?"

"The last four Demons Cole fought with are damaged," she whispered. "Permanently."

"Did he cheat?"

"He doesn't have to. He's a weapon even without his magic."

I rolled my neck, pulled my legs up to my seat and sat crisscross applesauce. Dixie gaped at me with concern.

"Astrid, this won't end well." She was a wreck and I felt bad for her.

"You're right Dixie," I told her. "It won't end well. Watch."

The sex gods bowed to Satan and began slowly circling each other. Ethan's perfect body was completely relaxed and excitement coiled in my stomach. Everyone, including the Devil sat forward in their seats.

Ethan refused to make the first move and waited patiently for Cole. Cole was stupidly cocky. He took Ethan's inaction as fear. Mistake number one... He smirked at the *Vampyre* and made his move. It was the most violent balletic battle I'd seen. They were well matched and utterly focused. A bomb could have detonated and they wouldn't have taken their eyes from one another. It was a mixture of martial arts and pure brute strength. Ethan was the deadliest fighter I'd ever seen and I hoped he didn't accidently kill Cole.

They parried, each getting kicks and punches in. Ethan deflected most of what Cole dealt out, but it was inevitable that he would come out scathed. My beautiful man was getting bored. Cole's moves, while powerful and potentially deadly, were predictable.

"You have nothing more than that?" Ethan asked in a disinterested voice. Cole sucked in a furious breath and attacked.

Ethan ducked to his left and Cole went tripping forward. His roar of fury made the hair on my neck stand up. Dixie's grip on my arm was going to leave a mark, but I didn't have the heart to peel her off. She was a mess.

Ethan was over it. As Cole charged, Ethan gave him an upper cut that sent him reeling backwards. He then aerial cartwheeled forward and scissor kicked his neck, dropping him to the floor. Cole jumped up and did a back tuck, aiming to land a foot on Ethan's spine to break it, but my lover was too fast. The crowd cheered and hissed. Cole came down so hard and fast on the mat that his foot, meant to maim, twisted beneath him. He grunted in pain and slashed out with his fist catching Ethan near his eye. It swelled shut almost immediately, but Ethan's reply was devastating. With right-left upper cuts, I heard Cole's jaw shatter and his nose crunch. The blood spatter would have been comical if it hadn't been real. The Demons gasped and chattered with glee.

Bleeding and broken, Cole refused to give up. Ethan had taken his fair share of brutality, but he was nowhere near the broken man that his opponent was. Cole came at Ethan like an out of control train. His wreck was imminent and I clutched Dixie in fear for Cole.

"Don't kill him," I told Ethan.

"Don't worry. He's a Demon. He'll heal."

"Of course he'll heal," I snapped. *"Unless you kill him."*

"Fine," he huffed. *"Shall I knock him out and end it?"*

"Yes, but DO NOT use the death touch. I know it doesn't work on Vamps, but it might kill a Demon."

"Good point. This is why I love you."

"Not for my boobs?"

He laughed aloud at my last transmitted message and I was sure everyone in the room thought he was insane. He wasted no time and Cole probably never knew what hit him. With Vampyre speed and the precision of a surgeon, my mate destroyed the finest Demon warrior in Hell. I idly thought these Demons needed some lessons, but I realized in battle they most likely used their magic. Ethan doled out punch after punch and kick after kick until Cole went down. The blood pooled around Cole's body, but Ethan had quite a bit of his own to wipe away as well.

The bell rang and the room went silent.

Oh shit. Were we about to get attacked by every Demon in the room? I rushed to Ethan's side and the noise started. Whistles and shouts bounced off the walls of the training room. The screaming and cheering made me want to cover my ears. Ethan nodded once to Satan, took my hand and walked back to our seats. He pulled his shirt back on, much to the sadness of the women in the room and took a seat. My instinct was to attend to his wounds, but I did nothing. Showing weakness was not an option. I'd fuss over him like a mother hen once we were alone.

"Impressive," Satan said as the crowd quieted. Several guards tended to Cole and took him from the room. "I was going to offer to fight the winner... "

"It would be my pleasure," Ethan said flatly, not fucking around or playing games. "We can go right now."

The Devil's eyes widened for a brief second—so quickly, I

wasn't sure I saw it. He was scared. Oh my God… Satan was scared.

His gaze narrowed and he stepped forward menacingly. His words were for Ethan only, but I was a Vampyre and heard everything. "You may be able to take me with your fists, but I could destroy you with a finger," he whispered.

"I'll keep that in mind," Ethan replied cheekily.

"Do that." Satan turned to his minions with a beautiful smile on his face. "Please make yourselves comfortable. Refreshments are being served in the dining room and the concert will begin in an hour." He gathered a pale Amanda to his side and left the room.

"Bedroom?" I asked my bruised and bloody mate.

"Yes," he replied.

As we made our way out we were given a very wide berth. Demons whispered and pointed. Several bared their teeth. Awesome. We had clearly become the new Power Couple in Hell. Unsure if that was good or bad, we held our heads high and walked out.

"I think everyone wants a piece of us," I muttered as I avoided the wet blood on the floor.

"Yes, I believe you're correct. Just smile."

"Will do." I smiled and nodded as we made our way through the throngs of Demons. The rest of the day would be tricky, but then again… what the hell in Hell hadn't been?

CHAPTER TWENTY-NINE

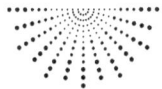

BUSINESS IN THE FRONT AND PARTY IN THE BACK.

"What did you say?" Ethan asked as we entered the ballroom. It had been converted to a concert venue for the evening.

We had rested and changed after the fight exhibition. General George had returned with my Baby Demons and they loved and kissed on Ethan until he insisted we lock them in the bathroom. They were unhappy, but found the tub to be an excellent pool. I left them splashing, screaming with joy and diving off the showerhead. I'd fussed over my Vampyre and made him drink a good amount of my blood. The only remnant of the battle was a slight purple bruise along his cheekbone. Vamps had amazing healing power.

"I didn't say anything. Wait, were you in my head?"

"Maybe," he answered cagily.

"Get out of my head," I snapped.

"Astrid." He stopped me on the side of the room, out of Demon earshot. "When you let me into your thoughts yesterday, something happened. I've been able to see inside you ever since. Completely inside."

My first reaction was anger, but I had let him in. Would I have done that if I knew he'd always have access, even without permission? In a moment of ridiculously mature adult clarity, I realized I would. My fear of rejection didn't exist with him and I wanted him to see me.

"This could be an issue on birthdays and Christmas." I grinned and he relaxed.

"I promise to stay out during the holidays."

I nodded and pressed a quick kiss to his lips. He looked mouthwatering in his black jeans and icy blue long sleeve t-shirt. I loved the casual dress code in Hell. It was in direct opposition to the décor, but I wasn't going to complain. I was deliriously happy in jeans, Doc Martens and a black fitted tee that hugged my body in all the right places.

"So business in the front and party in the back?" Ethan arched a brow for explanation.

"The mullets." I pointed to the cover band setting up on the stage and bit back my laughter. "Do you see how their hair is short in the front and long in the back?"

He nodded and winced.

"That's a mullet. Actually, those are some of the most spectacular mullets I've ever seen."

They were works of redneck art. One of the band members literally had a blond crew cut in the front and stringy long black locks down to his ample bottom in the back. Another had a short spiky red style going in the front and permed purple curls flowing half way down his back. The boys were also tatted and pierced within an inch of their lives.

"Words escape me," Ethan muttered and shook his head.

"Would you get a mullet if it turned me on?" I teased.

"No, I would not." He grinned and copped a feel of my ass as we seated ourselves along the outside wall. We wanted to be able to scan the room and watch for unusual activity. Sword stealers seemed to like an audience and this was a big event.

"The crowds have gotten bigger," I said as I searched for trouble. There had to be several hundred Demons here.

"Yep," Ethan agreed. "What game is he playing?"

I wondered the same thing myself. "Do you think it's a metaphor?"

"Come again?" he asked me, although his eyes were still on the crowd.

"The Sword. Is there an actual Sword or does it mean something else entirely?"

Ethan was quiet for a moment. "If it's a metaphor I will kick his ass."

"You won't have to—that ass will be mine."

As the room continued to fill with beautiful people I was relieved to notice that the dampening spell had been removed. My magic was alive and tingled with the need to come out. Satan arrived with his entourage. He was dressed in jeans and a Journey concert tee. I slapped my hand over my mouth and swallowed a laugh. No one was going to believe this. No one.

Amanda and the Sins, with the tagalong Dante, made their way to the front. I was surprised to see Cole. He hadn't healed nearly as well as Ethan, but he was able to walk and function. He shot a glance of pure hatred our way and Ethan waved.

"Are you trying to turn the concert into a brawl?" I asked as I elbowed him in the ribs.

"Just being neighborly."

That reminded me that Mister Rogers and Hemingway would be back for lunch with God tomorrow. Was it possible that one of them had taken the Sword? My brain hurt with all the possibilities.

"Let the concert begin," Satan bellowed joyously and held a lighter over his head. The crowd pulled out their lighters and fired up. Crazy. This was crazy.

The band was actually great. Blondie in the front with the black stringy locks in the back and the big booty was the lead singer. While no Steven Perry, he was really close. If I closed my eyes and blocked out the heinous hair, it was truly enjoyable.

"Movement," Ethan said. My eyes shot open and I stood.

Cole was moving toward an exit on the left side of the room. Greed and Dante were heading to exit the way they had entered. Shit, were they running off for more kinky icky? Their vibe was different and I didn't like it.

"I'll take Cole. You take Greed and the ass," he said, already moving.

"Yep." I slipped out behind them and quickly cloaked myself so I could stay close. They were headed to the library. I'd passed it several times, but had never been in.

"*Cole was a dead end,*" Ethan's voice rang in my head. "*I'm back in the Ballroom.*"

"*Roger that,*" I said and giggled. If I was going to play a cop, I was going to use the lingo. I could feel Ethan's eye roll. "*Over and out.*"

Greed and Dante were making out in the stacks. I was grossed out and out of here. I moved away slowly running my fingers along the spines of the books. The library was as massive as the rest of the Palace, but I felt more comfortable here. The magic was different, more creative, sillier, deadlier... Deadlier? WTF?

Still cloaked, I hightailed it back to Greed and Dante. Greed lay in a heap on the floor and Dante was nowhere to be found. I let my cloaking fall away and squatted by my cousin. She had a pulse, but there was a nasty gash on the back of her head and she was out like a light.

"Greed?" I shook her and her eyes opened slightly. She moaned and huge tears fell from her gorgeous eyes.

"I fucked... ," she whispered.

"I don't want to hear about your sex life," I said, searching her body for other wounds.

"No," she choked out. "I fucked up. He has the Sword."

Dante of big nose and dick had the Sword? "How?" I ground out. I was pissed and waited impatiently for her reply.

"He didn't believe it was real," she panted and winced in pain as she tried to sit up. Why wasn't she healing? "He told me to prove it and he would be mine."

It was still a mystery why she wanted him, but there was no time to go into that right now.

"What is he going to do with it?" He was a human. An angry dead human with no magic... how bad could this be?

"I don't know," she gasped as her bleeding increased.

"What the hell is happening here?" I asked her as I pulled my T-shirt over my head and put pressure on her gushing head wound. Thank God I'd worn a bra...

"I gave him my power." She cried even harder.

"What the fuck did you just say?" I yelled. So much for it not being bad.

"It's only for a half an hour. He promised to use it to make me come so hard I saw stars," she blubbered.

Greedy, stupid and sex starved was a bad combination. "Let me get this straight. You gave him your power to borrow, so you could have the mother of all orgasms... you showed him the Sword, he took it, beat you and left with it. He basically has the instrument to kill and the power to do it because you wanted to get off. Correct?"

"Yes," she wailed and threw herself back to the floor. "I am so fucking stupid."

I couldn't disagree, but I needed to stop her bleeding. I was unsure if I had healing magic, but was worth a try. She was in for a world of hurt with her father if we all made it through this. I closed my eyes and wished her healthy and whole. I felt the magic leave my fingertips and wrap her in a warm glow. The bleeding stopped, but her strength remained weak. I supposed that would come back when her power returned to her... in a fucking half hour. Shit, an angry dead guy could do a lot in a half hour.

"Where did you find the Sword?" I demanded.

"Den of Iniquity," she answered unsteadily.

Shitshitshit. It *was* the Sword...

"I'm leaving you here. You'll be okay."

"Thank you, Astrid. Can I ask one more thing of you?"

"Go ahead." She personified her name.

"Would you please kill him? I've had quite enough and if I can't have him, no one else can either."

I laughed. Hard. "You are all insane," I muttered as I raced out of the library. "Completely insane."

CHAOS ENSUED.

The ballroom was a shit show of enormous proportions. Someone using magic who had no clue how to control it was dangerous. Add the Sword to the combination and it was horrifying.

Demons were dying left and right—exploding and turning to dust. Terrorized screams and frantic running made seeing where the danger was difficult. I pushed through the throngs and saw Dante on the stage. He was wailing in fear and moving his arms wildly. He held the Sword and paced erratically. OMG, he had caused this and couldn't stop it. He shrieked at the Sword and covered his eyes with his hands to avoid the massacre his avarice and stupidity had spawned.

The Guards had surrounded Satan in a protective wall, but even they were exploding and turning to ash. Satan's lips moved and I knew he was chanting a spell, but time was of the essence. I spotted Ethan and Cole. They were removing Demons and tossing them to the exits. Their animosity forgotten, they worked together like a well-oiled machine. My relief that he was okay was profound, but I had a Sword to retrieve and a psycho to stop.

Too many Demons blocked my path. I hadn't wanted to show

all my party tricks to the population of Hell, but emergency bred necessity. I jumped and flew to the stage, landing and tackling Dante to the ground. I grabbed him by the neck and squeezed.

"End this bloodbath. Now," I said and squeezed tighter.

"I don't know how," he gasped and dropped the Sword to the ground. "I don't know how."

His wail of grief went right to my toes. If I destroyed him would the magic die with him? I had no freakin' clue. It would have been lovely to get to ask someone, but everyone was busy at the moment. Could I override his magic? I was unsure how much longer he even possessed it, but at the rate Demons were dying, even a minute was too long.

"What exactly did you plan to do up here?" I shouted in his face. Maybe if I knew his plan I could untangle it and stop the death.

"I wanted to humiliate him," he gasped. "Like he humiliated me." His voice grew stronger as his delusions of grandeur and ego took over. "I am the greatest writer of all time and he has made me look like a fool," he hissed. His eyes were wild and he truly was nuts. "I wanted to show him I could steal his precious Sword and kill him any time I liked." His eyes glazed over and he laughed.

"You were going to kill him?" I shook him back to the present.

"No. Never," he told me. "I just wanted to show his people how weak and laughable he was."

"You showed them alright," I screamed at him. "Look at what you've done."

His shrieking was pathetic as he watched the death and destruction of innocent people before him. I looked up and to my horror and darkest nightmares, I saw a family of Demons with small children and a baby detonate and blow up in front of me. Time stood still for the briefest of moments and the world tilted on its axis. A red-hot rage blasted from my soul and my skin turned sparkly black. Dante's eyes widened in fear and he tried to escape. He keened and groaned like an animal and grabbed for the sword to kill himself with the Sword. He sliced his skin several times and nothing happened. WTF? Another fake. All of this and the damn thing was counterfeit? The bastard was already dead, but right now I wanted him deader.

I put my hands on Dante and let the chant find me. *Sacrifice the one who sins for the lives of the innocent.* Would his death bring those children back? Probably not, but there were hundreds of others in the room who could perish in the twenty minutes or so he still had Greed's power in him.

I pulled from inside and I let my darkest of magic come to the surface. A sharp pain erupted inside my head and I dropped to my knees. A cage made of shimmering black and crystal white blades trapped the traitor and contained his stolen magic. The death and destruction around me stopped. The howling and weeping did not, but that would go on for eternity. Dante writhed in agony inside the cage and I watched him dispassionately as my pain disappeared and I slowly got back to my feet. I didn't care and that made me worry. I knew if I simply flicked my fingers he would be gone forever. I was unsure if I should actually show him that much mercy. Did he not deserve to burn in the Basement? Was I his judge? Did I want to be?

"Will you kill him?" Satan whispered in my ear and I jumped. Ethan had appeared on my other side and I breathed a sigh of relief.

"Did he lead a good life?" I asked as I watched him convulse.

"He did indeed," Satan said. "As you know, he's a card carrying member of my brother's house."

Right then I knew what I would do. He was stupid and driven by ego. His mistake came with a hefty cost, but the area was so very gray. I hated this and I wanted no part, but I was going to end him. Not for Greed, not for Satan and not for myself. He had committed unintentional manslaughter. He had not come in here to kill. He was distraught with what his greed had wrought.

Should he spend an eternity in the Basement for deaths he did not maliciously cause?

"You'll send him to the Basement?" I asked.

"Without a doubt."

I flicked my fingers and Dante turned to ash like all those he had killed today. He was no more. Should I have ended his suffering? I thought so today. Hopefully I'd feel the same tomorrow. To separate the man from the destruction he'd caused today and base his judgment on the body of the whole was harder than anything I'd had to do yet. But I did it. I bent down and picked up the sword. I held it out to my uncle and he glanced at me with questioning eyes.

"It's a fake."

"Really?"

"Trust me."

"And he got this and the deadly magic how?" he demanded.

"Ask your daughter, Greed." I threw her under the bus where she belonged. I was done here and I wanted my bed. I was wearing my bra and I was a fucking mess. I honestly was beginning to question the existence of the Sword. I wanted to meet God and I wanted to go home. Satan could find his own damn Sword. I was done.

CHAPTER THIRTY

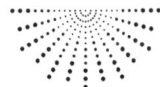

GOD WAS SO BEAUTIFUL IT WAS ALMOST IMPOSSIBLE TO LOOK
at him.

After a sleepless night, we'd dressed formally and made our
way back to the miraculously repaired dining room for lunch
with God. The General had spent a good portion of the morning
with us and the Baby Demons. I'd found out a number of
alarming things… he had taken my Babies to a strip club and they
been thrown out for lewd behavior. What that constituted in Hell
was mindboggling so I decided to push that one aside for another
time. However, the real kicker was when I learned that the
gestation for a Demon was two years. I offered to pay for the hole
in the plaster, but the General insisted he could have it fixed at no
charge.

Ethan paled at the thought of me being pregnant for years and
I nailed him with a vase. Luckily he ducked and I simply added it
to the growing list of things I'd destroyed in Hell. The only
consolation I had was that my baby was half Vampyre and since
he was the first of his kind, maybe the gestation time would be
shorter. I refused to even contemplate that it could be any longer.

There weren't enough items in Heaven and Hell put together for me to break if I really let my mind sit with that little nugget.

After calming down and locking the little monsters in the bathroom with a firm promise from them that they would stay, we went to the luncheon.

The dining room was laid out with the finest china and crystal I'd ever seen. An army of servants wearing all black hustled around and saw to the needs of the guests. This event was the first of its kind and clearly the Devil took it very seriously.

"This is one out of fucking control shindig," Myrtle said as she offered me a puffy looking pastry. Her grin was contagious and I wanted to hug her. Her total lack of manners and couth made me happy.

"You are correct." I smiled and took a pastry to be polite. "Are you, Carl and Janet working?" I sniffed the pastry and was delighted to find out I didn't want it.

"We're in charge," she said proudly. "Moby used to be, but Carl kicked his mean old Demon ass yesterday and now we're running the show."

"Wow," I said, unsure if that was the best way to maintain job security. "Congrats."

"Yeah, well, I have to go pass this shit around to assholes. Have fun," she chirped as she walked off.

Dixie approached and I was struck again by her beauty. "You good?" she asked as she gave me a hug.

"I'm good."

"Have you walked the room?" she asked and immediately began to pick at her polish.

"No. Should I?" I inquired and pressed the bridge of my nose. There was never a freakin' dull moment around here. Ethan was deep in conversation with my grandpa. When did he get back? I looked around for Gigi, but she was nowhere to be found.

"Well, um… " Dixie struggled for words.

"Tell me. I'm not in the mood for surprises at this particular time."

"It's better to show you," she said, took my hand and led me to the far side of the room. I was imagining all kinds of horrors, but I hadn't been prepared for what I saw.

A large cage made of some kind of glistening material sat on a platform made of gold. Demons milled around it, pointing and taking pictures. A strong dampening spell surrounded the cage and covered it completely. Thin razor sharp blades protruded from the bars insuring that no one stuck a hand or object in and no one stuck a hand or object out. It was positively brilliant in its structure and absolutely barbaric in its reasoning.

Inside the cage, seated on hard wooden chairs were three women I had hoped never to see again... Lust, Wrath and Greed.

They were dressed in formal gowns—they were sullen and humiliated. Refusing to make eye contact with anyone they stared straight ahead and said nothing. Satan was a sick cookie. This was one hell of a punishment. I wondered if he would let them eat.

"Why?" I asked Dixie.

"He wants his brother to see all of his children since God only has one."

"I'm kind of surprised he wants to show them off caged like animals. Doesn't say much for his parenting skills."

I walked to the edge of the cage and stared, knowing full well they could do nothing to me and I could destroy them. Lust stared back with hatred in her eyes and Wrath blew me an inappropriate kiss.

"Thank you for killing the bastard," Greed said. She looked better than she had yesterday, but I was not going to be fond of her anytime soon.

"I didn't do it for you," I said harshly. She was sorely mistaken if she thought I would take a life on a whim. My tone shocked her and she looked away.

Wrath considered me carefully and tilted her head. "You are more than what you seem," she said.

"Isn't everyone?" I shot back. "You all certainly are."

The silence was long and I wanted to walk away, but I refused to run.

"Come with me, Astrid. My father and Uncle God will be here soon. I just didn't want you to be taken by surprise."

With one last glance at the pathetic evil in the cage, I walked away with Dixie. I felt very little for the women—my cousins. I wondered if they lived in the same cage in Purgatory, but decided they didn't deserve any more thought.

The Sword was still missing, God was coming for lunch and it was the lunar eclipse. Hell was ripe for a showdown.

"All rise for Satan and God," a Guard yelled at the massive arched entrance to the dining room.

A hush fell over the crowd as a small army of Angels preceded the arrival of the big guys. Dressed in diaphanous white they seemed to float on air. They reminded me of my Angel, Pam—blindingly beautiful. They had peaceful smiles on their faces and they smelled like the wind on a rainy summer day. My body leaned forward in hopes of being noticed.

"Don't," Ethan whispered. "They're as crazy as the Demons, just in a different way."

"How do you know?" I asked, finding that hard to believe.

"A little first hand experience and the word from your grandfather."

I was instantly curious about his first hand experience and hoped it wasn't the same kind of experience he'd had with Lust. I tamped down my jealousy and simply gave him a look.

"No, it's not what you think," he said and put his arm around me. The heat of his body was comforting and I leaned in.

"Will we actually make it out of here alive?" I asked.

"Yes. We will," he answered. "Tonight if I have anything to do with it."

As much as I wanted to believe, I wasn't so sure. A promise was a promise. It didn't matter that the Devil didn't keep his. I was my own person and my word was good. I would find the Sword and I would leave.

"I'm glad you're wearing the necklace," he whispered in my ear. "You will use it if you need it. Promise?"

"I promise."

Again. God was so beautiful it was almost impossible to look at him.

God and Satan entered the room together and gasps went through the crowd. Angels and Demons alike were stunned to silence by the sheer power and beauty that stood before them. God was light to Satan's dark, but the similarities were uncanny. The mouths and noses and high cheekbones were almost identical. I was surprised his eyes were the same golden as his brother's. I suppose I thought they would be blue. His hair was blond and he wasn't bearded and robed as I'd imagined as a child. Nope, he was built like a brick shithouse, same as Satan. His appeal was far less overtly sexual than his brother's, but he was no less mesmerizing.

Several women passed out and I noticed they were of both Angel and Demon descent. The other Sins and Amanda stood off to Satan's side and several female Angels stood off of God's shoulder. I was hoping Cousin Jesus would come, but that would have to wait for another time.

Mister Rogers and Hemingway went to my uncles and paid their respects, then a line formed. God laughed at something Mister Rogers said and it rang like a symphony and bounced off the walls of the room. Satan rolled his eyes at the rabid hysteria his brother was causing, but did his very best to contain himself. Everyone wanted to meet God and everyone wanted a picture.

"Holy shit, did you see that?" Ethan chuckled and pointed to Satan making finger horns behind God's head in a series of photos. I burst out laughing and buried my face in Ethan's chest.

"Where did Grandpa go?" I asked as I watched Satan pinch his nose and act as if God smelled bad in a new round of pictures.

"He said he'd be back soon. He apparently forgot something."

"Should we get in line?" I asked.

"I don't think we have to."

"Why? We can't cut because that would be rude."

"We don't have to because they are coming to us."

"What? Oh, shit."

He was correct. They were headed straight for us and my knees were in danger of buckling. They made a brief pit stop at Dixie. God studied her for several minutes and then took her in his arms and gently hugged her. He seemed sad. It was odd and made me uncomfortable... like I was intruding on something I wasn't supposed to see. She blushed and hugged him back. Satan seemed bizarrely satisfied with this action. It appeared to mean more than just a simple hug to him. I tucked that away for future reference, but I was sure he would deflect.

My uncles approached me with a look of determination on their faces. God's gaze was gentle and filled with curiosity and Satan's was excited. A marching band quickly formed in my stomach and began practice for the first time. They were off key and they had no rhythm whatsoever.

God took my hand in his and led me to a platform on the middle of the room. How had I not noticed this? The three of us walked up seven steps and stood on top.

"Astrid, it is lovely to finally meet you," he said in a voice that filled every part of me with warmth and light. "I have heard so much about you from your Guardian Angel Pam and your nana."

My lips trembled and my smile was shaky. I had never been in a presence like his. I wanted to curl up at his feet and simply listen to him breathe. "You look different than I expected," I said and then immediately backtracked. "I mean you look great—better than great. I bet you have to beat the Angel ladies off and... Oh my God..." I slapped my hand over my mouth and wanted to die. I just implied God was a player and then took his name in vain while I was talking to him. Shitshitshit.

His laugh and the way his eyes crinkled with amusement calmed me a bit, but not much. I decided to keep my trap shut. I had no idea what might come out and I did not want to give God a reason to smite me.

Everyone in the room was watching with interest. The large doors to the hallway reopened and masses of Angels and Demons piled in. What was happening? I searched for Ethan, but he'd been swallowed up in the crowd.

"Ethan, where are you?" I asked frantically.

"I'm here, but your grandfather is being mauled by your cousins, I'm trying to get him to safety. I'll be right back."

"Okay," I said. *"But hurry... it's getting weird in here."*

"Tell me about it. I think they might have broken his ribs."

Holy Hell, Grandpa's cuteness was going to get him killed one of these days.

"Attention everyone," Satan bellowed. The room of over five hundred quieted. "You have been called here from both Heaven and Hell for a reason. We are here to celebrate the next True Immortal."

The crowd's chatter grew and the yelling began. I would have assumed it would be the Demons that would be the rudest, but the Angels held their own.

"Prove it," an Angel yelled.

"Why should we believe you?" a Demon shouted. "You invited a filthy *Vampyre* to Hell."

Alrighty then. A chorus of "yeah" and "purebloods rule" and "kill the Vampyre" assaulted my ears.

What in the hell was happening here? Clearly I hadn't gotten out much in Hell. I had no idea I was so popular... And why in the fuck was I on a stage with Satan and God? I tried to slink away. I didn't want my presence to cause a brawl. As I stepped back a strong hand grasped my arm and the chance for escape was gone.

It was God. He pulled me between himself and Satan and held me fast.

"Do you see the good or the bad in people?" he asked me quietly. Satan shot him an annoyed look, but God ignored him.

"What are you talking about?" I asked, bewildered.

"Just answer the question." His grip on my arm tightened and I realized Satan and Dixie and Grandpa were right. There is no such thing as pure good or pure evil. Period. Everything is gray and it's all in the interpretation.

"I see both," I told him. "Everyone has both."

"Everyone?" He raised his eyebrow and waited. His beauty was distracting, but I'd grown tired of all the beautiful without the substance to back it up. God may be full of substance, but in this moment he was after something that apparently I could provide.

"Yes." I looked him in the eye so he would know I was including him too. "Everyone."

He threw back his head and laughed. He reminded me so much of his brother in that moment, I laughed with him. He nodded to Satan and Satan winked at me.

"You may know of the Sword of Death," God called out.

"It's a myth," someone yelled.

"Doesn't exist."

"It's a joke," another chimed in.

"Oh no," God chided the audience. "It most certainly exists."

I shot Satan a glance. Did God not know it was missing? How in the world could Satan look so freakin' calm? This was a clusterfuck waiting to happen... Was he about to spring it on God in front of everyone? For real?

"Fred Rogers," Satan said. "Step forward."

The crowd parted as a shimmering dust exploded gently in the back of the room. God released my arm and I felt whispers curl around my body clinging to me and embracing me with a power that humbled me. It also froze me to the spot I was standing in. In a panic I looked to both God and Satan. They had put some sort of beguilement on me and I was planted—unable to run. The need to run was overwhelming, but the mechanics to do so had been taken away.

Mister Rogers walked forward. He held a sword in his hands and a halo glowed around his head. He smiled at me and I gasped. The magic coming from the Sword was so pure and so strong no one could look right at it.

"Mister Rogers stole the fucking Sword of Death?" I gasped.

"Oh no, neighbor. I am the keeper of the Sword. I live in the Den of Iniquity and I guard it with my goodness and light," my childhood idol said.

"Are you going to tell me Mr. McFeely lives there too?" I snapped sarcastically.

"No, no." He chuckled and shook his head. "Mr. McFeely is still on Earth, but when he ascends he will be in charge of the postal service in Heaven."

I was struck speechless.

"You bastard," Wrath yelled from her cage.

"You tricked me, you son of a bitch," Greed screeched.

Mister Rogers just smiled at them and waved. A very sick feeling settled in the pit of my stomach. The Sword had never been missing. This was a game. A horrific game played at my expense. Satan was in on it and from the looks of things God was too. I was going to die. The filthy half Vampyre half Demon was going to die. Grandpa had clearly been in on it too. He had lured Ethan from the room. I was going to die alone for the sins of my father. I closed my eyes and realized I had no one to pray to. Maybe this was my purpose... to atone for the sins of my father. Tears rolled down my cheeks.

"I'm sorry, my little baby." I touched my hand to my stomach. "I'm so sorry."

"Give the Sword to Compassion," God commanded.

Who in the fuck was Compassion? Was somebody new going to hop up here and chop my head off?

Mister Rogers stood in front of me and held out the Sword. Confusion didn't begin to cover what I felt. What kind of warped game were they all playing?

"*It's you, Astrid,*" Ethan said. "*You're Compassion. Take the Sword.*"

His voice rang in my head and I found him in the crowd. He was staring at me with wonder and love.

I was Compassion?

Me?

I slowly bent forward at the waist, as my feet still wouldn't move. I took the Sword in my hands. It was heavy and drenched with more magic than I'd ever felt. My head spun and I had to force myself to stand up straight.

"Behold the next True Immortal," Satan shouted.

"Wait," I hissed at the Lord of the Underworld. I felt the black gloves slide up my arms and I knew my skin had turned sparkly. There was a fine chance I was going to kick everyone's ass in the room… "What kind of bullshit did you put me through?"

"The kind of bullshit that will save you from centuries of bullshit in the future," he said and smiled. I so wanted to smack the grin from his mouth, but I realized what he had done. The anger inside of me remained, but it was tempered with something far more profound.

He had tested me and made me prove myself to those who would test me later. He was well aware that Wrath would eventually have his throne, but now she knew what I could do to her. The Sins may not like me, but they had a healthy fear of me— as did the rest of Hell. Satan was an ass, but he was a clever ass. I wasn't sure I wanted to be Compassion, but it appeared that I might not have much of a choice.

"You'll have to do a bit of work in Heaven too," God informed me and I shot him an evil glare.

"Both of you are pansy asses," I snapped. God was taken aback at my candor, but Satan chuckled.

"Prove it," a Demon cried out.

"I don't believe it," an Angel yelled.

God and Satan rolled their eyes simultaneously and I laughed. They looked so much alike, I couldn't help myself. They turned to me and simply stared. Shit. The pansy asses wanted me to prove it and there was only one way to do that.

The weight of the Sword in my hands made my fingers tingle —not in a bad or frightening way. A new and unusual way. I had no fear of the Sword and if I'd come this far I might as well go all the way. I caught Mister Rogers out of the corner of my eye giving me the thumbs up. WTF? But more importantly, I locked eyes with Ethan. He nodded and I knew everything was going to be fine.

I raised the sword and the entire room sparkled with what I would call Fairy dust. Iridescent crystals clung to all the Demons and Angels in the room. A strange purr of contentment burst from the crowd. I wasn't one for self-inflicted pain, but I figured the faster the better. I raised the Sword in one hand and extended the other. The breathing in the room had halted—even Satan's and God's. Holy hell, were they unsure I was really a True Immortal? The whispers came back and I was assured by both that they believed in me. The only one left that mattered was me… Did I believe in me? Could I do this? Hell, I didn't even know the job requirements, but if it simply boiled down to figuring out the definition of fair in a very gray world… I could do that. Yes. I could do that.

I sliced my arm and hissed at the excruciating pain. It burned like a motherfucker, but I didn't die. I mean, I was dead, but I wasn't dead-dead. The Demons and Angels went wild. Crying and bowing and wailing. Most of them dropped to their knees and begged my forgiveness.

I rolled my neck and looked directly at Satan. "I want to go home."

The room trembled and the walls began to buckle. Trees, grasses and flowering vines exploded out of the floor and walls.

Tables became boulders and the chandeliers dripped with flowers and fruit. Monkeys and birds hopped on the heads of Demons and Angels and everyone, including Satan and God, blanched and cowered in terror.

A huge pole appeared in the middle of the room. It went from the floor to the ceiling and at the top was Gigi.

"Astrid," she shrieked. "Look at me! I'm a pole dancer!"

"What did she say?" God asked his brother.

"I believe she said she was a pole dancer," Satan replied, completely baffled.

"That can't be right," God muttered.

"Oh, yes it can," I said, grinning from ear to ear.

CHAPTER THIRTY-ONE

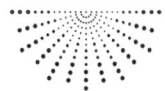

Mother Nature slid down the pole... kind of. It wasn't graceful. It wasn't pretty. It was difficult to watch, especially when she got stuck, hung upside down and cussed like a sailor for five minutes.

After three more stalled attempts she made it to the floor, and under the covert direction of Grandpa, the crowd went wild. She took eight bows and then did an abrupt about-face and narrowed her gaze on her sons.

"Hello boys," she purred. I even felt bad for them.

"Hi Mom," Satan squeaked. God couldn't even get his voice box to work.

As she moved toward them her skimpy pole dancer outfit was replaced by flowing robes. She was exquisite. Her hair blew wildly around her head and her animals darted around her.

"So what brings you here, Mom?" Satan whispered.

"I heard there was a party. My invitation must have gotten lost in the mail."

"Oh," he croaked. "I think God was supposed to tell you about it."

God shot Satan a look that was covered in 'I'll smite your ass later.' "No," he said in a voice that wasn't nearly as melodic as it had been. "It was all Satan's fault. He said he didn't want you here."

Satan tackled God and they began to pummel each other and roll all over the stage. Thankfully I had use of my feet again and was able to jump out of the way, or they'd have taken me down with them.

"Enough," she bellowed. They froze. The entire room froze. "So, Astrid darling. Was I amazing or what?" she asked, referring to her pole debacle.

"Gigi, it was okay. You need to practice more and I think you need to cut the cussing part back by a minute or so."

I'm sure I heard Satan and God whimper. Gigi considered me for a long moment and I wondered if my uncles knew something I didn't...

"Brilliant," she shouted and the walls rumbled. "I shall take those notes and incorporate them into my new routine. Do you see why I like her?" she demanded of her boys.

"Yes," they muttered meekly.

"She tells me the truth. Which is more than I can say for the rest of my family." She stomped her foot and the back wall of the dining room collapsed.

"Gigi," I admonished. "Chill out. If you want to be invited, you can't destroy your son's house every time you show up. Deal?"

"Deal," she said and pursed her pretty lips. "Would you people have me over more often if I didn't leave such a mess?"

"Um... sure," Satan said, looking to me for guidance. Even though he had fucked with me, I gave him a nod. He was a bastard, but I liked him.

"I'd be willing to host a family dinner every now and then," God offered in a shaky voice.

"Will you come visit me in Nirvana every Tuesday?" she inquired. "I'll cook."

Both men sucked in a quick breath and shuddered. "Can we bring take out?" Satan asked.

She gave him the evil eye and then laughed. "Of course. I can't cook for shit."

"Mom, Astrid is the next True Immortal," God told her. Satan flipped him the finger. Apparently he had wanted to spring the news.

"Tell me something I don't know," she cooed, letting them know that nothing got by Mother Nature. "I've known that since the minute the child was born. It was difficult to let her grow up the way she did, but that's what the Fates demanded. Those gals are bitches," she muttered and wandered over to the cage. "Why are three of my granddaughters caged like animals?"

"We had some issues. They'll be living in Purgatory for the next few years," Satan explained.

Gigi circled the cage and the Sins trembled. "I have a better idea," she crowed with excitement. Her robes billowed around her and her beautiful eyes lit up. "I shall take them home with me and teach them manners! Plus I need some new people to clean the monkey shit off of the furniture."

"Um... " Satan waffled.

"Excellent," she squealed. "We shall leave immediately. Bill, are you ready?"

Grandpa ran forward and blew me a kiss as he took his true love's arm.

"See ya, boys." He grinned and winked and they disappeared. Within seconds the room was restored to its former glory and the cage was gone.

"Did that just really happen?" God asked, dazed.

"It did," Satan said and ran his hands through his hair.

I felt Ethan's presence beside me and all was right with my world. He kissed my temple and wrapped his arms around me.

"I must take my leave," God said. "Astrid, it was lovely to meet you. I will assume this is your Ethan. You two have a very important job ahead." He touched my stomach and a warm burst of loving magic spilled into me. "A very important job." He turned to his brother and they embraced. The crowd was awed. I was awed.

God clapped his hands three times and he disappeared along with his entourage.

"Wow, people come and go so quickly here." I giggled at my *Wizard of Oz* reference, but nobody got it so I shut my mouth.

"Everyone clear the room. You are dismissed," Satan said. "Now." The room emptied quickly except for Ethan, myself, Dixie and the Devil.

"Goodbye, Astrid," Dixie said. Her eyes were full of tears and her hands shook. "I'll miss you."

She threw her arms around me and buried her face in my neck. I squeezed her and rocked her like a child. She longed for a mother like I did. It made my heart hurt. "Dixie." I lifted her chin and looked into her eyes. "I'll see you in six months. It's not that far away."

"You're right," she said and forced a smile to her lips. "Six months."

She hugged Ethan and her father and disappeared in a cloud of pink glitter.

"I have one thing left to do before I go home," I told Satan. He nodded his head and bowed to me. I turned to the man that made living for eternity worth it. "I don't want to do this alone. Will you come with me?"

Ethan brushed his lips against mine and whispered, "Always."

I took a deep breath, touched the amulet on my neck and turned back to Satan... but he was gone. In his place sat the General.

"*George?*"

"I answer to that." He chuckled and loped closer. "I also answer to Satan, Lucifer and the Prince of Darkness in a pinch."

I was speechless... almost. "You're a motherfucker," I gasped. "Does anyone else know?"

"No—well, Bambi does." He gave me a grin. I shook my head and tried to clear it.

"Does she shift to a Demon too?" I asked. I hoped with all my heart that Bambi wasn't Amanda.

"No. She's my Hell Hound lover."

"Of course." I rolled my eyes and laughed.

"Put your hand on my back, children and I'll take you where you want to go."

IT WASN'T LOUD. IT WASN'T DRAMATIC. IT WAS SIMPLY SAD. I CALLED her name and she came to me. Her beauty was still there, but her mind was gone. She thought she was supposed to lead. The amulet could kill one—the one who was meant to lead.

I told her I loved her and she just looked confused. She was broken beyond repair and I had one last gift to give her. The gift of mercy. I was Compassion and it was my gift to give.

I touched the amulet and it turned to dust in my hand. Her end wasn't brutal like her life had been. It was quiet and peaceful. She looked in my eyes and for the first time in my life I think she really saw me. She smiled and then... she was gone.

I turned to Ethan and I fell into his arms. "I will love you till the end of time."

"And I you," he replied and held me tight.

I pulled myself together and turned to Satan. He had transformed back to his breathtaking self. "I want to go home."

He held his hand out to me and I went to him without hesitation. He held me like a father holds his daughter and kissed me on my head. "Would you mind if the Babies stayed for a while? I find them quite amusing."

I looked up at the Devil and narrowed my eyes. "No strip clubs?"

"I promise."

I didn't believe him for a second, but I knew he'd take care of my little monsters. "One week and then you will send them home."

"Yes, one week. This promise I shall keep." He grinned and I giggled. "Are you ready?"

I glanced around the Basement one last time. I took Ethan's hand in mine and I nodded to my uncle. "Yes. I want to go home."

"As you wish."

— THE END (for now) —

EXCERPT: HELL ON HEELS

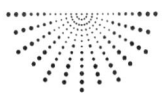

THE HOT DAMNED SERIES, BOOK 3

CHAPTER ONE

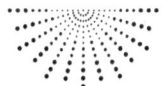

"WHAT EXACTLY ARE YOU DOING?" I ASKED MY FATHER. HE HAD A deck of playing cards laid out on his massive mahogany desk and he was putting tiny dots on the backs of the aces, queens, kings and jacks.

"It's Thursday," he replied.

"Yes… and?" I flopped down on the plush leather couch and waited.

"That bastard Hemingway won last week. That was unacceptable," he huffed. He put down the red pen and picked up a blue one.

"So you're going to cheat?"

He gave me a smile that had melted the hearts of thousands of women. Literally. "But of course."

Being the daughter of Satan had its challenges. This was only one of many. I knew that explaining to him that cheating at poker was wrong would be like running up the down escalator for eternity, so I kept my mouth shut. Furthermore I was fairly sure that Hemingway cheated too. Poker Night in Hell usually consisted of Ernest Hemingway, Mr. Rogers, my dad and occasionally Mother Teresa. Since all of the players, my father excluded, resided in Heaven they basically took a bi-weekly field trip to Hell for game night. For real.

He finished his deceitful art project and gave me his full attention. "So, my beautiful girl, are you ready?"

I picked at my nail polish and considered my answer. Pleading had not worked, nor had crying or throwing a tantrum. Actually, the tantrum was a total bust. We ended up laughing because it was so far out of my character and I sucked at it. I suppose I could try the truth.

"Dad, being deported from Hell is not my idea of a good time. I'm not ready. I have no real power yet and I know I'll disappoint you."

"Dixie, the only thing that disappoints me is that you will be graduating from Demon College as the valedictorian and your obsessive need to do good." He sighed dramatically and ran his hands through his jet black hair.

He was gorgeous. He was evil. And I loved him.

"Your sisters… "

"My sisters are thousands of years old. College didn't even exist when they were of age."

"Point," he agreed. "I just don't understand why you couldn't learn what you wanted and then flunk the tests on purpose. We have a reputation to maintain."

"I know." I let my head fall back and stared at the mirrored ceiling. What the…? When did he have the ceiling in his office mirrored? The reality was too much to take in. I shut my eyes and tried without success to block out what I'd just seen. I was from the most over-sexed family in history and I was a twenty-one year old virgin.

"I've done my best to help you past that little hump. No pun intended," Satan said innocently.

"Get out of my head, Dad," I snapped.

He wasn't lying, and he *intended* every pun he made. He'd thrown the cream of the crop at me. Of course they were smarmy and way too old. The last Demon he'd set me up with had ridden on the Mayflower, had no clue who Maroon Five was and smelled funky.

"Dixie, darling, all of your sisters popped their… "

"Hell to the NO," I yelled as I slapped my hands over my ears. It was beyond unnecessary to hear about the sexual exploits of my sisters, the Seven Deadly Sins. It was bad enough that one of them was named Lust.

"Dixie, I'm just trying to help," he pouted.

"Look, Dad… there is a guy. And, um… well."

There actually was a guy—an amazing perfect guy, but I had no intention of telling my dad about him. He would ruin it. My dad thought it was hilarious to threaten the lives of all my sisters' paramours. And what did it matter anyway? I was leaving. All Demon Princesses had to do their time on Earth and my number had come up. The only thing that made it bearable was that I'd get to see my cousin Astrid. She was very pregnant and furious that no one could tell her what the gestation time was for a half-Vampyre half-Demon baby. She'd apparently caused so much property damage that her mate Ethan had everything breakable in the compound nailed down.

"Do I know him?" my father inquired casually.

My stomach clenched. Nothing my dad did was casual. "Nope." I smiled and stood up. "And you're not going to. I don't like him anymore."

"This happened in the thirty seconds since you announced his existence?"

"Yes. Yes it did."

"Dixie, Dixie, Dixie, you are so like your mother."

Considering no one had the testicles to tell me who my mother was, his comparison drove me to grind my teeth. "And that's a bad thing?" I challenged, hoping for once he'd slip up and give me a clue.

He paused and watched me for a moment. "Not good. Not bad. Interesting."

I went back to work on my nail polish and bit back a nasty retort as the tears threatened.

"Will you attend the poker game tonight?" he asked as if nothing important had passed between us.

"Sure," I muttered.

"Bring your guy. I'd love to meet him." With that my frighteningly beautiful father disappeared in a blast of black glitter and smoke. He was insane if he thought I'd bring my *friend* —completely insane.

CHAPTER TWO

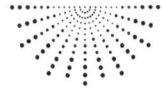

"How was the poker game last night?" my best friend Stella asked as we tried to find something edible in the college commissary.

"Dad won."

"Your dad always wins."

"He cheated," I muttered as I grabbed a sandwich and a bag of chips.

"So? He's Satan."

"Does anyone have morals here?"

"Dixie, we're Demons. We live in Hell. What do you expect?" Stella asked logically. The crabby Demon with the unibrow behind the food counter slid a nasty-looking bowl of what could pass for beef stew onto my BFF's tray. Stella, never wanting to cause a scene, accepted the offending bowl and moved on.

She was correct, and I didn't quite fit in. I never had and Hell knows I tried. I slid my tray quickly past the lunch lady and avoided the rank-looking stew.

"The commissary sucks," Stella lamented as she tried not to gag at the aroma rising from her tray. "I should have gone to college on Earth."

"Agree." I nodded as I made my way through the crowd to a table.

The Demon College looked more like a high school than a college—lockers and all. The commissary looked like a freakin' high school lunchroom because up until a couple of years ago it had been. Most Demons, if they chose to pursue a higher degree, went to Harvard, MIT, Princeton, Yale, or Northwestern on Earth. From what I understood Angels tended to prefer the party schools. Since my father decreed I wasn't ready to go to Earth four years ago, he created the Demon College—where my old high school formerly stood. While the education was top notch, the accommodations left a lot to be desired.

"Holy Hell, your boyfriend is staring at you," Stella whispered gleefully.

"He's not my boyfriend," I hissed.

"Does he know that?" Stella's smile broadened as she enjoyed my discomfort.

Glancing around the commissary, I spotted the person I dreamt about on a nightly basis and I debated my next move. Did I stay or did I go? Being near my secret fantasy made me stupid. I'd far rather be mysterious than idiotic. He made me feel hot, cold and tingly at the same time and I'd barely uttered a word to him all year. Go. I would go—just put my tray down and be out of the commissary in a minute flat—or I could dematerialize... but then I could end up anywhere. I didn't quite have the hang of dematerializing to places I was actually trying to go. Last week I tried to travel to the mall and ended up in my father's chambers while he was getting busy with his pregnant consort Amanda. Bleach couldn't remove that one from my brain.

"I'm out of here," I muttered as I started walking. Speeding up my pace, I hightailed it to the tray drop praying to every deity I could think of that I didn't run into the man of my dreams. In all of my inexperience I was liable to either drool or bodily throw myself at him.

"He's still watching you," Stella whispered as she followed close on my heels.

I rolled my eyes. "He's not watching me."

"Wrong," she trilled happily.

"Stella, hush. Someone will hear you." She was my best friend, and if I didn't love her so much I would take great pleasure in killing her.

"Oh please." She waggled her eyebrows and made smooching noises. Pretending I didn't know her was impossible and I seriously considered dematerializing, but a healthy fear of seeing my father's naked ass stopped me.

"He is totally gone on you," she informed anyone within hearing distance—which was everyone—as she chased me. "And you are so gone… watch out," Stella yelped.

I stopped short to avoid running into Vincent van Gogh, my art teacher. Dressed in a purple velvet cape and a frighteningly poufy hat, he was weaving his way toward the open bar. It was Hell, after all, where mixing alcohol and academia was the norm. Van Gogh had a very close relationship with his absinthe. When the great master died he had the choice between Heaven and Hell. He chose Hell, much to my Uncle God's disgust. Van Gogh, while brilliant and extremely funny when he wasn't morbidly depressed, was clearly intoxicated. Did no one notice or care about these things besides me? Much was overlooked in Hell, but drunk was drunk.

In an attempt to avoid body-slamming the great artist I veered left and unfortunately Stella had the same idea. She slammed into my back, covering what used to be my brand new hot pink Juicy sweat suit in rank beef stew.

"Shit," she moaned as she tried to remove the potatoes, carrots and meat from my hair and the inside of my hood.

I froze and closed my eyes. As a child I used to think if I couldn't see anybody then they couldn't see me. It didn't work when I was five and I was fairly sure it wouldn't start working at twenty-one, but one could always hope. I also used to think that there were actual people in the TV.

"Hey Dixie." An insanely sexy voice broke into my invisibility fantasy.

I pried open one eye, and much to my great horror and delight stood the object of my desire in the flesh. The most beautiful man I'd ever seen—Hayden Black.

"You okay?" he asked.

My stomach flipped, my tongue became sandpaper and I felt lightheaded. I shakily tucked my hair behind my ear in a move that I knew looked good on me and came back with a fistful of beef stew. "I'm great," I lied. The heat crept up my neck and settled squarely on my cheeks. Holy Hell, could it get any worse?

"I'm going to skip the rest of the day and go cliff diving south of town. You want to come?" He smiled a lazy smile that made my breath hitch and all my unused lady parts tingle.

"I can't," I stammered. "I have a calculus exam… and I smell like beef stew, and I don't have a swimsuit and I… "

"Another time then." Hayden grinned and my heart skipped a beat. He reached out and ran his fingertips along my jaw line and his thumb across my lips. The shock of his touch jolted through my body and my knees buckled a little. "Another time."

He stood for a moment and stared, then turned and left the commissary. I watched his perfect butt in his loose-fitted faded jeans walk away from me. I didn't like him walking away from me —it felt wrong. What the Hell was that about? Why was I so drawn to him? I was leaving and those were the most words I'd said to him in a year. My hand automatically went to my still tingling lips, which I silently vowed to never wash again.

"Dude." Stella bounced like a ball. "He just asked you out!"

"No he didn't. He asked me to skip class. You know I don't skip."

"You need to pull the steel rod out of your ass and loosen up," she chastised as she futilely attempted to remove the beef stew from my hair.

"I've been telling her that for years," my sister Sloth chimed in as she appeared in a burst of sliver glitter dust.

I rolled my eyes and smiled at my beautiful lazy sister. She was by far the nicest of the Seven Deadly Sins and I adored her. "What are you doing here? Is everything okay?" She never came to the Demon College. Academia gave her hives. Literally. Panic knotted in my stomach.

"Everything is fine," she assured me. "Dad's got his panties in a wad and he wants to see you. I've been sent to bring you to the Dark Palace."

"But I have a calculus exam and I… " I began to explain my schedule but petered off, realizing it was useless.

"And?" She raised her eyebrows as she began to scratch the welts that had popped up on her arms.

"Fine," I acquiesced quickly. As laidback as my sister was she got really grumpy and occasionally deadly when she was itchy. Furthermore, my dad waited for no one, certainly not his youngest daughter.

"You can't see Dad or Grandma like that." Sloth referred to my stew-splattered attire.

I paled considerably and clutched my sister for purchase. "Oh my Hell, Gigi is there?"

"Yep, and Dad is in a tizzy." She grinned evilly. "Let's get the unidentifiable lunch product off of you."

"That's my fault," Stella offered apologetically.

"No worries," my sister told Stella as she affectionately squeezed her cheek. Sloth raised her arms and flung them towards me. In a flash my hair was clean and my hot pink sweat suit was gone, replaced by the requisite black my father expected us to wear.

I hugged Stella goodbye and wrapped my arms around my sister. Sloth moved her hands in a circular motion. The glitter engulfed us as my beautiful sister and I vanished in a cloud of magic.

MY DAY WAS GOING FROM MORTIFYINGLY BAD TO REALLY SCARY BAD.

The Dark Palace, my father's main residence, was normally a gross display of wealth and questionable taste. At the moment it had been transformed into a wild garden that resembled a blooming jungle on crack as opposed to the lush manicured gardens that populated Hell.

I grasped my sister's hand in terror and peered through the vines and flowers. "Is she here?"

"I don't sense her yet, but she's definitely on her way. Her garden usually precedes her by about five minutes," Sloth mumbled as she disengaged her hand from mine. "Dixie, I love you, but I wasn't summoned by our certifiable granny. Do you mind if I go?"

"Um…"

"Great! Call me later," my traitorous sister said as she disappeared in a blast of glitter. So much for counting on a Sin. The smell of jasmine and lilies permeated the air. There was no trace whatsoever of the grand ballroom which was where I knew I stood. Mother Nature, aka my Grandma Gigi, had a very bad habit of destroying my dad's homes. My guess was that he had missed his weekly visit to Nirvana to kiss her butt and she was pissed, but that didn't explain why I had to be here.

"Dad," I called out in the largest whisper I dared.

"Over here," Satan said quietly.

I made my way toward my father's voice and found him hiding behind a large ivy covered rock. My stomach dropped to my toes. The most terrifying and powerful Demon alive was hiding from his mother. This was beyond bad.

"Um, Dad?"

"Dixie," he hissed and pulled me behind the rock with him. "Thank sweet Hades you're here."

"Why exactly am I here?" I asked as I peeked around the rock.

"Your grandmother is the definition of unstable insanity, and if I knew why she summoned us we wouldn't be hiding behind a rock," he answered logically.

"Dad, you're my rock and this is making me very nervous."

He considered me for a long moment and stood up. He was magnificent. He stood six feet six inches tall and has long raven black hair like mine. Our eyes were gold, although they turned ruby red when we got excited or angry. My skin was more peaches and cream in comparison to my dad's beautiful pale mocha color.

"You're correct Dixie, I am your rock. She's so damned horrific I forget myself. Everything will be fine—I hope," he muttered.

His total lack of conviction was unsettling. I rose to my feet and waited. What the hell did she want with me? She'd shown me no attention at all in my twenty-one years in Hell.

"Don't look her in the eye and stand at least ten to twenty feet away from her," my dad instructed. "She's crazy and prone to blistering and deadly fits of rage."

"I heard that, you little shit," a glorious melodic voice shouted. "Just because you're the King of the Underworld doesn't mean I can't take you over my knee and tan your ass."

I gasped and held on to my father.

"Son of a bitchass motherhumping asshats—arghhhh!" she screeched as she fell ungracefully from the sky. It wasn't until that moment I realized the roof of the palace was gone. The musical voice did not match the language flying from her mouth or the otherworldly glamour she possessed.

The disheveled beauty got to her feet and glanced around impatiently. She wore a gown of sheer golden gossamer that floated around her magically. Her hair was a mass of fiery red curls and her skin was a pale porcelain, but it was her eyes... Her eyes were the clearest blue I'd ever seen and they sparkled. She was quite simply the most gorgeous crazy woman in the universe.

Her power filled the room. It was earthy with a dangerous sensual undertone to it. I would give anything to be back in the commissary covered in stinky beef stew. Anything.

"Satan, you little bastard," she snapped as the gentle breeze in the room shifted into a slightly menacing wind. "I know you're here. I want to see my granddaughter. Now."

"Mother," Satan bellowed joyously as he stepped out from behind the rock. "To what do I owe this pleasure?" He placed me firmly behind him and waited for her next move.

"Cut the shit. You were supposed to visit me and I made a cake," she yelled. "You didn't show up and I ate it. I ate the entire cake. Do you have any idea how many hours I had to pole dance to work off an entire cake?"

"Seven?" he guessed.

She froze, stared at him for a tense moment, and then threw her head back and laughed with delight. "You're right! I always knew you were smarter than your brother. He guessed three."

My father stood even taller, clearly pleased with himself that he'd bested his brother, God. Forget about my Grandma Gigi—my entire family was nuts.

"Mother, while it's alarmingly wonderful and highly destructive to see you," he said, gesturing to the wrecked ballroom, "why are you here and what do you want with Dixie?"

"I want to see her," she pouted and stamped her small foot.

"You've not wanted to see her for twenty-one years. I don't see… "

"You know exactly why I've ignored her, Satan," she said in a deadly quiet voice.

My father had no reply. He bowed his head and shook it. What was going on here? Something was wonky and I'd bet my embarrassing virginity that no one was going to enlighten me.

"I know she's behind you. Dixie, come out and greet me," Gigi demanded.

My father turned to me and his golden eyes burned into mine. "It's all right. She won't harm you. Go to her."

Sucking in a huge breath, I stepped out from behind my dad and warily approached my grandmother. My fear disappeared and was replaced by curiosity... the kind that was deadly to cats.

"Oh my," she giggled, completely disarming me. "You are exquisite. You look like your father, but you have so very much of her in you."

She caressed my face gently. I automatically leaned into her warm and delicate hand. My maternal upbringing had been virtually nonexistent—attention from a mother figure was addicting, no matter how insane she might be.

"Do you mean my mother?" I asked tentatively, hoping she didn't remove her hand. "Do you know her?"

"Well of course I do. She's a crazy irresponsible assbuckle. The next time I see her I will... "

"Mother," Satan roared.

"Well, she is," she shot back. "Anyhoo, I got a phone with cells. Would you like to see it?"

"Um... " I was hoping she would continue her tirade on my mother. It was the most information I'd ever heard.

"You mean a cell phone," my father corrected her.

"That's what I said." Her gaze narrowed dangerously and the wind in the room kicked up a few notches. Her fingers began to shoot little orange sparks, and I worried for the health and welfare of my dad and his home.

"I'd love to see it," I insisted quickly before she caused a Hellquake or leveled the Dark Palace completely.

"I want you to take a selfie of me," she demanded as she handed me a jewel-encrusted cell phone.

"Um, a selfie means you take it of yourself," I explained as she shoved her new toy into my hand.

"Exactly. Take a selfie of me."

Deciding further explanation of a selfie could end in violence I took several as she posed obscenely with a flowering vine.

"While it's wonderfully disturbing to watch you hump the vegetation, would you like to explain your presence?" my father asked as he partially hid himself behind a boulder.

"Yes, of course," Gigi said as she disengaged herself from the plant and planted a huge wet kiss on my cheek. Glancing at her phone, she grinned. "These would go positively viral on YouTube."

"Mother," Satan warned as he stepped up next to me.

As calming as my father's presence was, I realized to my utter shock I was not at all afraid of Mother Nature. It was clear that she loved me, which only confused me more.

"Why haven't you ever wanted me?" I asked her and she froze.

My father tensed beside me and his magic began to swirl with his mother's.

"Dear sweet child," she cooed. "It was for your safety, but now since you're leaving I needed to see you and tell you... "

"Enough," Satan shouted. "You know the rules. Would you put her in more danger than she's already in?"

This was unwelcome news to me. I was in danger?

"You're such a douchewanker—I wouldn't say anything to harm her. I love her," Gigi shot back angrily.

"Then I think it best you leave," he said in a voice that made the hair on my neck stand up. However, his mother just giggled.

"Have her powers come in?"

"No, but they will," he snapped and advanced on his mother. "You will stay out of this. Do you understand me?"

"It's not nice to backtalk Mother Nature," she hissed.

"I thought it was fool," my father replied dryly.

"Whatever. I'm late for a marathon pole dancing exhibition, otherwise I'd smite your ass for being rude."

"You've done quite enough. Dixie, say goodbye to your grandmother. Now."

I scurried forward and embraced my slightly unhinged grandma. She hugged me tight and whispered in my ear, "Your father is an assmonkey. Don't worry about a thing. I will see you on Earth. I promise."

With that she disappeared, taking her jungle with her—almost. The roof of the palace was missing and I was quite sure that was not an accident.

"Son of a bitch," Satan yelled and stomped around, throwing a fit. "It had better not rain before I can get a new roof or I will send ten thousand giant goats to Nirvana to eat your gardens, you heinous woman."

"Um, Dad?"

"Yes, Dixie?" he answered as he reined in his tantrum with difficulty.

"What kind of danger am I in?"

"At this exact moment, none. But tomorrow is a new day."

"Is that supposed to help? Because it doesn't," I replied as I frantically began to pick at my woefully under-manicured fingernails.

"Dixie, look at me."

I did. He was magnetic and scary and beautiful and mine. I knew I would do anything for my father.

"I am sending you away from danger. You have a mission, but you are capable and ready. It's not for public knowledge because it fucks with my reputation, but I love you. I will kill for you and I would die for you. Now, your sisters? Not so sure, but I would not send you directly into the firing squad. You have to trust me."

Sucking in a huge breath, I nodded. "I trust you, Dad, and I love you too."

"Come here," he said.

I slid into his strong embrace and wished I could stay forever, but that was not how life went. If he said my powers would come, they would come. If he said I was ready... Hell, I just hoped he was right.

CHAPTER THREE

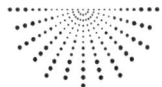

I GO TO GROUP THERAPY.

When you live in Hell and you're not considered to be evil enough, you have to do therapy.

I have to do therapy with a group of others who have an evil deficiency.

That group destroyed my cute bungalow yesterday.

They were insane misfits and I'd grown to love them in the same way one loves a puppy who chews up your couch and eats your walls. Prone to destruction, we'd been banned from meeting anywhere but privately. I'd spent every afternoon at three-thirty for the last year watching them destroy meeting rooms, offices, classrooms, convenience stores... you name it, they could trash it. The convenience store wasn't actually a session. We'd gone for Slurpees after a grueling hour of therapy and they thought the Demon at the cash register looked at them funny. It was bad. Our newest therapist—*we'd had many*—had threatened repeatedly to quit unless we started doing at home meetings. Hence my ruined house. And hence their solution.

I should re-name my group The Wrecking Balls. Janet the formerly Bearded Lady, Carl the Strong Man, and Myrtle the...

I'm not really sure how to explain her. I like her a lot, but she was difficult to describe. Basically she was a tiny Goth girl with more hair in her face than Cousin It. They were all quite funny but bordered on homicidal.

Today they arrived in a big van loaded with tools, wood, a window and paint to repair my bungalow in Hell. Yesterday's therapy session had turned violent when a debate over *The X Factor* versus *The Voice* ensued. Our therapist had been hospitalized for blunt head trauma from a toaster. Myrtle was one tuff cookie and psychotic to boot. She clearly thought the therapist was out of line when she commented on Simon's man boobs, hence the beating, followed by the destruction of my home. As much as I found my group amusing, their ability to trash every place we met was starting to ride my last nerve. Not to mention my horror that they were coming to Earth with me and posing as my family.

A furniture truck arrived soon after they descended on my home, loaded with brand new furniture to replace what they had demolished. The new stuff wasn't nearly as nice as my old furniture that they'd destroyed. When I tried to kindly explain this to the Strong Man *aka Carl* he just shrugged and began doing the Moonwalk. Normally he flipped people off, but he liked me. He was fond of flipping people off. It seemed to give him joy. He moonwalked for about thirty-two counts and then slid very slowly into the splits, arms raised above his bald head.

I stared at him in silence. I was definitely going to have a word with my dad about this group posing as my family on Earth. These people were C-R-A-Z-Y. It didn't help that Carl was wearing something akin to a mauve wrestling uniform with black socks and brown earth shoes. I had no idea how to respond to his performance. Was I supposed to clap or was I supposed to challenge him by busting out my own moves? In the end I nodded at him, he nodded back and I walked away. Quickly.

The furniture delivery guy, Wolf Boy, the hairiest Demon I'd ever seen, lined up all the new furniture on my lawn. I'd have to say Demons were a very attractive race. My therapy group and their friends were an anomaly. Wolf Boy then explained as he shed all over said furniture that he'd be back in a couple of hours to put it in my house.

After winking at me lasciviously, he meandered over to Myrtle and copped a feel of her butt. This earned him a bone crunching solid right hook to the face. She knocked his nose clear up into his forehead. *God, that had to hurt.* Amazingly undeterred by this painful rejection, I watched in shock as he then palmed her boob. Ya'd think he would have learned his lesson...

Myrtle easily picked him up even though Wolf Boy was twice her size and threw him to the ground. She then viciously crunched his testicles with the large hard heel of her combat boot. My dad would love that move. It made me bend over in sympathy for Wolf Boy even though our plumbing was entirely different.

Wolf Boy lay crumbled on the ground moaning for a long time. With his nose where his forehead should be and his testicles lodged somewhere near his chest I didn't blame him. All the others worked around him as if he wasn't there.

I sat down on the front steps of my bungalow and watched in horror as my therapy group turned my beautiful little house into a bad home-improvement project. I felt a cool wind on my face and I closed my eyes and smiled. The air shimmered around me and out of nowhere Blanche magically appeared on my front lawn. She stepped over Wolf Boy and made herself comfortable on my new and highly unattractive couch. She happily held one-sided conversations with a bunch of Demons that didn't even know she was there... because she was invisible. Blanche was mine and I was the only one who could see her. Although I'd told my dad and sisters about her, none of them believed me. Stella was the only one who was convinced of her existence. Stella loved hearing about Blanche's adventures and Blanche loved Stella. It pissed her off to no end that Stella couldn't see her. She would curse a blue streak trying to figure out a way to become corporeal for Stella. If I could behave a little more like Blanche, my dad would be so happy. However, every time I tried to copy her I either ended up with hives or laughing uncontrollably.

"Excuse me, Dixie," said Janet with the voice of a shy ten year old girl. Poor Janet was wearing a fake beard and mustache. Up until a few months ago her beard and stache had been real, but our former therapist had them permanently removed as punishment. Janet had been devastated. She'd been sporting her beard for hundreds of years and clearly felt naked without it. Her mate, Carl, loved her both hairy and hairless and had bought her an impressive array of beards. Focusing on her eyes instead of her lopsided facial hair was difficult, but she was sweet. "Would Your Highness like the walls the same color as before or do you want something new and fresh and not so dated?"

I was fairly sure I was just insulted by a child locked in a hairy adult's body, but I decided it was in my best interest to let that baby go. My hairy female friend was going to help me redecorate.

"I don't know. What do you think?" I felt my eyes go red with excitement.

"I think we should look at this!" She whipped out a color chart and squealed.

Blanche cleared her throat to get my attention and mimed shaving her face. Damn her, I was almost able to pretend that Janet was normal. Then Blanche had to go and ruin it by reminding me that Janet had more fake hair on her face than I had on my entire body. Well, screw her. Janet was my friend—she couldn't help that she was a hairy destructive mess.

While Janet and I bonded over paint colors, Carl and Myrtle got into three rather violent fights.

"Carl." I stopped him as he went to replace my window. "Why do you two hang out if you're just going to keep trying to kill each other?"

Carl paused, contemplated, flipped me off and then started break dancing. I was beginning to think he was brain damaged.

"Oh, for goodness sakes," Janet piped up. Her mannerisms were so dainty for such a hairy gal. "Carl is a little... well, he's just Carl. He's a wonderful Demon, just not a good conversationalist." She paused and waited for Carl to finish with his splits. That was how he ended all of his routines. As he wandered out of earshot Janet continued.

"Actually," she went on, "he's very smart and kind. He smells good and he's champion in the bedroom."

"Oh, Good Lucifer Almighty, no!" Blanche screamed as she slapped her hands over her ears. "That's disgusting." I was so glad that Janet couldn't see or hear my non-corporeal imaginary friend, but I had to concur. Blanche vanished in a huff of disgust.

"Oookay, Janet," I said, deciding to use this as a teachable moment for my hairy buddy. "That is way too much information. That's not really an image you want to create for others."

"You're right," she answered solemnly in her childlike voice. "No one should know that Carl is Superman in the sack. If anybody tried to steal my Carl away I'd tear their limbs off, decapitate them, shove a spike through their heart and burn them for the Hell of it."

She stopped for a moment, clearly considering what she just said. She was normally so sweet. I was positive she was going to yell "joking", but no.

"Actually I'd rip their limbs off first then burn them because they would be conscious for that and it would hurt." She seemed pleased with the new order of torture. "Then after they're dead I would decapitate them and run a spike through their heart to make absolutely sure they could never ever get a piece of Carl's manmeat. That goes for you too, so don't go getting any ideas." She was dead serious.

I was seriously unsure of why she was in my therapy group. That sounded pretty evil to me. I needed to reconsider the sweet thing. She was making it increasingly difficult to be friends. I could have possibly gotten past the fact that she glued on facial hair but this was a deal breaker. Janet the Fake Bearded Lady had succeeded where many had failed. She had rendered me speechless. Not to mention implanted visions in my head that would take years of therapy to erase. I really tried to speak, but my voice was gone.

Janet giggled and braided the left side of her mustache. "I think mustard yellow paint would be lovely in your den."

I nodded, still in shock.

"How about a mossy green in the bathroom, a candlelight yellow in the kitchen, and a warm peach in your bedroom?"

I nodded again. She could have said she was going to paint my entire house crap-brown or lime green and I would have nodded.

"Great!" She hopped up and hugged me, tickling my neck with her beard. It was not soft and silky. "It was soooo much fun talking to you. I'm going to go mix some paint, and if Carl's in the van… " She giggled. "Well, you know."

Oh Holy Lucifer, unfortunately I did know. I watched in abject terror as Carl did lewd hip-hop moves all the way over to the van —followed by Janet, seductively twisting her gnarly beard with her stubby fingers.

"Carl's really got moves," a wistful voice behind me said.

I whipped around to find Myrtle watching Carl longingly as he and Janet raced to the van for their love fest.

"Myrtle, if I were you I'd stay away from Carl," I said as I tried to save her from a sure death.

"Oh I know—Janet's already beaten up twenty-two low level Demons and a zombie over Carl."

"I heard she would mutilate and kill anyone who even looked at Carl," I casually informed Myrtle, fearing for her life. It was difficult to kill a Demon, but Janet's recipe would definitely work.

Myrtle laughed. "She wouldn't really kill anyone—she's too

sweet for that. Plus, I don't want Carl that way. I want to dance like he does."

Weird didn't even begin to describe that statement so I backtracked to something even weirder. "Did you just say zombie?"

"Yeah," Myrtle said, "and you think we're disgusting and gross."

"I don't think you're disgusting or gross."

Myrtle peeked out from behind her hair and stared at me. She took a long pause and simply said, "Maybe you don't, but everyone else does. We're the freak Demons—we're not beautiful like the rest of you." With that she picked up a hammer, stepped *on* instead of over Wolf Boy, and went back into my house.

Carl, Janet and Myrtle weren't freaks, they were just alarming looking semi-violent Demons who had the same problems that I did. Well, some of the same problems. My father would kill me if he found out how much compassion I felt for others, including my violent and bizarre little therapy group. Truth be told, I liked my therapy group and I did fit in with them. Why was life so damn complicated? Myrtle was a person, no matter how stinkin' weird she was or looked. She had feelings—they all did. I turned just in time to see the van roll over onto its side due to the disgusting and illicit activities within. Well, some of them did.

CHAPTER FOUR

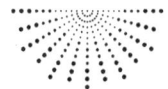

MY COMMISSARY DISAPPEARING ACT WITH MY SISTER SLOTH THE other day had caused quite the stir. I was going for a low profile today. Being Satan's daughter made it kind of difficult to blend in, but I tried. It was a little strange when underclassmen bowed to you, insisted on giving you their lunch money and offered to carry you. Not my books. Me. I shoved stuff into my messy locker and swore for the millionth time I'd clean it out.

"He's going to the library." Stella ran up and knocked me into my locker, causing an avalanche of the entire contents to come falling out.

I glared at her. "Stella, look at what you've done."

"I did you a favor," she retorted, grinning from ear to ear. "Now you don't have to clean it. Did you hear what I said?" she panted, out of breath from her sprint down the hallway and her flying leap into me and my locker.

"No. I was busy getting nailed in the head by my *History of Mortals* textbook," I sarcastically explained as I began to pick up the mess on the floor.

"I said he's going to the library," she repeated impatiently.

"Who's going to the library?"

315

"Your boyfriend," she yelled eagerly.

"Be quiet." I rolled my eyes. "He's not my boyfriend. I've barely ever talked to him."

"That's about to change." She yanked me up by the arm and shoved me into the middle of the hallway. "Okay, Dixie," she screeched at alarming decibels. "You go to the library like you said you were going to. You know, go to the library and… um… study. Okay? In the library, like you said."

Everyone in the hallway stopped what they were doing to watch our exchange. I had never wanted to die so much in my entire life. And every bone in my body sensed that Hayden Black was standing right behind me.

"So you're going to the library, Dixie?" Hayden chuckled, circling me until his entire beautiful self was standing in front of me.

"Um… well," I started, flustered and mortified.

"Yes," Stella shouted. "Dixie is definitely going to the library. She just said 'Stella I'm going to study in the library'. That's exactly what she just said. Just now."

We had entered the realm of shitty sitcom. "Stella," I hissed through clenched teeth.

"Yes?"

"You can stop shouting now."

"Oh, right." She laughed, clearly unashamed of her appalling behavior. "My bad."

"Well, it just so happens I'm going to the library too." He winked conspiratorially at Stella. "Can I walk with you?"

He turned his green gaze on me and waited for my answer. The speech part of my brain ceased to function. All I could do was stare at him like an idiot.

"Yes," Stella chimed in and gave me a push. "She'd love to walk with you and maybe even sit at the same table, regain her power of speech and exchange a few words."

Stella was evil. I gave her a look that would have scared most

Demons to death. I was Satan's daughter after all. She just stuck her tongue out at me and giggled. She was going to pay later.

"Shall we?" Hayden asked.

"Um… sure," I stammered and started walking toward the library.

"Dixie." Hayden's silky voice stopped me.

"Yes?"

"Do you want to bring some work with you?" His eyes twinkled.

I looked down at my empty hands and for the second time in a matter of minutes I wished I was dead. "Yes," I replied in a very businesslike manner. I made my way back to my locker, squatted down and picked up the first two things my fingers touched. "Okay." I smiled, having no idea what was in my hands. "I'm ready."

"Great." He grinned. "I was born ready."

SITTING ACROSS FROM EACH OTHER IN THE DEMON MAGIC SECTION of the library, I stared at my fingernails while Hayden stared at me.

"Dixie," he said softly. "Look at me."

"I can't." I continued my love affair with my fingernails. "I get stupid when I look at you."

"I find that extremely flattering and very sexy," he said.

My eyes shot to his and my stomach dropped to my toes. "No, you don't."

"I do." He captured my chin in his hands and forced my gaze to stay on his. "It's not every day that the most gorgeous girl I've ever seen in my life gets all flustered around someone like me."

"Are you kidding me?" I gasped. "Someone like you? You're the most… " I slapped my hand over my mouth before I permanently destroyed any vestige of cool I might own by telling him I loved him and that I had memorized every single thing he'd worn to class—*down to sock color*—for the last three semesters.

"I'm the most what?" he asked quietly.

Change the subject, change the subject. "So why don't you have a girlfriend?" *Help me Cousin Jesus, did I just say that?*

His grin was lopsided and the hottest thing I'd ever seen. "Haven't found the right girl yet."

"Oh." I was usually more eloquent.

"I'm working on changing my status." He let go of my chin and took my hands in his. I felt a tingle run through my fingers and all the way up my arms. Not only was I physically attracted to this guy, apparently I was chemically attracted too. "Do you have a boyfriend?"

"No." I was caught in his web and couldn't get away if my life depended on it. "I'm working on changing my status too," I whispered. Was I flirting? Oh my Hell, I was. My sisters would be so proud.

His eyes flashed red with desire and his smile broadened in approval. "Am I in the competition?"

"Do you want to be?" I lowered my eyes and watched his thumb caress my knuckles. His hands were beautiful and strong, slightly calloused and very gentle.

"More than you'll ever know," he replied with such seriousness my eyes shot back up to his and my insides did a triple lutz.

Whoa Betty, I needed to slow down or I was going to tackle him to the ground and see if his lips were as soft and tasted as good as they looked. My entire body thumped like a heartbeat and the need to lean into him was overwhelming. I disengaged my hands from his and tried to regain some composure. His smirk made me think he could read every thought in my head.

"I'd like to take you to dinner," he said, watching me closely.

Stella was going to freak. "But you don't even know me." I really wished the idiotic dumbass in my brain would stop talking.

"We could remedy that," Hayden leaned in.

318

Hades, he smelled yummy. "How?"

"Well... " He took my hands again. "We could ask each other questions."

Damn, I was hoping he would say we could play tonsil hockey.

"What's your favorite color?" he asked, drawing me back in.

"Green," I quickly replied. The heat crawled up my neck as I realized I'd chosen the color of his eyes.

"Why's that?" He tilted his head, very aware of my reasoning. I couldn't speak. "Mine is gold," he offered. His emerald green eyes bored into my gold.

"Is it hot in here?" I gasped as I pulled my hands back and put them in my lap.

"Nope." He grinned, quite pleased with himself. "Tell me what you like."

"Well... " I needed some noncombustible territory here. I wasn't about to tell him I liked the way he filled out his jeans or that his mouth was beautiful and the way his muscular arms looked in his long sleeve t-shirt was making me weak. Nope, not going there. I decided to tell him about the real me. Which would probably end with him walking away in boredom, but... "I like animals, especially strays. I love to run. I adore my family and I read constantly." I knew my tone was defensive, but I couldn't help it. I waited for him to glaze over and fall asleep.

"I love to read," he offered quietly.

"You do?" I was surprised.

"Does that shock you?"

"Well... " I bit my lip in embarrassment. Hot guys could read too.

"Is it because I skip school, wear ripped jeans and go cliff diving that you think I'm illiterate?"

"That's not what I meant," I sputtered. My cheeks burned. How many times could a person want to die in one afternoon?

"Dixie, I'm teasing you," he said gently.

"Oh... okay." He had to think I was such a dumbass.

"I think you're amazing and beautiful and sweet." He walked around the table and sat right next to me. "I love to read. I collect first edition books. I have some that are thousands of years old."

That piqued my interest. "Like what?" I adored old books. My father's den was loaded with them. I'd spent a great amount of my childhood curled up in his den reading till my head spun.

"I have an original bound copy of *The Beginning of Time.*"

"Holy Hell, I didn't know that even existed."

"It does. I'd love to show it to you if you'd like."

"I'd like." I smiled. "What's your biggest fear?" I asked. Now that the door was open, I wanted to know a few things about him. He might be hot, but maybe I wouldn't like him. Maybe he was a jerk…

"My biggest fear," Hayden repeated as he ran his hands through his thick blond hair. "My biggest fear is being alone through all eternity."

Damn, that was deep. I was going to say spiders.

"What's something you dream about doing?" He changed the subject to something far lighter.

I took a long pause while I considered my answer. The first thing that came to my mind was silly, but if he could be that honest, so could I. "Flying," I answered shyly. I knew Demons couldn't fly, but that's what I dreamed of. "I've always wanted to be able to fly. Sometimes when I run and I feel the wind race around me and through me and in me I pretend I'm flying."

He was quiet for a moment, just watching. "Perfect," he murmured softly. "Please, Dixie, let me take you to dinner tonight. I promise I'm a good guy and I like you a lot."

"Hayden, do you know who my father is?" I assumed he did, but maybe not.

"Yes Dixie, I absolutely know who your father is."

"And that doesn't… um, bother you?"

"No, should it?"

Was he crazy? Everyone was terrified of my dad. Wait… Didn't

Satan tell me to start being promiscuous? Something I had no intention of doing, but a date... I could go on a date. I wanted to go on a date. I'd never ever been on a date. No one had been brave enough to ask me. I wanted to go on a date with Hayden, and against all odds he wanted to go on a date with me.

"I'd love to go to dinner with you," I blurted a little louder than I intended. I wanted to nail down my acceptance before he changed his mind.

"I'll pick you up at seven." He looked so happy I started to giggle.

"What should I wear?" I asked as my mind raced through my closet.

He got up, gathered his books and whispered in my ear. "Flying clothes. Wear your flying clothes, Dixie."

— VISIT THE WEB PAGE FOR MORE INFO —

ROBYN'S BOOK LIST

(IN CORRECT READING ORDER)

HOT DAMNED SERIES
Fashionably Dead
Fashionably Dead Down Under
Hell on Heels
Fashionably Dead in Diapers
A Fashionably Dead Christmas
Fashionably Hotter Than Hell
Fashionably Dead and Wed
Fashionably Fanged
Fashionably Flawed
A Fashionably Dead Diary
Fashionably Forever After
Fashionably Fabulous
A Fashionable Fiasco
Fashionably Fooled
Fashionably Dead and Loving It
Fashionably Dead and Demonic
The Oh My Gawd Couple
A Fashionable Disaster

GOOD TO THE LAST DEMON SERIES
As the Underworld Turns
The Edge of Evil
The Bold and the Banished
Guiding Blight

GOOD TO THE LAST DEATH SERIES
It's a Wonderful Midlife Crisis
Whose Midlife Crisis Is It Anyway?
A Most Excellent Midlife Crisis
My Midlife Crisis, My Rules
You Light Up My Midlife Crisis
It's A Matter of Midlife and Death
The Facts Of Midlife
It's A Hard Knock Midlife
Run for Your Midlife
It's A Hell of A Midlife

MY SO-CALLED MYSTICAL MIDLIFE SERIES
The Write Hook
You May Be Write
All The Write Moves
My Big Fat Hairy Wedding
Johnson Jones' Diary

SHIFT HAPPENS SERIES
Ready to Were
Some Were in Time
No Were To Run
Were Me Out
Were We Belong

MAGIC AND MAYHEM SERIES
Switching Hour

Witch Glitch
A Witch in Time
Magically Delicious
A Tale of Two Witches
Three's A Charm
Switching Witches
You're Broom or Mine?
The Bad Boys of Assjacket
The Newly Witch Game
Witches In Stitches

SEA SHENANIGANS SERIES
Tallulah's Temptation
Ariel's Antics
Misty's Mayhem
Petunia's Pandemonium
Jingle Me Balls

A WYLDE PARANORMAL SERIES
Beauty Loves the Beast

HANDCUFFS AND HAPPILY EVER AFTERS SERIES
How Hard Can it Be?
Size Matters
Cop a Feel

If after reading all the above you are still wanting more adventure and zany fun, read *Pirate Dave and His Randy Adventures*, the romance novel budding novelist Rena helped wicked Evangeline write in *How Hard Can It Be?*

Warning: Pirate Dave Contains Romance Satire, Spoofing, and Pirates with Two Pork Swords.

NOTE FROM THE AUTHOR

If you enjoyed this ebook, please consider leaving a positive review or rating on the site where you purchased it. Reader reviews help my books continue to be valued by resellers and help new readers make decisions about reading them.

You are the reason I write these stories and I sincerely appreciate each of you!

Many thanks for your support,
~ Robyn Peterman

ABOUT THE AUTHOR

Robyn Peterman writes because the people inside her head won't leave her alone until she gives them life on paper.

Her addictions include laughing really hard with friends, shoes (the expensive kind), Target, iced coffee with extra ice in a Yeti cup, bejeweled reading glasses, her kids, her super hot hubby and collecting stray animals.

A former professional actress with Broadway, film and TV credits, she now lives in the South with her family and too many animals to count.

Writing gives her peace and makes her whole, plus having a job where she can work in her sweatpants works really well for her.

Want More Info About Robyn? You can find her here...
www.robynpeterman.com
https://robynpeterman.com/newsletter/

www.ingramcontent.com/pod-product-compliance
Lightning Source LLC
Chambersburg PA
CBHW070207260626
47160CB00002B/479